PAIN

by

Al Rhodes

Grosvenor House
Publishing Limited

This book is published by
Grosvenor House Publishing Ltd
28-30 High Street, Guildford, Surrey, GU1 3EL.
www.grosvenorhousepublishing.co.uk

A CIP record for this book
is available from the British Library

ISBN 978-1-78148-923-9

Part 1

Pain

The pain had started again. Every part of his body ached. His stomach and chest felt as though the skin had been scraped by a blunt razor blade. The soreness was becoming unbearable. His skin was red and raw. Initially, it had started in patches – now it had spread. He didn't know what his body was covered with, and the doctors didn't know either. All they said was, "It will go in time; take these antibiotics." Antibiotics: the doctors' cure for everything. He had been in and out of hospital for over eighteen months. His private consultant, Dr Haswell, paid for by his wealthy parents, had performed every possible test. "Without the cause, we won't be able to cure," was Dr Haswell's favourite saying. Blood tests, skin tests, x-rays, and constant prodding, poking and cutting, test after test after test was completed; until finally, the doctors decided they could do no more. It was now a waiting game, a case of seeing how the illness developed. All that was left were the antibiotics and painkillers. There were still the monthly check-ups, but they were merely routine. He would collect his prescription and submit to a minor blood test to see if there were any changes in his condition.

After suffering for over three years, he knew his illness was getting worse. It was affecting him mentally and physically. He no longer cried, but lay awake most nights praying for morning to come, when he could feel human again and talk and laugh with other students at the school. He had many friends, but not that many close friends. Sleep was impossible; the pain was too much. He couldn't remember the last time he had slept properly. His eyes were becoming dark and sunken in their sockets; his face was drawn and white. Splashing cold water on his face, he peered into the mirror. He was not a vain lad, yet he hated the very sight of his reflection. If he squinted, he could imagine how he used to look. He used to be fit and tanned with dark, unruly hair, which came from his Irish descent. Some may even have described him as handsome, especially when he flashed his infectious smile.

There was no cure on the horizon. He would just have to live with his illness. Even the radiotherapy had not alleviated the pain; however, it was difficult targeting the pain when it was spread across his entire body. The only cure Dr Haswell had not tried was chemotherapy, although there was no logical reason to put him through a course of treatment which would undoubtedly have no effect on his illness and could possibly kill him.

As the illness developed, it was not just his physical appearance that had changed. His fitness had also diminished. Damien Harrington's life had totally turned around. Once a fit, athletic young man who had the potential to develop a career as a professional sportsman, now Damien sat watching from the side-lines, dreaming of what could have been.

Damien now struggled climbing a flight of stairs. How much more pain could he endure? At times, life felt unbearable. A few months back, he had contemplated suicide. He considered all his options, but in the end, he could not do it. He was not strong enough mentally. At one point, he emptied half a bottle of painkillers into his shaking palm, beads of perspiration running down his face, trying to build up the courage to pop them in his mouth. He tried crushing the pills, grinding them into a smooth white paste. He had tried so hard to swallow but still could not do it. He was a failure – a failure that could not even end his own pain, his own miserable, pathetic life.

Today was going to be another hard day. He could feel the severe depression crushing him, and on days like this, with the added pain and tiredness, he knew he was unbearable to be around.

A sudden ringing broke his depressed thoughts. It was the warning bell signalling time for school. Leaving his night-time hell, Damien left his residence hall and followed the paved quartzite track through the well-kept gardens to the main school building. He tried not to dwell on the thought that he would soon return to his personal prison cell, spending many insomnia-filled hours behind a closed door, twisting and turning in agony. He shook his head, trying to dislodge the waking nightmare. His only escape was to focus on happy memories. Negative thoughts always made the pain worse. Keeping his arms tucked in and head down, Damien trundled to school, hoping today nobody would catch his arms as they rushed to beat the second bell. *Why does everybody always want to rush? Don't we all get there at the same time?* Deliberating the reason, he suddenly found his own speed had increased. After all, he didn't want to be late. Damien was only seventeen years old yet his mind and body felt much older. Since his illness, he had matured rapidly to cope with the physical and mental stress and strains placed on his young body.

The old school building loomed in front of him. It was not a beautiful building. Very little was left of the original school building. The left wing had been demolished by a fire forty years previously. The original school was financed and named after Frank Worthington, a local entrepreneur who had made his money out of recycling plastics using a new water-based technology. Frank Worthington may have been twenty years ahead of his time with his extreme ideas; however, his designs had made him millions. A stone statue stood at the top of the steps in Frank Worthington's memory. An orange and white traffic cone was normally placed strategically on its head compliments of the sixth formers – today it was cone free.

Damien managed a faint smile. Once, he would have been the culprit shimmering up the statue at night, balancing a cone under his arm with his mates egging him on. Next day they would have felt proud of themselves as the ripple of laughter intensified from the other students at the silly spectacle. The head would give his routine speech for the culprits to come forward; thankfully it was an unwritten agreement that nobody would tell. It was all to do with respect and honour, although Damien guessed the head knew who it was. Who knows? Maybe the head found it amusing as well, which is why it was never taken any further.

Once again Damien glanced up at the statue. The large bulky head blocked the sky. He focused his attention on the oddly-shaped jutting forehead, which distracted his thoughts momentarily from the pain he was suffering.

His legs kept moving. They were on auto-pilot, tackling the steps. The statue was ugly. He had never noticed how ugly until today, although it still carried an air of regal authority. Behind the statue stood the school. It may have looked out-dated; however, the school had an excellent reputation. It was four storeys high with the ground floor covered in warped decaying wood, painted white. The storeys above the ground floor had been left unadorned, reminiscent of concrete slabs used in the old war bunkers. A figure stared out of one of the large picturesque windows on the second floor. Damien thought it was from the staff room but wasn't sure. Since his illness, most of the staff had been sympathetic, even giving him a key to the service elevator to reach lessons, which he used when his energy levels were low, like today.

The art building to the left was the newest building; modern inside and kitted out with large kilns and screen printing equipment. It was not a place Damien ventured into. Art was not one of his strengths, and truth be told, he didn't understand modern art. All the symbolic images – why could people not just appreciate a good painting based on how it looked? Why did it have to have some hidden meaning, every brushstroke analysed, every colour reflected upon? The art building's external walls were painted blue with a bright orange wave fading to yellow. A splash of lemon finished off the design. Two years ago Ms Todd, Head of Arts, had been instrumental in designing the mural, no doubt reminiscent of her summer holidays – sea and sand.

To the far side of the main building lay a bungalow in which the caretaker resided. The ivy clung to its walls, almost covering the two small windows facing the steps.

Damien dreaded to think what creatures lay in that jumbled mass. Both buildings looked like they had been built more recently than the original school, which created a disturbing mishmash of designs. It all looked how he felt, worn out.

The twenty-five steps to the oversized entrance felt like one hundred and twenty-five steps today. Hearing a shout, he spun around to see Laurel.

"How are you doing, mate?" Laurel shouted, crashing his hand down on Damien's back.

Damien hollered out, "How many times do I have to tell you not to do that?"

Laurel looked sheepish, as he did nearly every day. He was forever causing his mate to suffer unnecessarily. Twenty steps to go. Damien wished he had brought his wooden walking stick, but it made him feel so old and feeble. The walking stick with its carved handle had been purchased by his well-meaning mother. Damien knew the stick was not cheap; nothing ever was with his mother. Would a modern Leki walking pole have made him feel different? He doubted it.

"I see you aren't doing your granddad impersonation today," joked Laurel.

"Ha ha, very funny," was Damien's sarcastic response. "If I could, I would thump you."

Laurel danced around him, punching the air. "Come on, granddad, take a punch if you can."

"Laurel, I mean it. I'm not in the mood for you today." Fifteen steps and everybody's pace was quickening except his. Damien was slowing down until he halted completely, struggling to catch his breath as his breathing turned to a wheeze. Damien placed his hand on Laurel's shoulder for support and then slowly continued his battle with the steps. A battle he was determined to win. Ten more steps. Nearly there. Today's progress was exceptionally slow. He was glad Laurel was with him – despite his teasing, he was a good mate.

Despite Damien's dark moods, Laurel had stuck with Damien even when some of his other friends had deserted him. Laurel was like a brother. They had been close friends since primary school. Both lads now resided at Worthington High School, much to the annoyance of Damien's mother, who wanted her sick son to stay close to their family home. After days of anguish and arguments, his mother had finally relented. Damien guessed his father had intervened. Damien stayed at Worthington High so as not to disrupt his education on the condition he could stay as long as he could take care of himself. Nonetheless, his education had been disrupted with all his hospital stays and appointments, and academically he had started to struggle.

"Are you coming to watch me train this afternoon?" Laurel asked.

Damien shrugged his shoulders. "I don't know. I'll see how I feel."

"Come on, granddad. We could go to the gym afterwards if you want. See if I can get you onto the man's weights and off them girlie weights you always opt for, or I could cut your hair. The Samson idea just isn't working for you."

Damien managed to smile. "You are a sarcastic sod. You know the Doctor said I can't strain myself; anyway, I don't want to start looking like you."

"What's wrong with me? This body is a temple and should be worshipped! Don't you think I am starting to look like Andy Farrell with my broad shoulders and thick bull-neck?"

"More like thick head and very vain," Damien laughed.

Laurel laughed and kissed his biceps.

"You forgot to mention your daily gym sessions, and you mention them every day," Damien reminded him.

"Well, I am stronger than everybody else on the team."

"Who says?"

"I do."

"Doesn't Farrell have dark hair?" Damien remarked.

"Yeah, well."

"Well, you look more like a skinhead with that short-cropped blonde top."

"You're only jealous."

"Maybe jealous that you are the one that secured a trial with the Wigan junior team when it should have been me; however, I am not jealous of that thing on your head." Damien joked, yet he showed no animosity about his friend's success. Laurel's life was dedicated to rugby league, and Damien lived vicariously through Laurel's success, knowing full-well playing rugby was a distant memory for him, and a trial an unreachable dream. Five more steps, and the top was in sight.

Damien paused again and squeezed Laurel's shoulder.

"Oy, cut that out," Laurel demanded. "You're nipping me."

"Sorry, mate. My stomach was starting to cramp up."

"You get more and more like a girl every day. Cramps? Are you sure you aren't pre-menstruating? And when did you start nipping? You'll be slapping me soon."

Damien gave him a shove. "Were you put on this earth to torment me?" he smirked.

"Yep, that's why you were a left centre three-quarter and I was a left wing three-quarter."

Damien smirked again, "We did make a good team, didn't we? It was my speed."

"I think that was my speed."

"Well, it must have been my agility and quick thinking on the pitch then."

It was Laurel's turn to smirk, "We won tournament after tournament, didn't we?"

"Have you been over to the sports hall lately to inspect the trophy cabinet?"

"Don't you mean the aquarium?"

"More like a goldfish bowl since the girls' netball team started displaying their trophies."

Laurel gave Damien another friendly shove. "Have you seen their new goal shooter?"

Damien shook his head.

"I am telling you, she is hot."

"All women are 'hot' in your eyes. Anyway, I haven't been over since William took my position."

"William Blakewell is not a bad player. He's powerful and aggressive when he tackles," said Laurel thoughtfully.

"Thanks, mate. They replaced me a little too quickly for my liking."

"If it helps, he hasn't quite mastered the miss two fast wing ball creative move, although he has mastered the Gauntlet Criss Cross."

Damien sighed. The Gauntlet had always been his weakest move. Standing on the last step, he let out a gasp in relief. The first hurdle had been conquered.

Glancing to his right, he caught a glimpse of Angel. At least, he thought that was her name. Her head was hanging down and her arms were tucked in, not due to illness, but probably due to confidence or rejection from the other kids. He pondered this thought for a moment.

She was an outsider as well, with few friends, although sometimes he would willingly give up Laurel's friendship with his heavy hand. His back was stinging from Laurel's playful arrival. He prayed another blister had not formed, or it would be another painful night. Damien tried to focus his thoughts on something other than his pain. Was she in his English class? He was having trouble concentrating so was unsure of the answer. He made a mental note to speak to her this week. Since his illness, he understood what it was like to be an outsider.

The Refectory

Morning class had passed quickly; however, lunch was always a challenging time. Angel sat at the end of a large refectory table that was designed to accommodate twelve students. A red plastic tray lay in front of her. In the centre of the tray lay two similar sized apples. Visually they were symmetrical, measured to perfection. The apples were placed six inches from the side of the tray – evenly spaced. Their stalks pointed to the polystyrene tiled ceiling. A single bite had been taken from the right apple, although this was not visible from Angel's angle. Turning the left apple slightly, she picked it up and took a bite. The apple crunched in her mouth as she bit down on its crisp, juicy flesh. A nutty after-flavour tantalised her taste-buds. Placing the apple back on the tray, the next few seconds were spent adjusting the subdued autumnal coloured apple's position. Eventually, both apples sat back in their symmetrical position. Angel closed her eyes to block out the clanking of the lunch plates, the scraping of the cutlery and the loud, vulgar voices that filled the room. Every day she suffered the refectory. One hour of torture was written in her daily calendar. Angel went through the motions of school. She attended class, turned up on time, completed homework. She caused no trouble as she drifted, waiting for Edward to return.

A young lad bumped Angel's table as he rushed to grab the last seat next to his friends. There was no apology. The impact disturbed Angel's daydream. The visual symmetrical beauty of the apples now lost. Looking up, she saw that nobody else was sitting on her table – this wasn't uncommon. People tended to keep their distance, scared of the rumours that surrounded her. Focusing on the right apple she took another bite, but the taste had soured. The apple was dead but had fulfilled her requirements.

Life used to be so different. Angel closed her eyes again, trying to recall some of those happy memories. When there were no distractions, she could drift back in time, feel the warmth of her family home. Edward sat staring out of the window, drawing the nicotine from his cigar. Inhaling and absorbing the chemical mixture into his bloodstream before exhaling the smoke into the air, dispersing it into the atmosphere within her mother's living room. Edward appeared so peaceful when he smoked, as though he was savouring every second of the experience. Angel often wondered if he could make smoke rings like Maggie Duke's father at junior school. She never dared to ask. A child should be seen and not heard, in Edward's opinion.

Edward was strict and controlling, and now she was beginning to understand why. She craved information to learn, to understand her role, and only Edward could do that. Edward was different. She was different, too, yet they were not alike in their differences. Edward was always in control, deceitful and devious; never a kind word to say about anyone. "Tall and standoffish," Bessie, a girl at her old junior school, had once described him. A traffic accident killed Bessie's father days after she spoke those fatal words. Edward said nothing. From that moment, Angel had often contemplated the thought – is it better to have known and lost your father or to have never known your father in the first place? Not knowing who her father was or what he looked like was hard to comprehend. Even her vivid imagination could not create a man she wanted to call Dad. Deep down, she hoped her father did not look like Edward – moustaches were creepy. The hairy creature took over Edward's face. The head and tail moved in different directions when he spoke, as though it were alive, controlled by an evil force.

Eighteen months had passed since she had last seen Edward, and still she could picture him to perfection, visualise his peculiarities. A long dark brown mackintosh with a wide collar adorned his large muscular frame, his dark hair greased and combed flat – no parting; Edward didn't like partings. A parting showed a person's weaker side, according to Edward. His voice was sharp, words blunt and abrupt. A hiss escaped from his lips when he spoke, giving a sinister quality to each and every sentence. An S sounded like "sh," which used to make her secretly snigger as a child, much to the annoyance of her mother.

Now she could smell her mother's baking, taste the freshly baked apple and cinnamon cookies, relive those happy times in her life. However, with good memories, there were always the other memories, the bad memories that she needed to explore, to understand.

Angel opened her eyes wide and stared at her hands. For one single moment, she could feel a sticky substance between her fingers, see the crimson red of a haunting horror.

"Not again. Please, not again," she whispered.

The Library

Damien stopped and grabbed the edge of the bookcase. Tears began to form in the corner of his eyes.

"Are you alright, mate?" Damien glanced up. Laurel was standing next to him.

"The pain is ripping through my stomach and chest like a force ten hurricane," Damien managed to stutter. "I don't know how much more I can take, Laurel. I'm thinking about going back to live with my parents."

"No, you can't," Laurel protested. "What would you do there away from all your friends? At least here you have me."

"I know, but it is getting harder to cope."

"Don't do anything foolish. Sit down and tell me what books you want."

Damien grabbed the nearest seat and passed his mate the list of books. He watched Laurel disappear up one of the book aisles. Damien placed his head in his hands and rubbed his eyes vigorously until they were red. *Come on. Pull yourself together. It doesn't hurt; it doesn't hurt,* he kept telling himself. He lifted his head and glanced around the modern facilities. Computers on every desk, books stacked high on every table, students busily working away; everybody in their own academic world, preparing for the approaching onslaught of exams.

Damien leant forward to relieve the pressure. He lifted his shirt slightly, making sure nobody else could see his chest and stomach. No wonder it was hurting. His skin was raw, just a mass of blisters. He quickly pulled his shirt down to cover the offensive sight. Scanning the room, he determined that everybody was clumped in their little groups. It's strange how similar types group together. He wondered how people saw him and his friends. Only one person in the room was by herself, and that was Angel. Twice in one day he had noticed her, which was unusual.

Laurel returned with a pile of books and plonked them down next to Damien. "Who are you gawping at?"

Damien indicated with his head.

"Ah, the murderess."

"I was merely wondering what she was thinking about. I can guess what most people are thinking about, but not her."

Laurel's head turned towards the door. Three young blondes had entered the room. "Totty alert."

"You are so easy to read, Laurel." Damien turned his head and admitted, "The one on the left isn't bad."

"She's all yours," Laurel said graciously. "Just look at the legs on the one in the centre."

Damien glanced again, "Not bad, but too much make-up."

"Do you mind if I wander over and say hello?"

"Be my guest, but don't bring them back here."

Laurel laughed, "Ok, and the answer to your question, I bet she is thinking of who to hack to pieces next."

"That's gross." Damien opened the book on the top of the pile and started to browse through the contents. The pain had eased once again.

The Third Child
Six Years Earlier

Angel wasn't the first girl to be ostracized by her classmates. Six years before, there had been a girl named Crystal who'd had a hard and unconventional childhood. She was different from the other children, although not just in looks or personality – Crystal had the ability to heal. Initially her ability made her feel special – it had been fun being the most popular child at primary school. If a child fell in the playground, she could instantly make them feel better. The other kids worshipped her. Everybody wanted to be her friend. The local comprehensive was when the problems started. Kids from all the local villages attended Redmond Comprehensive, the only secondary school within a twenty-five mile radius. Crystal's healing power was seen as freakish. Shunned by the kids she once called friends, Crystal became an outsider. Her close-knit community had diminished, and now she was often found alone.

As time passed, Crystal became more and more of an outcast – not only in school but also in her town and eventually in her own home – so when Crystal found out the people known as Mam and Dad were not her biological parents, it wasn't a shock. It was almost a relief. Crystal could now concentrate on finding her real parents and why she possessed the ability to heal through touch. There was no love left in her current home. Crystal was a demon child possessed by an evil entity according to her father. He woke one morning, had two boiled eggs and a round of thick buttered toast and went to work, never to return. She was only eleven years old at the time. Crystal would never forget what he called her for as long as she lived – 'a demon.' The words were imprinted in her mind. Her own father had turned on her because of what she was capable of. At first her mother stood strong, dismissing the neighbours' snide remarks, arguing, protecting her adopted daughter, but slowly over time, the woman Crystal had always known as mother began to change. There was distrust and resentment in their conversations. Crystal's mother could no longer cope. To block out all that was going on, she turned to alcohol. Did her mother care about her? Crystal doubted it. After all, it was because of Crystal that her mother had lost her husband.

Much to Crystal's annoyance, the social workers were always snooping around her home. Her mother rarely acknowledged their presence. Instead she always lay slumped on the sofa, watching the tiny box they called a television, muttering. Crystal tidied their small two-bedroom terrace and hid the glasses and bottles for the duration of the social workers' visits, but they must have realised her mother was an alcoholic. Everybody knew. The house was dirty and stunk of alcohol, which was now embedded deep into the carpet.

Crystal's mother sunk into the abyss of no return, where life was pure and simple – no feeling, no imagination, no real-life. A blank dark cinema screen, a life without a life, a mind without a thought. There was no quick solution. It would take more than a click of a switch to change this picture reel.

Crystal and her mother received no maintenance payments, and the state benefit they received did not stretch far. The staff at the post office had finally agreed to let Crystal collect the allowance on her mother's behalf. "Mother still ill?" was the cynical query. Crystal never answered. There were always enough nosey parkers in the small cramped post office who were more than happy to gossip life away in the small mining town. Crystal didn't want to give them any more ammunition. She would have loved to respond, "My mum? Oh, she is running the London marathon today" or "My mum is travelling around the world," but Crystal knew sarcasm would not help. It would only alienate her more.

Mentally stronger than many children her age and certainly not shy, Crystal held a ferocious temper that could quickly flare up. Her fiery red hair was pulled back from her face in a tight ponytail. Her clothes were not of the latest fashion and were often stained with mud and grass from the latest fight. Crystal could have been a pretty young lady, given the right care and attention. Her face was pleasant when not scowling. Her facial features were soft with gentle sparkling eyes, and her lips were full in a natural heart shape, but nobody except Margaret Riley saw this side of her. All the town folk saw was a wild, unruly child who needed to be disciplined.

Margaret Riley owned the small town's only off-licence. She was a small rounded lady who provided the booze Crystal's mother desperately needed. Margaret had always had a soft spot for Crystal, who had been her daughter's closest friend nine years ago, before her daughter had been taken away from her by Willie Reynolds. He had been drinking during the day – a vice he often pursued with his mates. November 15th was etched forever in Margaret's brain as the day when her life changed. The day when Willie Reynolds mounted the pavement in his small white transit van and tossed her little Jessica like a ragdoll into the air. The impact killed her immediately.

Crystal had been with Jessica that dreadful day. The two young girls were walking back from the newsagents with their bags of fruit-flavoured sweets. Margaret had been surprised that Crystal had only sustained a couple of cuts and bruises from the impact of the van. A couple of months after Jessica's death, Margaret had decided to purchase the off-licence. Many of the town folk reckoned it was Margaret's way of reminding everybody of the perils of alcohol. Every time they bought alcohol from her they would think twice about drink driving. Her daughter's face would be fresh in their minds, aided by a framed photograph that hung on the wall behind the till. Whether it was coincidence or not, there had been no other deaths caused by drink driving in the last nine years in the small town of Redmond.

Margaret never let a drop of alcohol pass between her lips. It was the devil's poison in her eyes, the goblet of death. Even at the local church, she always refused the wine of communion. How could it be the blood of Christ? This part of the sermon always angered and confused her. Every Sunday she sat in the third row and listened to Vicar Holloway preach from the bible. She always took the bread and placed a coin in the sterling silver offering plate. Another young man was always seated at the opposite side of the church to Margaret, on row five of the hard wooden benches. Willie had served his time for the death of Margaret's child. The desire to speak to Margaret and express how sorry he was for what had happened was always with him, but words did not come easy. He had written numerous letters, but the misspelt words and the grammatical errors could never convey his true feelings of remorse and guilt.

Many of the letters had found their way to his waste basket, while the others lay on his dining room table, screwed up into balls or ironed flat again. The creases were a reminder that the letter was not perfect. He worked hard every day, scribbling and rewriting every word. His life would never be able to move on until he had spoken to Margaret. Willie was now teetotal and lived like a recluse, only venturing out on a Sunday for church and Wednesday to collect his social security allowance to buy his week's food rations. He still heard the village gossip; it was impossible to escape. Once, he would have given them enough to talk about and maybe still did.

Willie knew Crystal's mother was an alcoholic – the whole town knew. If he had been strong enough, he would have given Crystal's mum a fierce shaking, to try and bring her to her senses, make her see what she was doing to her only daughter. The kid was turning bad, and it was going to end in tears.

Margaret's conscience had always been tugged in different directions with Crystal. It was wrong to give alcohol to Crystal, especially as she was under age. However, Margaret also knew how violent drunks could be, and if the young child didn't take alcohol home, who knows how her mother might react. At least if she sold alcohol to Crystal, her mother would more than likely leave Crystal alone. For the last few years, Margaret had regularly contacted the social workers to try and have Crystal removed from her mother, but for some strange reason the authorities never did anything. They would pay their routine visit and leave satisfied that Crystal was in no apparent danger.

Margaret could see Crystal was struggling. The once wide-eyed bubbly young girl had gone. Now she was becoming an aggressive child who the town folk no longer cared for; a child who cared little about life and how her actions affected others. Margaret's heart wanted to help, yet her hands were tied by the authorities' systems and procedures. She often sat and watched Crystal from her shop window, milling around, doing very little. Margaret had watched as the tall stranger approached Crystal. Goose-bumps had appeared on her arms when she had spotted them together. A cold chill ran down her spine, and she wasn't sure why. With no parental influence, Margaret was concerned what Crystal was getting into, but all she could do was worry.

Crystal was the second portage for Edward to nurture. Observing Crystal from afar during her early years had pleased him. She was strong and had mastered her gift quickly, using it to influence, dominate, and control her peers, which he liked.

Her mother – a drab, pathetic individual – was her only downfall. Edward realised he would have to take a more proactive role in bringing up his children if he wanted to achieve his goal and impress the Doctor. Their parents would always be their downfall. Edward pledged to observe the parents as much as the kids, and when the time was right, remove the parents from the equation and take over the child's upbringing. A task he would not relish. He could not see himself as a father figure. Edward knew Frank, his colleague in America, took an active part in bringing up his kids. Frank had proven himself to the Doctor, but wait until the game really started! Edward would please the Doctor. The Doctor liked games, and he would especially like the games Edward was planning.

Meeting Edward
Six Years Earlier

Edward approached Crystal a couple of times through her teenage years. Neither meeting had entirely gone to plan. The first was after one of Crystal's weekly fights with Denise Hudson, a stocky well-built girl, who used her weight as her main fighting tool. If Denise managed to pin her opponent down, then the fight was over – nobody would be able to move with that dead weight on them. Crystal towered over most kids her age, which she used to her advantage. She had the reach in her punch but lacked the strength to back it up. She was wiping the blood from her nose – a lucky punch from Denise – when Edward approached her.

"You do not have the strength in your punch, girl. What you need is one of these," Edward held up a knife. Not just any knife but a knife with a serrated edge and a hand-carved handle.

"F******g nutter," had been Crystal's only response as she ran off. Edward had forgotten Crystal had no idea who he was. They had never officially met before that day.

Edward smirked. Crystal not only had the power; she also possessed a fiery character and speed, and he liked that. The first meeting had not gone to plan, which niggled at the back of his mind. He had forgotten a basic rule – build trust. It was unusual for him to make such an obvious mistake. Planning was the key to life. Edward would find a way to capture Crystal's attention. He removed his glasses and placed them in a hard backed case kept in his chest pocket and set out to find Denise.

The mention of a knife had a strange effect on Crystal. She could feel a small stabbing pain on her left hip where a small scar could be seen. A small, pale pink-tinged scar shaped similar to a number three lay raised slightly on the skin. Crystal was unsure how she had got it. It was an inch in size and had never hurt before – so why now?

Denise Hudson's body was found a week later, slumped against a tree. A rotting apple protruded from her mouth. There was a knife wound in her lower abdomen, but no sign of the implement that had caused her death. A sign hung around her neck that read, "Take the knife over the fist." Denise's dead body was the talk of the school for weeks. Many parents set early curfews to protect their children. Crystal would have been surprised if her mother even knew what was going on in the world outside of their home. Crystal, like many of the other kids, was interviewed by the police, but she said nothing about a man offering her a knife. She was intrigued. Who was this man? Why had he felt the need to help her? It was an uncomfortable situation. She had never liked Denise, but death – that was a harsh punishment.

In some ways, Edward had done Crystal a favour. The other children were more wary of her. She was ignored more often than not, and her fights were less frequent. Rumours hinted Crystal was involved, that she had slaughtered Denise like an animal, the apple a form of humiliation. Others thought it, but said nothing. Nobody would say what they thought to her face. Even Willie Reynolds had his suspicions. He had heard the rumours. He would not have been surprised if Crystal had taken a knife to Denise. The kid was in fights every week with Denise so she was the prime candidate.

Margaret thought differently. Call it woman's intuition, but she knew Crystal was no killer. The stranger hanging around the High Street – he looked more like a killer. Margaret had watched him sitting on the bench in the bus shelter, observing what was going on in the small town. His eyes were always hidden behind his glasses, distorting the true shape of his face. He never came into her shop, but regularly went into the newsagent's next door to buy cigars. When her door opened, she sometimes had a waft of his cigar smoke if he had just passed. Margaret had contacted the police about him, but she was becoming known as a local busy body, always meddling in other people's affairs. Her suspicions fell on deaf ears, much to her annoyance. If the police did their job, then she would not need to keep bothering them. Dan Griggs' dog was always fouling on her front lawn, and she was sure Stephanie Khan took cuttings from her garden when she was at work. The police were not interested and so she had to report the same crimes weekly.

Edward's second meeting with Crystal was very different. This time she approached him as he stood outside one of the few retail outlets on the high street, watching her every move. She was a mouthy little b***ch, but she had a passion, a strength he could work with. Crystal had crossed over the road and had headed towards him, towards Mrs Hines' clothes shop with its grotesque manikins and their red pouting lips. The manikins modelled garish clothes, which were changed every two weeks for more garish clothes. The blank, lifeless stares remained the same. How she hated this shop and its manikins with their silly poses. Crystal stood only feet away from Edward and looked him straight in the eyes, a feat not common for teenagers.

"What do you want?" was her opening line.

"To nurture your gift," he responded, swiftly holding his hands in the air and wriggling his fingers.

Crystal understood immediately. "It's a curse," she hissed at him.

"Don't say that, Crystal. We can make a fortune. I can teach you how to be strong, how to enhance your gift, how to use it to gather respect from those in power. With your gift and my brain, we could rule this place."

It sounded tempting yet there was something about Edward she did not like, or understand. It wasn't that he had killed the fat cow that made her life hell – it was the apple that caused the concern. The police had said a bite had been taken out of the apple, and it was not Denise's teeth marks. It was another child's that they could not match, possibly a child around six or seven years old, due to jaw size and the shape of the teeth. Two strands of long, dark hair had been found on Denise's clothing, but again, they could not be matched.

There was something else more sinister about Edward that Crystal could not put her finger on.

"Leave me the f**k alone," she shouted at him.

Grabbing her arm, he drew a knife across her wrist. Crystal snatched her hand back. It was too late; blood appeared immediately. Pressing the palm of her hand on the cut, she shouted at him, "You bastard." Removing her hand from the wound, the cut disappeared. A small trace of smudged blood was all that remained, with no apparent origin.

"Ah, you are a lot stronger than my Angel, young lady."

"Sod off and leave me alone!" She ran back across the road and disappeared into the off-licence; Edward watched and smirked.

The bell on the door rang. Margaret's friendly face appeared from the back of the room.

"Ah, Crystal, what can I get you today?" Crystal glanced through the shop window out into the street. He was still there, still watching her.

"Vodka and whisky." She was still staring over the road as she spoke.

Margaret followed her gaze. "Is that man bothering you, my dear?"

"No. Can I have a bottle of vodka and a bottle of whisky, please?" Crystal emphasised the please as she remembered she did not say please the first time. Her attention was now fully focussed on Margaret, who took one last peek out of the window. Margaret sighed, disapproving of Crystal's request, but she would serve her anyway. She placed the contents in a brown paper bag, hiding a small bag of sweets at the bottom of the bag.

"For my favourite customer," she whispered before winking at Crystal.

"Thank you, Mrs Riley." Crystal was always polite to Margaret, and today was no exception. Crystal glanced out of the window as she spoke. The figure had gone; only the garish manikins stared back at her, now fully exposed, no longer partially hidden by the man with a knife. Crystal shuddered, unsure if it was caused by the manikins or her encounter with Edward.

*****

Crystal sat quietly in the living room, the television blasting out some obscure movie. She glanced towards her mother. Would she have the nerve to go through with it? What was the point of having the power of healing when you couldn't mend a broken heart! She watched her mother's chest rising up and down as she snored softly. Her body lay across the sofa, stocking feet pointing to the ceiling. Her mother's hair was dry and brittle from the lack of care she took with her appearance. Her head leant backwards, causing her mouth to gape wide open.

The more Crystal watched her mother, the more Crystal despised her. The noise from her breathing was deep and heavy, mixed in with the snoring. The gentle whimper when she adjusted her position and the smacking of her lips as her brain tried to send a message for the tongue to moisten the lips; her body was craving hydration fluids. Crystal felt more and more repulsed. Crystal's bag lay on the floor next to her feet. She didn't need to hide it. Her mother would not stop her. The front door was ajar, just waiting for her to walk out to a new life, an unpredictable, unplanned life.

Crystal's mother never saw or spoke to her again. At sixteen years Crystal ran away from home. With no qualifications and no prospects, Crystal walked away from the place she once called home. If she stayed any longer with her mother, a care home would be waiting. A free spirit should never be caged. She would rather be free, fending for herself, than stuck in some institution. Nobody followed her or tried to bring her home. In the town folks' eyes, the small community of Redmond was better off without her. To Edward's annoyance, he had lost his first portage.

Searching for Crystal for months without success, his anger built up inside him like a pressure cooker ready to explode. He began to search for his next victim. This time not for the cause but for his personal pleasure. The world was full of potential candidates, men and women who made other people's lives hell. He needed to release his anger, and a simple torture and death always helped. Informing the Doctor was not a pleasurable experience. Edward still had Dominique, Samuel and Angel; however, Frank had all four of his children. This was the first child he had lost, but not his last. Dominique would be next.

A Chance Meeting

The illness was worse today. The red marks were creeping up his neck. His neck felt stiff and even slight movements were making him grimace. Glancing down to his hand, he could see the red marks creeping past his knuckles where blisters were beginning to form. He wondered if this was what arthritis felt like – a constant pain which made gripping objects impossible. He could hardly hold a pen. How much longer could he go on with the constant pain?

At night when Damien couldn't sleep, he often dwelled on what had he done to deserve this illness. Teenage kids sometimes suffer from acne and, if they were really unlucky, eczema. Why couldn't he have acne like Laurel, like other kids? A couple of spots would be easy to cope with. Anything had to be better than sore red patches creeping across his skin, a minefield of weeping blisters and the excruciating pain he was prone to. If Laurel had a spot, it was the end of the world. Would Laurel have coped if he had Damien's illness? Damien doubted it. He knew his illness would eventually kill him. It was merely a case of when.

Damien had wandered away from the school grounds and now stood before a wide expanse of water surrounded by forests of pine trees. The water looked deep and cold. A couple of years ago, Laurel and he would have jumped in splashed each other and then raced to the other side – not much chance of that now. Laurel would have won; he always won when they raced. They would joke it was because Laurel's feet were like flippers, two sizes above average.

This place was a small paradise, away from the hustle and bustle of the school grounds which held the constant yelling of voices. There was a constant gentle buzzing of insects. A small brown and white bird high up in the trees sang out its song, whilst another squawked out a warning to its young, warning them of Damien's presence. A croak and then a splash signalled a frog diving back into a small stagnant pool. A flash of green, and it disappeared under a large white lily leaf. The water glistened as it caught the sun rays. Damien stood in awe for a couple of minutes, listening, trying to make out the various sounds. He could hear the bleating of a sheep but could see no fields, only trees – mostly pines, and a couple of birch and elm in the distance. He guessed sound must travel across the valley and become trapped in the dip where he now stood. He heard a rustle. A squirrel loped across the grass only feet in front of him. He had never just stood and listened to the sound of nature before.

Mr Barton, his first-year History teacher, once said your senses are heightened when you come close to death. This theory was backed up with a story of three hundred Spartan warriors led by King Leonidas in 480 BCE. They fought the Persian army led by the Great King Xerxes. Knowing death was close, their heightened senses kept the Spartans alive for more days than should have been possible. Unfortunately, the Spartan warriors were eventually defeated and died fighting. Damien didn't want to die, not today. If he were to die soon, he would go down fighting just like a Spartan warrior. Damien smiled. He enjoyed History, especially the stories of the Spartans and the Greek battles. Mr Barton always used the Spartans as an example to any point he made. The fight for freedom and democracy was the Spartans. Strong leadership was the Spartans. It was a shame this year's History teacher was Ms Dixon. She just didn't have the same passion for the subject that Mr Barton had.

Damien glanced around. Would he have the strength to walk around the lake? A quick calculation and he estimated two miles; maybe another day when he had more energy and less pain. Would he ever have less pain? A deep sigh escaped from his lips. Probably not. He was feeling more upbeat today so he was not going to let this thought dampen his mood. He could see a lone figure sitting on a boulder near the water's edge. He guessed it was female even though her back was facing him. Long, dark, wavy hair tumbled down a slender back. As he grew closer, a pale green woollen top became visible with metallic buttons that fastened a dark band near the waist. It was an unusual top, probably from Jays Vintage store. Most of the females seemed to buy clothes at Jays – not only were they cheap, but the store was a stone's throw away from the school. He often thought that calling the used clothes "vintage" was a clever marketing strategy from an obvious enterprising entrepreneur.

Damien could see a clear wide track round the lake with small sandy areas. To reach the figure, he had to cut through onto a rough track through the undergrowth.

Taking extra care and holding his arms in the air so as not to catch his hands on the thorns and nettles, he moved slowly towards the figure. It was more a precaution than anything else, as there appeared to be only ferns and grasses blocking the route; not the thorns and nettles he had anticipated.

As he drew closer, Angel lifted her head. Her eyes were bright yet black as coal, framed by thick and dark lashes. The murderess was directly in front of him. Opening his mouth he heard himself stutter, "Do you come here often?" It sounded like a chat up line; how stupid. He felt embarrassed that he could even think, never mind say, such a thing. He felt his cheeks warm.

Angel smiled. "All the time," she replied holding up a book. It was a soft back book with a yellow cover – *Tom Sawyer*. Damien smiled and nodded – homework.

"I'm Damien," he offered, holding out his hand.

"I know. I'm Angel," she replied leaning over to shake his hand.

"I know," he laughed.

"Do you want to climb up?" Angel invited. Damien inspected the terrain. How had she managed to get up onto the rocks? There didn't appear to be any footholds, and he wasn't sure if he would have the strength to pull himself up, and then he would look a complete idiot. His legs were feeling tired. He would have to sit down soon or he would fall down. The mile walk to the lake had really taken its toll on his energy levels. He leant his body over his stick to catch his breath. Damien hated it when people saw him with a walking aid, but it was too late now. Angel pointed to the far side of the rocks. Damien followed her finger. There was a kind of natural path he could climb. Without too much difficulty, he scrambled up onto the rocks to join her. She shuffled over to make more room. He placed the stick beside him, within reach if he needed to grab it.

Angel looked stunning, completely different from when she was at school. She was probably the last person he had expected to see, which is why she had caught him off guard. Here in the outdoors, she appeared vibrant and full of confidence, not like the downtrodden, meek individual she portrayed at school. *Split personality* crossed his mind, but Damien realised later that Angel's behaviour was intentional. She liked to keep a low profile so as not to antagonise the popular girls like Beth and her friends. He was aware, like everyone at school, of the history between Angel and Beth. Still, as he and Angel sat and talked, thoughts of murder kept running through his head. Could the girl sitting next to him be capable of murder?

Angel adjusted her position. Damien instantly reacted and swung his stick around, stopping only centimetres from her neck. She screamed and squeezed her eyes closed, waiting for the impact. Slowly opening her left eye and then the right, she realised she wasn't hurt. Angel stared at him in horror.

"I...I'm really sorry. I don't know what came over me," he stuttered.

She swallowed hard. A lump had formed in the back of her throat. The stick was still poised at her neck. Her hand was trembling as she pushed the stick away from her body.

"I'm sorry," he repeated again.

"What did I do?" she asked.

"Nothing."

"Are you scared of me?"

"No, of course not. I...I'm not sure what I was thinking." He felt stupid and embarrassed again. *I am a fool, listening to Laurel and his sordid stories,* he chastised himself. Looking away, he could still feel Angel staring at him.

"Do you want an arm wrestle? If you win, I won't kill you."

He turned slightly to face her. "Are you serious?"

She burst out laughing, but it was a forced laugh as she tried to diffuse the situation. "I'll warn you next time I am going to move," she promised quietly. Her hand was still trembling slightly.

"Thank you for taking that so well. I'm sorry, I didn't mean to scare you. I'm not normally violent."

"Can I see your stick?"

It was an innocent question, but Damien was unsure how to respond. He would look stupid again if he said no, but the stick could be used as a weapon. What if she was a murderer? He would have nothing to defend himself. With his brain and mouth working independently, the words, "Yeah sure," escaped from his lips. Reluctantly Damien passed the walking stick over. Angel took it firmly and then let out a loud growl. Damien sprang from the rock, tripped, and landed on his bum.

Angel burst out laughing for real this time, "I am sorry. I couldn't resist it."

"I don't...." He looked up at her. "Ow, that hurt," he said slowly getting to his feet and rubbing his bum and thigh. Angel burst out laughing again as he brushed the dust off his trousers.

"Ok, that was funny, and I deserved it," he said with a smile.

"I'm sorry. It was a childish prank. Being serious, I was interested in your walking stick." Angel turned it over in her hands and stared at the design carved into the wood. "Ah, courage and honour. It's written in Chinese. I thought it was."

"Really? I thought it was just for design," he said clambering back onto the rocks.

Angel giggled. "No, it's definitely Chinese."

"I don't know anybody who can read Chinese apart from the Chinese," Damien commented, impressed. "Can you speak it?"

"No, and I can only read a few characters. It's quite hard to learn. I am just interested in languages and accents. I can usually tell where people are from by the way they speak."

Damien took the stick back, inspected the symbols, which he now understood were words, and placed it to his far side. He was pleased she had relaxed again and she had got her own back even if she had made him feel stupid.

"Can you tell where I'm from?"

Angel nodded. "Say something else to me then I'll tell you."

"Ok," he uttered a couple of sentences before a palm in the air signalled enough.

"I think I have it. You were born in Ireland, but you moved at a very early age. I would guess around three, when you would have just learnt to speak but not much older as your Irish accent is hidden and only the first words you learned have an Irish twang. I would say you have spent most of your life in Yorkshire, probably Northern Yorkshire. You either have friends or family who live in Surrey. You have spent a fair amount of time there, although your accent is not strong, which suggests you have not been there recently." She paused. "How did I do?"

"That was fantastic, almost perfect."

"Almost," she appeared disappointed.

"I spent a summer in Scotland."

"How could I miss that?" she laughed.

"Can you recognise everybody's accent?" Damien asked.

"Usually."

"Wow, I am impressed. That's some party trick."

"The school weirdo gets weirder, eh?" Angel said with a self-deprecating shrug.

"Is that how you see yourself?" Damien asked in surprise.

"That's how others see me. I know your friends call me 'the murderess.'"

"Oh, I am sorry about that. Laurel can get a bit carried away. He is harmless and means nothing by it."

"No worries. It doesn't bother me what people think. I am who I am, and I can't and won't change that. Anyway I prefer my own company."

"Would you like me to go?" Damien asked, starting to get up.

"Oh no, I didn't mean that. I don't have much in common with the people at school," she gave him a warm, friendly grin. "You may be different."

"Should I feel honoured?"

"Yes," she laughed again.

"I am sorry about earlier."

"It's already forgotten."

Angel was at her happiest when she was near the lake. Back in her room she often felt claustrophobic, no doubt developed from her time spent at Stanfield. At the lake it was open and peaceful. Time stood still; the air was fresh, an untouched innocence created in the fertile landscape. She was happy to have Damien's company. They talked for a long time longer than either of them had realised until a sudden chill in the air reminded them both the sun was going down. It was still winter. The sun's small amount of warmth soon disappeared and the night's cold air closed in quickly.

Jumping down from the rocks to grab her rucksack, Angel slipped slightly on the damp grass. Damien immediately reached out to stop her from falling, and her hand automatically grabbed his arm. Pain shot through his body. He hoped he hadn't winced. He did not want to show her the pain she had just caused and he certainly did not want her to give him that sympathetic look; the look he received so many times from people.

This was their first meeting, a meeting on which their friendship was developed.

The First Time

The pain in his head was becoming unbearable. It was like a power drill burrowed deep into his brain, constantly hammering inside, stabbing at his temples. It was Saturday, a day of relaxation, and in his opinion normally a day of boredom. Laurel would be playing rugby league. Normally, he would go and watch, even though he found it depressing. Instead, today the plan was to go to the lake, where he hoped Angel, with her strange sense of humour and remarkable conversation, would be chilling. She didn't stare and make him feel like a freak; in fact, she never asked about his illness, and he liked that. The pain never quite seemed so bad when he was with Angel, although today the pain was already exceptionally bad.

Rounding the rocky outcrop, Damien saw that Angel was already there, feet dangling in the water, wearing a pale blue dress pulled tightly around her waist, a book in her hand. His prediction that she would be there wasn't so remarkable; she was always there. He tried to sneak up on her, but a snapped twig and a rustle of leaves gave his position away. Angel swung her head round to see Damien's silhouette. His white baggy shirt blew in the slight breeze. Lately baggy shirts had become the norm; they were roomy and didn't put unnecessary pressure on his skin. A welcoming smile crossed Angel's face. Butterflies fluttered in her lower abdomen as he approached. It was a feeling she had never experienced before she met Damien, and she liked it.

"I didn't think you were going to make it today," she said quietly. This was the fifth time in as many weeks he had met Angel at the lake.

"Neither did I," he grinned as he climbed up onto the small rocky outcrop and plonked himself down. The butterflies fluttered a little more, and her heart beat a little faster.

Damien's head was still pounding. The blood vessels in his temples swelled and throbbed. His vision was becoming blurred; white dots were beginning to form in front of his eyes. No longer a timid hammering, now a sledgehammer pounded against the back of his eyes. His eyeballs felt like they were squeezing out of their sockets as the pain intensified. Squeezing his eyes shut, he tried to release the pressure and ease the pain. He wanted to enjoy the company of his new-found friend and not have to worry about the pain pounding in his head.

After a couple of minutes of silence, Angel turned slowly towards him.

"Is it painful today?" she asked. This was unusual for Angel; they had never spoken of his illness and the pain. Damien had always assumed he had hid it well. He smiled. Today he would tell her everything. He explained about his illness, the constant pain, and how today his head was throbbing and was becoming unbearable. Damien had never suffered from migraines until his illness took hold, but he wanted to explain so she would understand why today more than any other day he was not going to be very good company. Silence again; Angel turned and faced him squarely and uttered the magical words that would change both their lives forever.

"*I can take away your pain.*"

"Sit in front of me and close your eyes, and don't open them until I tell you to." She was in a strange mood, but he obeyed. Damien was no longer afraid of what she was possibly capable of, and he was feeling relaxed. Her hands moved across his head. She ran her long slender fingers through his unruly hair and across his face while her knuckles kneaded deep into his temples. Her fingers moved upwards and outwards. Her thumbs stretched the skin behind his ears as her fingers moved across his cheekbones, gently catching his eyelids. Her fingers moved meticulously over his head as she applied compression to various areas. *If this was an Indian head massage, it felt wonderful,* Damien thought to himself. A cool tingling sensation surged powerfully through his body before his whole body went into a mighty spasm. He wasn't sure what she was doing, but it seemed to be working. A calm serenity flowed through his body. He was unsure how long she worked her magic – ten minutes, half an hour – but the headache was gone, replaced with a feeling of vitality and energy.

A small trickle of blue liquid dripped from Angel's mouth. She quickly brushed it away with the back of her hand before Damien saw it. She realised she had taken a risk, and if her mother were still alive, she would certainly have scolded her.

Angel missed her mother. Her mother had understood what she was capable of – she had always known. At night her mother would tuck her in bed and say, "Hide it well, my darling. Do not tell anybody or they will persecute you for the rest of your life," and that was exactly what happened to her mother.

Fortunately, Damien was so sure Angel had merely given him an Indian head massage that nothing unusual had been detected. He was happy, and she was happy she had helped a friend. They sat for a while in silence, both comfortable in each other's company. Suddenly, without warning, the wind started to pick up, blowing their hair and tugging at their clothes. Small ripples began to form in the normally static lake. The trees swayed gently. A symphony of music created through the movement of the leaves.

"I guess we are building up to a storm," his voice was low so not to compete with Mother Nature. She smiled at him, and her eyes caught his; they both looked up towards the sky. Grey clouds moved fast above their heads. Their shapes changed as they became one. A small droplet of water splashed onto his forehead. It was over a mile back to any shelter, and they recognised they would not make it back in time. A storm was not forecast; however, the weather was so changeable, especially at this time of year. Angel pointed to the trees to their left. The forest was dense in places so they could shelter there until the storm passed.

Damien jumped down from the rocks as though he had a new lease on life and held out his hand to support Angel in her jump. She didn't need help, but she grabbed his hand, appreciating the offer. His grip was strong and masculine, not as she expected.

"Are you sure we'll be safe?" Damien asked.

"It's only a bit of rain," she laughed. "We can sit on the pine needles beneath the largest pine over-looking the lake."

"It doesn't sound very comfortable."

"Trust me, it is. I have sheltered there before. A couple of months ago it was raining just like today. I took shelter, and before I knew it I had fallen asleep. I woke in the middle of the night, freezing cold, covered in pine needles. They were stuck in my hair. It took me ages to get them out. I thought I was going to have to cut my hair." Damien stared at her thick, dark hair. It would have been a shame to cut it short. Angel continued chatting as though she had known him all her life. "It was a right mess and then I had to find my way back to my accommodation. It was pitch black and I must have bumped into everything possible. Have you ever tried to climb a stile in the dark when you can't even find the stile? Now I come prepared," and she pulled a small torch from her rucksack. Damien laughed.

"You should smile more. You have a nice smile," she said as she glanced towards him.

"Thank you. I don't think anyone has ever said that to me before," a slight pink tinge appeared on his cheeks.

"Sorry if I embarrassed you. Mrs Simpson, my old school teacher would say to me, Angelica Wellingstone, you are not socially mature to say such a thing."

Damien laughed. He loved her impersonations. "You just caught me off guard. I can't remember the last time I had a compliment. That's all."

Angel smiled. Her eye caught his again, lingering a second too long. She looked away before he could see her blush.

He picked up a handful of pine needles and threw them at her. "I can be socially immature as well," he laughed.

Angel burst into a fit of giggles. "So can I," she said, throwing a handful back. Damien scooped up a large quantity of pine needles.

"No," she giggled, "that's too many." He looked at her, wondering if he should.

"Ok, I will be socially mature," he conceded, dropping them to the ground.

"But I'm not," and from behind her back she produced another handful of pine needles and threw them over him.

"Truce, truce, I give in," he shouted over the storm.

They plonked themselves down on the thickest carpet of pine needles they could find, and Angel was correct; they were soft. Their backs were resting against the old pine. His head felt so clear, and even his back was not hurting anymore. The rain drove down hard; droplets bounced on the lake one foot sometimes two feet high. The wind howled outside, but not a drop of rain fell in their shelter.

"Do you want an apple?" her hand was already rummaging inside her rucksack before pulling out two yellow apples streaked in red and orange. Damien smiled again. Every time they met, she had a different variety of apple in her rucksack, and she would always give him a run-down on the history of that particular apple.

"Ok, what should I be able to smell?" Damien asked.

"Some say it has a faint smell of pear, others just call it aromatic."

"And the taste?"

"Sweet and very strong-tasting – it's a Ribston Pippin. They are sometimes a little lopsided. See how the bottom is flatter than most apples. The fruiterer down in Sandalwood Avenue bought them from his supplier yesterday. He says most people do not appreciate apples anymore, so if he finds something a little different, he normally places an order for me."

Damien laughed again. "How do you know so much about apples?"

"Do you really want to know?" Angel asked, not wanting to bore him or freak him out.

"Sure."

Angel paused. She never let Damien get too close to her past, but the story of the apples was innocent. Surely no harm could be done along as she didn't delve too deep into the detail.

"Ok, when I was younger I had a friend called Stan who taught me everything I know about apples. He said every apple had a story – often a magical story. Every apple with their own personality: a grumpy Claygate Pearmain; the beautiful Beauty of Bath; the solemn Arthur Turner; the Flower of Kent, otherwise known as the Inspirer that inspired Sir Issac Newton to consider the laws of gravity. However, my favourite story was when Stan spoke of Adam and Eve and the forbidden fruits from the Garden of Eden, and how with just one bite from the apple plucked from the Tree of Knowledge of Good and Evil killed Adam."

"That's not a nice story!" Damien exclaimed.

"Why?"

"The young lad, Adam, died!"

"Oh, I never thought of that. Stan would joke that it must have been one of those foreign imports. I think he liked to make me laugh, although I never understood the joke until I was a lot older. Stan obviously thought it was a hilarious joke. I guess it wasn't funny if we were laughing at somebody's death."

"Sorry, I didn't mean to spoil it for you."

Angel appeared thoughtful for a minute. Then she smiled and continued, "We were always at an interesting part of a magical story when the dragon's voice would interrupt. 'Stan Cauldron, how many times have I told you not to talk to...'" she suddenly stopped. "That's not important. Stan would tell me about the slight variations in an apple's colouring, the differences in taste and smell."

"Who was the dragon?" Damien asked, intrigued.

"Nobody important," said Angel quickly. "Enough about me. Now tell me about you." Angel was desperate to change the subject, so Damien told her about his father, who was a Chief Inspector in Scotland Yard and his brother who was training to be a lawyer. He told her about Laurel's mother, Margo, who made the best apple pie and custard in the world, causing Angel to protest, "The world is a big place."

"Ok, I'll rephrase, the best I have tasted so far and far better than my mum's, who can't bake. Not that I have tasted yours yet," he added, giving her one of his cheeky grins.

"Is that a challenge?"

"Yep."

Margo's apple pie consisted of three types of apple and a large quantity of cinnamon encased in short crust pastry. Angel wanted to know the type of apples to help her with the challenge, but Damien didn't know.

"I only eat it, not make it," he laughed. Neither had noticed the rain had stopped, and the winds had died down. The sun was now warming up the land again causing steam to rise from the wet foliage. The faint trace of a rainbow could be seen just above Winslow Hill. The storm had passed.

The Third Child – The Train Ride Six Years Earlier

The freight train chugged slowly from town to town, only stopping to refuel and load its cargo. Crystal had no plan other than to get away from her current life; away from her sad, pathetic, alcoholic mother. She didn't know where she was going. The train would take her to the end of the line; to a new destination where she would start a new life, where nobody would know what she was capable of.

She didn't have a ticket – she didn't need one. She had travelled before without a ticket. Crystal never dared to venture into the first-class carriages. The other passengers would realise she wasn't one of them. They had snooty voices and over-priced clothes and jewellery; she had a dog-eared bag and ripped trousers. Second class was her normal mode of travel. This time she had chosen a slow, old freight train. An empty carriage reserved for animals would be her home for the next few hours. Some hay remained from a previous load, and the faint smell of the manure was surprisingly comforting, even though there was a draft from the gap under the door – at least she could sit and relax.

It was a clear night. The stars twinkled high in the sky. Through a small gap in the carriage ceiling, the Hunter with its Orion belt could be clearly seen. There was a chill in the air. Unzipping her bag, Crystal lifted out a long, dark-grey cardigan and placed it around her shoulders. Standing in the empty carriage, her body swayed in line with the movement of the train. Carefully she made her way to the wooden door and pulled it slightly open. A cold blast of air hit her in the face. Shivering, she closed the door. There was no way to tell which way the train was heading. The position of the stars meant nothing – her assumption had been that they were travelling north, yet she hadn't recognized the names of any of the stations they had passed. Sneaking on at Redmond, and then Bristol had been the easy part. Now miles from home, an ounce of guilt rushed through her body. It was the right thing to do. She had not taken the decision lightly to run away, to leave all what she knew behind.

The train began to slow as it pulled into another station. Once again she crept to the door and placed her ear on the cold, damp wood. She had to be ready to move if the doors opened. Just as she thought she was safe, she heard footsteps on the gravel. The door opened slightly. A white dirty hand grabbed the door frame while the other hand tried to pry the door open. Crystal backed away from the door. A gasp escaped from her lips. Her hand was too slow in stopping the noise escaping from her mouth.

She heard a gruff, gravelly voice, "Are you going to help me climb onto this thing or do you want me to give away our presence?"

Crystal swore, annoyed with herself. Everything had been going perfect. Reluctantly, she pulled the door open. Her bag was in her hand; she was ready to jump and sprint. An old man blocked her passage. A tea-cosy hat was pulled down low over his ears; wisps of his white hair stuck out from underneath. A white untrimmed beard tinged with yellow stains obscured his lower face and neck.

"Give me your hand, and pull me up before the train moves," he ordered, and without thinking, Crystal thrust out her hand and pulled him into the carriage. The woollen fingerless gloves that he wore were smeared in dirt and grime; his nails were encrusted in muck. The scabs and sores on his fingers appeared painfully infected. Red, hard lumps had formed between his fingers, preventing him from pressing his fingers together. By touching his naked skin, a small amount of healing power would have passed through her finger-tips to his fingers. Crystal quickly brushed her hand against the leg of her jeans to remove any muck or germs that may have been transferred – not that a germ would have any effect on her.

He wasn't heavy, nor was he very agile; however, his voice was fierce. Once he had clambered into the carriage, he barked an order to close the door. She thought about dismounting and running but instead closed the door. He appeared grumpy, yet harmless. Glancing over to the corner of the carriage, the stranger was now sitting down, rummaging in the pockets of a long overcoat.

"Do you have any food?" he asked.

Crystal shook her head as she sat down near the door, the furthest point from where her intruder now sat. A cold draft found its way under the carriage door, and the chill bit at her ankles and fingers. Keeping a safe distance from the stranger, she moved further into the carriage.

Lifting his head, he began to cough, a deep, grating, husky cough which came from deep within his chest.

He hammered his fist into the centre of his chest, coughed and spat a dark tar coloured liquid onto the floor. Crystal screwed up her face in disgust and pulled her cardigan tighter around her body.

"Here you go, kid," he said as a chocolate bar flew across the carriage. Crystal moved with agility, uncertain at first what had been thrown at her. He let out a howling laugh which ended in a coughing fit and him spitting some more of the tar coloured substance onto the floor.

The train once again pulled away from the station, continuing to its final destination, which Crystal was to learn was Glasgow. Her head rocked from side to side with the movement of the train as she tried to stay awake. Currently curled into a tight ball, the unwelcome guest had made himself at home. A large upturned collar sheltered his neck from the cold. Every few minutes, he rubbed his hands together to keep warm before coughing and spitting. After an hour, he slowly sat up.

"These things never get any easier to sleep in," he huffed. "The name is Fred."

"Crystal," she replied and then wondered if she should have given a false name.

"Welcome to first-class travel, Crystal. What brings you up here?"

"Work," she replied bluntly.

"Not much work going up here. You would have been better to go south to London."

Crystal sat in silence. She had deliberately decided not to go to London in case they were searching for her. Everybody headed to London; however, she wasn't going to tell a complete stranger her reasons. "That's a bad cough you have," she commented as she tried to change the subject.

"Bronchitis. Aren't you going to ask me why I am traveling north?"

"Ok, why?"

"I have decided to return to my roots to die. There would be no other reason I would be heading north in the middle of winter, too bloomin' cold, for starters."

Crystal managed a weak smile. She hadn't thought of the cold. "Do you want to die?"

Fred tugged gently on his facial hair before sighing. "Get off the street, kid. I have spent the last twenty-five years living rough, and it's not easy. Dying is the easier option. If the Bronchitis doesn't kill me, then the cold will. It gets into your bones, and then you never feel warm, even when the sun beats down on you. Your joints ache. It's not nice. Go home, kid, if you can." Crystal didn't say anything. She looked away and pulled her knees closer to her chest. Would her mother have realised she had gone yet? Would she care?

"Guess how old I am, kid," Fred challenged. Crystal glanced at him and shrugged her shoulders.

"Forty-two years going on sixty-two. I left home at seventeen. If I had known then what I know now, I would have done things differently." Crystal's stomach began to rumble. Un-wrapping the chocolate bar she began to munch on the soft-chocolate caramel. Skipping dinner before she left had been a bad decision. It was nice having company, talking to somebody who knew nothing about her previous life. She could be anyone and anything, an actress, a singer, an astronaut, a car racing driver – anything that took her fancy.

Fred started to cough again. With a clenched fist, he pounded it into his chest. "It releases the phlegm," he said almost apologetically. Healing the stranger, with his fierce irritating cough, would be easy; nonetheless, she had promised herself no more healing. Nobody must know what she was capable of. That's how it all started back home – the resentment, the names and finally being an outcast.

"Aren't you eating?" Crystal asked.

"Nah, I gave you my last chocolate bar. It looks like you need it more than me." Crystal popped the last piece into her mouth with a feeling of guilt. The small amount of nourishment was gratefully received.

"Thanks," she muttered.

They sat in silence for the rest of the journey until the train started to slow again. Fred slowly got to his feet and walked to the door. "When it stops at the next set of signals, I would recommend you disembark. If you ride right into the station, they will arrest you. Stick you in the slammer overnight, and it's none of my business, but I assume you are underage." He began to cough uncontrollably, spitting out the words between the coughing fits. "They will run a search on you, try and track down whoever and whatever you are running from. Think smart, kid," he admonished as spit dribbled from the side of his mouth. A fingerless glove reached up and brushed the corner of his mouth, catching his coarse beard; this time he spat two-foot to his left.

"I ain't going to live on the street. I am going to get myself a job, a house. Live like other people," Crystal quietly replied. Fred grinned a toothless grin. What was left of his teeth were black and stained.

"Good luck, kid. We all thought like that once. I still reckon you would be better off in London," was his advice. His deep husky cough stayed with her as they both disembarked and parted company. Despite the sweet chocolate, a bitter taste had been left in her mouth.

The Pain Worsens

No sign of Damien, which was unusual, although when the pain was bad he had started missing some classes. Angel had not seen him all day. The following day was the same – no sign of him. Plucking up her courage, Angel decided to visit his halls of residence. The male residential block stood tall behind a promenade of large oak trees. A delivery road to the left of the building serviced the school and separated the female and male residential buildings. A large wide open space to the far side of the building led to well-stocked gardens. Angel knew Damien had originally been on the fifth floor, but had swapped rooms to be on the first floor, where there were fewer stairs to contend with. Damien now spoke openly to Angel about his illness and the regular pain he endured. He tried not to dwell on it too much, and she did not judge him or treat him differently, which he liked.

It was early evening, so there were not many people around. A young lad of around fourteen years directed her to the right room. She tapped on the door, but there was no answer. The door was not locked; Angel pushed it open and entered the room.

"Damien," she whispered; still no answer. The curtains were drawn, and the room was in complete darkness. A figure was huddled in the centre of the bed. Angel slowly approached the bed; she could just make out it was Damien.

"I can't bear the pain, Angel," he said, pain evident in his voice. "It hurts so bad."

"I know; it will pass," she spoke softly as she placed a comforting hand on his shoulder.

Adjusting to the darkness, she could now see the hurt in his eyes. Curled into a foetal position, his body rocked gently. Without thinking, she whispered, "Damien, sit up. I will take your pain." He didn't quite register what she was saying, but he sat up anyway.

Angel moved quickly to the bedroom door and turned the latch. On her return to the bed, she flicked on the bathroom light. The sudden burst of light caused Damien to flinch. Thinking better of it, she closed the bathroom door. Later, after the treatment, she would need a clear route to the bathroom. Angel unbuttoned Damien's shirt. She prayed her fingernails would not scratch his tender skin. Slipping his shirt off, Angel also removed her top so her zip could not catch his skin. Standing in just her bra and feeling totally exposed, Angel moved quickly. Damien sat in a daze on the edge of the bed with his body slumped over his knees. Angel knelt behind him. Initially, he refused to bite down on the small black book Angel had found on the bedside table. Angel stroked the side of his face to help him to relax before trying again. This time he accepted the book – it would stop him screaming. Her touch would hurt at first before the soothing would begin. Slipping her arms beneath his armpits, she yanked his body towards hers. His body felt heavy, almost unresponsive. Placing her arms around his waist, her fingers reached towards his abdomen.

Damien felt Angel's warm breath on the back of his neck. A tingling sensation ran up and down his spine.

"Trust me, Damien. Don't fight me. Let my body enter yours. Let me take your pain," Angel spoke quietly, but she knew Damien could hear in his semi-conscious state. Her hands touched his body. He tried to scream except the book turned it into a deep growl. The book slipped from his lips; she prayed he would not feel the need to shout again. They didn't want any unwelcome company. Her hands started moving meticulously over his abdomen, fingers traveling in small circles, pulling and pushing the skin. Moving from the centre of the abdomen to the side of his body, the circles became larger. All the time, she was whispering, "Give me your pain." Damien was not fighting her. She was entering and probing with ease. The whole of his body lay open for her to touch, to manipulate and destroy the pain that was destroying his life. She could feel the pain surging from his body into hers; this was going to hurt. Damien was fairly resilient to pain, as he had been suffering for over three years, yet for Angel this whole experience was new. His head fell back onto her shoulder. The smell of Eucalyptus and apple blossom from his shampoo filled her nostrils. *Concentrate, Angel, concentrate.* His Adam's apple was now fully exposed. Gently brushing his cheek with her lips, she pulled him tighter to her body. Their cheeks now touching, his skin felt rough with a couple of days' stubble rubbing against her soft skin. He had not shaved for days – she did not mind. Her fingers now moved up his body to his chest and her methodical routine started again.

Absorbing his pain was tiring. Her body struggled with the procedure. How much more could she take?

Without warning, a feeling of relief surged through her body. Damien's back arched before locking. His body spasmed, signifying the end of the session. Angel eased him onto his back. His eyes were closed, his face no longer twisted in agony. A thin film of perspiration lined his brow. Angel moved her finger across his hairline and down the side of his face. As she reached his jawline, she noticed his lips were slightly parted, just waiting for her to kiss. Moving her face closer to his – she had wanted to do this for so long – she thought that she could claim it was part of the pain removal. It was only a small white lie. Angel quickly placed a kiss on his lips. She did not want to linger too long in case he opened his eyes. They were soft, just as she imagined. One day she would linger longer, savour every moment. Hopefully one day Damien would respond, kiss her as though she was the only one for him. Dare she dream? Was this what she had been reduced to? Find a man you like, wait until he is semi-unconscious and then take advantage – steal a kiss.

Her eyes moved slowly across his body, studying the shape of every muscle. His body was stronger and more toned than she had expected. Angel's fingers skimmed his chest and abdomen. What was she doing? It was so wrong, touching his naked skin. At least before, she had the excuse of healing but now it was wrong. The blisters and sore red patches had almost disappeared from the front of his torso, although a bruise was beginning to form around the lower abdomen. That should not have happened. She had been rougher than she intended. Angel stared at his torso again, a little annoyed with the bruising. Then a small smile appeared on her lips. She had removed a major pain for the first time and hadn't done a bad job. She should feel proud, not disappointed.

Angel suddenly felt the sickness rising in her body. She rushed into the bathroom to relieve herself of the blue liquid. On her return, Damien was asleep. He had somehow managed to crawl back into bed. Angel was tired, her energy levels sapped. Hoping he wouldn't mind, she curled up next to him. Pulling the thin linen blanket over her body, she wrapped her arm around his waist before she fell asleep, the faint smell of apple blossom lingering in her nostrils.

The next day Angel woke early, a tenderness in her abdomen reminded her of the evening's events. She had been back and forth from the bathroom for most of the night. The sickening blue liquid had made a presence every time. When all the liquid was out of her body, the pain would subside. Damien was sleeping peacefully. Glancing over to the bedside table, the digital alarm clock showed 5:30. The green luminous numbers glared brightly in the darkened room. Damien had recently turned over in bed. His arm now lay across her upper arm, trapping her in the bed. His face was close to her face. A single centimetre separated their lips. His were so inviting. She wanted to place another kiss on them, to feel their warmth again, but if he woke she would feel so embarrassed. Feeling happy, she lay next to him a while longer. When he exhaled, his warm breath touched her lips. Her fingers moved to his wavy hair. She wanted to feel its texture and softness, but was afraid she might wake him. Taking a deep breath, she inhaled his breath once more, almost a kiss but not quite, before carefully lifting his arm from her shoulder. Tip-toeing out of the room, Angel darted back to her accommodation to shower and change ready for school.

Damien woke, half expecting Angel to be still in his room. He remembered her arriving early in the evening but not much else. The pain in his stomach had subsided. Excitedly his eyes skimmed his abdomen; it was no longer a crimson red, nor was it swollen. A faint blue tinge marked where a bruise was beginning to develop. Apart from that, his abdomen was beginning to look normal. Damien turned towards the full-length mirror to view his back. Disappointingly, his back was still red and sore. With a renewed energy, he felt ready to face school, and the onslaught of his final exams did not feel so daunting today. He only had one class with Angel, and that was second period today. Damien desperately wanted to see her to ask the many unanswered questions that were running through his head. He felt closer to Angel than he had ever felt before. He guessed she had just left his room as a faint smell of her perfume was still lingering on his pillow.

Two bottles of tablets filled with antibiotics and pain-killers lay on the bedside cupboard, their screw tops missing. Damien rarely screwed the tops back onto the bottles as the child safety device made it impossible to open, especially when he needed a tablet fast, and the pain was in his fingers. Picking up the bottles, he gave them a slight shake. They were both empty. Another trip to the doctor was needed. Last time he checked, there was at least a week's supply in each bottle. He realised he had taken more than the recommended dosage, but the pain over the last two days had been exceptionally bad. Making a mental note to collect his prescription from the doctors before 2:00 p.m. Damien set off for school. He hoped Dr Haswell would be too busy to see him. The Doctor would only shatter his dream of a total recovery, although Damien was aware his check-up was due.

*****

The shower was warm and comforting, caressing her naked body. What was she doing? The feelings were getting stronger. What if she had been caught in Damien's bedroom? Edward would have... She stopped. What would Edward have done? She was too old to be smacked. He could have shook her, shook her so hard her brain turned to mush. So why risk so much? She could have gotten them both expelled for staying overnight in the male halls, but Damien was in such pain. Angel couldn't bear to see him suffer, and now he would want to know what had happened. He would wonder why his skin was looking better. He would push her to find out more, and the worse thing was, it was only a temporary respite from the pain. Her mother could heal, take away a person's pain, give that person their life back. A look of disappointment crossed Angel's face. Damien didn't need a temporary fix. He needed a full healing. Where was her mother? She hadn't seen her in over six years.

"Why did you leave me, Mam? I am so confused," she whispered. Raising her face to the chrome shower-head, the spray splashed her face with a powerful force. Closing her eyes, she whispered, "Books can't help me. I need to understand."

Angel could see herself standing over a body, a knife clasped tightly in her right hand. She was staring at a lifeless figure – a young beautiful child, an empty vessel, the soul long gone. Collapsing to her knees, she pushed the blonde matted hair away from the child's face with the serrated knife's edge. The handle of the knife had a strange carved pattern, possibly a hunter's knife. The inscription meant something, but she was unsure what. Without turning her eyes away from the body, she placed her left hand on the body's forehead and murmured in a soft voice, "The pain will leave you." The skin felt cool on her warm fingers. She traced the outline of the nose with her forefinger, down to the lips. She heard a child scream. Looking up, she could see Beth screaming hysterically. The water had turned hot, almost to scalding point – the dragon's breath was burning her skin. Stepping out of the shower, she gently toweled her body dry. The images continued to appear. Angel glanced left. Somebody else was with her, hiding in the bushes. The leaves parted with a slight rustle, and the mystery person stepped deeper into the undergrowth and disappeared from sight.

A red sticky substance dripped through her fingers. The knife was in her hand. Beth's scream rang in her ears, "Murder." Confused, she stared at Beth and then at the lifeless figure. Sickness rose in her body. She flung the knife into the bushes. "I didn't do it," she uttered over and over again. Standing up, she again glanced down at her hands. The red substance was already starting to harden. A crowd had gathered, drawn by Beth's screams. Her mother ran towards her, but it was now too late. They would take her away just like Edward had said.

"I tried to take away her pain, Mum, just like you do." Tears formed in Angel's eyes. This was not her imagination, not a story from a book. This was what had happened to her eight years ago.

"I know, pumpkin, I know," her mother's words began to fade, the embrace slowly dissolved. They took her away. "I didn't do it," she whispered again.

The Third Child – Glasgow Six Year Earlier

It was cold, wet, and miserable. The snow had turned to a grey, wet slush that kept finding its way into Crystal's battered leather shoes. Crystal had trampled the streets looking for work, only to find there were very few retail outlets hiring. Those that were recruiting would not consider somebody without an address. It was a vicious circle. No address, no job, but you could not get an address without a job. When she raised this point with the snub bitch at the delicatessen, the woman laughed in her face. Then there was the problem with her National Insurance number – she didn't have one. It was a big mess.

The rain penetrated everything Crystal wore. Her clothes clung damply to her body. She was cold, wet and hungry. Sitting on a bench in Kelvingrove Park near the River Kelvin, even the ducks had deserted her. Crystal was no longer trying to keep dry. She was trying to work out her next move. Had she been right to leave home? Nothing was working out. One day she had hoped to contact an adoption agency to try and find her biological parents to ask them why they had put her up for adoption. To find them would cost money – something she did not have nor was likely to have soon. Deep in thought, she had missed the figure approaching from behind. A woollen 'tea-cosy' hat was pulled low over the stranger's ears to keep out the constant beating of the rain. His hands were tucked deep inside his pockets

"How's it going, kid? Have you found that dream job?"

Shocked that somebody else was in the park, Crystal quickly raised her head. Fred sat on the far side of the bench, sodden and looking worse for wear. Spit dribbled from the corner of his mouth into the coarse hairs of his tea-stained beard. Beads of water had found refuge in his unkempt facial hair. His skin was pale and gaunt from wandering the streets in the bitter, dark, thunderous rain. A chesty cough escaped from deep inside, rattling his rib-cage. The build-up of liquid gurgled in the back of his throat. Any minute and he would need to spit. Strangely, it didn't disgust her; it was almost a relief to see a friendly face, somebody who would not treat her like muck scraped from the bottom of their shoe.

"How are you doing, Fred?"

"Ok, and you?"

She sighed, "Not good; it's impossible. No address, no job. I hate to admit it, but you were right."

"All those dreams shattered?"

She nodded, "I'm not sure what to do now."

"How about getting out of the rain for starters? You'll get pneumonia."

"If only you knew," she muttered. There had been times when she would have loved to be ill. Pneumonia, chicken pox, measles, even a runny nose or sore throat – anything. She had stood next to the kids who were ill, drank from the same cups at school. Still she could not make herself ill. Her body repaired itself so quickly; it fought off any infection before it had a chance to get a hold. Bruises came and went just as quick. Fred wouldn't understand. Nobody understood. Her father had been right; she was a demon. Fred stood up to go. "Let's go, kid. I'll show you where there's a decent squat. Get you dry, or you'll be popping your clogs before me, and that's just so unfair."

Crystal managed a weak, lethargic smile as she rose. "You're not a perv, are you, Fred?"

"Nah, I grew out of that a long time ago. I prefer mine a little older."

Crystal scanned the park. Everything appeared to be dead. The tiny snowdrops that had fought most of the winter weather were either crushed under the weight of the rain or drowned in the small pools of water that were beginning to form on the grass. The rain was now in full force lashing down onto the path. The ground had become sodden underfoot. They made an odd couple as they walked out of the park together; two homeless people who were to develop a bond of friendship.

Fred sneezed.

"Please let me sneeze just once so I can understand what it feels like," Crystal whispered.

Fred turned. "Did you say something?"

Crystal shook her head. Droplets of water sprayed in all directions like a border collie shaking its damp coat after a dunk in the river. Strands of red hair hugged her cheeks while droplets of water dripped off the end of her nose and ran down her neck and beneath the collar of her thin coat. Crystal continued to follow the only person who had shown her any kindness in the last few weeks; a man she hardly knew who would soon become a father figure.

Crystal stayed with Fred, watching him slowly deteriorate. His cough got worse. The build-up of phlegm on his chest was getting more difficult to remove. The tar-coloured substance had now turned to blood.

"It won't be long, lass," he kept saying. The squat wasn't bad. People came and went. She often wondered where they went. Fred said London, but she wasn't sure if he was lying to her. Fred never tried to lay a finger on her, and she never invaded his space. Three feet was as close as they came to each other. Men ogled, but nobody bothered her when they knew she was with Fred. Crystal followed her mentor, observed his actions, and learnt how to survive. Fred didn't seem to mind; maybe it even gave him a reason to live, a purpose. The politics were confusing in the squat with many do's and don'ts, but she was a quick learner. It was a strange new world that she had unwittingly become a part of. There was always a hierarchy. "Keep the main man happy, and he will protect you" were Fred's words, and that was how she lived.

Last week, they had lived like a king and queen, divulging in strawberry yoghurts for breakfast, creamy with chunks of fruit. They were not the cheap yoghurts from the discount stores; these yoghurts put pounds on the waistline through smell alone. Crystal and Fred had given a customary share to the squat leader. Today there was no yoghurt. Crystal didn't dare go back to the Georgian terraces on Mount Stanton Grove even though raiding number forty-six again was tempting. "You don't shit on your own doorstep" were Fred's words, not hers. She could see his point, but she was the one who walked the distance early every morning in all weathers before the homeowners arose.

Today she returned with a loaf of wholegrain bread and a bottle of semi-skimmed milk courtesy of the milkman from Taybridge Road. Not a major feast, yet worth the walk. She almost picked up some cheese, although Brie was not her favourite, and the housekeeper had come to the door at the point of removal. Twice now she had been close to being caught. The doorsteps of the wealthy always had tempting products just waiting for people like her to take. They could afford it, maybe a little inconvenient for the owner when breakfast was not waiting for them, but that was not her problem – she only caused the problem. Anyway, she rarely targeted the same residences.

Crystal ducked down an alleyway and through a back gate hanging off its hinges. A wooden board gave entry through a back window of a house, where she was met by the big guy with deep set eyes and a thick umbrella eyebrow. His name escaped her. Crystal immediately offered some of the bread and milk.

"Fred's dead," were his blunt words. "We're moving the body, leaving it at the hospital door tonight." Crystal nodded, not wanting to show any weakness. Fred had warned her this would happen. It was the homeless way of paying respect to a life of one of their own. The authorities would cremate the body, scatter the ashes across the rose garden in Rolinson graveyard. No grave would be marked – just another lost soul feeding the many plants. Over the next fortnight people Fred had never met as well as those he had would visit the garden. They would bow their heads, utter a few words, and then leave, all of them knowing one day it would be them. Fred's clothing would be picked over by the vultures first. His body would be left with very few personal belongings. The coat and shoes would be argued over; however, it was the big guy's job to distribute the belongings.

Fred's death hurt Crystal deeper than when her father called her a demon. Now all alone, the thought of facing another bitter Scottish winter was frightening. Crystal swore never to get close to another living soul as it always ended in tears. First had been Jessica, then her parents and finally Fred. Soon after, Crystal moved to London. It was Fred's last wish. "More chance and more opportunity," he would insist. Time would tell.

The First Child
Seven Years Earlier

Across the Channel, a very different battle was being fought. The suicide note was sealed in a small white envelope and placed on the dining room table. It was not written to anybody in particular – he didn't have anybody to write it to. His parents had died two months earlier in a car crash and his friends, well, they were falling fast. An Airfix Piper PA-28-161 Warrior II model stood proudly beside the envelope. Its fresh coat of paint glistened in the sunlight. A Robin DR400 was placed to the right, framing the small envelope. He had always had a fascination with small propeller planes and had been collecting models of them since he was a child. His friends would describe him as a bit of an anorak – but it was his hobby.

His Cessna 172 was his favourite plane. The wings were much higher than the other single propeller planes. His intention was to one day own his own plane and use it for crop spraying or delivering supplies to small villages in Africa. Wherever the demand, whatever the job, he would go with his plane. He had now saved enough money from his job as a car mechanic for the first few PPL lessons, and although the pay wasn't high, he realised this job would help him understand engines. What he worked on now may not be Lycoming engines, but the principle of how an engine worked and the servicing was similar. This had once been his dream; now his dream was to leave this god-forsaken place. His life had become engulfed by death and sorrow.

The rope felt comforting in his hand – it would be over soon. An old woman had recently come into his life, although on closer inspection she was probably not that old, maybe around fifty years. She seemed weary and drawn, possibly a traveller, who had had a hard life. She was confusing him and complicating matters. Her dark, enquiring eyes held a sadness that said, Trust me. Her long dark hair was often tied in a bun or hidden by a patterned headscarf, and her manner was intense and serious. He couldn't understand what she wanted from him. The language barrier was a hindrance. It was as though she was telling him she was his mother. He was sure mother was *mère*. Languages were normally easy for him, especially English. The old woman was obviously deranged; trying to feed on his recent loss after reading the newspaper obituaries. No matter which way he turned, either the old woman or the guy with the moustache was there. They were constantly asking questions, pushing and harassing him. He would leave the guy and the old woman to argue. He didn't want to be part of their world anymore. This was the simplest way – the only way – to escape. He had tried everything else.

Dominique always knew he was different from the other kids, but he had kept a low profile at school and had blended in well. His difference was not obvious. He looked and acted like everyone else. It wasn't as though a big sign was tattooed across his forehead that read "freak in town." Nobody knew what he was capable of, apart from the guy with the moustache and possibly the old woman. His parents had their suspicions. It started when he had laid his right hand on his sister Suzy's forehead and told her he would take her cancer. After that, the cancerous cells disappeared. He showed signs of cancer for a while, but they left his body within a day of being detected. He wasn't sure how or why he did what he did. A voice inside his head told him what to do, almost controlling his actions. Dominique loved his sister, but at sixteen years she had run off with some meathead who called himself Zacho.

"He's Italian," his sister had once boasted. Italian – that was a joke; his real name was obviously Zak and by adding an o, he felt he could trick everyone. His sister was stupid and naïve. Zacho was ten years her senior, but he had turned her head. He could not give her a comfortable life; he did not work. He could not even afford to get his hair cut or his beard trimmed. They lived off the land, drifting like hippies, constantly harping about love and peace. Their parents had been distraught and blamed themselves for giving Suzy too much freedom. He could not help her, not anymore; he could not even help himself.

His sister was not the only recipient of his healing. Émile, his golden Labrador retriever, had trapped her leg in a small rabbit burrow when chasing the neighbour's terrier. At the time, his father was sure Émile's leg was broken from the dog's howling and the unnatural shape of the leg. Dominique had repaired the damage within seconds with just a touch. Émile died three months later, run over by a car as she chased the same terrier. Dominique guessed the dog's time was up. But now things were getting out of control. This man was hounding him, following him everywhere, telling him to do things. The stale smell of smoke always lingered in his presence.

He wasn't a killer. How could the man say it was his destiny? He had refused initially, then his colleagues and friends started going missing and death was soon to follow. Philippe and Jean-Paul were the first. Philippe, known as Wasa due to the strange noise he could make with a cupped hand and an armpit, had said he felt as though he were being watched. Dominique and Jean-Paul had laughed at him and told him it was paranoia left over from his latest booze binge. Jean-Paul and Wasa both died in a freak house fire. Investigators said the gas oven had been left on during the day, and with no flame from the ignition, there had been a major build-up of methane. As soon as the light switch was flicked – boom! The mix of the hydrocarbon gases had combusted – bringing the end of his two mates. He couldn't understand why his mates hadn't smelt the mercaptan odorant, the rotten egg smell that indicates a gas leak, when they entered the house.

The young blonde from the *boulangerie* was next. Dominique didn't even know her that well, although he would have liked to. His daily morning flirt had rapidly come to an end. Dominique did not even know her name until the newspaper released it. Christine Blanchard, a pretty name for a beautiful young lady. Her body was found behind the *boulangerie* in the early hours; a single stab wound to the heart and no sign of any foul play or theft. There was still a twenty euro bill in her goat-skin purse and a single theatre ticket for the amateur dramatic show *Mon Cherie* taking place at 7:00 p.m. that evening.

Dominique knew it was the moustached man – his tormentor – who was killing the innocent, killing anybody he came into contact with, and now the voices had started again. No voices for over seven years and then for no reason they had started again. They were telling him to do things, trying to control him. If this was his future, it was a bleak future that he didn't want to be part of. He saw death, destruction, and sorrow. Often a young girl appeared with the darkest hair and eyes he had ever seen. She had a strangely bewitching beauty. One moment happy and laughing, and in the next snapshot a dark cloud would form and blood would cover her hands. She would hold them towards him and whisper something, but Dominique could never quite make out what she said.

He drew the curtains; it seemed wrong to have bright sunlight streaming through the windows when death was in the room. The house had been tidied; bed made, plates washed before being placed in their rightful place in the kitchen cupboard. He was wearing freshly washed and ironed tan slacks with a crisp white shirt bought especially for Pierre's wedding two months ago. Dominique picked up the phone and dialled 17. He wanted his body to be found earlier rather than later. He had read about decomposed bodies being found months after they had died because nobody knew they were there. The smell would eventually give their position away. He didn't want his body swinging from a rope and slowly rotting for months. He wanted a Christian burial, which he assumed the Reverend would perform, and he wanted it quickly. A fist pounded on the door. Dominique froze; it was probably the kid from next door. His frisbee was probably in Dominique's back garden again. Dominique didn't answer. He wanted the last few minutes of his life to himself. The banging got louder. The kid's fist would break the tiny glass pane if he hammered much harder.

"Leave me alone," muttered Dominique. There was a clatter as the kid's shoes scraped against the fence as he scrambled to get over. Dominique relaxed again, savouring the last few minutes of his short life.

This was his release – the only way of escaping his destiny. The knot was strong and skilfully tied; it slipped up and down the rope smoothly. The Scouts had taught him well. *Thank you, Pierre Dumont, for those many hours you made me practice. I hated you at the time, but now you are my saviour.* Dominique stopped. Should he write a note to Pierre Dumont? No, he was just putting off the inevitable. Dominique stepped up onto the small footstool and placed the loop over his head. He glanced around the room for one last time. The note did not say much but then what can you say on occasions like this. In fact, to most people it would sound quite cryptic. *Le diable est venu mais il ne me prendra pas vivant* [The Devil came, but he will not take me alive]. He hoped Reverend Leclercq would understand, but he was also aware suicide was frowned on by the church. It was seen as a serious sin, a self-inflicted murder. Since his parent's death, the church had become his salvation, the Reverend a friend. Dominique had spoken of the visions and the voices, but not of his tormentor or the old woman, and he was unsure why. The Reverend had blessed him, told him the dreams would go away, yet the look on the Reverend's face and the eyes behind the thick-rimmed Harry Potter glasses suggested otherwise. Dominique knew the Reverend was lying. A kick of the stool and snap of the neck, and it was all over. His body swung lifeless from the beam. A small vertical scar could be seen just above his waist band. He had escaped. At only eighteen years of age, Dominique's life had ended. He was the first child.

The Investigation

Standing on top of the steps in front of the Frank Worthington statue, Laurel watched Damien tackle the final few steps up to school. Could Damien be on his way to a full recovery? In the last few weeks, Laurel had noticed Damien was moving much better. He also knew his mate wasn't taking the pain killers in the quantities he had been taking them before. Laurel smirked as his mate drew closer. Without thinking, he brought his hand firmly down on Damien's back.

"Oy, cut that out. It hurts you know." Damien was still in pain; his reaction to the pat on the back had made that clear.

"Are you going to watch me play rugby this afternoon?" Laurel asked.

"I'll watch the first half; however, I'll have to leave before it finishes. I am meeting Angel later, and I don't want to be late."

Laurel sighed and launched into a lecture about how crazy and creepy she was. "Everybody else can see it. Why can't you?"

Damien looked shocked. "What's wrong with you this morning?"

"She's trouble. I'm telling you," said Laurel.

"Don't be stupid. People don't know her like I do."

Laurel knew Angel made his mate feel great. His pain seemed to be miraculously subsiding, and deep down he knew he should be happy for Damien, but the rumours could not be ignored. Angel had killed Beth's sister in cold blood. Most of her childhood had been spent in a mental asylum.

"Don't you think I've heard the rumours as well? Rumours aren't always true. Even if they were, she's been punished. Everybody deserves a second chance," muttered Damien.

"Second chance? You must be joking! She *killed* somebody. What if she's psychotic? It could be you next time! I am telling you: once a killer, always a killer. Throughout history, offenders nearly always reoffend. Don't statistics show that forty out of every one hundred juveniles reoffend?" Laurel could think of many actual examples, but he didn't reel them off. His point had been made. Laurel was concerned for his mate. What was Damien getting himself into? He felt better now that his fears had been voiced, but Damien was blinkered.

"Angel is no more a killer than I have leprosy," was his rather blunt reply.

Damien then went on to remind his friend that three years ago in one of their swimming classes, Brian, another mate, had noticed the first of Damien's red patches. Brian was so sure Damien had leprosy that the swimming pool was emptied in seconds. It took him six months to persuade people he didn't have a contagious disease and certainly not leprosy. At the time, even Laurel thought it may be leprosy.

They dropped the argument for now, but Laurel couldn't leave it; he had a duty to protect Damien. They had always been like brothers, and they had always been there for each other. He needed proof before it was too late. Browsing through the newspaper archives in the local library, Laurel tried to piece information together. He realised he was breaking Damien's trust, and it could destroy their friendship. His excuses were becoming lamer as he cancelled seeing Damien again, not that he saw Damien much these days. He seemed to spend all his time with Angel. He hoped Damien would understand when the evidence was placed in front of him.

There did not seem to be much written about the case, even though it had been the brutal murder of a child. Headline after headline, but with no real substance. Next to nearly every relevant article there was always a news story about the petrol crisis, a crisis he had never been aware of as a child:

Young girl dies in a bizarre killing...Petrol goes up by another three pence per litre (*Grimstone Chronicle* – 17th October).

Stacey Wilson had her whole life in front of her... Shortage at the petrol pumps (*Weston Post* – 18th October).

Elizabeth Wilson, sister of Stacey, accuses school mate of murder...Lorry blockade – anger swells over rise in diesel prices (*Weston Post* – 19th October).

The news stories continued but as the days passed less was printed on the killing and more was written on the fuel crisis. The last few articles Laurel found were the most interesting as they came from a different angle.

Police are baffled...the child has shown abnormal strength (*News Beat* – 18th October)

What's my Motive? (*News Beat* – 19th October)

Angelica Wellingstone sent to the state sanatorium for observation and assessment (*Weston Post* – 1st November)

Laurel printed copies of all the news articles he could find and filed them neatly in date order in a black flip top file, including a couple of photographs of the dead child – Stacey Wilson – one photograph taken before the killing, another after the killing. He stared for a while into the dead girl's eyes. She looked at peace, not scared as one would expect. Laurel had found nothing from his research, but this would not deter him. Call it instinct, but Laurel had the strangest feeling Damien was about to get into a situation that would test his nerve. A deep, disturbing situation; trouble with a capital T.

Everything Laurel found was common knowledge in the school. Trying to blacken Angel's name was pointless. Damien was already hooked. The only other option was to destroy Damien and Angel's friendship by introducing his mate to a new woman, and that new woman would be Beth. Damien was besotted by Beth, and why not? Every other young man in the school was captivated by her beauty, including himself. Beth had grown into a beautiful young woman. At the age of sixteen her looks were the envy of most women. At the age of seventeen, men were queuing to take her out. She had long blonde hair like her younger sister had, deep penetrating blue eyes and a smooth complexion. She was confident and straight talking. Neither friend had made a move on Beth. There was a sign of mutual respect between them. Their male bond was stronger than any female interference, but Laurel was about to step over the boundary.

The underlying history between Beth and Angel would enable Laurel to use Beth in his plan. He hoped

Beth would want to help save Damien's life and at the same time have the satisfaction of hurting Angel. A simple plan was hatched; Beth would ask Damien on a date. Laurel knew his mate would not turn down a date with Beth. After all, she had been a childhood fantasy for both the lads since they started school. Damien would see it as a dream come true, a way of scoring points over him. Laurel smiled a wicked smile. Beth would keep Damien away from Angel, and hopefully once Beth had told him what she had seen as a child he would see Angel for what she was – a murderer. There was something about Angel he did not like, but he could not pinpoint exactly what it was.

As Laurel predicted, Damien was surprised and flattered and had accepted the date with Beth before he knew what was happening. Damien wished he could tell Angel about his date; rumours would spread fast in school. Not that he needed to tell her everything. After all, it was not as though they were a couple; they were just good friends. It was a shame there was a history between Beth and Angel as this made it awkward to share his initial excitement. He would have loved to ask Angel's advice on what he should wear and how to act. Angel would have the answers. She would have filled him with confidence, but the occasion to tell her never arose.

The days leading up to his date with Beth, Angel could not be found. Selfishly, Damien was thankful he did not have to put himself through an uncomfortable conversation. Anyway what could he say? "Oh, by the way I have a date with your enemy. You know the one who spreads all the rumours about you?" That would not bode well. The more he thought about it, the more he realised it would be better if Angel did not know.

Nerves and excitement mixed into one. Only two days to wait, but it seemed like a lifetime. When the time finally arrived, the disappointment of the actual event hit him hard. The date with Beth did not go as expected. There was no spark between them. There was no denying that Beth was beautiful. Long blonde hair full of body hung loosely down her back. A tight lemon mini dress accentuated her curves, emphasising her long slender tanned legs that seemed to stretch upwards forever, but she was not Angel. There was no strength or intensity to her personality.

The plan was restaurant followed by the cinema – Laurel's idea. "The perfect place for a kiss and cuddle," he had said with a wink. At the time it had sounded like a great idea, but they never made it to the cinema. Damien knew within the first half hour the date was not going to work; he had made a mistake. Beth tried hard, but the silences were uncomfortable. She tried to play footsie under the table, moving her naked foot down his legs and up to his groin. It did excite his feelings, and if he closed his eyes, she could probably make him explode, but once he opened them the feelings were gone. Damien moved his seat slightly back so she couldn't reach.

"Please don't, Beth. You are beautiful, but I can't do this," his voice was low so as not to be overheard in the crowded restaurant. He knew what would happen. He would be so sexually aroused they would go back to his room, or if they were feeling adventurous, then possibly a hotel. They would rip each other's clothes off and then she would see his body with the gross red patchy sores and blisters that his torso was prone to; then she would puke. It would be the end of their relationship. Rumours would spread fast around the school, and once again he would become a freak that no girl would want to touch.

"What's wrong? I thought you would be up for it."

"I am. I just don't want to do it right now." The uncomfortable silence hit again.

"Are you gay?"

"No."

"Are you a virgin?"

"No."

"You must be."

"I said I'm not," and even if he was a virgin, it was none of her business.

Beth leant over the small intimate table and whispered, "Why don't you kiss me? I know you want to. I know you have always wanted to." Damien could not deny he was tempted. Her glossy deep crimson lipstick enticed him closer, but the more he looked, the more he saw how fake everything was. Her lipstick and liner were drawn outside her natural lips, making them look fuller than they were. Thick foundation hid her teenage spots. Her complexion was not smooth as he had once imagined; he could see the flaws in her skin. Her tan was no doubt from a bottle, and if he looked closely there would be a couple of streaks. Fake tan always left streaks. Her long blonde hair that grabbed the attention of men was dyed with extensions.

"Can we just talk?" he asked.

"I thought that was what we were doing." Silence hit again. "Ok, what do you want to talk about?" she conceded.

"I don't know. Anything – politics, life, school – your choice."

Beth thought for a moment, "I know. I think we should talk about Angel."

"Why Angel?" a sickening feeling dug deep in the pit of his stomach. "Don't you think she has suffered enough?"

"Suffered? What do you mean suffered! She killed my sister." This was the first time during the date Beth had grabbed Damien's attention but not in a positive way; Beth's words seemed forced and rote, as if she had repeated them many times over the years. As she talked, he listened intently, not wanting to believe what he was hearing. He was unsure why Beth felt the need to talk about Angel. Had Laurel set him up with Beth? It would explain why she had chosen to go out with a sick kid. He started to suspect either it was out of pity or he was part of a wider joke. Could the whole school be laughing at him? Beth could have chosen any guy. Most lads in the school fancied her. Did Laurel hate Angel so much that he had planned this? On several occasions, Laurel had made it clear that he did not trust Angel, and Laurel had really pushed him to go on this date. Was Beth just a pawn being used in a game of love and hate? It hurt Damien that people thought they could mess with his emotions. He didn't care what had passed. He could be friends with whoever he wanted, even if they were a psychotic killer. He laughed. Beth looked at him in surprise.

"Sorry, private joke," he muttered.

Damien realised he wasn't been a great host. His mind kept drifting back to Angel, her laugh, a joke or some silly face she had made. If Beth wanted to talk about Angel, then he would oblige, but he wasn't going to let Beth slag Angel off. He was open-minded and would listen to any argument if there was proof.

"Did you see Angel kill your sister?" he asked a shocked Beth, coldly. She wasn't expecting such a direct question.

"Yes," had been her timid reply.

"No, Beth, did you see Angel plunge a knife into your sister?"

"The knife was in her hand, Damien."

"But you didn't see her plunge the knife into your sister. All you saw was her holding the knife," he replied.

"She killed my sister. I saw her; she was leant over my sister's body with a knife in her hand."

"No, Beth. You saw Angel holding a knife; a knife that she could have picked up off the ground. You didn't see her kill your sister."

"Then why was she touching my sister's face with a knife?"

"I don't know why. Maybe morbid fascination. She was an eight-year-old child who had just found a dead body, for goodness' sake."

"She killed my sister! I know she did," Beth started to weep. "You are cruel and heartless, Damien. Angel is dangerous. Her entire family wasn't normal, and Angel always had a violent temper. She murdered my sister; I know she did."

Damien placed a comforting arm around Beth's shoulders. "I am sorry, Beth. I am sorry your sister died, but I don't believe it was Angel," Damien spoke calmly and objectively, just like his father would have done when interviewing someone down at the police station. Unknown to Damien, he was similar to his father in many ways.

His arm ached; the pain had been on and off all day. The longer he kept his arm around Beth's shoulders, the sharper the pain. Beth was upset, and although he didn't agree with her comments, it was wrong not to comfort her. He had acted so coldly over the death of her sister, and this was not like him. There was no proof Angel had killed Beth's sister. It was all circumstantial. The horrible date wasn't Beth's fault. It was Laurel's fault for putting him in this embarrassing position.

*****

Angel had obviously heard the rumours. Girls liked to gossip, especially Beth's friends. The days leading up to the date, she had kept a low profile, too upset to talk to her new friend. Angel knew if Damien mentioned his date to her, he would see straight through to those deep hidden feelings she was now beginning to have for him, and she didn't want to ruin their friendship. Hoping the date would be a disaster, she disappeared for a couple of days.

The date had had a profound effect on Damien. He began to question his relationship with Angel. He had taken Beth to a decent Italian restaurant, yet he had never taken Angel out for a meal. They usually spent their time at the lake. He was torn. If he offered to take Angel out to a restaurant, it would be like asking her for a date, and that could change the emphasis of their relationship. Damien could not take a chance and destroy their friendship; he enjoyed Angel's company. It was nice to have a female friend who he could talk to differently to his male friends; a girl friend who one day maybe he could call his true girlfriend. If only he could be more like Laurel. If Laurel wanted something or someone, then nothing would stop him from making a move.

When alone Angel made him feel special; however, socially Angel reacted coldly towards him and to the other students. In lessons, she rarely mixed with the other students; always choosing to sit at the back of the class with her head down, to avoid the uncomfortable eye contact. When asked a question, the answer was always the same, "Sorry, I don't know," but she did know the answer. They had worked on their homework together. She could critique novels easily, back any argument with quotes from the book. So why she always said she did not know irritated Damien. Shyness or possible insecurity was the only logical explanation he had come up with. Sometimes he wanted to shake her. "Give her the answer, please, Angel," he would whisper silently. Angel was much brighter than what she appeared in class. Brighter than ninety-five percent of the students in their English class in Damien's estimation. Decision made. He would not take her out to a restaurant. He didn't want to change their relationship. What they had was too special to ruin. Damien regretted his date with Beth, and he prayed Angel would never find out, although he accepted this was unlikely.

Rumours were spreading, and Angel could not be found. Damien couldn't believe the lies that were being spread. The first rumour was possibly a fair interpretation – it had been a boring date. However, the second rumour was unacceptable. He hadn't slept with Beth. So how could she say he was pathetic in bed? He was the one that had blown her off. What was she doing, protecting her reputation by ruining his? Another awful thought crossed his mind. If Angel heard the rumours, would she still want to be friends? Damien wanted to see Angel, to try and explain and salvage their friendship, but he had not seen her for a couple of days, although this was not unusual.

Trying to extract any additional information from Damien and Beth had proved difficult for Laurel. Beth had reported she had told Damien about Angel as they had planned, but Damien would not listen, arguing continuously, finding fault in whatever she said. Damien was less open, reporting the date was ok, and she wasn't his sort of woman. How could she not be his sort of woman? Beth was the sort of woman all men wanted. Laurel moved on to plan B.

*****

"Are you sure it's not jealously?"

"What?" Laurel asked.

"Jealously. Look at it from our point of view. You and Damien are best friends. Since Angel came along, you hardly see him. He spends all his time with her. You have done nothing but try and split them up."

"Stuff you, Tim. It's not like that."

"I hope not, but I had to ask. I'll help, if you are doing this for the right reasons." Persuading Tim and Brian had proven harder than Laurel had initially anticipated. He wasn't jealous. If he was, then why did he feel like he was betraying his mate? He didn't want to let Damien down, especially if his life was in danger.

Brian and Tim were two of Damien's and Laurel's closest friends. Brian was a self-confessed IT geek. His skin was pallid from sitting indoors in front of the computer screen for hours. Brian possessed an unusual ability for hacking. He had once boasted he had managed to hack into the MI5 security systems when he was eleven years old. Nobody was sure if this was true, although it made an interesting story and sounded quite feasible when he spoke of how he managed to crack their codes.

"Hacking is easy," Brian would say. "People always choose passwords that are personal to them. The name of their sibling or animal, parent's first name or mother's maiden name, birth dates and car registration numbers being the most popular. It takes time but it is easy." Brian had continued to talk about company passwords, which he reckoned were easier to crack than personal passwords. "Company passwords are linked to the company. Sometimes a company name is used. Other times, for example, if they produce confectionary then the password would be more than likely their top selling product. If they include numbers then the date the company was established is used. If the company is extra cautious then their second best seller is chosen." Laurel guessed it was probably a lot harder than Brian made out.

Brian had an eye for detail, which was why he found hacking so easy. He could also take apart any electronic device and reassemble it to make it work more efficiently. Apparently Brian had been doing this since the age of five, according to his parents. Laurel guessed Brian was probably some kind of genius – not that he would tell him that. His head was large enough. Laurel was glad Brian had agreed to help. Without him, Laurel knew he would struggle to uncover any additional information. Tim was no loss if he had refused to help, but they were a team, and mates should always stick together in times of need.

Tim was very different to Brian, with no special skill other than looking five years older than his eighteen years. Admittedly this had been useful when fooling the guy at the off-licence or when ordering drinks from one of the many town bars. Tim was quiet natured with shoulder-length light brown hair which was always tied back in a ponytail; his sideburns were long, and a faint sign of stubble was always present. Towering over six foot, his facial features were sharp and his nose large; he was a handsome lad who could charm males as well as females.

Laurel convinced them that for Damien's sake, they needed to at least look into Angel's past. Everyone knew love was blind. They had to protect their mate from himself. Their research was to be kept completely secret from Damien. If they managed to find something that could indicate Damien was in danger, then they would raise it with their mate, who could then decide on his own action. If they found nothing, then Damien need never know what they had been doing.

The lads realised they should have been revising, especially as their final year exams were so close; nonetheless, they agreed a couple of weeks' break would not cause any harm. In fact, it might even help them to look at things afresh and focus their concentration. They started uncovering additional information to what Laurel had found fairly quickly. It started when Brian ran a search on Angel's mother, Winifred Wellingstone. Laurel had not considered researching Angel's family until Brian suggested this new twist. They dug up the birth certificates for Winifred and Angel a little too easily according to Brian. It had only taken a week to order and have a copy of the certificates delivered from the Barton registry office.

"See how easy it is to steal somebody's identity?" joked Brian.

"I know whose identity I would like to steal," Laurel spoke up wistfully.

"Andy Farrell," the lads said in chorus, giving Laurel a friendly shove.

The father's name had been deleted on Angel's birth certificate, but the occupation was clear, Magician. The lads looked at each other and laughed.

"Could it be Houdini?" smirked Tim. "It would explain why the name has disappeared."

"I was thinking more Derren Brown, all that mind control stuff," laughed Laurel.

"Angel Brown has a ring about it, and it would explain Damien's obsession with her."

"Seriously, there may be something in it," Laurel said, wanting to pursue every lead.

"Don't be stupid, Laurel," his mates laughed.

Brian found details of Angel's grandparents, and some very old newspaper articles stored on microfiche about Angel's grandfather, Aurel Wellingstone. He was accused of inappropriate behaviour with two young children. One child, called Bobby, was his grandson. Bobby was removed from his mother, Winifred Wellingstone, and later adopted by an American family. One news article accused Angel's grandmother of witch-craft. A month after Aurel was accused and convicted of touching young children in an inappropriate way, she died; assumption was of a broken heart. The next brother they found was a lad called Dominique, who had been registered and then later wiped from the records. Both brothers seemed to disappear into thin air from all UK census records, possibly due to adoption and name change according to Brian.

Thankfully Brian liked a challenge. If Bobby was in America, tracking him down would be easy. Records were much easier to track in America than in England according to Brian. He tapped into the adoption records in England and America, and he had soon conducted a search on Bobby and Dominique. Where the adoption records led would determine Brian's next course of action. Laurel wasn't sure why Brian wanted to find Angel's brothers, but he didn't argue. For Brian it was a challenge. "The hunt without the gore," Laurel laughed followed quickly by a chuckle from Brian. Tim did not join in; it sounded obscene. It was a human being they were hunting, a young girl that his mate had fallen for. Houdini was funny – this wasn't. Brian was copying Laurel; they all copied Laurel. As long as Tim could remember, Laurel had always got his own way. If there were two films and they could not decide which one to see, Laurel always made the final decision. Even when it was three to one, Laurel would somehow persuade them to see his choice.

Every group needed a leader, but this was wrong – Laurel was wrong. Nobody would seriously challenge Laurel, who was the alpha-male and well-liked by everybody. He was a self-named "babe magnet," and he was right; girls couldn't keep their hands off his well-toned body. They were normally good-looking girls with little personality, not that Laurel seemed to care. Tim tended to attract older women who were more fun and not normally bothered about matching eye-shadow and handbags, the colour of their nails or if a wisp of hair was out of place. Brian wasn't interested in women or men. Damien...Tim paused his thoughts; Damien had Angel, who didn't fit any of their categories, yet his mate was happy. He hoped their sleuthing wouldn't turn up anything horrible.

Eventually, Brian had traced both brothers through their death certificates. It wasn't just the strange set up of Angel's family that had interested them. When Angel was released from the psychiatric hospital, death always seemed to follow close by, and this was where their concern lay. They found many press articles which highlighted killings with similar circumstances to Beth's sister. Brian had also started to tap into the Stanfield hospital records, attempting to access the psychologist's report to see if Angel had been diagnosed as psychotic. To tap into the full database could take one, two, maybe three weeks, depending on its security, and this was time the lads could not afford to lose in revision, although this would not deter Brian. Their case was not as strong as they may have liked, but Laurel felt it was their duty to warn Damien.

"When should we tell Damien?" he asked his co-conspirators.

"Tell him what? We've found nothing, other than the fact that grandfather Aurel was a pervert," said Tim.

"What about the killings?" Laurel pressed.

"There is no evidence Angel was involved, and she would have been locked up when most of them were taking place."

"I don't know," said Laurel. "Why don't we give Damien the information and let him decide?"

"He won't be happy."

"Better unhappy than dead," responded Laurel.

The Second Child
Nine Years Earlier

Bobby had never kept any secrets from Frank; however, if he told him he had got a young lady pregnant, Frank would be disappointed. Bobby didn't want to let him down. For the last eight years, since his marriage to Bobby's mother, Frank had taken a fatherly role in Bobby's upbringing. When his mother had passed away unexpectedly, Frank adopted him as though he was his own flesh and blood. His mother's death certificate read, "Cause of death: myocardial infarction." In layman's terms, heart attack. Knowing then what he knew now could have saved her.

Bobby always felt a part of him was missing. It first started at the age of six years old with a brief spell of dreams. Later, at the age of thirteen, the dreams started again. He dreamt of a young girl with long dark hair and bewitching eyes. She would turn to him with her hands outstretched, blood dripping through her fingers. He wasn't scared; in fact, quite the opposite. He found her presence comforting. The girl reminded him of somebody, although he could not place her. He could feel the girl's pain and sorrow as well as her joy. Recognising his dream was significant but not understanding why was frustrating. Sometimes her lips would move as though she was talking to him – he could never quite hear what she was saying.

At the age of fourteen, she appeared again. This time sorrow and anger hung in the air, heightening his rage. With lips tightly clenched and eyes as black as coal, she stared. There was no blood, only a disturbing presence hovering in the stark, white room where she stood. Bobby rebelled against life and against all those who cared for him. Never before had he shown such aggression as he did through his teenage years. Only when he felt the girl's emotions calm did his own aggression subside. There was an unexplainable connection. He felt close, as though she held the answer to all his questions. Bobby never met the young girl in person nor did he dream of her again until he was dying.

Bobby was an only child. The death of his mother and the unsteady emotions created from his dreams caused a rebellion. He fought his stepfather Frank on every decision. They constantly argued, but Frank was patient, never lifting his hand to his adopted son even though he had been tempted many times. The evening the local police bought Bobby home, Frank realised he was losing control of his adopted son. If the Doctor found out, he would not be pleased.

Bobby had been fifteen years old when he was caught with Troll and Sonny drinking illegally. Troll, real name Tony, had lived with his nickname since the age of five. His father had been instrumental in creating the nickname, and all because Tony had been a small, clumsy child with large feet and nose. Troll had grown up to be a small, sturdy teenager who would stand his ground if challenged. His wild unruly hair was dyed blue in line with his nickname. Everybody knew Troll. "We are just misunderstood," he had once joked. Bobby figured Troll was probably right. They may have been known as the local troublemakers, and they had been involved in some petty crime, small scale burglaries, vandalism and hooliganism but no serious crimes of any significance. They had had many police warnings yet had never spent time in prison.

The night Bobby was brought home in a police car, Frank had almost phoned the Doctor, but common sense prevented such a hasty decision. Bobby had been found sitting in the town's only churchyard, sharing a bottle of Bourbon whisky with his friends and toasting a five-foot stone statue of the Virgin Mary. Not the worse crime, but Frank was disappointed; Bobby had so much to give to society. Thankfully, that day was a turning point. Bobby mellowed and started to treat Frank like a son should treat his father – with respect, which was why Bobby now felt he had let him down. Even though they never spoke of the future, Bobby recognised Frank had big plans for him. He hoped those plans were not ruined.

Frank Arcos appeared to be an agreeable man from the old school. His manners were exceptional. Frank, christened *Flaviu* due to his bright yellow hair when he was born, was tall and thin, his posture stiff and his face slightly pocked from a childhood illness. Frank had not dated since the death of Bobby's mother.

Assuming a fatherly role for over ten years, Frank taught Bobby many skills. At first, it was simple skills like how to fly a stunt kite; later progressing to Cardiopulmonary Resuscitation, a skill Frank had acquired from his job at the town's only hospital. Bobby learnt how to speak fluent French and Romanian before moving on to the harnessing and development of Bobby's amazing gift – the gift of healing. The gift was special and could not be shared with anybody without Frank's permission; so far that permission had not been granted.

The small town of Vanguard, New Jersey, had been their home for eighteen years. Although the town was fairly quiet, it still had a population of 22,000 and plenty for the younger generation to do. The town had half a dozen drinking establishments, restaurants, two clubs and a theatre that doubled as a cinema twice a week. In the same complex was a bowling alley and swimming pool. Monday to Thursday, most of the town's teenagers hung around the complex. The Wild Stag Club or the Zig-Zag Club were their weekend haunts.

Bobby Sutcliff met Carla Sanchez in the Wild Stag Club. Introduced by mutual friends, they clicked as soon as they met. It was Carla's infectious high-pitched laugh that caught his attention. Carla's flat features and fine, shoulder-length, mousey-brown hair would not turn a man's head; however, her personality more than made up for any shortfall in looks. Carla was now three months pregnant. After the customary morning sickness, she was now actually starting to enjoy being pregnant. On Bobby's wish, her pregnancy was kept secret from family and friends. The extra weight she carried had so far concealed her pregnant belly. Bobby insisted Frank should be the first one to hear about her pregnancy. Carla had respected Bobby's wish; unfortunately, the right time and Bobby's courage had not coincided, so Carla's pregnancy remained a secret.

As Bobby lay on the firm hospital mattress, all he could do was reminisce. Today he was thinking about the time when Carla first told him she was pregnant. He had guessed something was bothering her. They had only been together six months, but Carla was fairly easy to read. He hadn't handled the news very well. "Are you sure it's mine?" had been his immediate response. If he could have chosen any words to upset her then those were the words.

"I am no slut," was her angry reply. It should have been a happy time for them both.

"I am sorry," he backpedalled. "It's just a shock. I thought we had taken all necessary precautions."

"So did I," she quietly replied, but from the refusal to look him in the eye, he guessed Carla had forgotten to take her contraceptive pill. Later she admitted forgetting to take the pill for four days in a row. How could anybody forget that many times? Surely it was planned.

"What are you going to do?" he asked, another awkward question that should have been worded differently.

"Shouldn't that be what are *we* going to do?" had been her response, quickly followed by, "I want to keep it. It's our baby, something we have created together."

Bobby remembered smiling, "You're right, Carla. She is our little girl."

"Little girl?" she had asked.

"I have a feeling it's a girl," he had responded.

"You will make a great dad," she had replied as she stood on tip-toes to kiss him. "Do you think she will have that funny scar you have? The one shaped like a snake?"

"I hope so as that would make her extra special, especially as scars are not genetic," he had whispered. "As long as she has her mother's looks and not my looks she will be a little stunner." He had nearly continued with "...and hopefully my brain and not her mother's" but he stopped himself. Sarcasm was pointless; it was as much his fault as Carla's. Once he got used to the idea of becoming a father, the prospect was exciting, although Bobby knew in his heart he would never see his own child. He hoped she would have dark hair, just like the girl in his dreams; just like him.

The Second Child – Death Will Follow Nine Years Earlier

Bobby had been in this room many times but never as a patient. That changed three days ago. Like his uncle Frank, Bobby had managed to secure a job in the local hospital only fifteen minutes from his home. It was his dream job where his gift could be used under Frank's protective eye. He only used the gift when Frank was present. Frank controlled who Bobby should and should not heal. As a trainee nurse Bobby had access to nearly all areas of the hospital and patients, which had proved useful. His healings were spread around the hospital and so could go undetected. To train as a medical practitioner was Bobby's long-term goal. He had applied for a scholarship and entry into three of the leading medical schools across America. He would know in two weeks if he had been accepted. Tuesday the 15th was printed in his memory. To Bobby's surprise Frank had not said much when he had unveiled his plan. He assumed it was because Frank would miss him.

Bobby was now relying on Dr Bryant to find a cure for his strange illness. A cure by the 15th was what Bobby wanted. The illness had taken over his life. A new-born baby would also take over his life. A small sigh escaped from his lips. Carla's pregnancy would confuse things. Paying for a child whilst studying would be difficult. Would Carla go with him or would she insist on staying in Vanguard? He had not revealed his plans yet to Carla. After all, he may not be accepted into medical school. Suddenly Bobby gasped for breath. What was happening to him?

He loosened another button on his shirt. It was becoming harder to keep cool. A desktop fan had been placed next to Bobby's bed. A gentle hum buzzed from its tiny motor as its head turned from left to right. It was almost hypnotic in its movement. The fan was no longer keeping him cool. All feelings had gone from his body, until he could not detect even a slight breeze on his skin. His strength was slowly being drained from his body, no doubt due to the lack of food being digested.

Bobby's worst fear was that the illness was connected to his gift. For the last six months, he had concentrated on healing children, usually under the age of twelve years, but lately Frank had pushed him harder than normal. He had cured many children at the small hospital, usually on a weekly basis, but Frank wanted the healings to take place on a daily basis. It was easy at first. He had not felt fatigued. All he had to do was lay his hands on the affected area, and the illness would disappear.

"I feel like god," he had once told Frank. "It makes me feel so powerful. I want to help all the children, to give them back their life. It is so unfair. Why should a child suffer from an illness when they have their entire life in front of them?" The overwhelming joy on the child's parents' faces when they were told their child was cured gave him a feeling that a normal person would never be able to experience, but then, he was not normal.

One of his last healings had not felt correct. He was trying to cure a young boy of six years who had been born with a hole in his heart and was prone to fits. On occasion, the child's little heart stopped beating. The child had been in and out of hospital for as long as Bobby could remember, waiting for a donor – his condition was deteriorating rapidly. He had spoken to the child on many occasions; Sid Bennett was his name. A name he would never forget. He had never tried to heal Sid before as his illness was riddled with difficulties, but Frank felt he was ready, and he trusted Frank's judgement. His gift was practiced and polished; there was no reason why he would not succeed. The healing would take his skill to another level. He could become the top doctor in America with his gift.

As he laid his hand on Sid's tiny chest, the child's body jerked, and his heartbeat stopped simultaneously. Bobby carried on with the healing, not realising what was happening. Only when his own body refused to co-operate did he realise something was wrong. The garbled messages his brain was receiving caused panic, instead of his normally relaxed attitude to healing. A piercing pain stabbed at his chest, like a blunt screwdriver forcing its way through the fleshy muscle of his heart. Bobby immediately pulled away from the child whose body now lay lifeless. Shocked, he fell to his knees and wept. He had never lost a child before. Frank had come to his senses first and dragged him by the collar out of the room.

"Leave him," he hissed.

"But I killed him, Frank. I killed him," Bobby wept. Since that day, almost two weeks ago, Bobby had not felt quite the same. It was a feeling he could not explain.

This was also one of the few times he had seen Frank display a coldness to a lost life.

The illness started as a stomach bug. His initial diagnosis had been food poisoning. As he grew weaker, the hospital bed became his home. Dr Bryant was struggling to find a cure. Bobby's body was now rejecting liquid food as well as solid food. Anything taken into his body was rejected and vomited within an hour. Then there was the strange blue liquid that kept trickling from the corner of his mouth. They hid the seepage from Dr Bryant. According to Frank, the liquid was part of his gift, part of the healing process, not the illness. His body had started to eat itself as it tried to survive.

One by one, Bobby's organs began to close down. His body tried to focus its energy on keeping his heart beating and his lungs taking in oxygen. His stomach sunk deeper and deeper into his body; his ribcage became more prominent as the skin stretched tight over the skeleton of his body. There was no pain. Towards the end of his life, he could hardly lift his hand to wipe his nose. He had made a mistake. He had not been ready to heal such a complicated illness, an irreversible decision.

When he saw the girl with the raven hair and dark bewitching eyes in his dreams, her arms outstretched, beckoning him to come to her, he guessed his life was over.

The Argument

"A gift for you, a curse to me," she screamed. They had met at the lake like usual, but Damien had never seen her this way. He was the one who should be annoyed. For five months since he had known her, she had hidden this ... this *gift*. What else could he call it? During this time, she had seen him suffer from pain. She had seen his skin become unbearably sore and seen his life slowly fall apart, and yes, she could have prevented it, or at the very least have given him a ray of hope. There was a cure – maybe not a traditional cure, but a cure all the same. Even now his hands ached with soreness. It felt as though a knife had been stuck into his right hand and was constantly being twisted by an evil force.

Angel wished she hadn't told him. Initially, he had accepted everything she had said. She had stayed with him all night because he was in excruciating pain, and she felt he needed a friend that night. She had explained she hadn't told him at first in case he was mad with her – they could have been expelled for her actions. She had told him she lay next to him, on top of the covers, and he seemed to accept that. He had said he was pleased she had stayed with him as he slept well for the first time in ages. He had asked her if he snored to which she had answered no. With a sparkle in his eye, he had said she could have snuggled down in his bed, and he wouldn't have minded. She had been embarrassed at the time so didn't say anything, and then Damien started pushing for more information; constantly asking questions until she had finally told him the truth.

Damien had realised the night she had stayed over was not a normal night. Small flashbacks of vague memory kept coming back to him – their naked skin touching; the gentle massaging of his upper body; the tenderness, the warmth and the love which oozed from her body. He remembered the kiss not only on his cheek but also his lips. The softness of her lips felt exquisite. This was one memory he didn't want to forget. He had been overdosed on painkillers, which may have affected his recall of the events, but the largest pieces of the jigsaw were still missing. How could his abdomen and chest lose their soreness overnight? Why did he feel so much better? And why had she not told him before of her gift? How could anybody call it a curse? He needed to understand.

Tears poured down her soft cheeks. Why did she feel this way? Was Damien right? Should she have helped him earlier in their relationship? She felt vulnerable and guilty. What should she do now? Angel reached out to grab his hand. Feeling betrayed and hurt, he yanked his hand from her grasp. They stood for a while in silence; the longer they stood, the more uncomfortable the silence. They were both angry with each other. A few more minutes passed and eventually Damien made a move; pulling Angel towards him, he tightly wrapped his arms around her body. He wanted to hold her close. He knew she was special; he had always known she was special. Placing her head into a gentle headlock, her head instinctively dropped, and she buried it into his shoulder. Placing his chin and hand on top of her thick dark hair, his left arm stayed tight around her waist.

"No more secrets," he said into her hair. Maybe he didn't understand her reasons, but he did know that he didn't want to lose her.

"No more secrets," she whispered.

The Scrapbook

If Angel was to tell him everything – in his words, 'no more secrets' – she would have to show him the scrapbook, and show him what she could do, although she wasn't really sure herself. She always knew she had a power, but the first and only time she had conducted a full healing was with Damien, and then it wasn't really a healing. It was just a pain removal. As yet, the level of her powers had not been tested. Everything she knew, she had learnt from secretly watching her mother, scouring pictures in books and the internet, and the rest had just been instinct. Damien's healing had been instinct. He was her closest and only friend, and she could not bear to see him in such pain, which was why his words had hurt her deeply. The unexplainable blue liquid secreted from her mouth after the healings was not mentioned on anything she had ever read. Angel could not be sure when she used her curse – or gift, depending on your perspective – it was not affecting her in some unhealthy way. She had recorded all the research she had conducted on her past and any information on her ability in a scrapbook. Her precious book, a book she had shown nobody. The book she was going to show Damien today.

That evening Damien was invited to Angel's room. As an older student, Angel had a room on the sixth floor, and it was for this reason Damien had never previously set foot inside her room, but tonight Damien had wanted answers. He would not normally be up to the feat of the six flights of stairs. Fortunately, the claustrophobic four-man lift was working. It creaked and groaned as it passed each floor, but it arrived at its intended destination within seconds of the door closing.

Angel's room was immaculate. The sheets on the bed were a crisp white cotton with the corners folded neatly and tucked under the mattress. Angel could see he was staring at the bed.

"Too long in hospital," she muttered, preferring to shorten the description to hospital or Stanfield than use the words *psychiatric hospital.* To his left was a small bedside table, similar to his own. On top was a small wooden picture frame, which he instinctively picked up to take a closer look. A woman was standing in front of a large house with a small child. On closer inspection, he realised it was a photomontage. The girl had been cut out very carefully from, he guessed, a magazine and neatly stuck next to a woman; in fact, both images had been taken from a magazine.

"My mother," said Angel, taking it from his hand and placing the frame in its rightful place. The resemblance was remarkable, the dark hair and eyes, even the shape of the nose and lips were almost identical. Damien didn't mention the fact it was a photomontage. He just felt saddened that Angel obviously did not possess a real photograph of her family. Angel had no other personal items on display apart from a small black hairbrush with strands of hair loosely wrapped around the bristles lying at a 45-degree angle to the picture frame.

Now that he was standing in her room, did she really want to show him everything? The whispered words *no more secrets* kept springing to mind. By showing him the scrapbook, she was revealing everything, revealing who she was, stripping away everything she had kept close to her heart for many years. Panic started to rise. She had only known him five months. Was this the right time, the right person to reveal everything to? Hands shaking, Angel lifted her thin mattress, ruffling the cotton sheet. A large scrapbook lay underneath; her hand reached out but just as her fingers skimmed the front cover, she quickly dropped the mattress and tucked the sheet back in place. She couldn't do it, not now.

Damien's back faced her as he looked out of the window. Hoping he hadn't seen her lift the mattress, Angel joined him at the window. "I don't want to argue."

"Neither do I." After she had taken his pain, when she was more prepared, then maybe she would show him the scrapbook. Placing his arm around her shoulder, he gave a gentle squeeze. They both stared into the large lush green gardens. The red-tiled roof of Worthington High School peered above the trees, and in the far distance, the high-rise blocks in the small town of Winston could just be made out. A fifth or sixth-floor room was one of the benefits of being an older student. These floors were supposedly quieter for revision, the rooms did not attract all the passing student traffic, and their views were stunning.

Time was ticking. If the warden found Damien in the girls residence after 9:00 p.m. he would be seriously reprimanded. She had been lucky recently as she had got away with it in Damien's residence, but Angel could not face any scandal. She needed to hurry him.

Out of the corner of his eye, Damien had seen Angel lift the mattress, but he couldn't bear to have another argument, so he kept silent. The photomontage had had a profound effect on his emotions, an unexplainable effect. He was not going to pressure her. Maybe trust was hard for Angel. He assumed, if the rumours were accurate at all, her history was not that of any normal teenager. Nonetheless, he believed when she was ready, Angel would open up to him.

For the next few minutes, they both stood in silence at the window, lost in their own thoughts. Without thinking, Damien began clenching his hand into a fist and releasing by spreading his fingers wide in quick successions – a habit that normally signified pain. Already knowing the answer, Angel moved to the edge of the bed and asked if his hand still ached. A nod was enough.

"Close your eyes; I will take your pain," she whispered, and like an obedient dog, Damien sat down on the bed. Placing his hands in her lap, Angel started to massage between his fingers across the knuckles, pressing down on the small bones on the back of his hand. Visually there were no marks to identify where the pain radiated from, but Angel could feel it in her fingers. Turning Damien's hand over, Angel's fingers traced his life-line followed by the line of health, reading every line with a sense of responsibility – a genuine palm reader exploring with an unrelenting enthusiasm. No silver had crossed the palm; Angel didn't need silver or gold to conduct her magic. She had the only thing she wanted; Damien's trust.

Touching and caressing Damien's skin always aroused Angel's sexual feelings. Their eyes met. His eyes said, *I want you, I want you now.* Collapsing on the bed,

Damien leant over Angel's body, pushing her hair away from her face so he could see every facial expression before pressing his lips against hers. His tongue started to tease her tongue and explore the inside of her mouth. She let out a small giggle. He smiled and pressed his soft warm lips firmly down on hers. They had never taken their relationship to the next stage. Caressing her body, his fingers moved slowly up and across her delicate neck. If she said no, he would back off, but tonight he wanted her so bad. She was responding. He slipped his hand beneath her blouse. Her stomach was flat and toned. His hand moved up to her breasts; his fingers slipped inside her bra. Cupping her breast, he stroked gently, almost nervously. They were small and pert and perfectly formed. Her body was beautiful. His heart pounded in quick succession. Damien's fingers no longer ached, making it easy to unbutton her top. His tongue traced down the centre of her body, down her cleavage and stomach to the top of her shorts. Angel's body arched and she could feel her pants start to dampen. Her body started to shake gently as her breathing changed to short pants.

"Oh Damien," she gasped as her hands grabbed the white cotton blanket pulled tightly across the mattress.

He slowly unbuttoned her shorts and located the top of her underwear. His forefinger uncovered a small scar in the shape of an S. She lets out a groan, and her body arched again. Her hands moved to his head. He kissed her scar and then her belly button before retracing the wet saliva trail his tongue had just left. His hand was constantly stroking and caressing her flawless body. As he reached her neck, he lifted her hands above her head and started to kiss her lips once again.

"You are gorgeous, Angel, and don't ever forget it," he whispered. She wanted him so bad, but she knew tonight was not going to be the night. Damien still had hang ups about his own body, and he needed to get over that first. Angel could wait. He made her feel so sexual with just a kiss and even more so when he caressed her body. She had never given herself to anybody so openly before as she had given to Damien, but there was something about him that made him special.

"It is after nine," whispered Angel.

"I know, but I don't want to leave you," he whispered back, scared in case they were overhead. Eventually she shooed him out and he snuck down the elevator and out the front door without being caught.

Their relationship still appeared so secretive. Damien had often questioned why Angel never spoke to him at school – was she embarrassed to be seen with him? The only recognition was a glance and sometimes a faint smile in his English class. Even when they bumped into each other in the refectory, Angel always refused to join him and Laurel; always with some feeble excuse, always in a rush. Usually apples adorned her tray. "I am not hungry, I just fancied an apple," she would say.

Angel's eating habits were quirky, including a passion for apples that could only be described as an obsession. A single bite and the apple could be disregarded; other times the specimen would be eaten slowly down to the core. A habit from childhood, she had once joked. "I used to love reading Snow White and the Seven Dwarfs. Did you know Snow White was poisoned by a Spartan apple?"

At the time, Damien had nearly choked with laughter. "It's a fairy tale," he laughed.

"Yes, but the apple was a deep red so reminiscent of the Spartan. It could be no other apple," she had paused for a moment. "Or it could be a Red Delicious," she had said after contemplating the two possibilities. The only Spartan Damien had heard of before that day was the Spartan warriors. Conversation with Angel was always entertaining.

Damien enjoyed spending time with Angel. She was so different when it was just the two of them. To make their relationship perfect, he hoped one day Angel would speak to him at school, to meet his friends properly and not hide away like a frightened animal. Living two separate lives was becoming difficult. Balancing his relationship with friends and Angel was delicate. He had to tackle this potential developing problem. Out of school, Angel gave him love and laughter, but in school she was so different. Laurel still didn't trust her; he hadn't said anything recently, but Damien could tell.

The perfect opportunity presented itself in the refectory. Cornering Angel before she had time to disappear out of the room, he grabbed and held her small wrists firmly, preventing her from rushing away.

"Are you embarrassed of me, Angel? You never speak to me at school," he accused. The words sounded a little harsher than he intended, but this was the only reason he could think of for her actions.

"Oh Damien, how can you say that? You are the nicest person I have ever known."

"So why won't you speak to me at school?"

She glanced around the refectory to see how much attention they had attracted. Lowering her voice, she whispered, "You have so many friends, and I don't want to alienate you from them. I know they don't like me."

"Don't be silly! They just don't know you like I do, and if they alienate me, as you say, then they are not friends worth keeping." Damien had tried to take her tray – the physical barrier between them, but she held it tightly. "Angel, please put the tray down," he had spoken calmly but firmly. She had looked into his eyes before placing the plastic tray down on one of the refectory tables. Turning her body towards him, he wrapped his hands round her waist and lower back and pulled her body towards his. His warm, soft lips came down to meet hers. Angel didn't respond immediately, but her arms moved up to his neck, and finally she caved in and kissed him back.

"Now everybody knows you are mine, so you have no excuse," he whispered.

"You shouldn't have done that," she replied.

"Will you join Laurel and me now?"

She glanced towards Laurel, who glared back at her. "Maybe another time."

Damien had hoped this talk would change things, but it didn't. Angel still kept her distance from him at school.

"Do you mind if I go?" she asked.

He could have taken her words the wrong way, but there was sincerity in her voice. "Of course not," he said, giving her a warm smile. "I'll catch up with you later." Angel popped the apples into her rucksack and placed the tray back onto its stand.

"How many varieties?" he asked.

"Forty-eight," was her quick reply. Damien smiled. When they first met, Angel had told him there were over fifty varieties of English eating apple, and she had tried thirty-four different varieties.

"Is the Russet still your favourite?"

Angel nodded. Damien smiled again. "Slightly rough with a greenish-brown colour, very sweet with a flavour reminiscent of nuts," he remembered her description of the Russet well.

"These are Kidd's Orange Reds; the Gala apple is a cross between this apple and a Golden Delicious. It's interesting how many of the apples are related, don't you think?"

Damien nodded.

"Are you going to the lake tomorrow?"

Damien nodded again. "Of course," he said, kissing her again just in case their audience missed the first kiss.

"Do you fancy trying to walk up Winslow Hill up through the forest from the lake? It has a beautiful view from the top."

"I don't know," he murmured. "I am not sure if I have the strength."

"You have." It was strange. He trusted Angel, yet there was no reason for it. If she told him, he could fly, he would probably believe her. She was good for him. He had changed so much since he had met her; he was physically and mentally stronger, life was enjoyable, and suicidal thoughts no longer crossed his mind. Damien was happy, but this was about to change.

Exposure

When Laurel arranged a lads' night at Brian's, Damien thought no more of it. It was to be a night of beers and laughs with the lads. Recognising he shouldn't drink too much with his medication, the plan was to indulge in a couple of cans and then fall back onto soft drinks. It was still possible to join in and have fun with his mates without being drunk.

Damien arrived last at the house, walking slower than originally intended. He didn't want to be the brunt of their jokes, so the walking stick stayed back in his room. Reserving his energy levels was essential. If previous nights were of any indication, it would be a late night. Normally he would have gone with Laurel, but Laurel had wanted to collect a book from the library and call in at the off-licence on the way. They agreed to meet at Brian's at 7:00 p.m. Brian lived two streets away from the school with his parents, although the basement had been converted into a pad for him so he could have some privacy. It even had a separate entrance so they would not be disturbed by his comings and goings. Very little natural light could find its way into the basement, but the lights Brian had installed more than compensated for this loss. There was very little empty wall space – most of it covered by characters from Marvel comics.

Brian had two major obsessions: Marvel comics and technology.

The basement was an IT geek's paradise. It was littered with various types of computer hardware; lights and images flicked on and off a range of screens, while processing equipment hummed gently in the corner of the room. A single bed was pushed into the corner of the room with a Spiderman duvet pulled haphazardly overtop; a small bathroom with a power shower was tucked under the stairwell. Seating consisted of blue and black striped bean bags strategically placed in the centre of the room and in the centre of the bean bags lay the black flip top folder.

Damien ascertained something was not right as soon as he entered the basement. The mood was sombre with a hint of apprehension in the air. Steering Damien to a bean bag, Laurel handed Damien a beer and said, "You are going to need this, mate. It's about your relationship with Angel." The showdown had begun. Brian had uncovered several deaths, one just after Angel had been released. It was close to where she was supposedly living. One of the news articles had made the connection, but there was no evidence to back up this speculation and so the case was left unsolved.

The next death was much more recent, and this was the one they wanted to bring to Damien's attention.

"We are sorry to do this, mate, but think back around the time you went on a date with Beth. Didn't you say you hadn't seen Angel for a couple of days?" Laurel asked.

"I don't remember."

"Well, I do, and you did. A young kid went missing during those unaccountable days. They found his body on Winslow Hill. Isn't that where you and Angel go?"

"So what are you saying? Don't tell me you think Angel was involved!" Damien cried.

"I am not saying anything. The facts speak for themselves. You must admit it is some coincidence."

"For god's sake, Laurel, this is ridiculous. That body was found on the East side of the hill. We can't get to that side unless we take the road, and may I remind you Angel can't drive and it's too far to walk. Or are you going to tell me she can fly as well as everything else?"

Laurel was on a roll; Damien was on the defensive, and when this normally happened, Laurel would win the argument. "Don't you see she is manipulating you? She pretends she has the power of healing and you believe her because you so desperately want your illness to go, like the rest of us, but this is not the way."

"I told you about the healing in confidence."

"Yeah, but your other mates deserve to know what a manipulative bitch she is."

"Don't, Laurel," Damien warned him, "or this will get nasty."

"Ok, that was out of line, but please leave it to the doctors, not black magic."

"There is no proof it is black magic," chipped in Brian, but a stern look from Laurel told him to hush. Damien glanced towards Brian, thankful for the intervention.

"She's probably using acupuncture or something similar that could take away the pain," said Tim, trying to be helpful. Tim was given the same look that Brian had just received. "I was just saying."

"I know what you were saying," Laurel said impatiently. "Let me continue. Once you start relying on her to ease your pain, you are trapped. You will do anything for her. Please don't be sucked in by her lies." Before this night, Laurel had rehearsed his speech over and over again. Now he had confronted Damien, the impact was gone. He wasn't sure if it was because Brian had butted in, but the words sounded lame. He had started strong, but now the information seemed weak. There was no evidence of any malice, just hints of something not right. Laurel knew his words were falling on deaf ears, but he had to try.

"We have her psychiatric records," Laurel finally blurted out. "Listen to this." Flicking through the black folder, he withdrew a file

"'...some days she even speaks like the characters. She lives in a fictional world which is far from reality. I do wonder if Angelica Wellingstone can distinguish real-life from her imagination. I have considered banning the books, but I am unsure how she will react,' Dr William Robertson."

"That proves nothing," Damien protested. "So she pretended to be different characters from books. You used to tie a red towel around your neck and run around the garden shouting, 'Superman,' and nobody said you were mad." Brian burst into a fit of giggles, much to Laurel's annoyance.

"Ok, what about this?" Laurel flicked through a few more pages until he found what he was looking for.

"'I cannot consider releasing Angelica back into society at this stage of her treatment. We have seen a violent side which could flare up anytime. She has overturned tables and chairs in the dining room. She has attacked Peter Holden, another patient. We don't know who started the fight, but Angelica scratched his face, leaving a nasty scar under his eye. The incident eventually caused him to lose partial sight in his left eye because her nail caught his cornea. I would be wrong to second-guess the motive or if she meant to cause such damage. Neither child has said anything, but what I do know is it took three nurses and a sedative to restrain her. Angelica had lost total control over her actions, and this is something that may or may not happen again,' Dr Henry Liddle."

"This Peter guy was six years her senior when the poor lad was attacked by her and it sounds like he never stood a chance."

Damien didn't say anything immediately as he searched for a smart reply. "It could have been an innocent fight that went wrong. We used to fight all the time at that age," was his final response.

"But I never ripped out your eyes," was Laurel's quick reply.

"Neither did she!" Damien yelled.

"You're hanging on to straws, Damien. Just face it, she's dangerous."

"I love her," Damien heard himself say. This was the first time he had admitted to himself that he felt more than just friendship or sexual desire for Angel.

Laurel laughed. "You don't even know what love is. She's your first girlfriend, isn't she?"

"I know more than you, Laurel. I know love is not about jumping in and out of bed with every girl I meet."

"For god's sake, man, can't you see you're only together because no other woman will touch you, and nobody wants her. You have been forced together through desperation, not by love."

"You bastard, Laurel," Damien said softly, his anger giving way to sad disappointment in his friends.

"You inconsiderate bastard. Why can't you just accept I am happy for once?"

Realising it was becoming too personal, Tim quickly jumped in, "All we ask is you listen to what we have to say, and then we won't mention it again."

In some ways, this was what Damien liked about his mates. There was no holding back. They always spoke their minds, and you know where you stood with them. He accepted they were concerned for him and what they were saying did sort of make sense. Damien turned to leave, but Laurel placed a firm hand on his shoulder. He didn't wince. In fact, he felt no pain at all.

"Don't do this, mate. Don't walk out on us. Just hear us out," whispered Laurel in his ear.

Damien turned towards them with a deep sigh and said, "Ok, what else have you got?"

Fourth Child One Year Earlier to Present Date

Samuel had just reached the fruitful age of seventeen years and Edward was torn who to concentrate his energy on. A flip of a coin and Samuel had come up heads. Samuel had shown as much promise as Angel, curing his stepsister Suzy of Leukaemia when he was seven years...or was that Dominique? He couldn't remember – too many of the brats to look after. If Suzy was Samuel's sister, she would need to die with her guardians, or it could get confusing. The alternative was to use Suzy as a pawn in his latest game of cat and mouse. He needed to think it through. He hoped Winifred would not turn up again; she was becoming a pain. It was because of her he had lost Dominique. At least Winifred had not been waiting for Angel at the hospital gate. He was the hospital's only contact, so Winifred wouldn't have known the release date. As far as the authorities knew, Winifred was a missing person, assumed dead.

Angel had not asked about her mother; this had surprised Edward, although his lies were prepared. A black plaque with a gold inscription reading, "In Loving Memory," had been placed in the cemetery garden off Townslow Road, near where they used to live. A tribute in many ways – it was the last place he had chosen a victim. In another way, it was stupid; he didn't like to kill near where he lived, or had lived, but sometimes frustration makes you do stupid things.

Edward removed his glasses and wiped the lenses with a clean, crisp handkerchief. Planning was essential. He would not make the same mistake he had made with Angel. Edward temporarily abandoned Angel whilst on his new portage – Samuel. The young lad had to be prepared and manipulated until he was fully controlled. This was easier said than done, as he had learnt from Angel. He had given the ungrateful cow a roof over her head, and she still got upset when he wanted her to do one little thing. So upset that she had run away twice in eighteen months. The first time it took him three weeks to find her. London was such a big, unfriendly place. The Cockney jackass propping up the Milestone bar was the victim on that occasion. He wouldn't stop whinging about the drop in car sales.

All Edward had wanted was a quiet drink to contemplate his next move, but the jackass would not stop talking. His miserable droning voice went on and on. No wonder nobody bought a second-hand car from him. The complaint about Edward's smoking finally sealed the jackass's fate. A knife in the gut, and the whining from the grotesque creature stopped. He probably did the fat grease-ball a favour and put him out of his misery. If Angel hadn't run away, then maybe the jackass would still be alive. Edward laughed a loud shrill laugh. No, he would have found him. He had a habit of finding them, and he would have killed him just like the others. He deserved to die for making everybody else's life a misery. Even if he had been a half-decent fellow, Edward would have still killed him; anybody wearing a donkey jacket in a public place deserved to disappear from this world.

Little Shaun was one who did not deserve to die – wrong place at the wrong time, that's all. His parents should have been looking after him better. The shocked look on Angel's face when he knifed the kid was a picture. What did she expect? All she had to do was bring him back to life, but instead she collapsed to the ground and started to vomit. He thought she was going to have a seizure the way she reacted. He had to pick her up and carry her kicking and screaming out of the forest. The kid had some strength for a small one. The only way to shut her up and stop the constant kicking and punching was to knock her out. He didn't even manage to check for missed details and prepare the death scene properly. This was his only niggle. He didn't like to leave his jobs only half-finished. It spoiled his game with the Chief Inspector.

They were lucky they had not been caught that day with all that noise she made. Morphine for nearly a week was the only way to keep her calm and under control. When he took her off the morphine, she ran away again, although she only got to the bus station that time. If she was his brightest protégé then they were in trouble. She had forgotten to take any money. There she was, sitting in the bus shelter, head in her hands, looking pathetic. The number 57 bus was pulling away from the kerb. Edward had sat down next to her, and said, "It's time to go home, Angel."

"I don't want to."

"Now, Angel," he said in a warning tone. She never argued with Edward, and she didn't on that occasion either.

Their relationship had changed, and she was never the same again. Edward tried again a couple of months later, pretending it was a holiday. This time she didn't scream hysterically. Instead, she stood over the body and stroked the young girl's forehead and asked what she should do. Eventually, he would wear her down. Angel was much stronger than her mother. She just didn't know how to channel her power. Angel could not only heal; she had the gift to bring life to the dead. Edward had seen Angel bring her hamster back to life when she was only three years old. Angel was much stronger now so a young child should be possible. It was just going to take a little time, and a few more deaths before she could master the procedure, but it would be worth it. Samuel would be just as good, older, so in theory his power should be more developed. Edward wondered, would Samuel be able to bring life to death or could he only heal? Angel was the only one who had shown any indication that regeneration was possible.

*****

Samuel was an American citizen, which made keeping track of him difficult for Edward. The Doctor's setup had been simple; the four gifted children who were to be brought up in the UK were Edward's responsibility. The four children in America were Frank's. This simple tracking had become complicated after the children were placed with their carefully chosen adoptive parents. One of Edward's kids had moved to America – Samuel – and

Dominique had moved to France at a very early age. These changes could have messed up the Doctor's experiment, but planning and confidence would dictate if it would work. The Doctor was always confident and well-organised in whatever he did. The eight children had to be brought up independently, and as close to natural as possible. The children kept in the clinics were fully controlled to enable a comparison to be made when the time was right.

Samuel had not turned out as expected. Already a violent lad with fire in his belly, he had walked out on his family at an early age. He soon became the leader of a small gang, who robbed, fought and terrorised both the young and old in the local neighbourhood. Nobody messed with him. Samuel would kill them if they looked at him in a disrespectful way. His parents were weak. How could he be respected with such wimpy parents? He left home after punching his father so hard his body had jack-knifed 90 degrees. His left lung was punctured, so every breathe became a constant reminder never to mess with or disrespect his adopted son. Samuel had taken nearly everything they owned. They did not want him back, nor did they want to see him again. A week after Samuel left home, both parents died in a house fire as they slept. Did Samuel start the fire? Nobody knew the answer, but there were rumours of arson. With the parents out of the picture, Edward's job should have been easy, but Samuel was a hard case to crack.

Edward would have to gain Samuel's respect if he was to control him and nurture his talent. Samuel obviously had a passion for killing; Edward would have to include this in his plans. Let Samuel feel the power of death. It was an addiction that needed feeding. Edward needed a new game specially designed for Samuel. An intellectual game was not appropriate. From observation, Samuel was not the brightest of kids. A game that required an ounce of intelligence would no doubt blow Samuel's last remaining brain cell – yes, a mind game was definitely out. More planning was required, a game to test the strength of Samuel's gift but still allow him the enjoyment of killing. A game with a religious twist could be fun. Edward had always been annoyed at how close Dominique had been to Reverend Leclercq. Had the Reverend corrupted Dominique's mind, made him weak? The lad should have been much stronger mentally. After all, he was bred from strong biological parents; they all were. Suicide was the coward's way out. It ensured nobody was a winner.

*****

Edward held the knife to Slasher's neck and slowly drew the blade across his throat. A faint red line began to appear. His eyes were tightly clenched closed. Slasher had shouted and hollowed, begging Samuel to stop the nutter, but Samuel was frozen in fascination at Edward's surreal calmness and the controlled rhythmic movement of the knife as it scarred the body. The blade moved vertically. Edward drew another line down his victim's throat, slightly deeper this time. The red line began to form droplets of blood that ran down Slasher's neck to stain his shirt. Slasher was crying, begging Edward to stop. His eyes stayed tightly closed. He could not bear to look into the eyes of his torturer. Those dark piercing eyes, normally protected with a glass barrier, now bore deep into his brain. Edward's glasses were tucked neatly into his chest pocket in their protective case.

A wet patch formed on the front of Slasher's trousers. It slowly crept down the inside of his leg.

"You filthy pig. Slasher has just had a slash," Edward hissed, and then laughed. "Your gang is weak, Samuel. Look, he has p****d himself. Join me, and I'll make you strong, give you a power. I'll teach you how to gain respect, and to kill creatively." Edward handed Samuel the knife, and ordered, "Now finish the job, son." Without hesitation, Samuel took the knife from Edward and plunged it deep into Slasher's fleshy abdomen. The body collapsed into a heap. Samuel stared at the knife, watching the blood trickle down the ivory handle into the carved shapes with a morbid fascination. He looked at Edward and smiled.

"I need to prepare the crime scene," hissed Edward as he pulled the body over the words *Carpe Diem* – "Seize the day" – that had been written earlier that afternoon. Arranging the body into a star shape, he scribed a range of numbers in red paint at each of the limbs. The left arm pointed to the number 280, the right arm 620, left leg 350 and the right leg 150. No letters this time; the map co-ordinates did not require letters. The clues were simple, but the police were not the brightest. The co-ordinates led to a church less than a mile away. Samuel watched in fascination.

"My trademark," smirked Edward.

Edward threw a two-foot-long metal bar to Samuel. The abandoned factory where they were currently conducting their game of torture was a haven of makeshift weapons. The metal bar was a leftover piece of scaffolding. It was perfect; lightweight and easy to handle.

"This will be your trademark, son."

"Can't I have a knife like you?" asked Samuel, looking disappointed.

Edward took his glasses out of his chest pocket and placed them back on his nose. "You are not a copycat killer, Samuel. You are too small a build to take on a large man with a knife. You don't have the reach. This bar will give you the reach, the power over all men."

Samuel smiled, an evil twisted smile; the idea of power over all men was appealing.

*****

The church stood proud in its own grounds. A graveyard surrounded the back and sides of the building and was slowly encroaching on the front of the grounds as more people were laid to rest. Soon there would be another body to bury. The spire stood proudly to the side of the church, dominating the skyline.

"A church is always open to its public," laughed Edward. "Remember, Samuel, this one is yours. Break a leg, let him feel the pain and then take away his pain. Break his arm, again let him feel the pain and then take away the pain. Do this six times and then tell him you are the Devil who has come to take his soul. Make him beg for mercy, make him curse Christ our Lord, make him worship you, the Devil, and then end his miserable life. Feel the power, Samuel; the power you now possess." Samuel swung his baton and walked through the large open door, a bounce in his step, a smile on his face as he entered the place where the priest would meet his fate.

*****

Edward didn't write to Angel whilst away on business. He wasn't a big writer, and what would he say? "Hi, kid, having a lovely time. Weather is hot. Visited the Empire State Building yesterday. Oh, nearly forgot! We battered a priest to death this morning, and tomorrow we plan to kill two more." He sneered. It would make an interesting read, but letters could be traced and vigilance was essential. Leaving Angel at this stage in her development had been difficult for Edward. He realised she was becoming stronger, and this was a delicate time in their relationship where trust was paramount; however, he now had a new problem to solve.

What Edward hadn't banked on was Angel developing a relationship with Damien Harrington, Chief Inspector David Harrington's son – the same annoying pig that had closed in on him a couple of times. When Edward received the message of Angel's exploits, he had been angry, and when anger took over, a new death always followed. Once his new protégé was fully on board, he would return to England, where he would sort them out. Edward sneered and smirked simultaneously, not a normal reaction for a man who was obsessed with death, but the thought of outwitting the Chief Inspector was always fun and the new twist with the Chief Inspector's son could be amusing. The game of cat and mouse was about to begin. He was the cat, but he had another mouse to play with, before killing it and tossing it to the dogs. It would just need a little more planning. After all, he had not been in touch with the

Chief Inspector for over eighteen months. It was time he looked up his old acquaintance to have some fun. Edward removed his glasses from the bridge of his nose, breathed on the lenses and gently wiped the surface. Soon it would be time to start the game.

Strange Reaction

Damien knew there was something wrong. Angel never normally met him before school. But she smiled as he approached.

"What's up?" he greeted her.

"Nothing. I just thought I would come over and say hello."

Now he knew there was something wrong. "Ok, hello to you too," he responded, puzzled. They walked in silence for a little while. He was moving quicker today; no stick was required.

"Damien," she said hesitantly. This was it – now he would find out why she had met him. "I am thinking of not going to lessons this week."

"Ok," he said, cautiously. There was more. He could feel it in his bones.

"If I asked you to ignore me for a couple of days, will you do that for me?"

"Why?"

'I would rather you didn't ask."

"Ok," he said slowly. "Are you dumping me?"

"Oh god, no! Please don't think that!" She grabbed his hand but not before glancing around. "Please, Damien, don't think like that. I just need some space. Oh god, that sounds bad. It's coming out all wrong." She took a deep breath. "Can you just humour me? Think of it as a game. Just ignore me; pretend I don't exist."

"I thought games were supposed to be fun."

She bowed her head before releasing his hand. Once again her eyes scanned the surrounding area. "I think he has come back for me."

"Who?" Damien asked. When she didn't respond, he pressed, "An old boyfriend?"

She shook her head.

"Then who?"

"Please, Damien. A couple of days and then everything will be back to normal, I promise." Her eyes scanned left then right again. "I have to go," she whispered. Angel could see Laurel approaching.

"Angel, wait," he called, but she had already mingled in with the other kids.

"What's wrong with you?" smirked Laurel as he brought his hand down on Damien's back in his standard enthusiastic greeting.

"I don't know. I just had the weirdest conversation with Angel."

"Women. They do that to us men, screw with our minds. Forget it. She'll be back to normal in no time. Or whatever normal is for her. Anyway, you know my opinion of your girlfriend."

"I know and didn't we agree not to go there again?"

"You started it, not me."

Reluctantly, Damien followed Angel's wish and ignored her for the next few days, and although they rarely spoke at school, it somehow seemed harder to play her game. After a week, as promised, their relationship returned to normal.

"What was all that about?" asked Damien as they sat near the lake.

"Me, just being silly. My imagination was playing tricks, that's all. I'm sorry if I worried you. Everything is going to be ok." Angel leant over and kissed him on the cheek. Damien responded by tickling her. She screeched with laughter before placing her hands on his shoulders and kissing him on the lips. "I will never leave you, Damien, not if I have a choice."

"You do say some strange things sometimes; you always have a choice," he whispered, kissing her again.

Missing

The pages of a small red book floated loosely on the surface of the water. The image of a woman in white adorned the front cover. Five minutes after he arrived at their meeting place, Damien had retrieved most of the pages. Turning the book over, Damien realised it was *Jane Eyre,* Angel's favourite. He smiled. Deep down, Angel was a romantic, but where was she, and why was her book in the lake? He adjusted his stance so he could see across the lake, past the white wisps of mist that had formed in the early morning. It would clear later; it always did. The lake wasn't visible so Angel could be out of his eye-line, running like she did most days. Sometimes, he wished he could have joined her with a lap around the large expanse of water, but he couldn't. His t-shirt would rub against his skin, making it extremely sore until it started to bleed. He remembered how his legs felt after a sprint across the rugby field, tired and aching, his shoulders heavy, yet his mind always felt fresh and alert. It was a wonderful feeling.

Damien climbed up onto the rock with thoughts of his favourite game, and although he could now see more of the lake, there was still no sign of Angel. Sometimes he wished he had probed more, questioned Angel when she said things he didn't quite understand. According to

Angel, she ran because she had to keep fit. It was the 'had to' that confused him. Angel often said strange things that meant nothing. At least, he assumed they meant nothing at the time. Now he was beginning to think otherwise. Maybe behind her strange use of words there was a hidden meaning. Sitting on the rock where they first met, he started putting the pages in the correct order, not sure why, just to pass the time. Half an hour quickly passed, and Angel had still not appeared. Leaving the papers to dry in the sun, Damien left, disappointed.

A couple of days later, there was still no sign of Angel. He had been back to the lake twice, and the leaves of the book were still laid as he had left them. She had missed the one and only class they were in together, English, and nobody had seen her for several days. Damien rarely went to Angel's room as he didn't want to cause problems with the warden, but he was beginning to feel desperate. Where was she? The pain in his stomach was starting to return, and he could really do with some pain relief. Maybe Laurel was right, and he was beginning to rely on Angel too much. Laurel had even suggested Angel was playing mind games, but he didn't really believe that. He desperately wanted to find her, to understand what was going on. As a precaution, he had decided not to ask Angel to remove the pain. Pain and suffering was part of his current life so a little longer would not be a problem. After all, he had promised his mates he would be careful and not rely on Angel too much.

Glancing up to the sixth floor Damien could see Angel's window; her room lay in darkness. The window looked closed, which was unusual for Angel, who craved fresh air, day and night. From Damien's angle, it was impossible to see if the blinds had been drawn.

There did not appear to be a light switched on in the bedroom or the bathroom, although his angle was not ideal to be one-hundred percent certain. Angel's room appeared higher in the building than he initially remembered; with the pain he was experiencing, he prayed the lift was working. If the girls' lift was similar to the lads' lift, there would be no guarantee it would deliver him to the sixth floor.

Thankfully, the lift worked, and the warden was nowhere in sight. Angel's door was not locked, which again was unusual. The door was always locked. It didn't matter if she was in or out. Angel was a very private person. Maybe it was her air of mystery that attracted him in the first place. Damien took a couple of steps into the room and found it was deserted. The bed had not been slept in. The sheets were still in their hospital-style folds. The photo frame and hairbrush had been moved from the bedside table, which made him worry. Snatching open the wardrobe door, his concerns were justified; her clothes were gone. Angel had left him, left the school. Damien had noticed she had been a little distant over the last few weeks, not her happy self. She did not always appear to be listening. There were times when she just stared into space as though she was thinking, or looking for someone or something that wasn't there. It had all started when she asked him to ignore her for a few days. Since then, they had both pretended everything was back to normal, but it wasn't. He had guessed there was something on her mind. His assumption had been exam pressure, but he hadn't guessed she was planning to leave.

He moved towards the bed and sat down, placing his head in his hands. This was the bed where they sat, when she had taken his hands in hers and removed his pain. Even though he was suffering again, the pain had not returned in full force. This bed was where she had shared her body with him – a sexual experience he would never forget. His mind drifted to the 10th May. They had been at their favourite haunt – the lake, deserted as normal. Angel was trying to entice him into the water. The waves were gently lapping against her thighs, and she was splashing the cool water towards him. It was a hot summer day. He was so sure he would catch an infection that he was holding back from entering the water. He remembered a lump had formed in his throat as panic rose through his body. *It's only water,* he kept telling himself, but he still held back. He trusted Angel with his life, yet he was still terrified. How could a little water appear so scary? He took a step forward. The water was cold, and he could feel the tiny pebbles under his feet as he slowly moved towards her. Three feet from the lakeside and the water had reached his knees. His legs shook, not because of the cold, but because he was afraid. He still continued to move towards Angel. He was sure she was moving further out into the lake. The water was now lapping gently against her waist, where previously it was thigh high. She turned her back to him and dove into the water, disappearing from his sight. Summing up the courage, he had taken a deep breath, and ducked down into the water. He swam to where she once stood.

Angel had still not surfaced. Suddenly, something grabbed his leg. As he pulled it away in surprise, a mass of dark hair appeared in front of him, and Angel popped up. She placed her hands on his shoulders and kissed him, a warm, wet, loving kiss. They had spent over an hour enjoying the lake's cool water before collapsing on the water's edge. He had done it. This was a turning point in his recovery. There were no side effects, no infection, just a bit of fun by two teenagers.

As they lay in the warmth of the sun, he leaned over Angel and kissed her gently. There was a twinkle in her eyes.

"How did you like your mental psychology?" she had laughed.

"As long as it is backed with a bit of physical psychology," was his quick response, as he kissed her once more. He loved it when she was in one of her playful moods. Now as he sat on the bed, memory after memory came flooding back. *My very own time-machine,* he thought. *If only it could take me to the future, as well as the past.*

He remembered Angel asking why he always kept his shirt on. "You know why. I don't want you to be disgusted by my body," he had hesitantly replied and then wondered if he had been too honest.

"How could I be disgusted? This is disgusting," and she had pointed to her second toe on her left foot. "Look how crooked it is compared to the others."

He glanced down and laughed. "That's just cute." He kissed her again, a warm tender kiss.

"No, it's disgusting," Angel had whispered as she responded to his passionate kiss. She was obviously making a point. Angel had changed tact since the last time she had brought up the subject.

"Let's not go there again," he said quietly. He remembered her going all serious on him and saying, "Damien, I don't care what your body looks like. It's part of you, part of the package. It comes with your brain, your personality; it is what makes you a whole person."

Damien remembered his response clearly, "Maybe one day."

"Can that one day be today? I'll show you mine if you show me yours," she whispered.

"What, here? Now?" he had asked, but Angel had already pulled the bow on her bikini top. Her hands had kept it in place, revealing nothing. He had panicked, quickly glancing around to see if anybody else was visiting the lake, but there wasn't another person in sight. Nobody ever visited but them.

"Promise you won't be turned off," he had whispered.

"You are so silly, Damien Harrington," Angel said, throwing her arms around his neck. With nothing holding her bikini top, it slipped gently down her body.

Damien had tried to smile, as he pulled his wet t-shirt over his head, before falling on top of her so quickly, and with such force he must have winded her. This was his way of hiding his body, not that her eyes ever strayed from his face. Her hands had moved to his shoulders. His body froze, not wanting Angel's hands to wander any lower and discover the disgusting sores and blisters. Angel must have realised. Her hands moved back to his neck, allowing him to relax and to enjoy the warmth of her body against his. It felt so good; something he had not realised was missing from their relationship until then.

Damien was about to leave the room when intuition told him to lift the mattress. To his astonishment, Angel's scrapbook was still there. Angel would never leave without her scrapbook. It was too precious – so precious that she had never shown it to him. Flicking through the book, he found the same articles his mates had found. Halfway through the book, he recognised the two images Angel had used in her photo frame. A small smile crossed his face. Towards the back of the book, several articles he hadn't seen before were stuck upside down. They were neatly cut out from newspapers, placed in date order and related to two child killings that had taken place a couple of years previous. The articles referred to a Shaun Barton, aged nine years, who was found dead in Waldorf Forest, Surrey, from a single knife wound – no witnesses – and Jennifer Villier, aged eleven years. Jennifer's body was found an estimated three months after her murder in an old abandoned farm building in the Ardenne region in the North of France. Police enquiries were suggesting a cult killing. According to the article on Jennifer, the body was placed in a ritual position. Her arms and legs had been spread in a star position, and the limbs pointed to various letters and numbers drawn on the floor. No suspects were being held, but enquiries were ongoing. Damien wondered if that was still the case, or had somebody now been arrested? A couple of articles were in French, but they added nothing to the English articles. French had been a beneficial option to take. It was French that had brought him closer to Angel when they had first kissed.

He remembered hearing something about the first killing on the news a couple of years ago, but the outcome escaped him. There didn't appear to be any connection with the earlier pages of the scrapbook other than a child killed in a forest. The same crime Angel had once been accused of over ten years ago. Damien put it down to Angel trying to prove her innocence or morbid fascination. Could there be a darker side to Angel that he had originally ignored? Maybe his mates were right, and she was insane. Maybe the institution had screwed her up. Even though Angel had gone, the scrapbook was not his to keep. He placed the scrapbook back into its rightful place and was about to drop the mattress back onto the bed frame when another object caught his eye on the far side of the bed, wedged between the mattress and the wall.

His hand grasped a small book. It was a deep blue in colour with no lock. A tiny metal clasp held the pages together. It was a diary. Why would anybody leave their diary? Damien knew he shouldn't look. It would be invading Angel's privacy, but it could help him to understand what went wrong with their relationship; why she had left the school and him without a word. He fought with his conscience, but the intrigue was too much. Sitting back down on the bed, he started flicking through the pages.

26th February

I still have not spoken to Beth. I want to say I am sorry for Stacey's death but I can't... Stacey was like having a younger sister. I miss her. I'll always miss her.

28th February

More and more jibes off Beth's friends. It doesn't matter. I expected it. Beth has lost her sister, and I a good friend...

29th February

I was pushed over in the corridor today. Tara is getting on my nerves. She is becoming more and more aggressive towards me. I want to hit her so hard, to hurt her like she hurts me, but I must not get into trouble. I must keep my head down. I promised...

At the bottom of the page, Angel had drawn a small caricature of Tara. Damien smiled. It didn't look much like Tara, apart from the spikey hair. Angel had obviously tried to make the image look as evil as possible. The eyes were small and situated close together, and the image had a large nose and horsey teeth. So this was the way Angel vented her anger, Damien smirked, not like Laurel suggested – by killing people. This had to be proof Angel was not violent. If only he could prove it to his mates.

A couple of sheets of paper were loose in the diary. They fell out onto the floor. Damien picked them up and saw they were all pencil drawings. The first was a drawing of the school. It wasn't bad, although the perspective was slightly out on the roof. There were a couple of other drawings, but again the perspective was not quite right, and they were drawn a little heavy handed and too dark for his taste. They looked like they had been drawn in charcoal rather than pencil. He wondered what a psychiatrist would make of the drawings. Could they tell the sanity of a person or what that person was thinking by looking at a drawing? Would it be wrong for him to remove one of the drawings and have it analysed professionally? The last sheet he picked up was a portrait of him. It was a remarkable resemblance, especially as she would have drawn it from memory. This was the only drawing that had colour on the page. Written diagonally in red was his name, *Damien*. The drawing was light and fresh; drawn in a very fine pencil line. It was very different from the other drawings. Particular attention had been given to his hair, smile and eyes, which she had captured perfectly. Damien placed the drawings back in the diary a little happier, but also a little sad at this finding.

He had once asked Angel what subjects she was studying. She had never answered before they were side-tracked onto something else, but now his educated guess would be Art. Angel spent time in the strange modern building with its bright external mural, which would explain why he did not see her around the school. Damien started to flick through the rest of the pages. Most of them had small drawings intermingled with the words. Damien promised himself that he would skip any irrelevant section, even if it had a reference to him. After all, he was worried what she might say. What he really wanted to understand was what was she thinking and why she left.

Damien was desperately trying not to look at April 10th when they first kissed. He had wondered if what he had said that day had caused her to leave. They had had a lot of fun since that day, and their relationship had moved on fairly quickly in his opinion, but had she thought more about his earlier words? He tried to think back to exactly what he had said. They were sitting at the lake, and Angel was testing him on his French, preparing him for his exam. She had spoken for a couple of minutes in French before finishing with "*Embrassez-moi, s'il vous plait.*" Her eyes looked to the ground as she spoke. He stopped and stared at her for a few seconds. He hoped he had translated her French correctly, or his next move would be very embarrassing. He had lifted her chin and moved his head towards hers, before softly kissing her on the lips. This was the first time they had ever kissed.

He remembered Angel apologising for being so forward, and he could see from the look on her face that she was concerned her actions would affect their friendship. He had smiled and kissed her again.

"Your French is coming on nicely," she had murmured.

"I have wanted to kiss you for so long, but I wasn't sure how you would react. You are a very difficult book to read sometimes," he said before laughing and following his comment up with, "I am glad you are forward sometimes." He had placed his arm around her shoulder and gave her a gentle squeeze. He could feel her soft bare flesh under his fingertips. He had been surprised she had not winced or pulled away, disgusted that he was touching her. He was an ogre in many females' eyes, all right to talk to, but nothing more.

The pain that day was becoming unbearable. It had moved up his side and into his shoulders. He thought, *Why does the pain have to be in my arms, today of all days?* He wanted to hold her longer, but he couldn't. Removing his arm from her shoulder, the pain had immediately eased. He hated how his illness controlled his life. If only he could have held her longer, like any other lad would have done in the same circumstances. Damien accepted their friendship had been developing. A closeness, a sexual tension, had been bubbling away beneath the surface for several weeks. He had seen the way she looked at him, and when she sat next to him, she always sat a little close, so their arms and legs brushed against each other. He wasn't complaining, He enjoyed their brief encounters. Damien had seen the signs, but he had never dared to believe that they could share anything other than friendship.

Angel had pulled her knees up to her chest and rocked her body slightly. He remembers he was pleased she had not tried to hug him. He sometimes felt she could read his thoughts, or at the very least knew where his pain was. The last thing he would have wanted was to tell her not to touch him because it hurt so much.

She had asked him if he thought Beth was beautiful. He had responded by saying, "I think she is very attractive. However, you are more beautiful internally and externally. You have a natural beauty. You don't need all that makeup to make you irresistible to me." Damien had never mentioned his date to Angel. He had often wondered if Angel knew about his evening with Beth. Was that why she needed reassurance? But why that day? Why the day he had kissed her? Angel's day at school had not gone well – that much he did know. He had heard through the school grapevine Angel had had a run in with Tara Hawkley, one of Beth's close friends. Damien remembers lifting Angel's chin again and looking deep into her eyes. He had told her if she was being bullied then he would step in and stop them. He felt she had answered him in a strange way.

"I deserve it," she had muttered, pulling her chin from his hand. Her eyes stared at the ground again, and her body rocked vigorously. He had launched into a lecture of whatever happened in your past should not affect your future, and she had responded by asking him to forget it. He had not pushed her any further. If there was a time when he should have given her a reassuring hug then that was the time; however, he couldn't because of the pain in his body.

Instead of a hug, he had kissed her for reassurance, and she responded passionately. Collapsing to the ground, they continued to kiss. Her long, slender fingers ran through his wavy hair. He had been thankful she had not moved her hands down his body. Instead, her hands had cupped his face – they did not wander. Never before had he felt such a loving feeling from a female as he had felt at that moment. He had laughed and sat up, making some comment about needing some air. He remembered stroking the side of her face and tucking her thick, dark hair behind her ear, a habit he would develop over the following weeks. He had stared at her for a couple of minutes before speaking. This was the part that may have scared her, so he needed to make sure he remembered the words correctly.

He had started by saying, "Please do not take this the wrong way, Angel. I have wanted more than just a friendly relationship with you for a long time, but I can't love you like I should be able to. I can't give you what you want. I want to hold you, except I can't because it hurts me too much. I want to be held by you, but my illness makes it impossible. The pain continues to get worse – much worse. When I am with you, admittedly I don't always feel the pain, and sometimes it can feel like it has gone. However, it always comes back. I cannot love you like a normal boyfriend. I can't even hug you when I know you are upset, and that makes me feel awful."

Angel had slowly propped herself up on her elbows and had responded by saying, "I don't care about any of that, Damien. I just want to be with you. I am sure the pain will go eventually." At the time he had loved her optimism. Now he understood why.

"Can we at least try and see how it goes?" she had asked. He had stared long and hard into her dark eyes before kissing her again. How could he have said no? It was what they both had wanted! Too much time had passed since April 10th. Damien decided it could not be that. They had argued since that day, but they had always kissed and made up. The air was clear between them, or so he thought. They had also shared the most exciting sexual experience of his life since that day, so why had she gone? Damien decided he would not look in her diary at the 10th; instead he would concentrate on the week before she had disappeared and work his way backward if necessary.

Curiosity eventually got the better of him. He didn't read the 10th. Instead he turned to the day he had lost control; the day he had shown his major weakness, his vulnerability. The entry was a lot longer than he expected, which was a concern. Taking his time, he studied every individual word; reading more into it than Angel originally intended. It was almost written like a novel, beautifully composed, every word carefully scripted, handwritten in fluid blue ink. It read...

24th April

...I moved my hands slowly to his shoulders. I wanted to caress his naked neck and the top of his shoulders. Damien's muscle tone is not as bad as he obviously thinks. He has a decent body shape – wide shoulders, smaller waist. He does not carry any additional weight, though this could be due to his illness. I told him he has strong arms and shoulders, but he did not take this well. He kissed me gently on the lips. He has a real nice kiss. He tucked his head into my neck. I could feel his damp cheek against mine. I know he was crying even though he tried to hide it.

I told him I was sorry. I know I went too far. I pushed him too hard. He looked deeply into my eyes and said I was too nice to him. I told him I was being truthful, and then he went on about the sores and blisters and how disgusting they were. It is silly, but I know he compares his body to his mates. He cannot see that people don't notice the marks. Damien has so little confidence, and I don't know why. He has so much life, so much to give.

I carried on pushing him, and I know I should not have. This has always been my downfall; I don't know when to stop. I want to tell him he has a small mark under his collar bone, shaped like a heart. I often trace the shape with my fingers. He has not noticed that I do this. On the back of his left arm there is another mark shaped like a bear's head. His body is beautiful yet he can't see this. If I tell him what I see, I think I will upset him. He prefers denial.

Damien moved to the mirror, undid his top two buttons and pulled his shirt to the side. He could see the heart she was talking about, one inch in width and slightly pink. He moved his fingers over the mark. It did not feel sore to touch it, and strangely enough he could feel Angel touching his skin. A faint smile crossed his lips. Sitting back down on the bed, he continued reading.

I asked him to sit up and remove his shirt so I could see his body. He begged me not to make him do this. Tears trickled down his cheek. He tried to stand, but I grabbed his arm. He has never been so rough with me as he was today. He tried to shrug me off, pushing me away. I grabbed his arm tighter and placed my arms around his waist. He managed to prise my fingers from his body, so I moved them higher up his body. Once again, he released my grasp. He was shouting at me to let go. I knew he would not hurt me, but I was not going to let him leave, not like this. Finally, his head collapsed onto my shoulder, and he cried long and hard. He kept saying he was sorry over and over again, yet he had nothing to be sorry about. I know he is embarrassed, but I was wrong. It was too soon, but I will not give in. I know he can get over this. I wish I could heal Damien, make everything better, make his life perfect. He deserves that. I cannot bear to see him upset.

He read it through again. He now remembered the whole event, clearly. Angel's record was so descriptive. This account was written in far more detail than the rest of the diary so it must have affected her severely. He had moved on since then. In fact, it had only been two weeks later, May 10th, when he had removed his shirt at the lake – unveiled his body and felt the warmth of Angel's body against his. He closed the diary. It was so wrong to read a person's thoughts, to pry into their inner feeling, but he needed to know why she had left him.

He opened the diary again. It fell open to the page that had one word written on it: *WHY?* It was heavily etched into the paper, almost ripping the page. He turned to the day before. *WHY?* And then to the page after: *WHY?* He stared at the word. *WHY* what? It did not make any sense. His eyes moved to the top of the page to the date in March. It meant nothing at first, and then it hit him. It was the day he had gone on a date with Beth. He had guessed Angel knew, and now the diary had said it all without saying anything. He flicked through the pages to the last ten entries. It was wrong, but he needed to know. He could explore Angel's feelings. He could flick through the diary and find out all Angel's feelings and thoughts, the day they first met, the day they first kissed, the first time they had sex, the dates were endless. He flicked through the pages to June 14th to her last seven entries and started to read.

After twenty minutes, he quickly slipped the diary underneath his jacket and left the room. He needed to see Laurel urgently. Rushing back to the halls, he climbed the stairs two at a time to reach Laurel's corridor. A couple of months ago, he had struggled to climb one flight of stairs. Today he was attempting to climb five flights of stairs in a hurry. His breathing was heavy, and he had to stop for a couple of seconds to catch his breath. His legs were tired, but apart from that he felt excellent; his adrenalin was keeping him going. He could have taken the lift – it was working – although the thought never crossed his mind. Damien hammered on Laurel's door, no answer. He was about to leave when the lift pinged signifying somebody's arrival. Laurel calmly stepped out.

"I didn't expect to see you until tomorrow. Did we change our plans?" asked Laurel.

"Edward, who is he?"

"What?" asked Laurel.

"Edward. You know, when you were talking about Angel, I am sure you mentioned the name Edward," by now Damien was almost shouting.

"Ok, ok, come on in. Let me check. What's all this about?" asked Laurel. Damien quickly explained his suspicions while Laurel checked his files. It turned out Edward was Angel's legal guardian.

Damien passed the diary to Laurel, "Read the last couple of days and tell me what you make of it."

Laurel laughed. "You're reading a woman's diary. Now that's just not cricket. Anything juicy?" He could see Damien was being serious, so he cut the wisecracks.

Laurel was quickly brought up to date: Angel's empty room, the book in the lake, the hidden scrapbook and diary, the lack of messages and eventually her disappearance. Laurel grabbed a couple of warm cans from the cupboard and threw one over to Damien. They sat down and started to go through the diary. Laurel opened it to the 14th June.

"Don't read the 14th or the 15th," Damien requested.

"A bit juicy, eh, mate?" laughed Laurel.

"Yeah, a bit juicy; start on the 16th." At last Damien was smiling.

16th June

...today I ran back to my room. I am sure I saw Edward near the school. I don't think he saw me... Why am I hiding from him? He has been so good to me.

17th June

Went to the lake... I know he is watching me. I can feel his eyes following my every move. Maybe it is my imagination playing tricks, but I am feeling scared. He said he would come for me when I reach 18, but I am not 18 yet. He shouldn't be here... I know I am doing the right thing, keeping Damien a secret. I am not sure how Edward will react if he knows I have a boyfriend... I did everything he told me. I have kept my head down, and I have worked hard.

"Laurel, do you remember last Saturday when Angel came over to see me in the refectory? She said she could not go to the lake the following day as she had something she needed to do, so instead I watched you stuff Staindrop Sixth Formers. Well, I thought it unusual at the time. Angel normally never speaks to me when other people are around, except this time she hugged me, and she said the strangest thing – 'Be careful, Damien.' I didn't take any notice at the time, but don't you think that's a strange thing to say? If you look at the 17th, she does go to the lake. She just didn't want me with her."

18th June

...I am still awake at 1:00 a.m. I think Edward is outside my door. I can hear breathing, and his footsteps are pacing the corridor. I have checked the door twice – it is locked. I have jammed a chair against the handle so he can't get in. Why is he still here? Why didn't the warden stop him? Why can't he leave me alone? This is the first time in my life where I have felt normal, like other people my age. I know he will take that away from me. I don't want to see him.

"I think she may have been crying. The ink has run in several places."

Laurel nodded in agreement, "Possibly." He turned over the page and carried on reading.

19th June

...Today I had a note pushed underneath my door. Edward wants to know why I am hiding from him. I don't know why myself, or maybe I just don't want to face the truth. He wants to meet me, I don't want to see him. He makes me do things that I don't want to do. He says I know what will happen if I don't stop playing silly games. I am scared...I am enjoying my new life. I want to disappear from his radar, but where can I go? I have no money, and he would only find me. He always finds me. I know I will have to meet him to try and make him understand things are different now.

"What is he making her do?" asked Laurel.

Damien shrugged his shoulders, "I don't know. She never spoke much of her past."

"Do you think it is sexual?"

Damien felt sick considering such a thought. Laurel just stared at him and then back to the words in the diary.

"Does she flinch when you touch her or does she appear to have any sexual hang-ups?" Laurel asked.

Damien shook his head. There were no sexual hang-ups that he was aware of. They talked it through for a while, although Damien wouldn't give Laurel any details, no matter how hard he pushed. Gentlemen do not tell stories. Anyway, how could he explain to Laurel that he had initially been the one with the sexual hang up, not Angel. Laurel would not understand. They came to the conclusion it was not sexual, although neither of them was 100 percent convinced.

20th June

I have managed to hide all day. I have spoken to nobody. Edward must never know my secret. Tomorrow I will tell Damien, but I don't want to put his life in danger. Edward can be so unpredictable. I know he doesn't mean to be...

"What danger?" asked Laurel in an urgent tone, but Damien only answered with another shrug of the shoulders, indicating he didn't know.

"The only connection I can make is a couple of weeks ago Angel asked me not to talk to her; to ignore her if I saw her. I wonder if it's connected. She also said something about him coming back for her, but she wouldn't tell me who."

"Do you think she was trying to protect you?" Laurel asked.

"After reading this, I think it is likely, don't you? The next bit sounds more desperate."

Maybe I should just disappear. Oh, I don't know what to do. I am confused...Edward is at my door again tonight. This time he is knocking and whispering my name. Why won't he leave me alone? I won't do it, not this time. If I meet him and explain, maybe he will understand...I have a new life now. Surely I am old enough to do what I want.

"No entry after the 20th, and today it is the 25th," said Damien. "I haven't seen her in eight, maybe nine days." They sat and talked for the first time in a long time. Angel was obviously scared and possibly hiding. Laurel even felt a small ounce of sympathy for her, although he did wonder if Angel was playing games with his mate's emotions. After all, she could have lifted the mattress knowing Damien would see her, to arouse his interest. The diary could have easily been written for his benefit. If she were psychotic, then this was exactly what a psychotic person would do. Laurel did not mention this to his friend. Since their frank discussion at Brian's, it was wiser to say nothing, especially after the episode with Beth. He was lucky Damien was still talking to him. Their friendship was too important to mess up on speculation.

Laurel placed a brotherly arm around Damien's shoulder. "Come on, mate. We will find her." Through the haze of tears, Damien nodded. He felt so pathetic crying in front of his mate.

"I love her so much. She makes me feel so good. She is funny and loving. I have never felt like this about anybody before," he rubbed his eyes on his sleeve before continuing. "I always wanted what you had, Laurel, to play rugby, to go clubbing and drinking, date loads of girls. I was jealous for years because I could not do any of it, and then Angel came along, and she made me realise I did not need any of that. I had a new life which I could enjoy just as much. I feel like I have lost everything again. What am I going to do?"

"We'll find her, ok?" Laurel promised. After a long discussion, they decided to speak to the warden in her halls to see if she had seen Angel. They would then walk down to the fruiterers where she frequently visited. It wasn't much, but at least they were doing something.

With Angel's past, Damien was unsure about informing the police, but if something had happened, he would never forgive himself. The decision was made, warden today, police tomorrow.

"Oh, and not forgetting the mathematics exam first thing tomorrow," reminded Laurel. Damien had forgotten about the exam, but one thing he did know, he wouldn't be able to concentrate. As expected, the warden was no help. She hadn't even realised Angel had not been back to her room, and the owner of the fruiterers had not seen Angel in over two weeks.

Damien appreciated how important a decent maths grade was for Laurel's career. Laurel's father was an Account Manager for PriceWaterhouseCoopers, one of the largest accountancy firms in England. It had always been assumed Laurel would follow in his father's footsteps and train as an accountant. Laurel was happy to pursue the profession; after all, academically he had a forte for mathematics and statistical analysis. Damien borrowed the black flip top folder and left his mate to revise. He wasn't sure what he was looking for, but maybe something had been missed, an obvious location to hide, or a relative to visit. He promised himself two hours maximum searching through the file and then the rest of the evening revising. This did not happen. Damien spent the night reading through the file. It made fascinating reading.

*****

Damien's paper lay on the table. The constant ticking from the clock filled the silence in the room of anticipative students. Damien was on a time limit. With pen poised and an overactive, drifting mind, Damien was surprised he had managed any of the exam paper, but the next algebra question had brought him to a standstill:

$$(a+5ea) + (3ae+a^2) =$$

The *a* and *e* kept jumping out from the page, reminding him of Angel and Edward. He needed to put them out of his mind for another hour. Concentrate, a couple more questions tackled, and then an awful thought hit him. Angel was not an only child. Two of her brothers were dead, and if his memory was correct, they died aged seventeen to eighteen years; one of Marasmus, an illness where the body gradually wastes away. The other brother through suicide. Did he also have Marasmus? Was that why he killed himself? Could this happen to Angel? Was this the law of averages or the probability theory? Is that why she had run away because she was ill like her brother? He must concentrate. Only half an hour to go. What did x stand for? What was he missing? Laurel's folder, the diary, and the scrapbook had all been scrutinised, but he had to be missing something.... Something so obvious, the y or x of the equation...concentrate... If $(2x^2a + xa - 3a^2x) + (-x^2a^2 + 2xa)$ then $2x^2a + 3xa - 3xa - 3x^2a - x^2a^2$...oh, damn, his mind was drifting again. In less than half an hour, it would all be over. They would be sitting inside the police station trying to explain their suspicions to an officer. They were intending to rush back to the halls, collect the diary and then head straight off to the police station. Last push, only one question to go and ten minutes left. He must concentrate.

The Showdown

A small hankie lay on the floor beneath his bedroom window. Bending over to pick it up, a strong smell hit the back of his throat and clogged his nasal passage. His body began to swoon. The smell was distinctive; he recognized the chemical composition. Damien dropped the hankie. Suddenly from behind, a hand wrapped around his throat, and his face was forced down onto the bed. Although he could not see the figure, he knew it was a male; the hands were large and powerful. A cloth pressed hard against his mouth and nose. Damien tried to get back onto his feet. The smell overpowered him, knocking him off balance. He felt his senses drifting, becoming weakened and then nothing but blackness.

Chlorophorm –
Easy to shoot

*****

Chief Inspector David Harrington paced the operations room. Today, a group of his officers were about to conduct their largest drug raid in the UK for over twenty years. The underground drug culture could be destroyed for years to come. A telephone call came through; however, it wasn't the call he was expecting.

"It's Edward," said one of his PCs. "He wants to speak to you, sir."

The Chief Inspector had not heard from Edward for nearly two years. "Put a trace on it now," he ordered.

"Already done, sir," a voice answered. Edward's voice was calm, but the Chief Inspector could tell he was excited about something.

"Good afternoon, Chief Inspector. Don't bother putting a trace on the call. You know as well as I do I am not going to be on the line any longer than necessary. I have your son." There was a pause as Edward waited for a reaction. The Chief Inspector said nothing, stunned into silence.

Edward continued, "And because he is your son I am going to give you three hours instead of my standard two and a half hours to find us. Find him within three hours, and he lives. After three hours, he dies, unless I am feeling generous, in which case we will move to another location and then the game will start again until I tire of it. Think mobile, Chief Inspector."

"You bastard," the Chief Inspector said with deadly seriousness. "You let him go right now, or I swear I will kill you with my bare hands."

"Temper, temper, Chief Inspector. Don't you want to know which son?" There was a pause. "It's your youngest," he laughed.

"Don't do this, Edward," David pleaded. "Let's talk this through. I'll give you whatever you want. Just don't hurt him."

"Two hours fifty-nine minutes and counting, Chief Inspector," Edward said, and the line went dead.

"Trace," shouted the Chief Inspector.

"Not long enough, sir," came the immediate response from the back of the room. The Chief Inspector thought for a moment. Edward had not left a clue of their whereabouts, and he always left a clue. Unless the word *mobile* was a clue; could they be in a van, a train? No, too wide an area to cover. Edward liked to make it challenging, but not impossible. No, think! He must detach himself from the situation, from his son, and think logically. *Mobile*, what did it mean if it was not transport? There was no shop, no town, with the same name? Then it struck him – of course, Damien's mobile. With a new focus and optimism, the Chief Inspector rang his son's number. It rang out.

"Contact the school and see if my son is there, and where is Stobbard?"

"Honeymoon, sir, somewhere in the Caribbean," another voice answered.

"Find him now! No wait. He won't have access to the relevant equipment. Who else can trace a person's location through a mobile phone?" They all sat in silence and looked at each other.

"Only Stobbard, sir," a quiet voice muttered.

"In the whole of the police force only one man can do the job. This is ridiculous," muttered the Chief Inspector. "Government flipping cutbacks."

"Ideas," he yelled, "and quick! Time is ticking. My son's life depends on you." There was more mutterings and whispering in the room and then silence.

"Sir, this is a real wildcard," began Inspector Strangeway; if he could rely on anybody to come up with an idea, it would be Strangeway.

"Come on, Inspector, give me this wildcard, and let us see if it is feasible."

"Remember that kid who hacked into the security systems eight years ago and you said one day he may have a future with the police force? I think you said better than any graduate coming out of University."

"Yes, yes, I remember. Get on with it, Inspector."

"We have been keeping track of him, sir. He has been looking up files on an ex-patient in a psychiatric hospital. He has the equipment to locate a mobile phone signal, and I think he goes to the same school as your son, sir, Worthington!"

"Inspector Strangeway, you are a genius. Get him on the line now. Tell him I will give him whatever he needs, passwords, codes, etc., and if he can locate my son within two hours, I will purchase any equipment he wants personally. If not, tell him I will prosecute him for hacking into hospital records."

Glancing upwards, Harrington prayed his son was carrying his mobile phone. Damien normally went nowhere without it, not that he tended to use it much according to the phone records. It was carried in case of an emergency, and this was an emergency. He blessed his wife for insisting on his son having a mobile, a compromise for letting him stay at the school.

*****

Damien woke with a pounding headache. His vision was still blurred; the chloroform hadn't worn off fully. He wasn't sure what had happened. He tried to sit up, but pain shot through his arms. He tried to move his left arm, but it was tied above his head, the same with his right arm. A rope was tightly tied around both his wrists. His ankles appeared to be bound as well. He couldn't quite make out his position, or where he was. The room was dark, although he perceived it was still daytime; a beam of sunlight bounced off the wall in front of him as it forced its way through a gap in a boarded window.

The more Damien tried to wriggle, the tighter the ropes felt. Realising his body was splayed in a cross and secured firmly to the wooden floorboards, panic started to overwhelm him. Was this some sort of sacrifice or ritual? Oh god, where was he? What was happening? Damien tried to shout, only to find somebody had gagged him. The tape across his mouth was firmly in place. Rubbing the edges of the tape on his shoulder made no difference. It was hopeless. Even a contortionist would not be able to remove the tape. The fastenings were solid; not even a slight give in the ropes was possible. Fear rushed through his body. Perspiration formed on his skin as he tried desperately to free himself. Warm, salty tears started to build up in his eyes. He was trapped. It was useless to struggle.

Damien would have to wait and see if anybody turned up. Was this what Angel meant when she said she might put his life in danger? It seemed like a lifetime just lying and waiting. No longer blurred, his eyes began to adjust to the darkness, which was a relief. The door opened, and the outline of a man's figure stood in the doorway. The figure moved slowly towards Damien until his legs were astride Damien's body. The figure slowly and carefully removed his glasses. He carefully placed them in a small case, before tucking it inside his coat's chest pocket. The figure slowly bent over Damien's body with no sense of urgency. His coat brushed against Damien's leg.

Sniffing the air, he whispered, "I can smell your fear, boy." The stale smell of tobacco hung on the figure's clothing and in the air. He removed a knife with a serrated edge from his belt and calmly carved a three-inch cut down the side of Damien's neck, not deep, but enough to bleed. Damien strained his neck as far from the knife as was humanly possible. His neck muscles were taut but he could not dodge the blade.

"You cut like a girl," the figure laughed a chilling laugh that burrowed deep under the skin. Another four cuts were made in Damien's lower arm; one curved, one horizontal and two diagonal cuts. The blood started to drip down his arm through the gaps in the floorboards.

"My initials," laughed the figure.

"What's this?" the figure slipped a thin latex glove on his hand before placing the palm of his hand on Damien's face. Pressing hard, he forced Damien's opposite cheek down until it was imprinted with the pattern from the floorboards. Slicing the top button off Damien's shirt was easy; it could have been paper with the ease the knife cut.

The figure once again laughed, "You're the sick son, aren't you? I knew the Inspector had a sick son. I could scale you like a fish. Remove the skin down to the bone. That would be a blessing for you, wouldn't it?" He pressed the blade flat against the skin, but not enough to cut. "Now why didn't my Angel heal you?" Damien started to hyperventilate. Sweat and tears ran down his cheeks as he tried to catch his breath. The duct tape was suddenly ripped from his mouth.

"Is that better, boy?" the figure laughed once again. The sound echoed through the empty rooms, making the laughter sound louder than it actually was.

Removing his glove, the figure stared at his palm. He removed a small pack of antiseptic wipes from his coat pocket and rubbed the palm of his hand vigorously with one of them.

"Cleanliness is important, don't you think," he observed.

Damien didn't answer. He was still trying to catch his breath.

Studying his palms to make sure they were clean, the figure turned his attention back to Damien. "I am glad you have regained your composure. You are going to talk. Do you understand?"

Damien nodded.

"I said talk, not nod," yelled the figure.

"Sorry, I meant yes." The knife was back in Edward's hand, waving above Damien's helpless body, slicing at his arms.

"I said, talk to me boy."

"No, please don't," Damien whispered, squeezing his eyes tightly closed. Suddenly he felt the tip of the knife's blade jammed under his chin.

"Look at me, boy! Are you scared?"

"Yes, sir."

"Tut, tut. At least you are honest. I like honesty." Edward began firing off his questions. "Did you think you could take my Angel from me?"

"No."

"Have you contaminated my little Angel?"

"No, sir."

"Ah, you are a well-mannered young man, Damien Harrington. May I call you Damien?"

"Y..ye..yes."

"Now don't stutter. I don't like boys who stutter. Your father is very rude to me, and I don't like rudeness. Do you like rudeness?"

"No," the tears were starting to fall uncontrollably.

"Today is a special day for me and you. I will make you famous. Do you want to be famous?"

Damien didn't answer. "Do you want to be famous?" the figure bellowed.

"No," he sobbed.

"Wrong answer, boy. Of course you do. Everybody wants to be famous." The figure stood up straight, removed the glasses from his coat pocket and popped them back on his nose. "Anyway, enough chit chat. I have somebody you may want to meet. If I don't return for whatever reason, I am sure the rats will enjoy feasting on your body." He smirked then leant back over Damien's prone form. "Be scared, my boy, be very scared. Shit happens to those that lie," and with that final comment the figure left the room.

Damien tugged on the ropes once more. His vision was clear, although his tears kept making the room blurred. If his hands could not be freed then maybe he could free his feet. Pulling his knees closer to his body, he pushed down hard against the metal stake holding his ankles. Pain shot through his body as the stake rubbed against his ankle bone. Twisting his body, he placed the full force of his weight onto the ropes and stake. Again no movement. He was only causing himself more pain. Damien glanced around the room. The damp on the walls that had caused the plaster to crumble in places was now visible. Cracks had appeared, and chunks of plaster lay strewn across the floor. He tried to reach a piece of plaster so he could rub it against the rope, hoping it would be sharp enough. The first piece crumbled into a powder. The smell of gypsum reached his nostrils, replacing the pungent smell of stale tobacco. His fingertips could not quite reach the thick, solid-looking piece that lay millimetres from his grasp. He pulled hard on the rope, annoyed with himself.

The brickwork on the wall to the right looked cold and damp. The Artex ceiling was yellow from years of neglect and appeared to be closing in on him. The corners of the room were black from the mould that had formed; the fungi live and poisonous. Green, brown and red wires dangled down where a light once hung proudly. If it had been his mother's house, the wires would have been connected to a crystal chandelier; his grandmother's, a strange cane contraption that was intricately woven. An old chimney was positioned snugly behind his head. A thin film of soot covered the floor. No doubt his body lay in the filth from the fire. The 1980's golden textured flock wallpaper above the fireplace was peeling away; once a family home, now a torture chamber. A cold prickly feeling ran down his spine. The cut on his neck was starting to clot, but he realised worse was to follow.

Damien waited another five minutes and then hollered and screamed as he tried desperately to attract somebody's attention; somebody who could help him. His throat became hoarse and dry until finally yelling was no longer an option. His wrists were sore. The skin had started to flay from the constant pulling at the ropes. A vibration in his pocket indicated his mobile was on silence. The small object vibrated gently against his body, a welcome but frustrating contact. If only he could reach it, tell whoever was calling help was needed. The vibration changed; a message had been left – text or voicemail, he was unsure. Maybe it was a message from god telling him his life was over. Damien shook his head. The sharp pain on the side of his neck was dulling, causing his jaw to lock. Tears started to swell in his eyes.

Damien wasn't sure how long he was left alone, but the next time the door opened, two figures blocked the doorway. The smaller person was the one to speak first.

"I am sorry, Damien. I am really sorry. Please forgive me." Immediately he recognized the voice. It was a relief to hear her tender tone, even though the words spoken were less encouraging.

"Remember what you need to do, Angel," said the male's voice.

"Please don't, Edward. Anybody but Damien. I'll do anything, but please not Damien." Angel jumped in front of Edward, blocking Damien from view.

"No, Edward," Angel's voice was starting to rise. "Please no." Edward removed his glasses, squinted then looked hard through her small body to his prey.

Bringing his attention back to the young girl standing in front of him, Edward smirked, "You like him, don't you?"

Angel nodded.

"Has he contaminated you, Angel?"

"No honestly, he hasn't. Please, Edward, don't."

"I know he has contaminated you, Angel. I need you pure. What did I tell you?"

Angel bowed her head and mumbled, "To keep myself to myself and not to draw any attention, and I did that Edward, honestly I did." She raised her head. "I didn't stand out. I blended in well, just like you said."

"But you didn't, did you?" he shouted. "You became contaminated by Harrington's son." Edward's face was red with rage. Angel had let him down. He had given her one order, and she had not obeyed that order. Her tears were now falling. Damien watched in horror. It was like a Shakespearian play being acted out in front of him, yet he was their only audience. He wouldn't have been surprised if the three witches made a dramatic appearance, with a clash of thunder and a flash of lightning, uttering the words, "When shall we three meet again..."

Edward pushed Angel to one side and approached Damien's body, revealing the knife once again. Angel lunged at Edward, trying to knock the knife from his hand. She did not even knock him off balance. The figure was powerful. With one swipe of his hand, he knocked her to the ground.

"If you like him that much, then bring him back to life. Show me what you can do, girl." Lifting the knife in the air with both hands on the handle to give him force and control, Edward plunged the knife deep into Damien's chest. Edward had intentionally missed his heart, but several blood vessels were severed. This was going to be a messy killing, and Edward didn't like mess. A single stab to the heart would stop the heart beating on impact. It was less messy. The blood immediately stopped pumping, and there was very little leakage from the open wounds – the perfect killing – but today he needed the lad to die slowly. He liked watching life disperse from the body, seeing the spirit rise. He often killed this way. It gave him a feeling of satisfaction. Thin medical latex gloves shielded his hands from the mess. The feel of rubber against his skin disgusted him, but he disliked the feeling of somebody's blood squelching between his fingers more.

Damien screamed at the top of his lungs. Angel joined in and screamed before throwing her body over Damien's.

Edward grabbed her wrists. "Your power is in your hands, girl." With one hand, he pulled her off Damien's body and then pulled the knife out of Damien's chest, before plunging it down again, deep into Damien's stomach. This time, even with one hand on the handle, he felt the blade hit the floorboard beneath the body. Edward smiled. The strength was in his hands. He was powerful; nobody could stop him. This time he twisted the blade rupturing the organs. Damien squeezed his eyes tightly closed, praying it was a nightmare. It would all be over when he opened them; he would find Angel in his room, in his arms sound asleep. This would not be the case. The horror was about to get worse. The pain was intense. As the knife twisted, he could swear his insides were moving, wrapping around the blade to intensify the pain. Opening his eyes wide, the nightmare was still happening.

"No," he screamed, "please no more." He started to cough.

"Goddamn you, boy," Edward spat. A spot of blood had soaked into the fibres of Edward's suit. Brushing the suit's fibres with one of the latex gloves, the blood dispersed deeper into the fabric, and across the sleeve. "Damn you! You have ruined my suit with your diseased blood, boy." Edward rubbed his sleeve again, obviously annoyed, before stopping and smirking. "I'll send the dry-cleaning bill to your father. He'll like that, won't he? It will confuse him, and I like to confuse your father." Edward's loud chilling laugh echoed around the room. "I think I'll pay a visit to your brother next, see if he wants to play a game. Then again, I may not give him a choice. You like games, don't you, boy?"

Angel sprang back onto her feet and leapt onto Edward's back. Her hands were tightly wrapped around his throat, desperately trying to pull him off Damien. Once again, Edward shook Angel off. She fell and rolled across the floor, banging the side of her head on the wall. More plaster cracked and crumbled and fell on the floor. Edward stood and turned towards Angel, who was ready to lunge at him again.

"Remember, Angel, the brain starts dying in three to five minutes without oxygen. I believe the countdown is about to start," he hissed.

Glancing towards Damien and then focusing again on Edward, she screamed, "I hate you! Why Damien? You could have picked anybody!"

Blood seeped through Damien's clothing. He started to cough and choke on his own blood. A red frothy liquid spurted from his mouth and ran down the side of his face. His shirt was now drenched in the red substance. A dark pool began to form beneath his body. Angel could see the life leaving his body as his eyes start to glaze over. He was fighting, but this was one battle he was not going to win.

"Now do your magic, Angel, and this time do not fail me," Edward hissed. Angel moved towards Damien's body. Tears rolled down her cheeks. She sat astride his hips to enable her to reach every part of his body without too much movement. Speed would be of the essence. Not knowing where to start, she glanced towards Edward for guidance.

"Four minutes," he growled. Glancing down at Damien's lifeless body beneath her, the tears came thick and fast. She tried to wipe her eyes on her sleeve, but the tears kept falling.

Concentration was impossible with his eyes staring lifelessly at her. The mischievous sparkle extinguished, though she prayed not for eternity. Angel moved slowly, closing his eyelids. She kissed her fingertips and placed them on his eyelids.

"I will take your pain and your death," she whispered in a tearful voice. She turned his head slightly to the side, and blood trickled from the corner of his mouth.

If she could give him life, then she didn't want him to choke again on his own blood. Placing her right hand on his forehead and the left on the wound, she tried to clear her mind, to summon the energy to bring life back to the body. She felt nothing at all, no sensation.

Turning towards Edward, she cried, "I can't do it. I don't know how to do this. Please call an ambulance, Edward, please."

"Three minutes to go," came the response. She quickly undid Damien's shirt. Of course, she needed to be next to his skin. A stupid mistake made under extreme pressure. Once again her hands touched his body. This time she lay one hand on his heart, and the other on his stomach wound. Gently moving her hand across his heart, she started to make circular movements with her fingertips, applying pressure and releasing, massaging the skin. Her knuckles kneaded parts of his chest when intuition told her to. She was beginning to feel something, a feeling she had not felt before, and again she uttered the words, "I will take your pain and your death; I give you my life."

It could only be described as a transistor radio inside her head. A single voice spoke low and gave her much-needed instructions. The volume control knob that started at one slowly rose as the intensity of the situation became serious. Now on three the voice switched from male to female, a child's voice, a town crier, an old man. The instructions leapt from one to another. The only common denominator was the voices were loud. The language English, the next second French, then Romanian, translating as quickly as her brain could process, the volume control switched to maximum. The raised voices in her head shouted and screamed out instructions. Her head hurt. She was losing control. Too quick, the voices were speaking too quickly, or was she too slow? Her fingers were tiring. Damien would not die; she would not let him die.

"Take me," she screamed. Edward stared in amazement. He knew Angel could do it. He had always had confidence in her ability. Controlling death was his payment for the hours of nurturing. He was almost giddy thinking of the financial rewards he would now receive, the power he would possess. The Doctor would be pleased.

Angel's left hand felt wrong. There was no feeling from his skin. Moving her fingers to his head, she started stroking his face. She always failed when she massaged the head and face; images of Stacey and the other kids came flooding back. Angel was slipping into a trance. Her fingers moved in patterns across his body. Unintentionally, without a free hand, she smeared blood from his stomach across his forehead. No longer looking down at her hands and with her eyes tightly closed, she mumbled words that could no longer be identified as English.

Edward watched in fascination and horror. The sight of blood on Angel's hands disgusted him, yet he accepted her hands had to touch the naked skin to be successful. When finished, he would make her scrub her hands in bleach, cleanse the skin and make her pure again. Her nails would need special attention; they would have to be scrubbed vigorously. That's where the germs and dirt would hide.

The messages came quick and fast. The voices pressed hard on Angel's temples, squeezing her brain, wringing it out as though it was nothing but a rag. *The heart pumps the blood to the brain, than I must move onto the chest and stomach whilst keeping my right hand massaging his heart.* The routine was going through her head. Her hands tried to keep up with the brain's processing. She was tired, and her fingers were becoming slower, falling behind her brain's messages. Angel was un-intentionally coming out of her trance. Finally, she could feel the power thrusting through his body. His body twitched. Her head was thrown violently back.

"Yes," screamed Edward. "Go for it, girl!" Glancing at his watch, he saw they had two minutes to go. She was going to do it. Angel felt Damien's body start to spasm. The messages from the voices raced around her brain. They screamed, *Don't let the body spasm.* Some of the voices were almost unintelligible, but they continued to boom out instructions. The languages became mixed with languages she had never heard before; and then silence, an abrupt eerie silence. No more instructions; no more translating. All she could now hear was her mother's voice.

"Let him go, Angelica. What you are doing will kill you. Please, pumpkin, let him go. Let him fight his own death."

A tear rolled down her cheek. Her body suddenly jerked and slumped over Damien's torso. She could feel a faint heartbeat.

"Hang in there. It won't be long," she whispered. Sirens could be heard in the distance. Angel prayed they were coming for Damien. Closing her eyes, she slipped into unconsciousness. Their bodies lay motionless.

Edward stared for a couple of minutes, the anger building up inside him. "You stupid bitch,; we could have had everything we ever wanted," he finally bellowed. The knife flew from Edward's hand with a force. It caught the side of Angel's arm before bouncing on the floor into a corner of the room. He did not retrieve it.

"I saw you bring him back to life and then you took it again," yelled Edward. Moving to her body, he grabbed a fistful of thick dark hair. He lifted her chin and stared at the lifeless face. Her slender neck would snap with ease. The head would lay twisted and distorted to one side, but breaking the neck would give him no satisfaction, only anger him more. When he released Angel's hair, her body fell back over Damien's body. Edward's foot lashed out, kicking her body as it fell.

"Bitch," he muttered, "you contaminated bitch."

Edward stormed out of the room, slamming the door, almost shaking it from the rotting hinges. He needed a drink and a puff of his favourite tobacco, although on this occasion a large cigar would have to suffice, until his next shipment. Eighteen years of waiting had been destroyed by a stupid bitch. She had been the strongest yet. The bitch had even ruined his game with the Chief Inspector, and it could have been his best game yet. The Doctor would not be pleased.

Part 2

Hospital

Dressed in a white hospital gown, Angel lay curled in one of the chairs, knees drawn close to her chest. A portable drip had been at her side for the last few days. She had waited patiently beside Damien's bedside as he was wheeled to the theatre. The surgeons were still trying to stop the internal bleeding, which was becoming an endless task. During the operations she sat and waited patiently for his return. Only then would she return to her own ward in the public wing. The nurses no longer bothered Angel, even though her daily visit to Damien's bedside was against their recommendation.

Angel moved back to Damien's bedside and stared lovingly at his handsome features. He was at peace. Placing her lips close to his right arm, she gently blew on the hairs of his arm. The hairs rose, and tiny goose-pimples formed and then disappeared. His skin responded, but he did not awake.

"Come back to me," she whispered. "I need you."

"Any improvement?"

Angel sat up and shook her head. "Not yet."

Laurel had just arrived. She moved over to the armchair to give him some time with his mate.

Laurel had only spent a few days in Angel's presence, but he could see her attraction. She had dark bewitching eyes, a mystical aura and a captivating personality that lit up the room. Laurel had guessed Angel would already be in Damien's room, either sitting on the edge of his bed or curled up in the chair, and for some strange reason he was pleased to see her.

Angel's state of mind no longer concerned him. Maybe Damien was right, and everybody deserved a second chance. The police had found Damien and Angel alive. Her body lay sprawled over his mate's body, shielding him from whoever had been in the room with them. Angel was protecting Damien. According to the police, they had no idea what had happened. Angel was saying very little. They knew Damien had been stabbed, and Angel's fingerprints were not on the knife. Laurel hated to admit it, but his initial diagnosis could have been wrong. Maybe Angel was not a killer, but it was obvious she was hiding something. Her account was sketchy. The police sensed she was withholding information. Selective memory, one constable had said.

Angel would not give a description of the attacker. From the minimal information the officers had gleaned, they deduced Angel must have seen the attacker's face, but with a story full of contradictions, it was hard to make sense of what had happened. Telling stories was a skill Angel had acquired from her early years in a psychiatric hospital, but she didn't want to speak to the officers. They spoke to her in such a condescending manner. What did they know? Who were they to judge or second guess what had happened? The more the officers pushed, the more Angel refused to cooperate. She kept reminding herself that it's all in the details, but she didn't care if they believed her or not. Protecting Edward had to be her priority, although why, she did not know.

Within seconds of curling up in the armchair, Angel fell asleep. In some ways, this would make it easier for what Laurel was about to do. A brown paper bag with string handles lay beside his feet. Inside the bag rested a dressing gown and slippers. How do you give your best mate's girlfriend a present without it giving out the wrong message? Now he knew. Placing the dressing gown over Angel's shoulders and slipping the slippers onto her feet whilst she slept was easier than having to explain his actions. There was a slight stir, but Angel didn't awake. Laurel recognised she was becoming weaker. Taking a step back, he smiled.

He waited patiently for Angel to wake up. Sometimes it was hard talking to his mate when his mate couldn't answer back, but when Angel was awake, time passed quickly.

Damien lay in a coma in the middle of the bed. His condition had now stabilised, and the bleeding had stopped. It had taken three operations. Damien's father was paying for around the clock medical supervision. The small private room was a mini intensive care unit with all the apparatus within arm's reach. The nurses checked every hour, the doctors every two.

After Edward's violent attack, Damien's father spent every evening at his son's bedside watching over him. He always waited until the young female and Laurel had left for the day. He could have joined them, but it felt intrusive. Instead he spent the evenings with his son, in the same armchair that Angel occupied during the day. He told Damien his life story. It was the longest time he had ever spent in his son's presence in one go. The room was peaceful; the constant blip, blip of the heart monitoring machine surprisingly comforting. He would sometimes sit and stare at the machine. A habit acquired from the girl, who would also watch the mini Matterhorn peaks appear and then disappear across the screen. They never appeared to change, just a constant, stable rhythm.

The girl spent nearly all day in his son's presence, sitting on his bed from early morning to early evening. He could not hear what she was saying, but she spoke to his son for hours. Her routine was the same every day. She arrived early, stroked the side of his son's face, combed his hair, kissed his forehead and stroked his chest and abdomen. Her fingertips moved in circular movements around the pads and bandages, before kissing him again. He never stirred. Angel always placed her ear on his chest and listened to his heartbeat for a couple of minutes. He had noticed the girl always sat on the right side of his son's bed, and she always finished her routine by stroking his arm, and holding his hand for hours, or until she needed to vomit. The small sink in the corner of his son's room had taken some abuse over the last few days.

From just watching Angel's daily routine, the Chief Inspector could see the girl was very close to his son. Later in the day, she would curl up in the chair next to his son's bedside and sleep. Laurel always visited his son in the afternoon, sometimes with other kids from the school, sometimes alone. On occasions, the young lady and Laurel spoke. Other times she slept. As time passed, he had seen her condition start to deteriorate; she looked weaker and slept longer.

For the fourth time in as many weeks, the Chief Inspector was helping himself to a glass of water from Damien's sink. The sight of the scars on his son's arm would always be a constant reminder of Edward's dominance over his family. The nurses had been told to keep the arm covered so he could not see it during his visit. Unfortunately, the nurses on duty appeared to have a short memory span. The arm had four neat cuts, three straight and one curved, Edward's initials – EV had had been cut deep into the skin, scarring his son forever. He couldn't bear to look. It was pure evil, a sick vengeance. As if his son hadn't suffered enough. If Edward had done this to get at him, he was succeeding. When Damien was better, they would discuss a skin graft to remove the offensive marks. At least the rope burns around his son's wrists would eventually fade and disappear. The Chief Inspector's face reddened. He was fuming. Edward was a sick psycho. Prison was too good for him. The death penalty was the only option for people like Edward. He should burn in hell for what he had done. Now it was personal. All rules and procedure were thrown out of the window. He would either bring this animal to justice or kill him for what he had done to his son.

It was Laurel who suggested the Chief Inspector return home, and maybe a little too eagerly he had agreed. He was in the middle of the largest case of his career, and there was nothing he could do at his son's bedside other than sit and wait. He felt guilty, but he also knew he needed to be there for Damien's mum. Laurel would call him if Damien awoke, or his condition changed. He was a good kid; he had always been a good mate to his son. Laurel kept his word. Within half an hour of Damien opening his eyes, the Chief Inspector had been informed.

The day Damien awoke, Laurel was reading a chapter on ancient Greek history aloud. Damien was fascinated with history, especially Greek history. The doctors had said a comforting voice sometimes helped the patient to come out of their coma after being traumatized. Laurel never thought of his voice being comforting, but he assumed the doctors meant a voice that could be recognised. Every day Laurel read a chapter of ancient history. It also helped him to revise, so he didn't mind. History was not Laurel's strong point, but when choosing their options, Damien had agreed to study Mathematics if Laurel studied History, which was why he was sat reading the battle of the Greek Spartans. Angel would often sit and listen, but the last few days she had spent more time just sleeping.

Laurel had just reached the battles of Thermopylae when he heard a faint voice. "Ah, the death of Leonidas and Artemisium and later the battle of Salamis." Glancing over to where Damien lay, Laurel could see his mate's oxygen mask had been removed, and Damien was looking at him. If anything was to awaken Damien, Laurel guessed it would be the Spartans.

"My god, you scared me," Laurel moved to the bedside. "You had us all terrified, mate. I was sure we were going to lose you."

They spent a couple of minutes catching up, although Laurel did most of the talking. Damien managed an odd sentence but had to keep placing the oxygen mask over his mouth and nose to breathe.

"Is Angel all right?" he managed to ask in between breaths. Laurel pointed to the chair, and Damien's heart skipped a beat. The heart monitor made a strange beeping sound before settling back into its constant blip, blip, blip. She was alive, but his joy was short-lived. Laurel filled Damien in on Angel's deteriorating condition before agreeing to wake her. He did not want his mate's hopes built up to be shattered ten minutes later. Angel was in a deep sleep. Laurel called her name, but she didn't awake. "Sorry, mate, I am going to have to touch your girlfriend."

Damien smiled. "Just this once, I'll let you off."

Laurel smirked, and shook Angel's shoulders gently. Any harder would have hurt her.

Angel's eyes gradually opened, and she protested, "I'm tired, Laurel."

"I know, but look," he gestured. Behind Laurel, Damien lay gazing at her. Angel sprang from the chair, the stand for the drip almost toppled over. Laurel grabbed the drip and then grabbed Angel as her legs collapsed under her weight. He lifted Angel onto the bed so she could sit next to Damien.

"I do this all the time. Your lass is always falling into my arms," Laurel winked at Damien as he spoke. His words were closer to the truth than Damien realised. The last few evenings Laurel had carried Angel back to the ward. The short distance was becoming difficult for her to cope with, especially after a full day at Damien's bedside.

"You look awful," whispered Damien.

"You don't look much better yourself," came the quick reply. Damien was right the last couple of weeks had taken its toll. Her face was pale and drawn with fatigue. Struggling to keep solid food down, she hadn't eaten in days. It was Damien's worse nightmare. He knew it was Marasmus. Angel seized his hand and lifted it to her lips. Kissing his hand tenderly, she lay it back down in her lap.

"I am sorry. I tried to stop him," she said.

His right hand reached towards her face and stroked the side of her cheek. He knew she had done everything possible. Damien continued to tuck her hair behind her ear so he could see her face more clearly. Her cheekbones appeared more prominent than he remembered and slightly hollowed.

Angel held up his wrist, drawing his attention to the coloured threads tied around his wrist. "It's a friendship bracelet I made it for you," she added shyly. "I know it's not something you would normally wear. I made it when I was waiting for you to wake up. I hoped it would bring you luck." He managed a weak smile. "It's the colours of the Irish flag. You don't mind, do you?"

He moved the mask to one side. "Why should I mind? It's lovely."

"Took me ages to find the right coloured thread. Angel is so picky; the colour had to be just right." Laurel winked at Angel who returned the wink with a warm, friendly smile. Damien looked at the bracelet that had been tied to his wrist and then looked up at Angel.

"Thank you. I'll wear it always," he smiled weakly. "Come here. I want to hold you."

A white spring-loaded clip nipped tightly at one of Damien's fingers, linking him to the machine. Taking extra care not to catch the clip and send the machine into chaos, he slowly steered Angel's head down to his chest. The wounds and pads that were connecting him to the life support had to be circumvented. Damien's arm felt like a lead weight. Resting his hand on her head so he could play with her hair, a small amount of warmth radiated from Angel's body. It felt wonderful touching her again.

Laurel was about to leave the room, but Damien signalled him to stay. Now that she couldn't see his eyes, which would give away the hurt he felt, he took a deep breath, moved the translucent oxygen mask to the side and calmly asked Angel if she was dying. The law of averages and the probability theory kept running through his mind. Why had he studied mathematics? It had only made him realise the numbers were not adding up in Angel's favour. His eyes filled with tears. The lump in his throat made it difficult to swallow. He knew the answer; this was the same age her brothers had died.

Angel's hand moved to Damien's heart. "A part of me will always be in here with you," she said. The lump grew larger and larger in Damien's throat. This was Angel's way of saying, yes, I am dying, but he still needed to hear her say the words not in a riddle, but in plain English. There was a long silence.

"Angel," he whispered. She tried to lift her head to look into his eyes, but his hand kept her head firmly on his chest. He continued to stroke her hair, wrapping his fingers around the long dark strands trying to put her at ease.

"I can't digest anything." She was fighting back the tears, her voice strained and husky. "My body can't fight it any longer. I took your pain, but I also took your death. I am not regenerating like I should be. I'm sorry, Damien. I am so sorry." She didn't pause for breath as she blurted out the truth in one go. Her tears were starting to flow. A damp patch formed on his chest. The wounds on his chest stung from the saltiness of her tears; tiny pin pricks bearing down on his body.

His own tears started to swell inside. No longer able to swallow his pain, he was desperately trying to fight the overwhelming emotion he was experiencing. The lump in his throat pressed against the larynx. His throat burned. The blip, blip of the heart monitor machine was now increasing at a radical speed. Damien tried to control and slow his heart rate by inhaling and exhaling slowly. The machine's change in sound would bring the nurses to his room, but he could not control it. The blip, blip was loud, beating against his eardrums. He could hardly hear anything else in the room. The beating of his heart pounded against the walls of his chest as if it were trying to escape from his body.

Why had Laurel told him? Why couldn't he have had ten happy minutes with his girlfriend without wishing he was dead; without feeling like his life had fallen apart? To hear that Angel had spent nearly fourteen hours per day by his side waiting for him to open his eyes had given him a warm feeling inside. Then to have it shattered seconds later by the words, "The doctors only let her stay in your room because she is dying," felt like a sledgehammer had slammed into his heart. Laurel had been so quick to explain Angel's illness and how he had overheard the doctors talking. Patient confidentiality was obviously not high on their agenda. Anybody could have heard their discussion.

According to Laurel, daily tests had been conducted on Angel's blue vomit. The chemical combination was still proving to be a mystery. The doctors had assumed her attacker had injected the substance, and Angel had told them no different. This part of Angel's illness did not worry Damien. He had become aware of the blue substance earlier in their relationship, even though she had tried to hide it. The wounds and the problem with digesting food was a concern. Two cuts that had mysteriously appeared on Angel's body were also baffling the doctors. One cut in the chest and the other in her stomach. A mirror image of Damien's wounds, although none of the medical staff had made the connection. The doctors were convinced the wounds were not there when she was first admitted into the hospital, although nobody would testify to the contrary.

Damien held her head down on his chest whilst he tried to compose himself. He assumed his rapid heart-beat would be giving his emotions away. Feeling ready he lifted her head and stared into her beautiful, dark, tearful eyes.

"Be strong. We will fight this together. I want you to go back to your room and rest, and stop worrying about me. I want you to do what the doctors say. Take the medicine they offer and please try to eat. I want you to do this for me. Will you do that?"

Angel nodded, but her tearful eyes said it would not work; it was too late. He wanted to take control, to place a kiss on her lips, but his body was weak. It had taken all his energy holding her head down and muttering some meaningless words. Tim was now standing at the doorway of the room. He had not wanted to interrupt their reunion. Initially, a wide lopsided smile had crossed his face. Now the smile had gone, his face expressionless, wondering what was happening. He could not hear what was being said, but it looked serious. Tim raised his hand without speaking, and Damien responded by raising his slightly off the bed. The gesture was welcom-ing yet serious.

At Damien's signal, Laurel scooped Angel up in his arms, ready to take her back to the ward. Her head fell against his chest as a child would do when being carried by a parent. She had fallen into a deep sleep. This would be the last time she would visit Damien's room. Tim grabbed the mobile drip and pushed it down the corridor to Angel's room. He hoped Laurel would update him on what had just happened, but Laurel said nothing. After pulling back the bed sheet, Laurel slipped off Angel's slippers. A smile crossed his face; her feet were warm and clean. The dressing gown was slightly more awkward. Laying Angel down on the firm mattress, Laurel leant over to kiss her forehead when he heard Tim's voice, "Remember, she is Damien's girl." Laurel stared for a while as she slept. A faint blue liquid secreting from her mouth. Turning back to Tim he muttered, "Come on. Let's see if Damien is ok." When they returned, Damien was fast asleep; the oxygen mask back in place; the monitor back to its constant rhythmic blip, blip. The police interview would have to wait.

The next time Damien awoke, Inspector Strangeway and Sergeant Morley from Scotland Yard were at his bedside. Inspector Strangeway was not part of the Criminal Investigation Unit so she rarely went on location, but the Chief Inspector had a lot of confidence in Strangeway's ability. Spotting minute details that other officers normally missed was Strangeway's skill. The Chief Inspector sensed she would make an exceptional detective, and she had only one more year left before she would qualify. In his haste the Chief Inspector had forgotten to tell her to leave his son's statement to him. He knew his son would not talk to anybody but himself.

Two uniformed officers had already gleaned some information from Laurel, who had explained about the mislaid diary. Now it was Inspector Strangeway and Sergeant Morley's turn. Currently, nothing seemed to make sense to the officers. It was obvious there had been a violent attack on the young lad, but the girl was being uncooperative.

The Chief Inspector had said the girl was romantically involved with his son, so the questioning should have been simple. Why was the girl contradicting her statement? Who or what was she protecting; and why? This was Inspector Strangeway's first big case, and she could not get past the first and easiest stage of the investigation. They were no nearer to catching the Chief Inspector's adversary.

Inspector Strangeway hoped Damien would be more co-operative, but this was not the case. Damien made some feeble excuse about being too tired to concentrate, and said he would only speak to Chief Inspector Harrington of Scotland Yard. It was another week before the police got their story.

*****

Angel was frustrated. All she had wanted was Damien to wake up. Four weeks in a coma was a long time, but now that he was awake she was stuck in the ward, banished to bed. Angel had begged Laurel to help her walk to Damien's room, but help was denied. Selfishly Laurel wanted to spend time with Angel alone. He accepted it was wrong, but he couldn't help it. "The nurses want you to rest" or "Damien is not up to visitors at the moment" were the excuses Laurel constantly used.

Angel's condition continued to deteriorate. X-rays were showing an unknown entity was coating her vital organs, although this didn't appear to stop the organs from working. The doctors were confused; the concept was unexplainable. They could find nothing remotely similar in any medical journal. Adding to the problem with the organs, the wounds on Angel's upper body kept opening and closing; internal bleeding was now evident. Angel was still vomiting the blue liquid on a daily basis. The amount of vomit had been reduced. This coincided with the amount of fluid her body took on. The opening of the wounds happened without warning. One minute she would be sleeping, the next minute she would be sitting up in bed with blood soaking through her gown and blood trickling from her mouth. The pain in Angel's stomach would cause her to double over in agony, screaming for the nurses. Morphine was pumped into her body to relieve the pain, but this made her vomit more. Her throat became sore and scratched, making it difficult to swallow.

*****

"I hear you are being very uncooperative and will only speak to Chief Inspector Harrington," a loud voice boomed. Damien swung around to see his family standing in the doorway. His mother rushed over, and gave him an almighty hug, kissing him repeatedly.

"I am sorry, Dad. You always told me not to talk to anybody but you if I was in trouble."

His dad laughed. "I remember. I think I said something like we don't want any young buck trying to make a name for himself early in his career." Damien managed to smile If he laughed it would hurt too much and possibly burst the stitches that were holding him together. He was happy his parents were with him as he could focus his energies on them, and stop himself from constantly thinking of Angel.

Damien had not seen his family for an extended period of time; not since his condition had worsened. His mother had moved to the area when he was going through the tests for his illness. She had flapped and mothered him so much that he had felt claustrophobic. He knew he hurt her feelings when he asked her to leave. He just wanted to be treated normally, not have his every move scrutinized and questioned. *Should you be doing that? Why don't you do this?* His mother went back to Surrey. At first, regular letters dropped through his hall's post box, but he continued to distance himself from his family. During the school holidays there was always a reason why he could not go home. This reaction inflicted more pain physically and emotionally on him. Why, he said and did it he didn't know. He accepted he had been cruel to his mother who was only trying to help, but now all that seemed to have been forgotten. Damien wanted to say sorry, but apologies did not come natural. Damien hugged both parents whilst relaying what had happened.

His mother fussed around him. She hugged, kissed and smothered him with love and affection, and although initially welcome, the attention was tiring. Damien glanced towards his father for support. He didn't want to be the one to upset his mother again. Picking up on Damien's glances, his father turned to his mother and said, "Good god, woman! Give the kid a break. Go and grab us a couple of coffees and take the long route back." Damien smiled. There was no way he could have said that to his mother without offending her, yet his father had happily got away with it. His mother left the room, happy she had been reunited with her son.

When she had gone, his father turned to Damien. "You were lucky, kid. I think you may have just had a run in with Eftemie Vladimirescu or even Édouard Vasser."

"Edward Wellingstone," corrected Damien. "He is Angel's uncle and legal guardian."

"He uses many aliases, son, which is where my difficulty lies; I have been trying to catch him for nearly ten years, but he has a habit of disappearing whenever I get close. He is one slippery eel – and deadly. I believe he has killed at least four people, maybe more. Thankfully you are not one of his numbers." He gave Damien a manly, fatherly hug, "I thought I had lost you, son."

Neil stood and watched. His cashmere overcoat and silk scarf hung neatly on his frame. Only three years apart, Damien had always been close to his older brother. They had shared a common interest in rugby league, although Neil did not have the same passion Laurel and Damien had for the game, preferring to watch rather than play. Neil had always been the intelligent one who was destined to do well. The entire family had celebrated when he was accepted into Cambridge University to study Law. This had been the start of Neil's six-year plan to become a barrister. Currently he had passed the exams with ease. A blue collared profession was a career option Neil would never have considered. Damien was different in that respect. Since his illness he had come to appreciate life in general. He was not materialistic like Neil, who always looked like he had stepped out of the latest fashion magazine. Damien did not need much to survive. Take away his illness and the excruciating pain, and he would give up everything he owned.

For the last few years, Damien had received a monthly allowance direct to his bank from his parents. Too ill to spend it on nights out, and with his accommodation already covered through his parent's term payment, he hardly touched the money, and a substantial lump sum had built up. Damien had considered changing his accommodation, upgrading to a one-bedroom apartment with its own kitchenette like Neil had done when he was at Worthington High. Maybe Damien was more sociable than Neil, but he preferred to be in the company of others, although he missed more meals from the canteen than he ate due to his stomach pains. He had lost a stone in weight in less than a year. His doctor had put it down to muscle waste, so it was nothing to worry about. He wondered how many more pounds had been shed with his latest stint in hospital and would it still be classed as muscle waste.

"What have you got yourself into this time? First the illness, then this. Some people will do anything for attention."

Damien looked over to his brother. "You never change, still the big brother with the smart comments and the designer suits."

Neil laughed, "And you're still the scruff of the family."

"Now lads," butted in their father, "we have things to discuss before that mother of yours returns."

There was a slight pause before Damien spoke, "He is going after Neil next."

"Are you sure, Damien?"

"I know what he said, Dad. He is insane." His dad nodded his head slowly in agreement as he processed the latest revelation. A plan of action was required, although the final plan was not that elaborate – protection was arranged for both lads. Neil didn't say anything else.

His attempt at humour hadn't worked. He hadn't expected Damien to tell him he was the next target. His brother was in a bad state and was lucky to survive. Would he survive if a similar attack came his way?

Damien was still very ill and although off the critical list, he was unable to move from his bed. He was attached to a machine that monitored any change in his condition. A machine fed him and gave him morphine on a constant drip feed. His body had little energy to do anything else.

*****

Laurel often watched Angel from the doorway, normally for only a minute, maximum two. During that time she usually slept, hair wild and strewn across the pillar. There was an amazing energy in the room, which had been enhanced further when Angel was in his mate's room and he first opened his eyes. There was an electric spark that he had never experienced before, and the look Angel had shared with his mate. No woman had ever given him that look. He couldn't describe it. There was happiness, excitement, affection, love and even sex mixed into that look. If Angel, or any other woman, could give him a little of that look, he would give up everything. He paused and then smirked, maybe not everything. A place on Wigan's Rugby team – he would not give that up, that went without saying, but that look, the energy in that room was amazing. Angel always looked happy when she saw him; however, the rest was not there.

Laurel became the daily courier, delivering cryptic messages between the young lovers. The messages put a smile on Damien's face, especially when Angel told him his best mate was reading a chapter of *Pride and Prejudice* to her every day, and she didn't have the heart to tell him she had already read it five times. Damien guessed it was difficult for Laurel, but at least he was making an effort to be nice to his girlfriend. The thought of Laurel reading a romantic classic was highly amusing. Laurel also gave Damien daily updates on Angel's deteriorating condition. Both lads knew without discussing it Angel was slipping away from them.

During one of Laurel's daily reports Damien had seemed brighter. "Laurel, will you do me a big favour? Will you order a Breedon Pippin over the internet? I want to give it to Angel as a present. Before you ask, it is a type of apple." Laurel burst out laughing. "I am serious, Laurel. I know it will mean a lot to her."

"Why an apple?" laughed Laurel.

"It's a rare English apple that I know she has always wanted to try. Angel likes apples." Without thinking he heard himself say, "Did you know there are over 7,500 varieties of apple worldwide?" Damien laughed. He sounded just like her. "Watch Angel when you give her the apple, Laurel. You will love her reaction. She can be so weird, so loveable. It's that weirdness that I love. She's not like any other girl I have ever known." Laurel could see Damien was entering his dream world. He was pleased to see Damien was more upbeat. The last few days it had been hard trying to raise his mate's spirits.

The day Laurel gave Angel the present from Damien, she had opened the little gift box slowly. Her eyes lit up and a large smile had crossed her face. She had let out a gasp. Laurel watched carefully. Damien would want to know everything she did and said in fine detail.

"He has found me a Breedon Pippin apple," she whispered, holding it up for Laurel to see. "It is so rare. Look, the skin is a dull yellow with tinges of autumn colours running through it." A little card was tucked into the box. The message was simple – It read "love, Damien." A tear trickled down her cheek. "Please thank Damien for me. I will definitely try and eat it. I don't care if it makes me ill."

"Damien said you have to wait five days before biting into the apple. It's not quite ripe yet."

Angel nodded and took the apple out of the box. "Can you smell it, Laurel? How different it smells to the common English apple." He inhaled, but to Laurel it smelt like any other apple, but he still nodded as though he understood what she meant.

"Did you know the Breedon Pippin originated in the nineteenth century in Berkshire? It is so rare. When I bite into the apple you will see a deep yellow flesh and it should taste similar to a pineapple." She stared for a couple more minutes. "Oh, thank you, Laurel." Placing her arms around his neck, she gave him a hug. Laurel could feel the warmth from Angel's frail body pressed against his. He could have held her longer and tighter, but he didn't, he knew it would be wrong.

Pulling away from the hug, Laurel insisted in taking a photo for Damien. Angel held up the apple, placed her thumb in the air, and blew a kiss. Her hair was tousled, sticking up in some places and flat in others, and although ill there was a sparkle in her eyes. This single photograph had captured Angel's personality and beauty. Laurel stared at the photograph. He wanted to keep it for himself, but he realised he would have to show it to Damien. After all, she was still Damien's girlfriend.

Laurel was the only visitor to Angel's bedside. Usually he arrived earlier than the visiting hours dictated. The nurses still allowed him to sit and read to Angel quietly. He remembered Damien once mentioning she was reading *Pride and Prejudice* by Jane Austen so he had picked up a copy so he could read her a chapter every day. It wasn't his type of novel, but he kept telling himself he was doing it for Damien. Laurel loved looking at Angel's dark bewitching eyes. It gave him a warm feeling inside. Many times he wondered if Angel was looking for a Mr Darcy. Did she want an aloof wealthy romantic hero, or was she drawn more to the Mr Bingley type, a sociable, wealthy charismatic character like the ones in the book?

Sitting on the edge of Angel's bed, they would talk for as long as she could manage before sleep took hold. Laurel never mentioned the characters in the book or the thoughts he was having. He guessed it would spoil the mystery, and it was that mystery that attracted him to her. Angel spoke slowly. Her voice was becoming huskier, and he could tell it was difficult for her to talk. Angel always made an effort when he visited. Sometimes Laurel felt he understood her well and other times not at all. The stories she told were enchanting, especially when she spoke about France. She didn't always finish the story as fatigue sometimes kicked in earlier than he would have liked. Her eyes would close and then open with a jolt as she desperately tried to fight the drowsiness.

Sometimes the stories seemed so far-fetched that Laurel once asked Angel if she was telling the truth. She had laughed, even though her throat was painful, concluding in a coughing fit.

"Is Nontron in the Ardenne region?" she had asked.

Laurel was confused. "No," was the simple answer.

"It's all in the detail, Laurel, in the detail."

He still looked confused so she had explained further. "Nontron is not in the Ardenne region, so it's a white lie," she laughed and Laurel had nodded as though he understood.

"So did you really use a different name when you lived in France?" he had asked.

"If I had given you a fabricated French name then it would have been a lie, so it was true. I was known as Andrée Arceneau. As I said, it helps you to fit in. The French accepted me because they thought I was French," Angel had replied. Laurel stared warmly at Angel. Damien was correct Angel was unusual – not like the normal females he dated. She was playing with him. Poking fun, yet he didn't mind. He enjoyed her teasing, playing her strange game. Damien had never mentioned Angel lived in France, and she could speak French fluently, but then again Damien never spoke about Angel's past, not since their frank discussion at Brian's.

Intriguing and surprising, Laurel could not understand why Angel never studied French at school. She would have found the exam easy. Instead she choose German as one of her options. When questioned, her response was simple, "I can already speak French so they can't teach me anything new, but I can't speak German," a strange answer which emphasised their differences; most people would have chosen the easier option. To Laurel's disappointment, as the days passed their conversations became shorter and Angel slept longer.

*****

"How is she?" asked Damien.

"See for yourself." Laurel flipped up the cover on his mobile to reveal the photograph he had taken on the tiny screen. He was careful not to reveal all the other photographs he had taken of Angel in case Damien got the wrong idea. He just found her fascinating.

"God, she is beautiful," Damien murmured under his breath.

Laurel smiled, "You will see her soon, mate," although deep down he wondered if Damien would ever see Angel again. Earlier that day he had noticed a ventilator had been moved into Angel's room. She was not connected to it, not yet, but he could tell she was struggling to breathe. It was only a matter of time before she would have to rely on it.

Selective in what he told Damien and not wanting to depress him further, Laurel knew his mate was frustrated not being able to see his girlfriend. He updated him daily on Angel's progress, although sometimes it brought Damien down into a deeper depression. For example, Laurel felt the episode with the white roses was an overreaction. A dozen white roses had been left on Angel's bedside table. No card was tucked in the bouquet, but the aroma the flowers left in the room brought the outside freshness back into the small cramped room. When Laurel mentioned the roses, Damien had sent him back to Angel's room to remove them before Angel saw them.

"Angel believes the white rose is a symbolic sign of death. If she sees them in her room, she will assume her life is over," Damien had tried to explain to a baffled Laurel.

"They are only flowers."

"I know, but please, Laurel, do it for me. I can't take any chances." Closing his eyes, he could remember word for word a short poem she would recite whenever she saw somebody with a white rose. With her eyes shut, she would whisper: "Beware of the rose, the deeper the red, the deeper the love but when the rose holds no colour, the rose flourishes no more, the life disappears from all it beholds."

Damien wished he hadn't sent Angel back to her room so early that afternoon. He could have spent at least another ten minutes in her company maybe longer. It seemed so unfair that his best mate was able to see her yet he couldn't, a mate who didn't trust his girlfriend. He needed to get better or at the very least have the ludicrous wires removed from his chest and arms so he was mobile. The blip, blip of the heart monitor was now becoming extremely annoying, the companion that was with him day and night, a constant rhythmic sound that never changed. Doctors were still monitoring his heart rate. The stab wound closest to the heart was constantly causing problems. Various drugs were being pumped into him to help relieve the pain, but he was sure the pain was starting to ease. He had tried to tell the nurses, but his words fell on deaf ears. Damien was so desperate to be mobile that he had almost disconnected himself from the machine on one of his 'down' days. Four days later, Damien received the dreaded news Angel had slipped into a coma and had been moved into intensive care. The doctors estimated she had only a couple of days to live. His heart sank. He was not religious, but he had prayed day and night she would start to recover. Obviously nobody had heard his prayer.

Laying alone in his room, the memories flooded back to the time in the halls when he lay on his bed in agony, wrenched in pain. This time the pain was different. Tears flooded down his cheeks as he realised he was losing the one person he loved. As he lay in his darkened room, head turned away from the door, a figure entered his room, moved slowly to the monitoring equipment, looked at his chart and then moved slowly to the side of his bed. He could feel eyes watching him. He held his breath, not wanting the nurses to know he was crying.

"Look after my Angelica," the voice whispered. Realising it wasn't a nurse, he swung around to see who had spoken just in time to see the back of a female exiting his room. He called out, but there was no reply.

An hour later, a commotion broke his restless sleep. Outside his room, feet rushed up and down the corridor. Voices spoke in hushed tones so as not to wake the patients. He wondered who was being brought in or taken out.

A nurse popped her head around the door. "Everything all right?" she asked, and then quickly disappeared to the next room to ask the same question before he had time to answer.

Finally disconnected from the equipment – free at last, although weak – Damien persuaded Tim to grab him one of the wheelchairs stored in the corridor next to the lift. Damien's intention was to head towards the intensive care unit so he could cast his eyes on Angel for the last time. He wanted to hold her hand as she slipped away from him, so she would know she was not alone as she left this world.

"I hear somebody died in your corridor last night," piped up Tim. "Rumour has it a woman carrying no identification was wandering around the building. How can somebody wander around and not be challenged? Your dad must be paying a fortune for your treatment and anybody could get in and attack you. Security is getting worse in this place..."

Damien was only half-listening. He was focusing and preparing for what he would say to Angel when he saw her. If Tim had mentioned the body in the corridor had blue liquid trickling from its mouth, he would have taken notice, but the blue liquid was never detected by the medical staff on duty.

As they rounded the corner in the corridor and pushed through the double doors into the intensive care unit, they found four out of the five beds occupied. A nurse scuttled over and tried to get them to leave.

"Please, I just want to see Angel Wellingstone," Damien said, almost in an authoritarian tone, until his emotions took over. "Please," he begged tearfully. The nurse looked them both up and down and then directed them to the middle bed.

"Don't be too long," she whispered. The large windowless room felt claustrophobic. Life-support machines were connected to patients who appeared to have no life left in them. Damien swallowed hard. It was a place where death lurked.

Whispering came from behind one of the curtains.

"It sounds like a final blessing," whispered Tim.

Angel looked fragile. Her arms were thin. Sharp bones protruded through a thin layer of skin, ready to break the surface. "Do you think the priest has blessed Angel?"

Tim shrugged his shoulders, "Is she religious?"

"No, I don't think so."

"Let us hope not then."

"I feel scared Tim. I don't want to lose her. Not here, in this place. It's haunting and depressing. Death lurks everywhere." Damien touched Angel's hand her eyes opened.

"I knew you would come," she whispered. Both Tim and Damien jumped.

"I thought you said she was in a coma," gasped Tim. A weak smile crossed Angel's face. She was about to speak but instead coughed, a deep-chesty cough. Closing her eyes, she swallowed slowly and inhaled deeply so she could suck the oxygen back into her lungs.

Damien stroked her hand. His fingers moved across her knuckles and between her fingers, massaging and exploring every small detail of her hand and wrist. It felt remarkable being able to touch her again. "How are you feeling? No wait, don't speak if it hurts."

Angel's eyes opened again. "Have five days passed yet?"

Damien stopped stroking her hand and then smiled, "I knew the thought of eating a Breedon Pippin would keep you going," he murmured, lifting her hand to his lips before tucking her hand between his cheek and neck. The nurse returned to inform the lads they had ten more minutes before they would have to leave. The doctors were on their way. A feeling of overwhelming relief surged through Damien's body. The dark cloud had lifted, and the heavy weight on his shoulders had disintegrated into thin air. His prayers had been answered. *I will never doubt again,* he thought. *Miracles do happen.*

Too many wires prevented Damien from hugging Angel. He wanted to hold her so badly. He pulled himself up out of the wheelchair and flung his arms around her frail body. The unexpected hug sent the monitoring machine into chaos.

"You'll be in trouble," Angel laughed, before another coughing fit started.

"Got to go; I can see the nurse coming," he whispered, quickly pecking her on the cheek as he left.

In the afternoon, with Laurel in tow, Damien paid another visit to Angel's bedside. There had been a change in shifts. This time the nurse on duty did not approach them. Instead, she lifted her head, 'clocking' their presence from the nurses' station. Angel looked much better. When she spoke, there was no coughing. Damien knew Angel was going to recover. Marasmus was no longer a threat. She had beaten it.

"Last night I had the strangest dream," said Angel quietly. "It was as though my mother was right next to me, standing where you are right now. She was telling me everything was going to be all right, that I was a lot stronger than she would ever be. She told me I was going to get better, that my life was mine again, but in return for my life she wanted me to carry out her instructions; instructions that she would leave next to the bed. Can you see anything, Damien? I know she left them here." Damien steered the borrowed wheelchair out of the way and quickly scanned the floor and the top of a small cabinet next to her bed. Laurel checked the far side of the bed. When they found nothing, Angel looked disappointed.

"Probably just a dream," said Damien. "I am sure you will see her again." He failed to mention his night-time visit, or the voice telling him to look after her; even though it was the same night of her dream. Perhaps coincidence, perhaps not. Either way, Angel would read too much into the event. It would be some omen. He did wonder if the two events were connected. Did Angel's mum visit his room, or had it been his imagination? His visitor had definitely been female with dark hair, but he was heavily drugged at the time. It was a strange night full of commotion. Then, according to Tim, there was the body found in the corridor, although he had been only half-listening when Tim was relaying the story earlier in the day.

The Truth Can Hurt

Angel had refused to co-operate with the police, and when she did speak to them, the information she gave was minimal. Damien hadn't commented on her lack of co-operation, even though the hatred he felt inside and the constant pain was a reminder of Edward's sick brutality. When his father asked for his help, he knew he could not refuse.

"Why is Angelica so uncooperative?" asked his father.

"I think she's just scared of figures in authority. Angel has been through hell for nearly ten years, and her past just keeps on catching her up," Damien replied, defending her actions.

"Will she talk to you?"

"Possibly," and that was when Angel and Damien came to argue again.

Damien did not like the idea, but he desperately wanted to capture the guy who had tortured him, permanently marked his skin with his initials and tried to take his life. He wanted to catch Edward as much as his father did.

"I'll wear a wire, but I don't want Angel to know. I feel like I am betraying her," he had told his father. Strict instructions were given on what questions to ask and how to extract certain pieces of information.

"Don't lead," his father kept saying, but having a two-way conversation naturally was challenging if you couldn't lead on occasions.

Angel had now been transferred to a single recovery room. Damien walked slowly through the door. He felt uneasy, and the wires sat uncomfortable under his shirt. His dad had said they were the old-fashioned type, not the new modern ones that clip on to your clothes, but that was all his dad could get hold of at short notice. When Damien moved, the pads pulled gently on his skin. If they pulled too hard, his wounds would re-open and it could possibly do permanent damage.

Damien shuffled uncomfortably to Angel's room and sat as he did every day on the edge of her bed.

"I hear your parents are visiting you."

News travels fast, he thought, "Aye," was his response. "Angel, we have been together for several months. Will you tell me about your past with Edward?"

"You know everything," she sighed.

"Not everything. Tell me where you were brought up, about your time with Edward and what he's like. Tell me about his past. I really need to know, and please no more secrets."

"I have no secrets."

"Then tell me," his voice was quite stern yet held his love for her.

"You know everything."

"I don't know everything. Angel, talk to me," he said again, "and no more secrets. I just need to understand."

"I have told you I have no secrets." They were going around in circles, and he was beginning to get frustrated.

"Are you helping the police?" she asked.

Unable to lie, Damien nodded.

"I thought so," there was a sigh followed by a short pause. "Edward is my genie. He said he would teach me to bring life to death. I didn't believe him." Damien didn't say anything. This was going to be one of Angel's long stories. She would eventually get to the point. What she was saying would make sense in her mind, but to anybody else it was a strange fantasy. "Every day Edward sat in our dining room in his favourite chair, a faded cream and floral covered chair with polished wooden arms. The chair always faced the window and looked out over the south-facing gardens. I think he liked our Hydrangeas. The day he told me he was my genie, I was playing with a small ceramic teapot from the kitchen. I was imagining the smoke from Edward's cigar was a serpent, a good serpent, a genie who would grant me three wishes. The teapot was placed perfectly, when Edward threw back his head and blew the smoke in the air, the smoke looked like it drifted out of the spout of my magical lantern. I remember Edward leaning forward so his face was two feet from mine, and he said he would show me how to bring life to death. I was annoyed. That's not real magic. I wanted to live in a magical kingdom, I answered. Edward said no more. He leant his head back and blew the final remains of his cigar's smoke into the air. I was young. I did not understand what he meant; however, the more time I spent with Edward, the more I started to understand. Anyway, I was brought up by my mother and Edward in a small village called Barton on Stowheath.

"Edward didn't reside with us, but he was always at my mam's house. From eight in the morning to ten at night he took residence in our home, never a minute before nor a minute after. Edward was always very precise in what he did. Standing or sitting, staring out of my mam's dining room window, smoking a cigar, was his normal position. Small black round-rimmed glasses sat neatly on the bridge of Edwards's nose. They magnified his small eyes, shrinking the rest of his facial features. When he doesn't wear glasses, he looks so different. He used to clean his glasses daily, gently breathing on the lenses and then rubbing them with a clean white handkerchief that took residence in his chest pocket. His hand would move from the nose piece outwards in swift movements. I would sit cross-legged on the floor ten feet from wherever Edward sat, watching the simple but obsessive routine. Sometimes he lifted his head and looked at me through squinted eyes. He very rarely spoke. He preferred the company of adults to a child.

"The smell of tobacco always clung to Edward's dark brown suits and immaculately pressed and bleached shirts. I often wondered if his shirts hung in his wardrobe next to his suits or inside his suits, possibly above a line of black leather-laced shoes. There were no spots of dirt on Edward's shoes. They were as clean as the day he bought them, so highly polished that you could see your face in them.

"I used to wear blue-buckled shoes. The toes were always slightly scuffed, and there was usually some mud on them from playing in the garden. I once tried to shine my shoes like Edward."

Damien smiled. He could imagine Angel polishing her shoes.

"I often wondered if Edward owned seven pairs of shoes. Edward was a perfectionist, so he probably did; everything laid out and planned perfectly – that was what Edward liked.

"When I came out of hospital," she paused for a second, trying to find the right word, she looked into Damien's eyes; he nodded he understood. Damien wanted to ask about her time in hospital, as she never mentioned it, and he had always been curious, but sometimes people need their privacy, and he shouldn't invade this privacy. But what was he doing now? This was not the time to ask or his father's business. He must stick to the information his father required.

Angel rephrased the sentence she had just started. "At the age of fourteen years, I was released into Edward's care. *Released* is a strange word, don't you think?"

Damien nodded, not really understanding why.

"Anyway, six years after the hospital door was closed, I was free. I remember walking out of the building to where Edward stood waiting."

"Away from insanity into the devil's arms," muttered Damien.

Angel ignored the sarcastic comment and continued. "Edward was surprisingly charming for the first few weeks and tended to my every need. One of the last things my mam said to me was not to have any contact with Edward, but I didn't have any choice.

"A one-bedroom second-floor apartment was our home which was not ideal as I had to kip on the settee, but the arrangement somehow worked. We never stayed long in one place, which was why I was home tutored. Edward said I was vulnerable and would be easily influenced by other children. *Naïve,* he called it, which was why eighteen months after leaving the hospital I was surprised when Edward announced I would have to go to boarding school. Urgent business across the Channel was his explanation. Edward promised he would be back for me on my eighteenth birthday. He came back early. I remember, he helped me pack and dropped me off at the bus station. For the first time in a year, I could smell the stale smoke on his clothes."

"Was that when you came to Worthington High?"

Angel nodded. "Edward said external influences could easily corrupt my mind, which was why he chose the same boarding school Beth attended. He said if Beth was around, then I would more than likely keep my head down and keep myself to myself. He knew I always blamed myself for Stacey's death. We travelled everywhere together, always on the move, never staying in one place for long."

"Where did you live before you came to school?" he asked in a softer tone. She gave the address and then gave another half a dozen addresses, two in France – one on the outskirts of Reims in the large town of Epernay, and the other in Nontron in the Dordogne area, Southwest France. Angel also gave four towns in the United Kingdom.

"Do you need their full addresses?"

Damien nodded. She couldn't remember all of the addresses, but she remembered enough for their previous homes to be traced.

The Chief Inspector listened, delighted with the information. He had some new leads and a couple of new addresses to visit. He would catch this animal if it was the last thing he ever did. Relevant personnel were dispatched to the locations as soon as it was physically possible. The Chief Inspector was particularly happy and annoyed simultaneously with the next piece of information as this had puzzled him and his staff for a long time.

"Is Edward part of a religious cult?"

"I don't think so. Why?"

"Before Edward stabbed me, he placed my body in a star position," Damien bit his lower lip as soon as the question had been asked. A small drop of blood began to form. It was too personal. The question was bringing back too many unpleasant memories. Damien knew the information was important to his father and important to catching Edward. He licked the blood from his trembling lip and waited for the reply. His father listened, feeling his son's agony, knowing this was difficult for him to discuss.

Angel gave a sigh and placed her hand on top of Damien's, "The letters and numbers your hands and legs pointed to were map co-ordinates. He was leading you to the next point where he can be found."

"Which map, Angel?" Damien asked with a certain amount of urgency.

"He won't make it that easy for them. That is for your father to work out, but if you take the letters in the star that are not part of the co-ordinates, they will make the name of a country and town. The numbers left will give you the map reference. It was a game we used to play when I was a kid. Edward would draw the Star of David with two interlaced triangles with the letters and numbers scribbled at the six points. I would then pinpoint the location on a map. I used to be so quick."

"Where, Angel, where is he now?"

Angel closed her eyes. "If I remember correctly, the letters were BKEA, LPNN, AOGD and COLL and the numbers – wait, I have got it. Blackpool. I think it's Blackpool, just outside, near the beach heading towards St. Helen's. I used to be able to pinpoint the location without a map. I can't remember the map grid like I used to."

"Will he still be there?"

"I doubt it." There was an uncomfortable pause. "Two days maximum, and then he would move again, with no clues this time, Damien."

"Yes."

"If it helps, Edward normally used the pink Landranger maps for a Great Britain destination and the *Institut Geographique* national maps when in France."

"Oh, Angel, why didn't you tell the police this before? We could have caught him."

She shrugged her shoulders. "I don't know. I don't like the police."

He gave her a disapproving look. "If you told them, they might have been able to catch him before he kills somebody else."

She gazed towards the window in the small room.

"Never mind. What's done is done." He tried to muster a smile, but it was difficult. "So why was the word *Mazel tov* etched in the centre of the star?"

"Sarcasm," replied Angel. "It means *good luck*. I'm sorry, Damien. He shouldn't have done that to you. Edward once told me the police are stupid. He always leaves a clue to his whereabouts. Sometimes the clues are easy, sometimes hard. Edward found it amusing that the police could never work out the clues. The death of Shaun Barton was probably the easiest clue I think he ever gave them. He blamed me for that. The train in Shaun's hand, his left arm 45 degrees from his head and his right arm 270 degrees. Shaun's body was displayed in a clock face. We caught the train at 2:45 p.m."

"Did Edward kill Shaun Barton?"

Angel nodded. "But it was my fault," she whispered.

The more Angel spoke, the more annoyed Damien became. She was giving them some fantastic information, but there was a naivety to her words. "Edward is a good man, deep down. He wants to help people to stop people dying. I failed him, which was why they died."

Her words had shocked Damien. "You didn't fail anybody, Angel! He is a lunatic who should be behind bars." His face was reddening with anger. He had never thought of Angel as stupid or naïve until today. He could feel his voice starting to rise, and his father's voice telling him, *Don't argue. Don't lead her. Just keep calm, or we won't be able to use the information in court.* Taking a couple of deep breaths he tried to calm down; his irritation disappeared as quickly as it came.

"Who else has died, Angel?"

She looked at him for a couple of seconds. "Remember the rumours in school?" she whispered. "They were so close to the truth. I was so close to bringing Stacey, I mean Stacey Wilson back to life, and then Beth started screaming, and I couldn't concentrate. I had a knife in my hand but…" her voice trailed off.

"I'm sorry, Angel, but I really need to know. Did you kill Stacey?"

"Yes," she replied without hesitation. Why had he asked? This was the one word he didn't want to hear. Now he would have to face the truth. "I could not save her, Damien, even though I did try."

"You actually killed her?"

Angel nodded.

Damien looked away to compose himself. He felt repulsed.

"Do you hate me Damien?"

"No, I don't hate you. I am surprised. I..." he hesitated a moment. "I just can't believe you killed somebody." Everybody had warned him, including his mates and Beth. Even Angel had previously hinted, yet he had taken no notice, dismissing any suggestion that she could have been involved. The truth had been standing in front of him all along. He had to now make a decision. Did he believe she could kill again? Could they still be together? After all, she was the same person he fell in love with, and he had always harped on about her past being irrelevant.

He cupped her face in his hands, "Please listen carefully, Angel. I am going to ask you one more time. Did you stick a knife into Stacey?"

Angel stared at him in disbelief. "No, of course not. I should have brought her back to life, but I couldn't. I was so close. I just wasn't sure what I was supposed to do. I killed her."

"Stop it, Angel. You did not kill Stacey. She was already dead. You said yourself, you were supposed to bring her back to life, which means she was already dead, and that's not your fault." He still held her face in his hands. The relief that was now surging through his body was unexplainable.

"Angel, who stuck the knife in Stacey?"

Angel raised her eyes to meet his. "Edward," she whispered.

"Did you tell the police?"

A slight shake of the head indicated no. "Edward said the Keres would come after me if I told them."

"The Keres are mythical creatures."

"I know that now, but at the time I believed him. I never lied. I just told everybody I couldn't bring her back to life."

"Oh, Angel, if only you had told them the truth."

"I tried to later, but they told me if I didn't accept what I had done then I would never be released, so I told them it was my fault." At that moment, Damien wanted to hold her closer than he had ever done before. He was relieved and also disappointed in the authorities. An innocent child had been punished for something she hadn't done.

Unaware of the emotions Damien was now going through, Angel moved onto the next killing. Damien no longer held Angel's face, afraid it would interfere with the sound quality. Instead, he sat awkwardly on the edge of the hospital bed. The corners of the linen sheets were not folded as neatly as Angel would have done. Damien was surprised Angel hadn't adjusted them; normally she would have.

"There was Shaun Barton and Jennifer Villiens. Jennifer died when we lived in France. Edward had taken me on holiday to Ardenne to see the Cathedrale Notre-Dame de Reim and the Celliers Ruinart. I thought it was just a holiday, but Edward had other plans. I know now he didn't want to take another life near where we lived in case I failed again, and I did fail," a sadness appeared in her voice. "I didn't know what I was supposed to do until it happened to you." She raised her finger-tips to his lips, which he kissed slowly but not passionately. "I am not a bad person, Damien, and neither is Edward," she whispered. "If I had done what I was supposed to do, nobody would have died."

Damien didn't respond. He could see what she was saying, but she was wrong – very wrong.

"Did you see Edward Wellingstone kill Jennifer Villiens?" Damien could have kicked himself; he should have used the name Eftemie Vladimirescu, but it was too late.

"Yes, it was quick. Did you know Edward always uses the same set of knifes? It's a beautiful set with ivory carved handles. He buys them from Nontron. I once went with him when he bought the two smaller knives." How could Damien forget the knife? Angel was twisting one inside him right now. How could she be so insensitive?

Angel continued, oblivious to the hurt she was causing. "Edward told me that my great grandfather lived with the Yanomani tribe in the Amazon for six months. My great grandfather often went there to cleanse his body and mind. The last time he visited, he came back fully cleansed, and he also came back with a child, my grandmother. Edward said he didn't meet the Doctor until many years later, and that was when he learnt his destiny. I am part of that destiny." Damien didn't comment; he could feel himself getting angry again. "Edward reckons it is easier to capture the shamanic spirit with a knife than a gun. He sees these spirits through the hallucinations caused by *yopo* and the potent strains of wild tobacco he smokes. The *ebene*, at least I think that's what he called it, is supposed to be blown into the nasal passage rather than smoked. Edward reckons it does not matter if it's inhaled through the nose or smoked. These shamanic spirits give the participants the gift to heal and the power to harm enemies. I assume that is how my power was developed, passed down through generations. Don't you think it's a fascinating story?" she asked. Damien didn't respond so Angel continued, "Edward said if we can bring people back to life then there would be no more sorrow in the world."

"But people have to die," interrupted Damien, "or the world would be overrun by people, and we wouldn't have the resources on this planet for everybody to survive."

"But what if we could choose? What if we had saved President Kennedy? Lyndon B Johnson would not have taken over the presidency and then fewer men would have been sent to Vietnam to fight; maybe fewer lives would have been lost," she replied.

"Get your facts right, Angel. Kennedy had already started the war in Vietnam, and he would have sent more men eventually." Angel realised she should not have used a historical event to prove a point. Damien would always have a smart answer to counteract her argument.

"He will come back for me, you know," she said, trying to change the subject.

"I know. Have you heard the name Eftemie Vladimirescu?" asked Damien.

"No," was the adamant answer.

"I will keep you safe, Angel. Don't worry. You can talk openly to me. I will never judge you."

She didn't answer but turned her back to him. He assumed their conversation was now over.

Leaving her room, Damien felt a sense of pride. His father now had some new leads to pursue. The way he had extracted the information made him feel less proud.

"I would have told you. You didn't need to wear a wire," she called as he closed the door. Damien didn't go back to his father. Instead he leant against Angel's doorframe and took a deep breath. He couldn't leave it at that. Removing the wires and stuffing them in his pocket, he pushed the door open and entered her room again.

"If you would talk to the police then I wouldn't have worn the wire," he shouted angrily. He hadn't come back into the room to argue if he should or should not have worn a wire. He came back because he was annoyed at her ignorance. She was still not facing him, but that did not deter him.

"How can you say Edward is a good man?" he demanded. "He tried to kill me in cold blood for no other reason than I know you. I had not done anything to him. Do you know what it feels like to be tied up, not knowing if you are going to live or die while a psycho prances around you slicing at your skin? Do you know what it feels like to have a knife thrust into your body, to feel your life disappear whilst hearing his insane laughter? Just think, Stacey, Shaun and Jennifer, and god knows who else, went through what I went through. He should be strung up for what he has done. Edward is insane – a lunatic – and you are no better than him if you think he is a good man. Do you love me, Angel? Because you have a funny way of showing it! I feel like you are taking Edward's side, as though I mean nothing to you, after all I have been through."

She still didn't speak, which angered him more. Their relationship had been so perfect before Edward had come into their lives, and now it was all collapsing around him.

Damien was about to leave the room when he heard a quiet voice. He turned around. Angel now lay on her back watching him. "I'm sorry. I don't want to upset you. I didn't think. I just blocked out the attack on you as though it never happened."

Damien moved back to Angel's bed. "I wish I could block it out like you, but I have the marks." Damien rolled up his sleeve. "This means I can never forget what he did too me." Edward's initials jumped out on his skin. "I have to live with this, Angel, live with what he did to me."

"I know, I'm sorry. I could try and remove the scars."

"But that's not the point, is it? The point is he did this to me."

"But…"

"There are no buts. I don't want you to try and heal me again. The next time will probably kill you. I know you will say Edward was trying to push you. He knew you could bring back life, and by using me you would do everything possible, but that's not acceptable, Angel. He carved his initials in my arm. That is the sign of a mad man. It has nothing to do with bringing back life." Once again, he thrust his arm back under Angel's nose to strengthen his point. "I can't wear short sleeved t-shirts because I see the marks all the time. He has scarred me more than just physically, Angel, and you think he is a good man!"

Tears began to form behind her eyes. He had never seen Angel cry, she always appeared so strong, so in control, but today there was a weakness he hadn't expected to see.

"I can see your point, but I can also see Edwards'," Angel managed to stutter, as she fought back the tears. "Edward was wrong for what he did to you, I know that much. The rest, I don't know what to believe."

Damien studied her face. Lying to him would have been the easier option, yet in some ways he respected her honesty.

"Please think about what I have said," he said in a gentler tone. She gave a slight nod. The tears didn't appear. Damien wasn't going to push any harder, nor was he going to comfort her. It would not have felt right. Damien's hand moved to his stomach.

"Does it hurt?" she asked.

"A little," he gave her a forced smile. "I'll survive." He left Angel's room but did not walk out of her life.

*****

Dr Ben Wilson was not expecting to spend too much time in his newly acquired position. His current boss was paying him well, and that was all that mattered. Monitor Angelica Wellingstone was his brief; find out as much as possible about her medical condition and family. Ben was sure he had read about a similar medical case in America, several years ago. If he remembered correctly, a young lad had an illness that ate away the body. From what Ben could remember, it appeared similar to Angel's condition. Minor details could be found in the medical journals, but information was still sketchy.

Dr Wilson visited Angel daily. Her condition was fascinating. She had been so close to death one minute and then experienced a miraculous unexplained recovery. He wanted to know more, and so did his boss. At first Angel had been co-operative but Dr Wilson's continuous visits were wearing her down. Every day, more blood and tissue samples were taken for tests. Then there were the constant questions about her family: Who was her mother? Where did she live? Did she have any brothers and sisters? Question after question. Angel needed to get out of the hospital as soon as possible before Dr Wilson became a problem and discovered the truth.

Her mother had warned her of what would happen if people found out what she was capable of; even now, too many people knew the truth.

Dr Ben Wilson was young, ambitious, and highly intelligent. At the age of twenty-six years, he had completed his medical training, two years earlier than most students. At University he was awarded the title of "Student Most Likely to Succeed." Two years later he had been a finalist for one of the Shipston Awards for his contribution to improving medical science through the treatment of patients. He changed his medical focus to get away from the strict hours laid down by society, and being allocated a number of patients to treat had never excited him. A year later he was once again recognised by the Shipston Foundation in a field he was passionate about. He received the Hownslow Medical Research Award for the genetic manipulation of human DNA after detecting specific DNA sequences amidst the numerous organisms' genomes.

Dr Wilson was onto a major break-through when the funding was withdrawn. His partner, Dr Troy Eastwick went one way, and he went another. Now in new territory, he found the prospect of identifying a new gene found in a chromosome or a new nucleotide sequence in the body exciting. He had signed a confidentiality agreement so that any findings could not be published or discussed in public. His boss had been very thorough on that front, but recognition was not everything. He was giving him access to some interesting subjects, and some inspiring medical research; and if he could impress the redhead at the same time, that would be a bonus.

His elderly boss knew exactly what he wanted, and how he wanted it done. There was no flexibility, no discussion. His boss had cursed him loudly and aggressively when he mentioned his plan to find the American practitioner who had tried to cure a similar condition several years previous.

"I was only trying to save time," he had argued.

"I am not paying you to save time. I am paying you to do what you are told. You tell nobody, and you discuss this with nobody. You are under contract, my lad," his boss had warned. Never before had Ben seen his boss so angry. His face was red and sweaty, his body shaking. A cold shudder ran through Ben's body. He was not used to people disagreeing with him. The redhead had just looked at him in her disapproving way. When she shook her head, her hair fell effortlessly, caressing her shoulders and back. Her hand lay on his boss's shoulder, no-doubt trying to keep him calm; stop the old geezer from having a heart attack.

Ben did not want to mess this chance up. In the last few years he had become disillusioned with the medical profession, bored with the routine. All challenges had been removed, and he needed to be challenged. Give his brain a workout. Todd had found him in South America and had offered him a chance to escape the routine, or so he thought. There was still the daily routine but this time with a hint of ground-breaking research mixed in.

Angel didn't mention Dr Wilson to Damien as she didn't want to worry him. If she continued getting better, she would be out of hospital soon. Damien and Angel were well on their way to recovery. Edward's name was not mentioned for a long time, and although they spent as much time as they could together, their conversation had left a large void in their relationship. Damien had never heard Angel utter such rubbish as she had done that day. The coldness she had shown was disturbing. For some reason, Angel worshipped Edward, not recognising the evil he was inflicting, believing in all he stood for. Damien could not forget that. His father had also found her comments disturbing.

"Brain-washed" had been his father's explanation, followed by, "It's similar to the Stockholm Syndrome, where the kidnapped has positive feelings towards the kidnapper, like that Jayne Cuthard, who was locked away for fourteen years in her kidnapper's cellar." Then he had commented on Angel's story about the shamanic spirits. Damien had asked his father to ignore this story.

"Angel has a vivid imagination; it's an escape mechanism she uses," had been his excuse.

His father then reminded him of a young lass called Sabrina who had followed him everywhere, "your very own stalker."

Damien remembered the incident and laughed. "She was only ten. I don't think that can be classed as a stalker," Damien had pointed out.

No matter how far-fetched it sounded, Damien did believe in Angel's story of the shamanic spirits, although he also appreciated his father would not be able to comprehend such an idea. His father did not believe Angel could ease his pain, and he certainly did not believe she had taken his death, so shamanic spirits were certainly not comprehendible. Damien had probably made Angel sound like a complete nutcase, and maybe she was, but it was the only response he could think of quickly in response to his father's comment.

Damien had now been sent home with the strict instructions to relax, although he spent most of his time back at the hospital with Angel. Damien may not have liked what she had said, but he just wanted his old Angel back again. Angel rarely mentioned Edward by name unless she was asked something specific. She was aware she had said too much that day. When Edward had spoken of her family ancestry, she had been fascinated, wanting to share it with Damien at the earliest opportunity; now she realised it had been the wrong time. Angel was disappointed Damien had not shared her enthusiasm, and maybe she had come across as cold and heartless, but he was the one who had pushed her hard for answers, just like Inspector Strangeway had done and for what‽To score brownie points with his father – a father who had not been around, a father who had never taken much notice of his son before. She hated it when they argued. Although their arguments did not last long, it always saddened her.

Damien's parents wanted their son to move back home, and although tempted, his stubborn streak surfaced and instead he insisted on staying close to Angel. He couldn't face going back to his old school room, – too many unpleasant memories. Nightmares were also starting to haunt him. Scared to be alone, he ended up at Brian's pad.

It wasn't until a week had passed that Angel found the letter from her mother tucked deep into the pocket of her dressing gown. It was a letter that answered many questions and created many more. As she read parts of the letter aloud to Damien, he sat and listened intently. He asked no questions; instead he mulled the information over, trying to make sense of what the woman had written. Angel skipped the section about Edward, which was a no-discussion area with Damien, and another section that was very personal. She needed to digest its content before sharing the information. Angel guessed Damien would say she was being secretive again, but she couldn't help it. If Damien knew she missed out sections, he didn't say.

My darling Angel,

This is probably the hardest thing I have ever had to write, and I don't know where to start. I hope this letter will help you to understand who you are. As you now know, you are special, very special; you have a unique power that very few others possess. I think there are five of you left who possess a similar gift to mine, spread across North America and Europe. As you probably realised from your childhood, I have the power of healing, even though I tried to hide it from you. Unfortunately, the wrong people also found out what I was capable of.

I don't understand why and how I can do what I can do. As I grew older, this power changed and became stronger. I assume yours will as well. Don't be scared; embrace this power. It is god's will.

The following section she skipped for Damien's sake.

I fell for Edward in my teens. He was a handsome young man whom I worshiped. When Edward met the Doctor, he changed. The Doctor turned his head, gave him a power, showed him things until I had lost his love completely. I was an outsider. In his eyes, I was a job. I tried to bring love back into our life, but to no avail – I had lost him. Edward became violent, unpredictable and dangerous, which is why I asked you not to have any contact with him. As you no doubt have guessed from my feeble words, Edward is your father. Maybe now you will understand why I never told you who your father was.

Edward is my father? It is impossible! thought Angel. *Why didn't he tell me? Why hide it from me all these years?* The revelations in the letter continued.

This will also probably surprise you, Angel, but you are not an only child; you also have an older sister, two older brothers and one younger brother. They told me your sister and one of your brothers were stillborn. I never held them in my arms like I held you. I always had a feeling they were alive, and later Edward confirmed my suspicions. I know Dominique is now dead. I met him a couple of times. I tried to explain that I was his real mother, but he was a scared young man who was sceptical of my words and of me. I could not make him understand. He had beautiful dark hair just like you, my darling. I am unsure about your sister; I have no information on her whereabouts.

Then there was Bobby; I started to bring up Bobby. He stayed with me for the first few years but then they took him away. They have a manipulative power, Angel; they can make things happen. Bobby should never have been taken from me – it's a game to them. They don't care who they hurt. A couple of years later, I gave birth to you, Angel. I was allowed to keep you as long as I agreed Edward could have daily access into our lives, whenever he required. I tried to bring you up as a normal child; please don't feel angry with me. I did my best; I did it for you, pumpkin. I don't know and will never know if all my children have a similar power to you and me. I assume that is why they wanted my children. When I would give them no more, they took my eggs and created their own. You see, it gets more confusing. According to Edward, in addition to the five of you, there are three more children. I don't know who they are or where they reside.

I know there are many children with gifts – some similar to you, while others are very different. I know there are two young lads who attract metal. They are like magnets. And I know there are children and grown-ups who can control a person's thoughts. My brother has the power… [Angel was frustrated because this sentence was never completed.] *I don't know how many more people have these gifts, and if they are connected or just coincidence.*

I would never have intentionally abandoned you, Angel. In the hospital I knew you were out of harm's way. They could not get to you in there. I made sure you were protected and you did not suffer. A guardian angel watched over you at all times. You must understand why I had to leave, my darling. My intention was only for a couple of weeks. Then outside events took over; events I could not control. My other children needed my help. I am sorry, Angel. I never meant any of this to happen.

I am giving you my life as I can no longer fight. *My energy is fading fast. Please look after Warren for me. I know he will be their next target. I can no longer stop them, but you can you have a renewed energy, a fighting spirit which you don't often see in a child. Please keep my other children safe, Angel. I am entrusting you with their lives. I have already lost Bobby and Dominique. How many more, I don't know. I was never privilege to such information. Sometimes Edward divulged minor information. I think he took great delight in telling me about my children, knowing I couldn't see them growing up, but I digress. Soon you will meet the Doctor, Angel. Don't let him corrupt your innocence. He ruined my life. Don't let him ruin yours.*

Warren's last known address is North Hampden Street, Barnstable, Massachusetts.

I'm sorry, but I do not have the addresses of any of your other brothers and sisters. There is a Samuel somewhere in Connecticut, in America, and the twins, who must be close to twelve years old, and I know there is your older sister, if she is still alive. I don't know her name. How sad is that? A mother who doesn't even know her own daughter's name.

Angel immediately broke from the letter. "Damien, I am not an only child; I have brothers and sisters. I have Dominique and Bobby," she flicked the letter over, "and Warren and a sister, and there are others, Damien! There are others."

"Don't build up your hopes up too much, Angel. Yes, you have brothers and sisters, but your mam was unsure if they were still alive." Angel wasn't listening. The excitement of having a family had taken over.

"Do you think they will look like me?"

"Nobody could look like you," he smiled, not wanting to dampen her mood. Angel let out a giggle before returning her attention back to the letter.

I have enclosed the only item I have left to give you. Wear it with pride. It holds a stone known as a Citrine stone. It will protect you and give you strength and courage. You have grown into a beautiful young lady, who I am very proud of, but please be careful, Angel. Keep your gift secret. Trust nobody. It's a sinister world.

I will always love you.

Mum

In the envelope was a small gold locket inlaid with a tiny golden yellow stone. Angel fumbled clumsily with the clasp, trying to open the small golden heart. Her hand was shaking. Damien offered to help, but she drew the locket closer to her body, reminding him of an obsessive child who did not want to share. Angel almost dropped the locket, but the chain caught between her forefinger and thumb. With trepidation, she managed to open the small clasp. The locket was empty. There was no photograph inside, and Damien could see her disappointment. He too was disappointed, as he knew how desperately she wanted a photograph of her mother.

Tucking the letter back into her dressing gown, Angel sighed, "My mum was here. I knew she was alive. I knew she would come. What do you think I should do?" There was excitement and a hint of disappointment in her voice.

"Just get better, Angel. We will discuss it when you are out of hospital." Damien hoped she would forget the letter, although this was unlikely. There were many things about the letter Damien was uncomfortable with – not just the content, but what it was suggesting. The words that read, 'I was allowed to keep you' disturbed him. Why couldn't a mother keep her own daughter? Why take her brother away from his family? Who had this power? Was it the authorities, or was it someone, or something, more sinister? Who was the Doctor? How could a mother put such a large burden on her daughter's shoulders, entrusting her with her brothers' and sister's lives? It was surreal and very wrong. Could this be the start of something he did not want to be part of? His mind started to drift. He knew he did not want to meet Edward again. Next time he may not be as lucky. It felt like a never-ending nightmare, and the nightmare was about to get worse.

*****

As soon as he said it, he knew he had said too much. "How do you know about my grandfather?" Damien didn't want to lie, but by telling her the truth, he knew she would be upset.

"You must have told me."

"I didn't," she quickly replied.

Just admit it, he thought. *Honesty is the best policy. You always get caught in the end.*

"I'm sorry, Angel. I have a file on you, with items and articles on your ancestry. I'm sorry," he repeated.

Angel stared at him. She couldn't believe what she was hearing. "You have a file on me. Why?"

"I'm sorry," is all he managed to say.

"I thought I could trust you, but you are just like everybody else," her voice was calm, but there was a slight quiver as she tried to supress the anger rising in her body. "I feel so violated. How could you do such a thing?" she whispered.

Damien tried to hold her, but she pulled away.

"Don't touch me. Don't even speak to me. I feel sick with disgust," her voice was starting to rise. She was losing control. Any minute he would see her anger.

Tim and Laurel stood next to Damien; neither had said a word.

It was Tim who finally interrupted, "Don't blame Damien. It was us. Damien had nothing to do with putting the file together. In fact, Damien was furious when he found out." Angel stared at Tim and then back to Damien.

"You were all in on it. Did you all have a good laugh at my expense?"

Damien shook his head, "It wasn't like that."

"Did you read about my medical condition or my time in the psychiatric hospital? Did you have a real good laugh when my psychiatrist said I was a violent child, or when they couldn't find a straight-jacket small enough to fit me! Was it amusing to see how far you could push the school nutter? I don't believe any of you. You are all sick. Edward tried to warn me. People are evil and not to be trusted." Now would have been the perfect time to storm off but there was nowhere to go.

Damien grabbed her arm. "Angel, please don't. It wasn't like that. I only looked at the file because I was worried about you. For goodness sake, you had gone missing. I looked hoping to find a clue on your whereabouts." He glanced towards Laurel for moral support; Laurel said nothing. His actions said everything. Shifting uncomfortably, staring at the ground, no doubt wishing it would open up and swallow him. Damien felt terrible, but he guessed Laurel would feel just as bad. It had been Laurel's idea to create the file.

Tim finally spoke. "We put the file together because of the rumours in school. We wanted to make sure Damien was safe."

"Who do you think I am? What do you think I was going to do?" she accused them.

"I am sorry, Angel," said Tim calmly. "I know it was wrong."

Angel now glanced towards Damien, "Why did you do it? Why do you want to laugh at me? I have done nothing to you. In fact, I have done nothing to any of you." With hatred and anger in her eyes, she eyeballed them all in turn.

"I know," Damien assured her. "We aren't laughing at you. I told you before, Angel, I don't care about your past; it's the future I am interested in. I'm sorry. I didn't mean to upset you." Damien reached out again. This time she did not pull away. Her small fists beat gently on his chest. It hurt more than it should. She missed the stab wounds, and the sore patches that were beginning to form again, but still he could feel the pain. Was the pain from his illness, the attack, or from the pain he was causing to the one person he loved? Her anger was beginning to subside. She buried her head into his chest.

"I'm not sure I will ever trust you again," she whispered.

"You can trust me. I'm sorry for what I did, Angel."

There was a long pause before she pulled away from his grasp. "Please leave me alone. I want to be by myself."

Damien was about to argue, but instead he kissed her gently on the forehead.

"I love you and don't ever forget that," he spoke quietly, without his normal confidence. Slowly he got up to leave, and his mates followed his lead.

Still struggling to walk without assistance, Angel discharged herself from the hospital that afternoon, much to the disappointment of Dr Ben Wilson, who would have to break the news to his boss and the redhead. The one person he was supposed to study had left the hospital. He was no closer to discovering her true identity and the strange ability her body had to protect itself. It had been a bigger surprise to Damien who had visited the hospital as normal, only to find Angel was no longer a patient. Angel went back to her school room, locked the door and didn't come out for twenty-four hours.

*****

"Please, Angel, let's talk."

"Leave me alone, Damien. I need time to myself."

"I am not going anywhere until I have seen you," Damien said. He was met by silence. "I'm sorry. I was wrong, but I was so worried about you. I didn't know where you were. I know so little about your past; I didn't know where to look for you." Silence again. Damien slid down the wall and placed his head against the door. The pain from the knife wounds dug deep in his stomach. The painkillers had little effect.

"I can't live without you," he whispered. Angel's shadow moved closer to the bedroom door, and by the noise he guessed she was sitting behind the door.

"I feel so alone, Damien."

"You have me," he said and waited. Silence and then a sigh.

"I have a family I've never met. The only member of my family I know has let me down so badly. I don't even think Edward cares about me. Edward shouldn't have done that to you."

"I care about you," Damien said sincerely.

Angel sniffed.

"Don't cry."

"I'm not," she argued. "I have a runny nose."

"I thought you said you had never had a cold."

Silence again. "I know I am overreacting, but I can't help it. I think it's just a combination of everything. I need time, that's all."

"I'll give you time, but let me see you and hold you first."

"Tomorrow, when my head is right; when I look better."

He gave a faint laugh. "How do you look at the moment? You haven't turned into an ogre have you?"

Sensing he had made her smile, Damien squeezed his fingertips under the door, just catching the side of her hand. She didn't pull away, but still the door stayed closed.

"Damien, what if I'm like Edward?" Angel worried.

"What do you mean?"

"It's just that I have similar traits to Edward. Do you think I have obsessive habits?"

"Like the apples and the way you fold the sheets on your bed? Oh, and not forgetting how you angle everything as though it's on display."

"Yes."

"Then yes, a few, but nothing extreme. The apples I would probably class as a passion rather than an obsession. I clean my teeth every morning, and that could be described as an obsession."

"Edward had obsessive habits."

"That means nothing," Damien said. There was silence again.

"I also like games and so does Edward, and I find languages easy to learn, and Edward can speak fifteen different languages."

"That proves nothing."

"What if I tell you I have thought of killing somebody?"

"Who?"

"It doesn't matter who."

"But you didn't kill them did you. Was it Tara or Beth?" His question was met with silence.

"There is a difference between thinking it and doing it," Damien assured her.

"Have you ever had those thoughts?" Angel asked, looking for reassurance.

"Probably, I don't know. I can't remember if I have."

"Sometimes I look at my hands, and I can see blood on them. I'm scared that I'm like him."

"Angel, listen to me. You are nothing like him. You are a good person. If you live with someone then you are bound to pick-up some of their ways, but not killing. Live with me and then you'll pick-up some of my habits."

Angel sniffed again, but managed to joke, "But you are so messy."

"Ah, at last you admit it. Is that why you fold the towels in my bathroom?" Sensing her head was now laid on the door, Damien did the same. "Are there any more of my imperfections you would like to raise?" He got a sniff and then a slight giggle. Damien smiled. This felt normal – they had always teased and joked with each other. There was hope for them. "Angel, please open the door." There was another long pause. "Open the door, please." There was a longer pause before Angel spoke again.

"Tomorrow, I'll talk to you tomorrow, I promise. When my head is right." Her shadow moved slowly from the door. The noise from Angel's mattress springs suggested she had retired to the bed.

The halls of residence were almost empty of students; many had made their way home to parents for the summer holidays. A few girls were still hanging around, prolonging the inevitable. They saw him sitting and talking outside the door, but they were too enthralled in their own lives to care what was going on. This time he moved from Angel's door. Tomorrow he would arrive early.

*****

The door was already open, awaiting his arrival. Angel was sitting on the bed, staring out of the window with her back to him. Before entering the bedroom, Damien gently knocked on the door. Angel slowly turned around. A calm serenity engulfed the room. The room hadn't changed since the last time he had visited. Bare and impersonal was the only way to describe it.

"Are you alright?" he asked nervously. Angel nodded.

"Are we ok?" She nodded again.

"Have you been meditating?"

"Is that what it would have said in my psychiatrist's notes?" she asked, quickly followed by, "I'm sorry. I promised myself I wasn't going to mention the file. I just feel let down, and totally exposed, as though everybody knows my life story." She turned to face the window, a sadness in her voice.

"They meant well, you know."

"I know. I guess you are lucky to have such loyal friends who care about you." A forced smile crossed her face as she turned to face him again. "But it doesn't stop the hurt I feel."

"I have more I need to tell you," he whispered taking a deep breath. "I have seen your scrapbook."

Angel nodded.

"I saw it had been moved," she spoke hesitantly.

"I have also seen your diary, but I only read the last ten days when I couldn't find you. I promise I didn't look through the rest of it. I know diaries are very personal." Damien waited for her reaction; there was none. He couldn't even tell if she was angry with him. "I know you care about me, Angel. Please don't let my stupidity spoil what we have." Angel still did not speak; instead, she moved slowly towards him, placed her arms around his waist and gave him a gentle squeeze before placing her head on his chest for a couple of seconds.

"Shall we go out for something to eat?" she asked.

Damien was glad she had taken the news well, but there was a coldness to her embrace which disturbed him. Placing his arms around her body, he gently pulled her dark hair so she had no choice but to look him in the eye. "I love you," he whispered. His lips came down to meet hers. Angel wanted to pull away teach him a lesson, but she couldn't. Her body melted into his arms, and she responded passionately. This was a breakthrough. Her fingertips slipped under his shirt, and she gently caressed his skin.

"I bet this is one habit you didn't pick-up from Edward," he commented, and she let out a small giggle. "Have those silly thoughts gone?"

"Gone but not forgotten," was her only response, and in a colder manner than he would have liked. "This must be hurting you," she said after a moment, and her eyes rose to meet his.

"Maybe but the pain is worth it." They held each other for several minutes. Warmth transferred between their bodies. Neither spoke, both were enjoying each other's company. Kissing her forehead, his eye caught sight of the object next to her bed.

"That's a pretty brush." Angel glanced over to the object on top of the bedside cupboard that Damien was referring to.

"It's a present from Laurel; it has a mother of pearl back and handle."

"From Laurel!"

"Yes, he bought it so he could brush my hair when I was in the hospital."

"Really? That's not like the Laurel I know."

"It is pretty, isn't it?"

"Yes, it's lovely." Damien was trying not to show any jealousy. He was still treading carefully, trying not to break the eggshells further. Laurel had never mentioned buying Angel a present and brushing her hair surely was his job, not Laurel's. Could he be reading too much into the situation? It wouldn't be the first time he had misread the situation. Angel was so open, so dismissive, about it that she obviously did not see it as wrong. A kiss on his cheek broke his thought process.

"Damien, can we leave the food? I have something I need to do."

"Sure, what do you need to do?"

"Oh, something and nothing."

"Can I come with you?"

She looked at him. "I don't think so. You would be bored."

"I don't mind. I just want to spend some time with you."

She smiled. "I am going home."

"What to Barton on Stowheath?"

She nodded.

"But that's over an hour away by bus," Damien protested, "and you're so weak. If you are going home then I am going with you to look after you."

"I think you're weaker than me, Damien."

"Then we will look after each other," said Damien, determined not to let her go alone. Angel handed Damien an apple from her bedside cupboard.

"My mam used to say an apple a day keeps the doctor away."

"You are funny," laughed Damien, taking the greenish yellow apple from her hand. Today it was an Ashmead Kernel.

Mrs Beakes

The bus ride and the short walk to Angel's house was relatively straightforward, but Damien wasn't expecting the sight that met him. They stood outside a burnt-out shell, staring at her old home.

"Welcome to my past," Angel said. This was the first time he had accompanied her to the house or anywhere else with a link to her past.

"Did you know it had been gutted by fire?" he asked sadly.

"Yes, but I sometimes think my mother will turn up here looking for me. I usually come here to think. I used to come here to try and find out who I am. Something more than what's written on paper. A bottle of my mum's perfume, one of her dresses or a doll, anything really. Did you know all my belongings can fit inside a carrier bag? I own nothing from my past. This house holds all the secrets. If only it could talk to me. I think that's why I was so upset about the file. My life is all on paper, and now everybody knows as much as I know, maybe more."

"You have your memories," Damien suggested.

"But memories fade over time," Angel said sadly.

Angel stared at her old home, willing it to speak – an impossible task for an object without life. Subconsciously, Damien curled a couple of strands of Angel's hair around his fingers, creating ringlets. When he released the curl, its weight caused the hair to fall straight. Angel had talked a lot on this trip; Damien had mainly listened. He didn't mind. It was nice to hear her talk.

Damien moved his hands from her hair and placed his arms around Angel's waist. He stood slightly behind in the gap where the gate once stood and rested his chin on her shoulder. Nuzzling into her neck, he kissed it gently, trying to give her the reassurance she was not alone. Glancing down the road, he saw a parked car. It was the same make and model that had followed their bus. His father's men were watching and waiting in case of another attack. Damien turned towards the house and the large overgrown garden. There must have been five or possibly ten years' growth. An old rusty swing peered over the long grass. The swing looked as though it was suspended in mid-air. Thoughts of Angel swinging as high as she could go immediately sprang to mind.

"Did you try to swing over the top?" he asked, pointing to the swing.

Angel giggled. "Yes. Did you used to do that?"

He nodded.

"I wonder if anybody ever succeeded."

"I don't think the force of gravity would allow it."

"Always Mr Practical," she giggled again before digging him in the ribs.

"Ow. I am still a little sore, you know."

"I used to sit on the freshly mowed lawn over there," Angel pointed to an overgrown area in the centre of the garden. "I like the smell of freshly cut grass. I used to sit and comb my doll's synthetic hair at least once a week. Their hair easily knotted if I didn't comb it. I remember glancing towards the patio doors where

Edward and my mother were arguing. I remember scowling. My forehead felt all wrinkly like an old person. I was angry with them; I remember wondering what they were arguing about. At the time I was playing with my dolls, Maisie and Violet, but they felt stupid. I pulled hard at Maisie's leg. It popped effortlessly out of its socket. It made a strange popping noise, like popcorn when it expands in a pan." There was a pause. "I remember throwing both dolls down on the lawn. I never saw my dolls again. I skipped next door to see if Beth and Stacey were doing something more interesting. I was still very angry," Angel suddenly stopped telling her story. "Anyway that's not important."

Damien was so tempted to ask why, but he guessed he already knew the answer.

"Do you want to come in?" Angel asked after taking a deep breath.

"Is it safe?" Damien worried.

"Of course. Follow in my footsteps, and I'll show you around. I left a letter for my mam on the mantelpiece, so I want to check if it is still there. Afterwards, we can visit Mrs Beakes. You will like her. She was my mam's best friend."

"Why the sudden change of heart, Angel?" Damien had to ask. "You've never voluntarily told me anything about your past before."

"I know, but trust is important. You said no more secrets, and I want to show you I'm not a total loser. There is more to me than what's written on those pieces of paper."

"I didn't think you were," Damien assured her.

Mrs Beakes was only a couple of minutes' walk from Angel's old home. "She never locks her door," uttered

Angel, stepping into the entrance hall. "Mrs Beakes, it's Angelica," she called as they moved further into the hallway. "Mrs Beakes?"

"I'm coming, my dear." He heard a croaky voice from the back room. An old lady with ghostly white hair rushed to greet them. "Hello, Angelica! What brings you here?"

"I thought you might like to meet Damien, Mrs Beakes," Angel said. The old lady viewed him with an air of suspicion.

"Is this the young man you were telling me about?"

Angel nodded.

"Well, come in, young man. Grab a pew. Where are my manners? Please call me Stella.... Stella Artois," she chuckled. "Oh dear, I find that name so funny." All her suspicions appeared to have evaporated.

"Should I make a drink, Mrs Beakes?" Angel called from the kitchen.

"Oh dear. Yes, please do, Angelica. Where are my manners?"

Damien sat for a few minutes glancing around the living room. It was old-fashioned yet very homey. Lace doilies sat underneath a large collection of ceramic horse ornaments. They looked like Royal Doulton, like his grandmother's.

"Come closer, my dear. Let me take a good look at you. My eyes are not as good as they used to be."

Damien complied, and she observed, "My, my you are a handsome young man. What a handsome young man you have, Angelica."

Angel popped her head around the door and winked at Damien, "Where are the tumblers, Mrs Beakes?"

"Oh dear, let me think. Ah yes, I remember. The tall cupboard near my fridge. I had to move them, you know.

I am too old to keep climbing up to the top cupboard. I might fall one day."

Damien smiled. "Do you see Angel often?" he asked innocently.

"Oh yes, but not as often as I would like; normally Christmas and whenever she is passing. Now, let me see. A couple of months ago Angelica stayed with me for three whole days. It was so nice to see her again. Are you staying over tonight, my dear?"

"I don't think so."

"As I was saying, Angelica was having some boy trouble. He had gone off with another young lady. Oh yes, I remember, she used to live down the road; the big house on the left with a real pretty sun-house in the garden. I don't think I am the right person to give her advice on dating. I am a little rusty you see. Did you know I am seventy-two?"

Damien smiled. She was a dear.

"Anyway, I told Angelica if she wanted this young man then she should go and get him. If he didn't want her, it was his loss not hers." Angel had returned, balancing a tray of three large tumblers and a jug of fresh lemonade.

"Now, my dear, did you ever capture that young man's heart?"

Angel blushed. "This is Damien, Mrs Beakes."

"Oh dear. Yes, yes of course. I am seventy-two, you know."

"Have you seen my mum, Mrs Beakes?" Angel asked, trying to sound casual.

"No, oh dear no. It's a shame about your house, my dear."

"I know it is, Mrs Beakes."

"I gave your mam all my savings to help her get away from him. Edward controlled your mam. I told her to leave him years ago, but she worried about you my dear."

"I know she did. Do you want me to fix the blind in your kitchen?" Angel was moving a small white stallion on the sideboard as she spoke.

"Oh dear, yes. That would be nice." She turned to Damien. "When Angel's mother left, he held a knife to my face, and he said, and I remember his words quite clearly, 'If you don't tell me where she has gone, I'll cut your f***ing nose off, you f***ing b**ch."

Damien nearly choked on an ice-cube that he had just popped into his mouth and started coughing uncontrollably.

"Oh dear, dear me! Are you ok? The ice-cubes always make me cough as well," Mrs. Beakes sympathised.

Damien just nodded as he tried to stifle his laugh.

He looked over to the kitchen and could just make out Angel clambering on top of the kitchen units to fix the blind. Should he offer to help? he wondered. No, he decided. She looked competent in what she was doing. It was hard to believe it was the same person who less than two days ago was in hospital, and only a couple of hours ago looked so weak that lifting her mattress would have taken all her strength. Angel was laughing, full of life – just how she used to be.

*****

"I am glad I came with you. She is amazing your Mrs Beakes. Or is it Stella...Stella Artois?" They both laughed.

"Now you know where I disappear to," Angel explained. "She is an adorable old lady, don't you think?"

Damien agreed. "Thank you for taking me. It's been a lovely day. Will you do something for me?"

"I'll try."

"I know I am asking a lot, but will you spend time with my friends? I want them to get to know the real you, not the person in some stupid file, or on a piece of paper. They are not all bad, and I know Laurel is quite taken by you." Angel didn't answer; Damien guessed the answer was a reluctant yes.

"Will you burn the file?" Angel finally asked.

"Is that what you want?"

She nodded.

"Ok, consider it burnt." He had given the file to his father to see if it would help him find Edward, so burning it was going to prove difficult. If Angel realised he had passed it to somebody else, he dreaded to think how she would react. One thing was for certain, she would not speak to him again.

True to her word, Angel started to join Damien and his friends. The file was forgotten, and they moved on with their lives. Sitting outside of Café Ruben in the small town of Winston, the conversation had turned to their future. All the sixth formers congregated at the café. It served decent strong coffee, although most of the students ordered Frappuccinos, especially the strawberry flavour. Angel was different; she always ordered apple juice, even though she complained it tasted nothing like apple.

The café had a friendly, comfortable atmosphere, with large cane chairs and sofas scattered haphazardly in the outside space. Off-white parasols covered in a weatherproof membrane were available when the weather was too hot, or when the rain started to fall. The owner, a large burly ex-military chap, ran the coffee house. He was soft-spoken yet stood no mischief.

Laurel and Tim had applied to Kingston University, so if their grades were decent their next three years were planned. Brian was currently engrossed in some IT project, so was once again missing from their select gathering. Damien had never thought of his future; his illness had prevented such thoughts. Surviving was his only goal. Surviving this long had been a surprise, and Angel, well she was drifting and seemed quite happy with no clear goal.

Today was the day Damien had been dreading. Angel's thoughts had returned back to the letter.

"Can I borrow some money?" she asked almost apologetically. "I need to go to America to find my brother – Warren – however, I cannot afford the flight. I promise I will pay you back."

Damien wanted to say no, but he realised he couldn't. Angel had never asked him for money before – even change to buy a snack – so he guessed she was desperate. And he did have more than enough in his bank account to easily spare the fee. His thoughts returned to the letter. Maybe Warren was the only family she had left, and it was unfair of him to keep her away from him, especially if he could reunite them. He still didn't believe Angel's mother had written the letter. He would not have been surprised if it turned out to have been Edward, playing his games. The delivery of the white roses at Angel's bedside was also still unexplained. It had to be Edward. Who else could it have been? Ever since Damien's attack,

Edward played on his mind. He was sure he would come back to finish what he had started.

Damien stared warmly at Angel, wondering what he should do. She only had a couple of weeks left on her accommodation, so it made sense, especially as he felt uneasy her living in an almost empty building. They were still under surveillance by his father's team of officers in case Edward made another appearance; if Angel knew, she never let on.

"Why don't we all go and have a holiday before university? It would make the summer fun," said Laurel, winking at Angel.

Tim pondered this idea for a minute. "I could afford to go as long as we camp; hotels may be pushing my budget."

"Angel's too ill to go this soon," muttered Damien backed up by, "it will be a long stressful trip." As normal he was out voted; Damien was weaker than Angel, not that he would admit his weakness to his friends. His wounds were still healing, and he didn't feel as strong as he would have liked to undertake such a trip.

The decision was made; they were to fly out to New York, catch the Greyhound bus to Massachusetts, and then hire a camper van for the rest of their journey. Angel had not expected everybody to travel with her, but at least she could fulfil her mother's wishes, meet her brother, and maybe the trip could be fun as well as productive. Jumping onto Damien's lap, she threw her hands around his neck and kissed him.

"Thank you," she whispered, giving him the largest squeeze she could muster without hurting him; he responded instantly. Since the hospital and the visit to Mrs Beakes, Angel had been a little distant. Today it felt like old times, which they were both happy to rekindle.

It was hard to be affectionate, knowing you were being watched by undercover cops. Cops, who no doubt reported back to his father every movement they made. He felt like a child of ten rather than a man who had just turned eighteen years. Some eighteenth birthday, spent in hospital attached to a life support machine – but at least he was alive. His father did not believe his story, although he did listen. It did sound impossible: a woman who could miraculously take away pain and bring life to death. Maybe he needed to be locked up for believing it himself, although he deemed it was true as he had witnessed it first-hand.

"I only have one condition," said Damien, staring directly into Angel's smouldering eyes. "I want you to put some more weight on. You're all skin and bone." To demonstrate, he started to tickle her. Shrieks of laughter interrupted the otherwise quiet café. If nothing else, it would give the cops something to report, although he realised he would have to telephone his father and let him know what they were doing. His father would no doubt tell him it was a bad idea.

The Streets of London

Stepping from the train, Crystal was greeted by music drifting through the air. She smiled. Maybe Fred was right – she should have come to London earlier. Was this an omen? The sun was out, and music filled the air from a nearby parade. The streets of London finally became Crystal's home. During the day, she begged. Rarely did she steal, even though the fruit and vegetables from the market stalls in Covent Gardens were an easy target. Fred had taught Crystal to target supermarkets and eating establishment waste bins where food was thrown away in abundance. Crystal estimated a supermarket's weekly disposal could feed a platoon for a day. The food was relatively wholesome. Even if the sell by dates were past, the merchandise was normally still within its use by date according to the stamp on the carton or packet.

Keep away from fresh meats and frozen products had been Fred's advice. Slowly rotting meat was never pleasant; the smell alone said leave it. Packets, tins and fruit with a removable skin were the ideal products to scavenge from the bins. Friday night was pizza night; leftover cheese and tomato or pepperoni pizza in flat packed boxes from the local take-away was always a welcome luxury.

Crystal no longer raided the doorsteps of the wealthy. She found that people were willing to give her money if she begged; her age probably had something to do with it. Nobody liked seeing a child on the street. In London, it was a common sight. Many children a lot younger than she had made the street their home. Glasgow had been very different. People were tighter with their money. In London, giving a few pence no doubt made the rich feel better. The small contribution cleared their conscience and allowed them to retire to their comfortable homes guilt free.

Initially, Crystal slept in shop doorways before building up the confidence to join one of the homeless groups. The worse times were the cold winter nights when there were fewer daylight hours, and the chilling winds blew from the North. These nights were frequently spent in the abandoned subways where the homeless lit fires to keep warm. There was a hierarchy in the homeless camp, just like in the squat. *You have to earn your place* had been Fred's words of advice. Crystal was not privileged to the full heat from the burning barrels. The strong hogged the heat; the weak moaned and groaned as they fought for their cardboard boxes. Against the walls and pillars lay stacked boxes reminiscent of a bookcase leant on its side. Boxes were kitted out with blankets, bubble wrap and cut-offs – anything to keep the cold from entering their body.

Crystal did alright for herself. After gaining the confidence of Wenlock, the unofficial leader of the camp, her time on the streets was more comfortable – she had earned her place. Crystal made Wenlock's life easy. Fit and athletic, she could easily scale the ten-foot wire fence into the compound to check out the Lowercroft supermarket bins. Lowercroft always threw a lot of food away. Sunday was the best day for scavenging; more food was thrown away on a Sunday than on any other day of the week, no doubt in preparation for the week ahead and the upcoming delivery. There were no Alsatians or Rottweilers guarding the compound, only an overweight security guard who was too lazy to take chase. Sometimes the guard opened the gate to stop the wire fence from sagging under Crystal's weight. If the fence started to show signs of being scaled, the owners would realise their security guard had lazily abused his position.

It always amused Crystal that the security guard turned his back on her for the duration of her visit. Was he embarrassed that a human being had to resort to scavenging? Was that why he turned away, or was the television too much of an allure that he could not avert his eyes from the screen?

Billy Barncroft enjoyed his job. It was easy, and it paid well. Watching television all night in a small room the owners called the 'security office' was no hardship. There were four cameras, without recording tapes, covering the whole of the yard. His job was to monitor the security screens. Watching a security image which never changed from one second to the next for eight hours was mind numbing. Wednesday night was his favourite TV night – non-stop comedies. His weekend visitor did not cause any problems, and she broke the monotony. Sunday was a rubbish night for television. Billy didn't like to watch her too closely, though, because it felt wrong watching a child searching through the bins. Why shouldn't the waste products help another to survive? When the weekly visits stopped, Billy wondered for many years what had happened to the red-headed child with her foul mouth and cheeky grin.

Crystal brought carrier bags of food back to the camp courtesy of Lowercroft. Wenlock would take a share of the food and in return she was given heat from the fires. If she brought smokey bacon crisps, a luxury Wenlock had a passion for, then she would have the benefit of the full heat from the fire – much to the disgust of Kate, Wenlock's woman.

Wenlock was a strong-headed individual with long, dry, braided hair. Surprisingly, his speech was articulate; he could tie people in knots with his words, a skill always worth watching. He took part in all the demonstrations, especially political demonstrations campaigning against the Government. Arrested more times than he could remember, Wenlock was always released without charge. The camp was strict and fairly ruled. In the camp, there was a strong community, all fighting for survival, and everyone was willing to protect each other if needed. The streets felt safe. There were some weirdos around who tried to prey on their vulnerability by offering money for a blow job or a quick grope in the back of a car. Some of the homeless obliged. Crystal often wondered if they ever contracted diseases from any of the sicker clients. She assumed so, but it was their decision. Rich men in their large oversized cars were the most persistent, offering very little financial award yet expecting a lot. Crystal kept away from them. She did not need to pleasure any man to survive – not yet.

The first time Crystal met Todd, he seemed different from the others. He asked for nothing. He placed ten pounds in her open hand as she sat begging at the mouth of Piccadilly Tube Station.

"What do you expect for this?" she had replied bluntly. Nobody gave that much money unless they wanted something.

Todd did not reply but continued to the tube station. Next day Todd dropped another ten-pound note into her hand, this time with a photograph; he still did not speak. Crystal watched him disappear down to the tube station before glancing at the photograph. Two figures stood in front of a house – one female with thick, dark hair; the other an older gentleman. Recognising neither, she placed the photograph into her back pocket. Next day the mystery man did not appear. The following day he appeared again.

"Do you want a coffee or something to eat?" he offered, signalling to the café over the road. Crystal shrugged her shoulders, so he placed another ten-pound note next to her and disappeared down the tube station.

"Who are the people in the photograph?" she asked next day.

"Coffee first, then I'll talk."

"Do I get food as well?"

"Ok, food as well."

As she tucked into her burger and chips, Todd watched her shovel the food into her mouth. "Is your name Crystal…Crystal Ceasar?"

"Who wants to know?"

"I've been sent to find you."

Crystal spat out a mouthful of chips. "What the…"

"Don't panic," he said thrusting his business card across the table. The words *Todd Bradshaw, Private Investigator* written in blue ink jumped out from the card. Situated in the top right corner of the card was a green eye with a pale blue outline that seemed to follow her around the room.

Following his uncle's advice, Todd had been a private eye for over twenty years. Well-known in the trade, he worked closely with the police, as well as the newspaper reporters when it suited him. Todd could do things that sometimes the authorities could not, due to their strict policies and procedures. He was a cheerful individual who had never married. His working hours were not conducive to having a relationship. He enjoyed his job, felt close to those he worked with, and had a bond with colleagues in the same profession. He required nothing else. What you never had, you will never miss was his motto.

"You don't have to shovel your food down that quick," he told Crystal. "It's not going anywhere."

"What do you mean?" she managed to spurt out with a mouthful of food. Turning the fork over had been a brilliant idea; more food on the surface at any one time.

"Why don't you try a serving spoon next time?" said Todd slightly irritated.

"Soz, mate. I haven't had burgers and chips for a long time."

"I am not your mate, Crystal, and if you are going to meet the person I want you to meet then you will have to learn some manners."

"What do you want?"

"Answer my question first. Is your name Crystal Ceasar?"

"Yeah, I'm Crystal," she wiped the ketchup from her chin onto the back of a slender hand and took another large bite from the sesame-seed bun. Todd tossed a paper napkin in her direction.

"You have sauce all over your face."

"Not made for baby's bums, this stuff," Crystal commented, but used the napkin.

Todd nodded in agreement. That was one way of saying the napkins were rough. Although she was coarse and rough around the edges, Todd still quite liked Crystal. He saw a child acting tough, pretending not to care, yet something deeper inside said give me a chance, and I'll show you.

"That photo you gave me," Crystal asked again. "Who are the two people?"

"Your grandfather and mother."

"Really?" Crystal fished out the photograph from her back pocket and stared at it again. "They don't look like me!" she muttered, shoving the photograph back into her pocket.

Crystal shifted uncomfortably in her chair. What did the private-eye want? A thin film of grime from vehicle pollution obscured the view out of the window. Inside was not much cleaner – a film of grease covered the window-sill.

"Who sent you to find me?" She stared out at a busy bus-stop over the road. Passengers were boarding and dismounting the steps of the double-decker. Old people were taking their time as they rummaged through their purses for change, or a travel pass. The nutter – it had to be the nutter. Who else would send a private-eye? Nobody else cared – what did he hope to achieve? Crystal squinted hard out of the window, but the grime made it impossible to see clearly. The nutter with the knife was over the road, back facing her, wearing a long mac with a briefcase in his hand. No, it couldn't be him. A briefcase was not part of his attire. The nutter carried nothing apart from a knife hidden beneath his coat.

"Your grandfather sent me," Todd answered her. Crystal heard the words, but still the thought of the nutter played on her mind. Was the nutter her grandfather? No, it couldn't be. He was too young to be a grandfather, and the photograph was of a different gentleman, an older gentleman. Crystal took another large bite of her burger and then turned her attention back to Todd.

"Tell me more," she requested.

Over the following few weeks, Todd continued to buy Crystal burgers and chips regularly. He spoke about her family, yet asked little about her. Crystal was happy. A decent hot meal without begging was always welcome. Crystal hoped one day to find her true parents. Now there was a chance she could meet her long lost family. Decision time. Could she trust the self-confessed private-eye – the man who bought her burgers and chips every day? Curiosity eventually got the better of Crystal, who succumbed and agreed to meet the man who said he was her grandfather; the man who sent Todd to find her. This was her way off the streets.

Massachusetts, USA

Massachusetts had many places to camp and really they didn't need a camper van. However the van gave them the security and the flexibility to travel where they wanted, when they wanted. Massachusetts was thick with forests and made a great place to camp, as long as they kept away from black bear territory. They spent their first evening in a local club with lots of country and western music. Damien and Angel danced the first few dances and then collapsed back into their seats with Laurel and Tim. Ice-cool Miller was on tap. Even though they were underage drinkers, nobody quizzed them, no doubt due to Tim's mature appearance.

"May I whisk your young lady to the dance floor?" asked Laurel. Angel was already on her feet.

"Of course," said Damien winking at Angel.

As soon as Laurel and Angel were out of earshot, Damien turned to Tim and asked, "Is there something going on with Laurel and Angel that I should know about?"

Tim's immediate response was no, but Damien was still unsure. Laurel always took Angel's side, which was beginning to make him feel like an outsider. He had seen how Laurel looked at her, and now his hands were tight around his girlfriend's waist. Her body was pulled close to Laurel's as they danced, and she didn't seem to mind.

"Remove those thoughts," said Tim, glancing over to Laurel and Angel. "It's your imagination. Sure, they became close when you were both in hospital. I just think Laurel is trying to make an effort for your sake. You should be happy they get on so well. Laurel is a flirt and always has been. You know he doesn't mean anything by it."

Tim hoped Damien could not see through his lies, as he too had started having similar thoughts. He had seen how Laurel stared at Angel in the hospital.

Laurel was handsome and charismatic, a seducer of women. They fell at his feet, spellbound, hypnotised by every word he spoke. If Angel was falling under Laurel's spell, Tim would not have been surprised.

"Anyway," said Tim, "how many women would give you their life?" Not that he believed the story. Pain he could accept; the body had many pressure points where pain could be relieved, but for Angel to bring Damien back to life was too surreal. The obvious explanation was Angel had massaged his heart, which kept it beating. It was just another form of cardiopulmonary resuscitation.

"Angel loves you. It's written all over her face. Don't mess it up," said Tim.

"I know," said Damien sulkily. "I'm being stupid."

"Anyway, how is the pain?" Tim asked, changing the subject.

"Not brilliant," came the reply. Tim could not understand why Damien did not let Angel help. After all, she was confident the episode in the hospital was a one off. Damien knew what Tim was thinking.

"It will kill her next time," muttered Damien. Tim did not reply for a few moments as he tried to find the right way to phrase his words without causing offence.

"If you meet Edward, you are not going to be much good if you are doubled over in pain," he said softly.

"If I meet Edward, the pain is the least of my worries," Damien admitted. "Tim, I'm petrified. I didn't want to come on this trip. If you had seen him when he looked at me – his eyes were soulless. He cut me so calmly, like I was a piece of meat. He is evil, pure evil. I know he will try to kill me next time, and this time he will succeed." Tim could see Damien was physically shaking as he spoke.

"Listen," said Tim. "Laurel and I will be with you for the next six weeks. I won't leave you alone; we can even go to the toilets together if it makes you feel better. Hopefully, we won't meet him. Who's to say he's even in America? If he is here then he will have me to contend with, and if we don't see him, Angel will meet her brother and we will all have a nice holiday."

Damien smiled, "Thanks, Tim. You're a mate. However, the toilet maybe going a little too far." They both laughed. Damien decided to retire back to the tent. His pain was starting to become unbearable. A good night's sleep and he hoped he would feel better. They signaled to Laurel and Angel that they were leaving. The signal came back, *another fifteen minutes and we will join you.*

A little later that evening, Angel crawled into the tent. Damien lay on his side. He slowly rolled onto his back and kissed her tenderly. "Did you have a good night?" he whispered.

Ignoring his question Angel returned the kiss. "Please, Damien, let me take your pain."

"I'm fine," was the response. Angel knew he was lying. For the last three days he had been ill, no matter how hard he tried to hide it. She knew him too well. His personality always changed when he tried to hide his pain.

"I will take it anyway," whispered Angel.

"No, it could kill you."

"It will not kill me. I know where I went wrong last time. Please, Damien."

"No."

"I feel strong."

"I said no."

"You are no good to me or to anybody else. What happens if we meet...," she paused a moment before continuing, "thugs? You will stand no chance against them."

"No," said Damien firmly.

"In which case, I am sorry, but I am going to take your pain anyway. Maybe it is a violation, but I will not see you in pain and struggling when I can help."

With these words, she lifted his top. He wanted to stop her, but to stop her, he would have to hurt her. Her hand went straight to the pain and with only a slight massage, his body went into a spasm. He arched his back and let out a loud cry of passion. A giggle started in the other tent.

"It's not what you think," shouted Damien.

"Not yet," whispered Angel. Laughter started again.

"A little too loud, Angel," laughed Damien. Moving his body on top of her that night, they had a sexual experience that neither of them could have dreamed of. It was soft and tender. Their bodies entwined as they quietly and slowly made love.

The gentle rumble from Tim's snoring kept Laurel awake. Tonight he had messed up. Why had he made a pass at Angel? Thankfully, she had laughed it off and blamed the drink, but he had only had two beers, and she knew this as well. He had gone to kiss her. She had realised and instantly turned her head, which meant he had only brushed the side of her mouth and cheek with his lips. How could he have been so stupid? What if Angel told Damien! He didn't want to upset Damien. After all, Damien deserved some happiness, especially after the last three years of hell he had been through. The last six months had given Damien a new lease on life, and Laurel nearly took that away tonight. He didn't want to hurt Damien. After all, he was his best mate. As he lay in his tent, all he could think about was Angel – those bewitching eyes, and behind those eyes an uncertainty, an unpredictability that drew him to her. Could Damien also see this: was that what he loved about her? The only sensible option was to keep his distance from Angel, or else he may do something stupid that he would later regret. He didn't want to hurt his mate; nonetheless, Angel deserved better.

Laurel snuggled down into his sleeping bag, not because he was cold, but because he hoped it would help him to forget this unforgiveable attraction. He would keep his distance, and hopefully Angel would forget the attempted kiss. Laurel had not anticipated how difficult it would be to keep his distance from Angel. Laurel realised he would end up trying again. He couldn't help himself. So when Angel started looking for her brother, Warren, Laurel was relieved they only saw each other late evening which meant he could fight his urge to make another move. The lads spent the days swimming and fishing. When early evening came, Angel spent a couple of hours alone with Damien. Normally they sat in a small sandy spot next to the slow flowing river sharing what they had done during the day.

Angel habitually sat with her back to Damien, allowing him to wrap his arms tightly around her body and nuzzle into her neck; kissing it when he felt the urge. "I think he is watching us again."

"Who?" asked Angel.

"Laurel, of course. This is the third time this week."

"Maybe he's lonely."

"Shall we give him something to watch?"

"What are you thinking?"

"A kiss and cuddle, nothing else. Play along with me I'll show you." He gently rolled her over onto her back. Moving his body gently onto hers, he kissed her.

"Are you ready?"

"Ready," he moved his hand down her side.

"Oh Angel," he said loudly. "What are you doing to me?"

She looked into his eyes with amusement. She could see a mischievous sparkle in them that she loved so much.

"Lower, lower, oh yes, give it to me, babe," Damien moaned, and she started to giggle. A finger immediately went to her lips.

"Can I have a go?" Angel asked.

"Be my guest."

"Oh yes, yes, yes, harder, harder, you bad boy," she said in mock passion, and they both collapsed into a fit of giggles.

"Bad boy!" Damien cried.

"I couldn't think of anything else."

"Enjoy the show," Damien shouted over to Laurel. There was no answer. "He's gone," laughed Damien. "Our very own peeping Tom." It was a perfect holiday for the small group of friends, full of jokes and laughter; however, this changed when Damien met Edward again.

Damien was standing in front of an open green area with his back against a large pine tree. The warmth of the sun was beating down on his shoulders. Young children were playing in the distance, running around squealing in delight. A mother pushed a double buggy over the rough track that had formed through years of use. Two dogs chased a ball that their owner threw over and over again across the large expanse of grass, always tumbling over when they reached their goal. Damien smiled. The owner would tire before the dogs. Tim was purchasing coffee from a nearby kiosk as Damien stood waiting. He closed his eyes for a second and lifted his face to the sun to catch the warmth of its rays. The smell of stale tobacco drifted up his nostrils. Damien swung around. A couple of feet from him stood Edward.

"Good afternoon, boy," hissed Edward. "I see Angel has worked her magic."

Oh, how Damien hated being called 'boy.' It always reminded him of a naughty child. "No chloroform today?" asked Damien as calmly as he could manage. He was surprised at his own audacity. Damien took a small step sideways as Edward reached into his pocket and produced a small bottle.

"I don't go anywhere without it. Anyway, down to business. Where's my Angel?"

"She is not your Angel. She is my Angel," answered Damien firmly. "You were the one that killed her, remember?"

Edward leaned forward until he was only a foot away from Damien's face; the stench of tobacco was overwhelming, making Damien feel physically sick.

"Don't lie to me, boy. You've got guts, I'll give you that. Maybe we should have a closer look at those guts of yours." He drew an imaginary horizontal line across Damien's stomach as though he was cutting it open with an invisible knife. Damien's legs felt like jelly. Ten seconds for a 100 m sprint may have been possible if his legs could have moved – *Look out, Usain Bolt; here I come,* he thought giddily. Instead, paralysed by fear, he found himself having a surreal conversation with a mad man.

Edward squeezed the butt of his cigar between finger and thumb, extinguishing the remaining life from the object. Damien hoped this wasn't an omen. Edward tossed the butt his way. It bounced off his shirt and fell to the ground. His legs had frozen, and it felt like his body was sunk deep into the ground. He tried to look like he was bravely holding his position and not show this mentally insane man any weakness. His bladder was close to bursting. *Please don't pee yourself!* thought Damien. *Not in front of this lunatic.* Where the hell were the police? His legs started shaking. Suddenly, he could stand no longer, and he fell to the ground heaving.

By the time Tim had arrived with the two Styrofoam cups of coffee, Edward had gone. Damien was still shaking from his encounter. He was glad of the bitter coffee Tim bought for him. It removed the foul taste left in his mouth. He relayed the event to Tim, missing none of the gruesome details. The same information was communicated to his father, who balled out his American colleagues who were supposed to be keeping an eye on his son and friends. Later that evening, Damien informed Angel and Laurel. Angel listened without commenting. It took another week before Edward's name cropped up again.

*****

Alone with Angel Laurel was once again trying to make her see sense.

"How can you say that, Laurel? Damien is supposed to be your best friend!" hissed Angel.

"Damien would probably agree with me. He's a drifter with no career prospects; he'll be a burden to you. His illness will eventually kill him, and if it doesn't, you'll end up nursing him for the rest of his life. Get out now, Angel, whilst you can, while you still have a life," urged Laurel.

Angel looked amazed. "Damien is not a burden. He is funny, friendly and loving, and I am lucky to be with him."

"Don't be a fool. I am here for you, and I am fit and healthy. I am telling you he will be a burden," muttered Laurel.

"Who's a burden?" asked Damien catching the last part of the conversation. Angel glared at Laurel, her eyes icy cold.

"Oh nobody. We were just discussing who are the biggest burden, cats or dogs," Angel said, grabbing Damien's hand to make a point.

"Oh, that's easy," said Damien. "It has to be dogs."

"Or sick people," piped up Laurel. Angel glared at him again. "Think about it, Angel. You don't have to give me your answer yet."

Angel couldn't believe how Laurel could stab his mate in the back. He was blatantly trying to destroy Damien's happiness. It was a selfish act. He was so self-centred, so absorbed in himself, a trait she had not noticed before. In the hospital, she had looked forward to Laurel's visits, but now she saw the real Laurel. She had thought no more of the attempted kiss, but now she realised there was more to his actions. It wasn't just an innocent act. When Edward came back onto the scene, Laurel's advances were soon forgotten.

The Meeting

The smell of freshly cooked sausages wafted through the air. Fat spat on the fire, and sparks danced in the air. Tim had taken the role of Chief Cook for most of their holiday. His culinary skills did not stretch much further than sausages and burgers, but nobody minded. Sitting around an open fire as it crackled in front of them, conversation flowed as easily as the beer. Common sense prevailed, and Damien still kept to the soft drinks. They were happy chatting about anything and everything.

"You're quieter than normal," whispered Damien to Angel.

"Edward wants to meet me," she whispered back. They all stopped in mid-conversation and stared at her in silence for a few seconds, digesting what she had just said.

"How do you know?" asked Laurel.

She sheepishly passed him the hand-written note written on standard lined notepaper:

Angel,

We need to talk and clear the air. Meet me at Grogna Supermart off Grimblay Straight 9.00am on Friday. Come alone, as Warren wants to see his big sister.

Edward

"When did you get this?" asked Damien, snatching the note from Laurel's hand.

"Karaoke night, a waitress passed it to me. I thought I saw Edward at the back of the room. By the time I had made my way over he had gone."

"Two nights ago! We could all be dead by now because of you."

"You saw him, too," Angel replied.

"Yes, and we moved the campervan immediately, or have you conveniently forgotten that? Stollen bar is less than half a mile away. We could all be dead. He could have killed us while we slept," he repeated again.

"Don't be silly," was Angel's quick response.

"Why didn't you say anything earlier?"

"I knew how you would react. I have decided to meet him. I think I can talk to him. He will listen. I know he will," she hesitantly muttered.

"You can't meet him, Angel. He is dangerous! You heard what he said to me," snapped Damien.

"With the greatest respect, Damien, that's what he said to you, not me," she replied.

He ignored her comment and responded by pointing out that there was no Grogna Supermarket or Grimblay Straight.

Angel smiled. "It's code; we used to send messages to each other in code. That's why he gave me a couple of days to crack it. This one is really easy. It says..." but Damien had already interrupted before she had time to finish. A move he would later regret.

"This is not some stupid game," he shouted. Angel was stunned. She had never seen him so angry. Rarely did he raise his voice. Even though Damien was shocked by her attitude, he realised shouting was not the answer and switched to a softer tone.

"You can't seriously be considering meeting him. He is a nutter."

"I have to, Damien."

"I have never begged for anything before, but, Angel, I am begging you, please don't go. He's dangerous."

She just stood and shook her head. "I'm going."

"Then let me go with you."

"No," was the blunt reply. "You know he will kill you; he has already threatened you." She had now admitted for the first time Edward was dangerous, yet she would still not back down.

"He will manipulate you, Angel, just like he did before when you spouted all that crap in the hospital."

"I am not stupid," she snapped.

"Then stop acting stupid," came the curt reply. "Why can't we have a normal relationship like normal people? Why does everything have to be so complicated?" Damien wished he hadn't said that. He knew what was coming next.

"But I am not normal; I have never been normal, and I never will be normal. If you want normal then maybe you should have stayed with Beth. Maybe I am not the one for you," she said calmly.

"For goodness sake, Angel, I don't want Beth. I have never wanted Beth! I don't fancy her."

Laurel cleared his throat.

"What now, Laurel?" Damien sighed as he saw Laurel pull a face. "Ok, I did once fancy Beth. I was probably twelve at the time, maybe thirteen. She was the first girl at school to develop physically into a woman; every lad fancied her." He looked towards Laurel, who nodded his head in agreement. "I did go on a date with Beth. I never told you because there was nothing to tell.

I was embarrassed, but I'll tell you now if it stops you thinking such stupid thoughts and maybe I can prove for once, and for all, I want you."

Angel didn't move; she sat quietly waiting for the story she had wanted to hear for a long time.

"I went on one date with Beth. I took her to Pepitos, the Italian restaurant in town." This was stupid, Damien thought. Why should he have to justify his actions? He glanced towards Angel, who was waiting for him to continue. From the corner of his eye he could see Laurel and Tim had adjusted their positions so they could hear the full story. A story he had told nobody.

"Can we have some privacy, guys?" Tim got up to go, but Laurel grabbed his arm and pulled him back down.

"No, I want to hear this," Laurel stated.

"You can be a right prat sometimes, Laurel. Ok, she, I mean, Beth and I went on a date," Damien began.

"We know that," butted in Laurel.

"Ok, there was no chemistry between us, yet that didn't stop her, I mean, Beth, from making moves towards me, saying she was up for it if I was."

"Wow," gasped Laurel. "You lucky bugger! Sorry, Angel."

"Ssh, Laurel, please."

"I told her I didn't want to, and could we just talk?" Damien said, remembering that awkward night.

"What, talk! I seriously need to talk to you, mate," gasped Laurel.

"Please, Laurel," he paused, waiting for another interruption – there was none. "Beth asked me what I wanted to talk about, and I said it was up to her. She said Angel; I spent the rest of the evening talking about you, Angel." He gave her hand a quick squeeze.

"I argued with Beth for the rest of the evening that you were no killer; that you hadn't killed Stacey. I then walked her back to her accommodation at around 9:00 p.m."

"What about Beth's story?" asked Laurel. "She said you slept with her and..."

"I know what she said, and none of it's true. Angel, you know me. You know I'm telling the truth. You know how I felt, and still sometimes feel about my body. I can't sleep, and I don't want to sleep, with other females. It was that night I realised I wanted more than just your friendship. I wanted you."

Angel was looking relieved. The tension in her body had evaporated.

"What did you think happened?" Damien asked.

She shrugged her shoulders. "I don't know. I always felt like second choice. You couldn't have Beth, so you chose me instead."

"Did I ever make you feel like you were second choice?" Damien asked with concern apparent in his voice.

Angel shook her head. "No, I don't know why I thought that. Tara said...." Her voice trailed off. "I guess I was having insecure thoughts like a normal person would."

Damien smiled. "I can't believe you have been listening to gossip. That's not like you. No more green-eyed monster."

"No more."

"Will you stay here with me and forget this nonsense with Edward? I will phone the police and have him arrested or at least a restraining order issued, so he can't come anywhere near us. I'll also report he has kidnapped your brother."

Angel raised her eyes to meet his. "I am sorry, Damien. I can't. I know you don't understand, but I need to go."

There was an uncomfortable silence. She was right; he didn't understand. He looked into her eyes. There was no coldness, only affection. Was his next move stupid? Would she laugh in his face? He would do anything to keep her with him. He still had one card left up his sleeve. The ace of spades or the joker – he was soon to find out. He didn't think it would work, but anything was worth a try. Going down on one knee, he grabbed her hand, "Marry me, and I will give you a normal and happy life away from all this madness. I love you too much to lose you."

Laurel nearly choked on his can of Bud Light. "Come on, mate! This is going too far."

"Shut up, Laurel." Damien was trying everything. Maybe it was not the most romantic proposal, but Laurel still couldn't believe what his mate had just done. Angel stared into his eyes – Damien was deadly serious. Joining him on her knees, she kept hold of his hands before throwing her arms around his neck and hugging him.

"You know I can't," she whispered. "I would never forgive myself if my brother died because I was too concerned with my own happiness, and you would never live with yourself if that happened."

"Please, Angel, don't go," he pleaded.

"I have to, Damien. What about Warren? He needs me. I don't want to lose another brother. You would do the same for your brother."

"But you don't even know your brother." He could have kicked himself as soon as he said it. He sounded so heartless, and he knew he had touched a raw nerve. She pulled away from him.

"Which is why I am going," she answered sternly.

That night the arguments came thick and fast. Words were said that shouldn't have been said. The final straw came when Damien accused Angel of never loving him. She had never said the words *I love you*. He accused her of being in partnership with Edward and described her as being selfish and a heartless killer. He even went as far as saying that he wished he had never met her. Arguing was useless. There was nothing left to say. Deep down, he prayed the police would protect her; although he wasn't confident in their ability. After all, he had seen no sign of them in the last four weeks, and twice now Edward had been in close vicinity to his friends and him.

They argued well into the early hours. Angel was hurt. Damien was right. She had never said she loved him, but she did love him. She started falling in love with him the first time they had met at the lake. Her love for him had grown, and she hated being away from him. He had hurt her so much when he went on a date with Beth. She had prayed that it would not work out, and not because she was religious. She was smitten by him, and she didn't know what else to do. She didn't tell him all this. If she did, then she wouldn't leave him to meet Edward, and she needed to protect her brother. Angel knew this was something she had to do; it was her destiny. It was what her mother had wanted. *Selfish* was a cruel word to use and so uncalled for; she had nearly died for Damien.

Tim and Laurel retired to their tent around midnight, finally giving their friends some privacy. The tiny gas lamp burned brightly in their two-man tent. Neither felt like sleeping. They could hear Damien and Angel arguing into the early hours. They figured Damien would lose this battle as Angel's mind was already made up. When Damien walked out of the camp, Laurel grabbed his denim jacket and joined his mate. It was going to be a long night. Medication forgotten, Damien headed to the nearest bar. It wasn't one of his wisest moves, mixing medication and alcohol; fortunately, it had no adverse effects. Damien just needed to get away from Angel to drown his sorrows. Tim joined Angel at the campfire. It felt wrong leaving her alone. She was upset, and just like Damien, probably needed somebody to talk to. He wasn't sure who had got the short straw tonight – Laurel or himself.

"Damien didn't mean what he said," said Tim.

"I know, but it still hurts. Do you think I am wrong to meet Edward?"

"It is not my place to judge your decision, but as an outsider, yes I think you are wrong."

Angel fell silence, "Tim, if I tell you something, will you promise never to tell Damien? Maybe you could talk to him without telling him what I am about to tell you."

"I don't know, Angel. I don't want to get involved and take sides. Damien is my mate."

"Please, Tim." There was another silence. "Edward is my father."

Tim looked at her. "Did you say your father?"

"Yes, that's why I have to go, but I can't tell Damien that. How can I tell him my father tried to kill him? He wouldn't understand. I don't even understand. He'll think I am a 'nutter' from bad blood."

Tim smiled; Angel had a strange way of phrasing things. "Wow, that's serious. It makes more sense now. Damien will understand if you tell him."

"Really!"

Tim bit his lip. "Maybe not. I don't know. I won't tell Damien, but you should seriously consider telling him yourself. He will find out one day." They continued talking for another hour, mulling over if she should or should not have told Damien. Tim had never spent much time alone with Angel until tonight, and for the first time he could see why Damien loved her.

At five in the morning, Angel left the camp. She had packed a few personal items and on Tim's recommendation slipped Damien's mobile phone into the back pocket of her jeans. "Phone if you need assistance," was Tim's only piece of advice, although she had been adamant help would not be required. Damien had his back to her, still sulking from the night before, pretending to be asleep. Angel was not sure what time he returned, but it was very late. He could have chosen to sleep in the campervan, so she was thankful he had at least chosen to sleep in their tent. Angel could smell the booze on him, which was unusual as he never drunk much. He was stubborn. She only intended to go for a day, possibly two. The argument was childish and hurtful. He would never agree to her decision, and deep down she could see Damien's argument.

"I am sorry. It's my destiny," she whispered to herself.

Damien had no intention of turning over. He didn't want to say goodbye, as goodbye always sounded so permanent. Running her fingers through his hair, she gently kissed his head, inhaling deeply to capture the scent of his shampoo. Sometimes silly things like the smell of apple blossom made life feel so simple. She pulled on her boots, unzipped the flap of the tent, took a deep breath and stepped into the cool, fresh morning air. Damien nearly called out, but he didn't. He couldn't.

Laurel and Tim heard the zip on the tent. Neither had slept much.

"I think she is making a big mistake," said Tim, and with those words, turned over, each lad deep in his own thoughts.

Getting Back on Track

Over the next few days, Damien waited for Angel to return. The anger had subsided; he was now concerned. All she had originally asked for was one or two days. Had he scared her off with all the venom he had spouted? Did she have any intention of returning? Was she safe? Damien wished he had stopped her from going. Then again, how could he have stopped her without physically restraining her? No matter how much he disagreed with Angel's decision, he would never hurt her physically. He had tried so hard to work out where Grogna Supermart was; he had failed miserably, and it was now time to leave.

"Give me the keys, Damien."

"Please, Laurel. Five more minutes! That is all I ask."

"She's not coming back."

"She'll be back."

"Have you tried her mobile again?" piped in Tim.

"Of course, I have been trying it every fifteen minutes. It's still turned off."

"Give him five more minutes, Laurel."

"We'll miss our flight if we're late!"

"Then you are going to have to drive a little faster to the airport."

Laurel stuck out his bottom lip, making it clear he was sulking. Knowing he was beaten, he grunted and climbed back into the driver's seat of the camper van to wait out the five minutes.

Angel didn't make the flight back to England. Damien pleaded for his friends to wait as long as they could. He had been adamant they could not move the camper until the last minute, and when they arrived at the airport, he had paced up and down the airport lounge like a man obsessed.

"He will kill her! I know he will. He is evil. Her brother is dead, and she's probably in a ditch somewhere. Why did I let her go? I could have stopped her! One to two days was how long she said she needed. It's now five days." His ramblings continued until they boarded their flight.

Tim felt awkward. Why had Angel told him her secret? What was he supposed to do with the information? What was he supposed to say to Damien?

"Maybe she had her reasons, Damien," was the best he could manage.

"What did she say to you, Tim?" Damien asked, feeling there was more. "I know you spoke to her that night."

"Nothing, mate. Honestly. Think about it. Angel lived with Edward for many years. He didn't hurt her then, so why would he hurt her now?" Tim suggested, but he knew his argument was falling on deaf ears.

"Did I scare her away, Tim? I know I was awful to her."

Tim shook his head. "Stop punishing yourself, mate. She knew you were upset. When we spoke, she had every intention of coming back." Damien continued to pace the lounge until he heard the final call. His mates were sure he would not get onto the plane, but he did.

*****

Nobody heard from Angel. This was her first promise she had broken. Life continued for the three lads. Tim and Laurel started University, and Damien moved back home with his parents. Six months had passed since their trip to America. With Damien's pain intensifying and his previous encounter with Edward, he was finding it harder to leave the comfort and protection of his parents' home. His mother dragged him shopping at least once a week, and on occasion, when forced, he had dinner with his parents' friends.

It had come as a complete shock to both his parents when Damien announced he was going away for the weekend to see Laurel and Tim. Damien realised he needed to get out and re-build his life, and meeting up with old friends would certainly help. They could laugh and reminisce, discuss school friends, rugby league and University life. Maybe he too would consider applying to university.

*****

"Hiya, mate," shouted Laurel, bringing his hand firmly down on Damien's back. Laurel pulled away quickly, waiting for Damien to react like he used to. There was no reaction. "Did that hurt?"

"Like hell."

"Don't you want to bawl at me?"

Damien shook his head. "No, I'm just glad to see you."

"That makes two of us. Come on, mate. I have a great weekend planned, and one of the highlights is going to Quinet, our University club. The women are hot there, mate. You'll see tonight."

Quinet was a cheap venue aimed at the student market. Based close to the University campus, nobody would guess it was a nightclub from the outside. Graffiti and posters covered the exterior walls. There were no windows, only four faded-red double doors along the East wall. The students did not seem to mind that the venue wasn't decked out with the latest technology. They played decent music and served cheap booze. It had been good for Damien to get out again and experience a young man's lifestyle. Thankfully, his pain had subsided in the last few days. The pain in his abdomen was still bubbling under the surface of his flesh, but today it was bearable – just a dull pain, not the piercing pain he was prone to.

An unspoken decision had been made between Laurel and Tim not to mention Angel in their conversation. Instead, the decision had been made to have a lot of fun and introduce Damien to other women. They realised if Damien started to date again, maybe he could forget her.

"Where's Damien?" Tim asked.

Laurel pointed upstairs and laughed. "Getting ready for tonight. Call me Cupid, but I have an idea."

"Don't push him too hard, Laurel," said Tim just as Damien descended the stairs.

Laurel placed his arm around Damien's shoulder. "Let me give you some advice. Tonight, go with the flow. The girls are going to be all over you, especially when they know you are my out-of-town mate." Tim shook his head; Laurel was once again in charge.

Damien smiled, "I'll take your word for that." Looking over to Tim, he nodded as if to say, *Here we go again*.

*****

Damien was introduced to a young blonde Business Studies student – Sophia. In Laurel's opinion, she was a great laugh and wore the smallest, tightest denim shorts known to mankind, which had caused Tim and Damien to explode with laughter. When Damien met her, he knew what Laurel meant. Damien had got on well with Sophia especially after he had relaxed. It was surprising how a couple of beers can help, although the idea of dating still felt alien, the whole concept scary. He kept hearing Laurel's words, *go with the flow,* but it was hard. He danced a few numbers and drowned a few drinks. The medication caused him to react strongly to the drink. Soon he was woozy, and his head spun. Laurel's words stuck in his mind: *have fun, let your hair down.* Kissing Sophia gently on the lips, he tried to block out all the noise around him.

Pretending it was Angel that he was kissing was wrong and surely unfair on Sophia. If this was the only way to kiss another woman, what choice did he have? As soon as their lips touched, he realised he had made a mistake. There was no emotion, no passion. He felt awkward, almost embarrassed. His world felt as though it was falling down around him. The smell of smoke clung deep in his nasal passage. His head was spinning, and he felt physically sick. Damien quickly excused himself, leaving Sophia sitting on the thread-bare sofa talking to her mate. He went to find Laurel, who was cuddled up with a couple of females on a nearby sofa. Tim was up on the dance floor, making the mandatory fool of himself. *Things never change,* thought Damien.

"Laurel, can I have the keys to the room?"

"Sure. Are you ok?" Laurel asked with little sincerity. "I'll come back with you unless you are taking Sophia back to the room."

"No, I'm just tired."

"If you don't like Sophia, there is always Caroline. She has a tattoo on..."

"No, honest, mate. I'm just tired," Damien replied, trying to muster a smile.

*****

Back in Laurel's room, Damien slid off the bed onto the floor and placed his head in his hands. Why couldn't he get Angel out of his head? He looked down at his wrist, but the friendship bracelet made of green, orange and white thread was long gone. Damien had been heart-broken when he realised he had lost the bracelet; it had disappeared into the abyss of all missing objects.

Unzipping a duffel bag which held his clothes for the weekend, Damien sighed. At the bottom of the bag was a small white top with the words *if pigs could fly* written across the front. The word *pigs* was emphasized with a visual representation of three pink pigs flying. A gold thread ran through the wings of the pigs linking them together. This was the last t-shirt Damien had seen Angel wear. Holding the t-shirt close to his face, he inhaled. The smell of perfume was beginning to fade. He may not be able to see her, but he could almost picture her there with him. Screwing up the t-shirt, he cried into it. Where was she?

The Call

Chief Inspector Harrington sat looking over the city of London from his office window in Whitehall Place. It was a fine day; white feathery clouds drifted slowly across the pale blue sky. The last few months had been fairly quiet. No major disturbances had taken place, and for the first time in many months he was relaxed. The phone had been fairly quiet all day, but its shrill high-pitched tone echoed around his office, breaking the silence. If he had known where the instruction manual was, he would have changed the annoying ringtone a long time ago. He let the phone ring five times, a custom he always followed before picking it up. After all, he didn't want his staff to think he wasn't busy.

A woman's voice was on the other line. He assumed Inspector Strangeway, as she often took the calls. He smiled, "Yes, inspector." The sound of authority in his voice always impressed. The Inspector was fairly small, yet highly intelligent, seeing things other police personnel would often overlook. Strangeway had a peculiarity not only in looks but also in stature. She lopped from side to side as she moved around the office, shoes squeaking on the wooden floor. A smirk replaced a smile, which no doubt annoyed many of the police staff. She was a hard worker, probably one of the hardest workers on his police force. He had to admit she was one of his favourite officers, a soft spot he could never vocalise. Ever since her wildcard idea which had saved his son, he had treated her differently. That had been over six months ago, but her lack of success in finding Edward and the lack of clues left at the crime scene had disappointed him. Strangeway had found nothing new to go on. Edward had disappeared into thin air, or to America according to his son. Even the information about the map clues had not helped track him down.

"I have a call for you, sir," said the woman's voice. "It is collect from America. Somebody called Angelica. Do you want to take it or should I get rid of it?" Harrington pondered. The only Angelica he knew was his son's ex-girlfriend; whom Harrington believed was Edward's accomplice. He pondered for a while–Angelica could be the key to the case. She may even have information for him, and he wasn't busy.

"Accept the call, Inspector." There was a clicking and then a bleep as the call came through.

A softly spoken, distressed female voice was on the end of the line. "Is that Inspector Harrington?"

"It is, young lady, and whom do I have the pleasure of speaking to?"

"Angel, I mean Angelica Wellingstone." He was right. It was the young lady who had screwed up his son. He was tempted to put the phone down, although that would be unprofessional. "How can I help you?" he asked, but the tone in his voice had changed. It now sounded abrupt, much sterner.

"Sir, we need your help. We are scared they are going to kill us."

"Who is going to kill you, Angelica?"

"Samuel and Edward," came the reply. There was another long pause. Was this a stupid kid's prank? She did sound distressed, but she could also be working alongside Edward. Could he afford to ignore this lead? It could be the breakthrough he had been waiting for.

"Talk to me, Angelica. You have my attention. Who is with you and why do you think they are going to kill you?" he also wanted to ask who Samuel was, but that could wait.

The Chief Inspector sounded like Damien, and the more Angel thought about this, the more the tears welled up inside.

"How is Damien?" she blurted out. Pact broken. She had vowed not to ask the Inspector about his son and lose control of her emotions – too late, she needed to know.

"He's ok," was the rather curt reply. He wanted to add, *And who do you think you are, screwing up my lad? He doesn't just have to deal with physical pain; he now has to deal with emotional pain.*

Angel was getting more agitated as the call went on. Mentioning Damien had been a mistake. The disapproval was evident in the Inspector's voice.

"They have taken my passport and everything I own. We can't get home. They will be looking for us now; I know they will kill us." Tears started to stream from her eyes. All composure had vanished. Angel had promised herself she would not break down on the telephone. Getting Warren back to the UK where she could try and sort the mess out was her only goal.

Suddenly there was a loud scream.

"What the hell was that?" shouted the Chief Inspector.

"I'm sorry. Warren grabbed my hand. He forgot I am in pain. I think my hand is broken. Oh, please help us, Inspector. I don't know who else to turn to."

"Who is Warren, Angelica?"

"My brother," she sobbed.

"Tell Damien I'm sorry," she whispered. What a dilemma. What should he do? Should he trust Damien's ex-girlfriend? Deliberating for a few moments, he realised he had to make an immediate decision. He had many close friends in the American police force. If it was a wild goose chase, he could visit some colleagues over the ocean; not much else was happening where he was now.

"Angelica, I want you to stay where you are. I am sending an unmarked police car to pick you up. They will show you their id, and take you to the nearest police station. Tonight you will stay at the police station, and tomorrow I will fly out to speak to you. Together we will decide what is best. Do not speak to anybody, not even the police. Tell them your name, and nothing else, do you hear me? Don't mess me around, young lady."

"I won't sir and thank you."

Decision made; he wasn't sure if it was the right decision, but he would soon find out.

A call from a phone box was always easy to trace. He would phone his counterpart in the US in an hour to see if they had picked Angelica up, then he would arrange the flight. The call was received within half an hour: a young man and a distressed woman had been collected from the location he had given.

Today was going to be a day of dilemmas. Should he tell his son that he had spoken to Angelica and that he was flying out to America to see her? His wife would disapprove and say in her broad Yorkshire accent,

"Leave her to rot. She has been nothing but trouble for our Damien." The Chief Inspector smiled. His wife was so grammatically correct, spoke the Queen's English, but when annoyed, her Yorkshire accent always became prominent. The Chief Inspector sighed. He still had to decide what to do. Surely Damien was old enough to make his own decisions. Maybe it would help him to move on with his life, give the lad closure. There was also the possibility his son may pick up where he had left off with Angel. Brian had said he had never seen two people so much in love. Surely bringing that happiness back to his son was worth the risk. After all, the lad was not moving on with his life. It was as though he was still going through a period of mourning.

The Chief Inspector sighed again. He had not been a hands-on father; his career had taken all of his time and energy. As his sons, Damien and Neil, were growing up, he had been working his way up in the police force. His sons never went without – he fed and clothed them – but he never felt part of his own family. The lads always turned to his wife for advice and comfort. They shared jokes which he never felt part of. If there had been one thing in his life he would have changed, it was the amount of time he had spent with his sons. He always felt he had missed out on them growing up. One minute they were in nappies, and the next they were grown men. If he could help Damien in some small way which wasn't money related, he could give something back to his son that maybe nobody else could, and help fill that gap in his own life.

*****

"Well, son, you only have one hour to decide. I leave tonight. I have a spare ticket if you want it." Damien removed his headphones completely and turned to face his father.

"Are you sure it was Angel? Why did she phone you? What did she say? Did she ask after me?" He had so many questions, but there was not enough time for any answers.

"Come with me, and I'll fill you in on the way. Once we get there, if you want to see her you can. If not, it will at least get you out of this house." Damien didn't need much time to decide. He was packed and downstairs within ten minutes and on the plane within three hours. He had packed shirt and tie as his dad had instructed and enough clothes for five days.

*****

"How long has she been like that?" Chief Inspector Harrington asked his American counterpart, Captain Henley.

"Just over two hours. When we heard you had landed, we moved her and the young lad to the interview room. We expected you earlier." They had stopped off at the hotel to freshen up on the way to the station. After all, eight hours was a long flight.

Ignoring the obvious dig, Chief Inspector Harrington continued, "Have they eaten or had anything to drink?"

"Girl refused; the lad has had a Coke," came the reply. It was a sorry sight through the one-way glass. Angel had her head resting on her arms on the table. Thick dark raven hair had fallen over her face, hiding her dark bewitching eyes and slender arms. Warren sat close, his hand rested on Angel's arm. She was obviously crying, and according to his counterpart had been for the last few hours.

"Maybe she needs to relieve all the emotions and pressures that have been building-up inside for so long," said the Chief Inspector.

"Are you going to tell me what is going on?" asked Henley.

"Patience, old chap, patience." They had known each other for nearly twenty years and often played these games with each other.

"Before you go into the interview room, you may want to take a look at this." Henley placed his hands into thin latex gloves before pulling a small white t-shirt out of a plastic bag. As he unfolded a blood stained t-shirt, a knife caked in dry blood was revealed.

"Do we know whose blood it is?"

Henley nodded. "There was a killing in Central Park a couple of weeks ago. We found a mutilated body of a young girl. She had been strangled by her dog's lead, and then stabbed. The dog is still missing. Her neighbour said it was a black terrier, not that the dog has any significance to the murder. We have been able to match the blood samples, and the wounds are consistent with the blade of this knife. Looks like Edward's work!"

"Isn't it unusual for Edward to strangle his victim first?" The Detective Inspector asked rhetorically.

"That's what we thought; however, the rest of the killing follows the same pattern – a straight stab wound followed by a second knife wound where the blade is twisted. Edward always makes sure the victim won't survive."

"Was the body displayed?"

"No, we assumed he may have been disturbed. It's more public than he normally opts for."

"Where did you find the knife?"

"Your young lady had it hidden in a small plastic carrier bag with a few other clothes and personal possessions."

"Have you asked her about it?"

"No, I thought I would leave that to you."

"It's definitely consistent with one of Edward's knives; it has a serrated blade and carved handle."

"Something else you need to be aware of. It has Angelica's fingerprints on the handle."

Damien sat down. "It can't have."

Both the Captain and the Chief Inspector looked across to where he sat. The Chief Inspector had forgotten his son was with them in the small room.

"Sorry, son, it does," said the Captain.

"Can I have a couple of your men in case we need to act fast?"

A look of excitement crossed Henley's face. "It's Edward, isn't it? You're close to finding him, aren't you, and those two kids in there are going to help you?"

"Oh yes, with no thanks to your guys. How could you lose him? A trained chimp could have followed him!" The Chief Inspector gave his friend grief, although he knew Edward disappeared like fog.

Henley ignored the dig. "Don't smash up my car this time, and let me know what you are up to," was the only response as he left the room. Harrington could see he had touched a nerve. Turning his attention back to Damien, he grinned.

"He's a decent chap, and it was only a scratch on that precious motor of his. I just can't get used to driving on the other side of the road. It is just not natural." Placing his arm around Damien's shoulder, he gave him a squeeze. "Are you ok, son?"

Damien nodded. He hadn't taken his eyes off Angel since he had arrived. He had missed most of the banter between his father and Henley. She looked so helpless and vulnerable. He hadn't seen her like this since the hospital. Tears were building up behind his eyes as he watched. He wanted to hold her and tell her everything was going to be ok, yet he couldn't. She had obviously found solidarity in Warren. He realised he was now an outsider. A hint of jealousy ran through his veins.

"Stay here. I'll be back soon. I have some interrogation to do, I mean."

"It's ok, Dad. I know what you mean," butted in Damien.

The Interview

Chief Inspector Harrington glanced over to Lieutenant Sanders. The look said, *Let's get this over with.* It was always wise to have two interviewers in the room. Sanders had been told to sit, listen and not to intervene. This interview was going to be difficult enough without any additional interference. Harrington was aware his son would be scrutinising the interview. If he pushed the girl too hard, his son would turn against him. If he went too easy, then she would not divulge the information he needed. Was he right to bring his son on this trip? The whole experience was difficult for his son, who obviously still had feelings for Angelica.

"Good afternoon, young lady. Do you know who I am?"

Angel lifted her head and quickly rubbed her red puffy eyes on her sleeve.

"No, sir, I do not." She looked tired. The lad also looked tired, but he showed no emotion. If they were brother and sister, there was very little resemblance. In fact, in many ways they were like chalk and cheese. The slightly-built lad had fair, wavy hair and pale skin, a few freckles across his nose and round cheeks that made him look younger than he was. The lad stood as soon as he entered the room but quickly sat back down when

Harrington introduced himself. His hand grabbed Angel's hand again; for comfort or protection, Harrington wasn't sure which. The female did not move.

The Chief Inspector opened with the most obvious question. "Tell me: when you rang you said they were going to kill you. Who is going to kill you and why?"

Angel leant over the table and spoke quietly so as not to be heard by anybody else. "They said I was almost ready for harvesting."

"Harvesting!"

"Yes, what do you think they meant?" Angel chewed on her lower lip.

"I don't know."

"It sounds bad, don't you think?"

The Chief Inspector nodded.

Angel sighed. "Oh sir, I don't know who I am, or what I am."

"I don't understand what you mean, Angelica."

"I know you don't." She sighed again. "And I can't explain it."

Damien shook his head. "No, Angel, don't go there," he muttered. He wanted to bang on the window, shout to warn her she was about to lose his father's trust and attention. His dad would never understand. He would dismiss all she was about to say as utter nonsense, a teenager with an inventive imagination, a nutter.

The interview started slowly. There was a lack of trust between all parties, but as Angel continued to talk, the Chief Inspector was drawn further into her story. Angel did not hold back. She told the Chief Inspector everything. Most of the information was new to him and well worth the flight across the Channel. Angel started with the letter she had received in the hospital. This time, she covered more of the letter's contents, not selecting sections as she had done with Damien. Standing, she revealed the small scar on her hip and told him she was the fifth child, and Warren revealed his scar – the number six was clearly evident.

"We are branded like cattle, so we don't forget who we are," she explained, anger apparent in her voice. The Chief Inspector noticed the young lad squeeze Angel's hand tightly at this comment. Angel spoke of the killings. When the subject of Warren's parents arose, she asked if the Lieutenant would take Warren for a sandwich and drink. Even now, Angel was protecting her brother, not wanting him to hear the gruesome details of his parents' killing. The Chief Inspector admired that quality in her.

Warren gratefully took the opportunity to leave. He needed a break. It was over five months since his parents had died in a house fire. He didn't want to relive that time. Edward had told him his parents would have to die, and without question he had accepted it. He had been too wrapped up in who he was – the special child that must be looked after. His parents were now obsolete; they had done their job, according to Edward. Angel hadn't said much, even though she was at the house when it caught fire. He didn't want to know what had happened, not yet, not until he had come to terms with their death. In fact, that was the way he had coped. He didn't think about it, blocked the episode out. He hadn't even gone to their funeral, although this was not by choice. Edward had stopped him.

Since their death, he had visited his parents' graves with Angel, where they had laid flowers picked from the local park, a mixture of yellow and red tulips. Edward was so annoyed that they had disobeyed him. Angel had been severely punished. A direct hit from Samuel's lead bar across her lower body, followed by 96 hours in a locked room, had been her punishment. Edward had said she should use the time to think about what she had done in going against his decision. It was the first time Angel had disobeyed Edward, but not her last. Warren was not punished. Initially, he thought it was because he was younger than Angel, but now all evidence was pointing to Edward being scared of punishing him. Warren smiled. Did he have a power over his new family?

*****

Damien listened as Angel's story unfolded. Her clothes were dirty, her hair a dull mangled mess, face pale with puffed-up, red, blotchy eyes from the tears that had been shed, but Damien saw only her beauty. His hand moved to the one-way glass. At one point he could have sworn Angel looked directly at him. There was no way she could have known he was there.

Very little shocked the Chief Inspector. He had seen and heard many things during his twenty-five years of service, but what Angel said next he was not expecting.

"I killed Warren's mother," she said coldly.

"Can you repeat that?" said the Chief Inspector.

"I killed Warren's mother," she repeated. This time her voice was trembling and her body was beginning to shake. "Not now," she uttered under her breath. He looked up and studied her face carefully. He thought she had said something else, but he must have been mistaken.

"Do you realise what you have just said?"

She nodded.

"Angelica Wellingstone has nodded her head in agreement," he said aloud for the benefit of the tape recorder. It was customary for two interviewers to be in the room; however, there was still no sign of Lieutenant Sanders' replacement. He did not want to stop the interview and lose the momentum. "How?" he asked.

"Edward asked me and Samuel to go and see Warren's parents. I didn't ask why. I just did as I was told," she was still shaking and her voice quivered as she spoke. "I knocked on the door. When Warren's father answered, Samuel hit him hard across the face with a metal bar. The force knocked him over. I know his jaw was broken on impact." Angel didn't want to go into too much detail. She was unintentionally visualising the scene as she spoke, and was beginning to feel queasy as she relived the experience. She remembered seeing his teeth scattered across the floor from the impact of the bar. His blood had splattered against the wooden panels of the staircase and on the thick-pile beige carpet where he fell. Thankfully, the Chief Inspector did not ask for the details, and she didn't give him any additional details beyond what was necessary.

Angel was still shaking as she tried to explain what had happened. "Warren's mum was crying," she whispered. A lump in her throat was beginning to form, causing difficulty in not only swallowing but also speaking clearly. "Her hands were tied behind her back, and she was kneeling on the living room floor. Samuel had dragged the body of her dead husband into the same room and propped him up against the wall. He looked like he was watching us, but his eyes were lifeless," she sniffed. "It looked like his mandible had smashed through his zygomatic bone and broken the skin."

"You mean the jaw bone went through his cheek bone?" repeated the chief Inspector.

There was a nod before she continued, "I was kneeled in front of her, I mean, Warren's mother. Her eyes were pleading with me not to do it. Samuel held my right hand so tight," she sobbed. "The knife was in my hand, and I couldn't let go. He held it so tight," she said under her breath, "and he made me draw that knife across her neck. Oh god, she didn't die instantly. It went on and on. The blood, her eyes staring at me, and then the fire..." Angel covered her mouth with her hands; her body trembled as she relived the moment. Tears started falling once again. "Please don't tell Warren," she whispered. Angel realised what she was saying would implicate her as an accessory to murder, maybe even point to her as the murderer. After all, she had been holding the knife, but she wanted to be open with the Chief Inspector, everything laid on the table.

"Did you try to stop him?" the Chief Inspector asked.

"Of course I did," she replied. "I'm no killer, no matter what you may think. I fought him as hard as I could; he broke my arm during the struggle." She pointed to a bone on her lower arm. "I couldn't stop him, sir. I did try. Honestly, I did try." He looked at her arm; there was no sign of a break, but five months had passed, so it would have healed.

"And the fire?" he asked.

"Samuel found a can of petrol in the garage, so we burned the house to a shell to destroy all evidence. I could not get rid of the smell of petrol. It was on my clothes, hair and hands. Even now I can still smell it," she replied. Her hand had moved up to her eyes as she tried to wipe away the tears before they rolled down her cheeks.

"Take a deep breath, and carry on. You are doing well." He realised he sounded hard; nonetheless, he could not afford to show any sympathy. If Angel broke down, the connection would be broken, and all information suspended. This was the closest he had come to Edward; the slippery eel was in the Chief Inspector's grasp. Sniffing a couple of times, Angel took the hankie offered by the Chief Inspector, dabbed her eyes, and carried on as instructed. This time she concentrated more on her elder brother, Samuel, who in Angel's opinion was more dangerous than Edward.

After all the years of hearing such horror stories, the Chief Inspector thought he would be inoculated against such evil – he wasn't. The Chief Inspector did feel for Angel. No child should have to endure what the young girl sitting in front him of him had endured. Angel was eighteen, still a kid, with no mother or father. It was just her and the young lad. He thanked god his two sons had loving parents to support them when evil came their way. Damien still had the nightmares; during the night, he sometimes heard him screaming. Damien had refused any external help, which hadn't surprised his father; he was an independent lad. He wondered if Damien was still listening to the interview, and if he was, what thoughts were going through his head. He hoped he had made the right decision bringing Damien with him. His wife was not happy with him. It was very rare they ever argued, but they argued over what was right for Damien.

"Tell me about this, Angelica," The Chief Inspector laid the knife in front of Angel. She stared at it for a while.

"It looks like one of Edward's," she replied looking up at him.

"Do you know where we found it?"

Angel shook her head. "No."

"In your bag," he said softly.

"How did it get there?" Angel asked.

"I don't know. That's for you to tell me."

"I didn't put it there, sir."

"So how did it get there?"

"I don't know."

"It was used in a recent killing in Central Park."

"I don't know anything about that."

"Don't lie to me, Angelica."

"I'm not."

"It has your fingerprints on the handle."

"No, it can't have."

"Can you explain to me how your fingerprints got on this murder weapon?"

"No."

He stared at her, trying to work out if she was telling the truth. "Ok, we'll move on for now, but I want you to think carefully on how your fingerprints would come to be on this knife." He removed the knife from the table and placed it back in its bag.

Warren returned for the last hour of the interview. He sat quietly next to Angel, holding her hand for comfort. He didn't move unless Angel gave him an instruction. It was an unusual relationship, a fifteen-year-old boy who did everything an eighteen-year-old girl said. He was completely controlled by her, yet he didn't appear intimidated. Angel talked for over three hours and had gone through four tapes by the time she had finished.

Chief Inspector Harrington was stiff from sitting on the wooden hard backed chair, which was not made for comfort or for long periods of sitting still. Next time he would ask Henley for a comfortable chair. He leant back, trying to stretch his back and shoulders. He had more than enough information to nail Edward and his new accomplice Samuel – if Angelica was telling the truth. He had no reason not to believe her. The story was too full of detail, which was not normal when somebody was lying. Many years of interrogation had taught him this. In the Chief Inspector's opinion, the word *interview* always seemed a bit wishy washy. Maybe because he always took the hard, violent cases, but he preferred *interrogation,* where you got the truth with no embellishment. He wasn't into torture – that was one step too far, back to the dark ages. He stared long and hard at Angel. She looked him in the eye when she spoke, and he liked that about her. All he needed now was to capture Edward, and the bait was sat here in front of him.

"I think we need to get that hand of yours seen to, young lady. I am surprised they didn't fix it up last night." Glancing down, he saw her right hand was a mess, all distorted and discoloured. The way she held her hand suggested intense pain. It could be a permanent injury. The hand was useless – a dead weight hanging off the end of her arm.

"You told me to give my name, and not tell them anything else until you arrived. I didn't want to disobey you, sir." He stared at her again; it was interesting how she had taken his words so literally, spent the night in pain so as not to upset him. He was about to say, *I didn't mean …* but he stopped himself. "I'll ask for the police medical physician to take a look. In the meantime, young man, how would you like a Dairy Queen? Any flavour, with any sprinkle." Warren glanced over to Angel, who nodded her head in agreement.

The small interview room now appeared deathly quiet and eerie. She felt like she was being watched. Glancing around the room, she homed in on the mirror. It was obviously a two-way mirror, so that was probably the cause of the uncomfortable feeling. Angel stared long and hard at the shiny surface. Her drawn face reflected in its surface; tears ran down her cheeks. Angel sniffed and laid her head back on the table. Cushioned by her arms, she wept. She hoped the Chief Inspector believed her. She had told him everything. All she wanted was to get back home to England.

*****

"Well, Damien, do you want to see Angel or not? I can give you ten minutes before I send in the physician," his father offered.

Damien nodded his head. "I want to see her; I just don't know what to say. I have rehearsed over and over again, if and when this occasion ever arose, but now all the words seem so wrong."

"Go in and say whatever comes naturally, but Damien, please take it easy. She's tired and frightened. I think she is self-harming. Check out her wrists and arms. It's a control mechanism. I have seen it hundreds of times before."

"Her damaged hand, is that through self-harming?" Damien asked.

"I doubt it; I think everything she has told me is true. It's what she hasn't told me that I am more concerned about. For example, on her left arm there are several small fresh pin pricks directly in line with her veins."

"Drugs?"

"Possibly, although her pupils are not dilated, so she is clean at the moment."

"Angel is not the type of person to take drugs."

"So what type of person takes drugs?"

"I don't know, not the Angel type."

"Everybody has a weakness."

"Not Angel."

"You see her through rose-tinted glasses, son. People change."

"I don't believe it."

"You see a lot when you interview as much as I have. You get to know what you are looking for, and she has definitely taken something.

"Your Angel concentrated on what she thinks I want to know. See how she is constantly fidgeting, even when she is crying. I think she is close to a total meltdown. If she had not had the young lad to focus her energies on, I don't think she would be sitting in that room today."

"If you think that's the case, Dad, then why didn't you take it easy on her?"

"I gave her what she would have expected from me. I also needed the information. She is not expecting to see you, so I don't know how she will react. Ten minutes."

Damien nodded.

*****

The door of the interview room opened again; less than two minutes had passed. Angel lifted her head and dried her eyes before turning to the door.

"Angel," a voice whispered. The voice was one she had been longing to hear for months, yet she also knew she was tired, and her imagination could be playing tricks. Turning fully, she saw Damien standing in the doorway, staring at her. She was unsure how to react. He looked handsome, healthy and so confident. She had never seen him in a shirt and tie before – it suited him. He had a leather jacket on top, which she always loved him wearing. In a split second she had gone through surprise, excitement and finally anticipation. Angel took a step forward just as her legs gave way. She began to fall. Damien reached out and grabbed her. Pulling her close, he hugged her with a passion that he had held inside for so long. This was not planned, but he didn't intend to let her go. He wrapped his arms around her body, and Angel's arms became trapped. She placed them around his waist and held him tight. His grip was firm – any closer and she would suffocate. He could see the marks she had told his father about on her neck. There was a deep red oval shape left from a thumb that had been pressed down with an ugly force. He didn't want to think about what could have happened, and instead concentrated on feeling the warmth of her body.

Angel ignored the pain radiating from her hand. "I am sorry, Damien. I tried to get back to you; they wouldn't let me. I love you; I'm sorry I never told you. I was sure I was doing the right thing." Tears of happiness roll down her cheeks.

He stared into her red, tearful eyes; there was still a hidden sparkle in there. Maybe his father was wrong, maybe she was not as far gone as he thought.

"Don't cry," he whispered. "You will set me off." With dull, lifeless hair and clothes that looked like they had been slept in for the last week, Angel was a mess, yet he didn't care. He had been unsure if he would still have the same feelings for her; now there was no doubt. He did love her, no matter how hard he had tried not to.

"I am sorry for what I said, Angel. You hurt me, so I wanted to hurt you."

She could feel the warmth of his breath on her cheek, and the faint smell of aftershave reactivated her senses and emotions. Wrapped in his arms, it was the first time in a long time Angel had felt safe.

"Can we wipe the slate clean and start again?" she asked hesitantly.

Gazing into her eyes, a warm feeling flowed through his body. "Do you come here often," he said in his best chat-up voice.

"All the time," she answered with a short laugh.

Bringing his lips down to meet Angel's, he kissed her tenderly. She responded passionately, drawing her body even closer. They did not hear the door open behind them until a male cleared his throat.

"Sorry, mate, the young lady nearly fainted. I just caught her in time." Damien winked at Angel and then slowly backed away to the side of the room.

"I may be old, but I'm not stupid," the new arrival said. "I was young once, you know, and even I know you don't normally catch somebody with your tongue."

Angel's cheeks reddened; Damien laughed and patted the medical physician on the back.

"Well," said the physician turning Angel's hand gently over, "my first impression is your right index finger is dislocated at the proximal interphalangeal joint, and your next two fingers are either broken or dislocated. It looks like the distal interphalangeal joints have also had some damage. A couple of your metacarpal bones in your hand are broken, possibly crushed. We need to get that hand of yours x-rayed and see what other damage there is, and then we can decide how to repair it.

If it's just dislocation, we'll have you back to normal in no time." Angel managed a faint smile. With the physician's attention, her fingers were now starting to throb. Tears started to well up in her eyes once more.

"I don't want to go to hospital," she sniffed tearfully.

"You have to go, young lady."

"They'll be waiting for me."

"Nobody will be waiting for you, and we have to get that hand seen to," the doctor insisted.

"Damien, please don't let them send me to hospital," Angel pleaded.

"Angel, you have to go. We need to repair that hand of yours."

The Chief Inspector put his head around the door. "Everything ok in here?"

"Yeah, apart from the young lady refusing to go to the hospital," the physician reported.

"Do you want to go back to England?" The Chief Inspector asked.

Angel nodded.

"Then you are going to hospital." He closed the door before she could argue, and disappeared down the corridor to find Henley. Teenage tantrums were not something he was used to dealing with, and Warren had just told him something that needed acting on immediately. Another vicar was about to lose his life.

Damien moved closer to Angel. "They won't let you travel with a damaged hand unless it has been seen to professionally." Her eyes were welling up with tears once again. Focusing on her arm, she started to scratch at the scabs. The wounds opened up again causing them to bleed. Damien placed his hand over her arm, preventing her fingernails from reaching the scabs.

She looked up at him. He looked away, ignoring her obvious intention to harm herself. She was so different from the girl he first met at the lake. A young, bubbly, confident girl he had fallen in love with, who was not bothered what other people said or thought. There had been some signs of vulnerability, but not somebody who would self-harm. Six months was all it had taken to change Angel into a fragile, helpless, scared individual. The uncertainty in her tearful eyes and the lack of confidence and control she now possessed was quite apparent.

"Damien, promise me you won't let them put me to sleep."

"I promise," he said. "I don't think they will have to for a broken hand."

"And if Samuel is there...."

"He won't be."

"But if he is," she paused before rushing her words. "Samuel will guess I need to go to the hospital with my hand."

It was Damien's turn to pause. "Ok, if he is here, he won't try anything, not in the open, and you have me and my dad with you, so don't worry. You really need to have it looked at."

She could see the concern in his eyes; arguing would be pointless. Angel sighed and stood up. "No time like the present," she muttered, giving him a weak smile.

Angel was right. She was being watched, but not by Samuel. The unwelcome presence of the watchful stranger burned deep in her soul, although she saw nobody.

MacGregor Hotel

The waiter stood patiently. He had listened to them changing their order for the last few minutes. The evening diners were always the same with tonight's table being a rare exception. This evening, lobster was exceptionally popular with most of the diners. *Plenty of money around tonight,* he thought. He hoped they would tip well. *Keep smiling,* he told himself. For the last twenty years, he had taken people's orders with an artificial smile plastered across his face. Only five more years left to retirement. What was worse, working, or spending every minute of every day with his wife? A difficult decision.

A female voice interrupted his thoughts. "Can I have a Greek salad please?"

"Why not try the chicken?" whispered Damien.

"I can't cut it, remember?" Angel lifted her hand, which was now heavily bandaged and placed in a sling.

"I'll cut it for you," he whispered, placing a quick kiss on her cheek. The waiter sighed a little louder than he intended. How much longer would he have to wait before the small group made a decision on their entrees?

Damien was desperate for Angel to eat more. She was still so thin, even thinner than when she came out of hospital. Marasmus kept springing to mind, and how

Angel's brother had died aged eighteen years; his body had just wasted away. Damien prayed it wasn't genetic. He had been close to losing Angel to the same condition six months ago. He couldn't face it happening again. Losing her would kill him. Even now, he was unsure how she had managed to recover. He was not a non-believer, but had her mother really given Angel her life? Then again, several months ago, he had been sure Angel had given him back his life by sacrificing her own. This was not reality – only trauma-induced fantasy. Time had made him realise this.

"How about pasta? I can eat pasta with my left hand," Angel replied tearfully.

"Hey, come on. No more tears." Damien placed a comforting arm around her shoulder. "You have what you want; it was only a suggestion." Chief Inspector Harrington, Warren, Angel and Damien were sitting in the hotel restaurant, discussing their evening meal. The dining room was full of Henley's men, who were obviously relishing their role of diners. They were ordering the finest food on the menu, at the expense of the tax payer; British or American still had to be decided. The intention was for the group to stay in the MacGregor Hotel, where Damien and his father had checked in earlier. A couple of Henley's men were keeping a watchful eye on proceedings, and were ready for any trouble, if it occurred. But none of them noticed they were being watched.

*****

In the adjoining bar, the stranger sat positioned in a window booth. From his location, he could watch the street as well as the restaurant. A copy of the *New York Times* lay sprawled across the small, round table. Wet rings had formed on the pages from the numerous drinks that had been downed. He wasn't inebriated. Celebrations would come later. Now was the time to sit, watch and learn. A business crowd had gathered at the bar. The barman busied himself preparing their many drink orders. Joyous laughter filled the small room, giving him more cover. Office staff celebrating the end of the day. He watched for a few minutes. A feeling of disgust sat uncomfortably in the pit of his stomach. Filthy bitches, in their tight skirts, bursting out of their see-through blouses.

A woman sat at the end of the bar. Her posterior hung over the mushroom shaped stool. Grey pantaloons were not the most flattering item of clothing for her shape, gripping and enhancing all those areas that should be hidden from sight. The stranger stared. The rear of an elephant sprung to mind. With a sip of red wine, he mused there was no sophistication with a rear that size. Rolls of fat hung from her once firm jaw. She watched the business crowd with interest, no doubt wishing she was in the in-crowd rather than a fat lump waiting for yet another blind date. Life can be cruel for people like her.

Drawing his attention back to the street, he saw another yellow cab pulled over to the kerb. Two men disembarked, one carrying a large gentleman's umbrella; the other, a briefcase. Both entered the restaurant. The rain had started to fall, blurring his view. The window had become a pattern of blurry coloured lights, seen through circles of water that constantly changed. Drops of water snaked down the glass pane, gathering pace as the snakes expand in size, gobbling greedily on the lone droplets. Reds, greens and oranges mixed into one. The cab pulled away, another passenger, another fare in tow. He read the headline again. It was the fifth time tonight he had read the same headline and still it seemed dull, uninteresting drivel.

Glancing back over to the woman, he saw she was now on her third glass of Cabernet Sauvignon, still alone, no sign of a blind date. He probably took one look and was now sitting in the back of one of those taxis or hidden in the toilets, scared to show his face. Scared she would eat him alive, poor cow. How could people let themselves go like that? At least her flesh was hidden, not like the other bitches at the bar. He'd leave her to fantasize of true love, which she would never find.

Time to retire to room thirty-five. The Wallace Suite was waiting for him. Two doors down from Ms Angelica Wellingstone. Nothing much learnt tonight, apart from the bitch liked chicken, salad and pasta.

*****

Angel ate three mouthfuls of pasta. She pushed the rest of her meal around the plate for well over forty-five minutes. Damien watched as she built a small tower out of the pasta, followed by two smaller towers, which were knocked down a lot quicker than they were built. Eventually the Fusilli pasta dish was pushed to one side of the plate; Angel had finished her meal. The Chief Inspector signalled to Damien, who had already 'clocked' Angel's actions. Angel had wiped her knife on a napkin, concealing it up the sleeve of her baggy grey cardigan, before sitting back in her chair. The knife had been taken quite openly. There was no obvious intent to conceal her actions. His father would say it was a cry for help. This was not the time to confront her, not in front of Henley's men. Embarrassing somebody in public was not the way to handle such a delicate situation. They would discuss her actions later when alone.

*****

"Give me the knife."

Angel swung around, not expecting to see Damien standing behind her in the bedroom.

"The knife. Now."

She stared, not moving, bottom lip trembling. "Stop shouting at me," she cried.

Damien approached her slowly, unsure how she would react and gently grabbed her wrists. Rolling up her sleeve, he pulled out the concealed knife. "So you want to self-harm, do you?" He pulled the knife gently across her arm, not hard enough to draw blood, yet hard enough to leave an ugly red mark. "Is this what you want? Is it?" His voice was angry. "Look at these marks. Angel, what happens if you catch the Ulnar artery? Do you want to kill yourself? Is that what you are trying to do?"

She shook her head as she tried to pull her wrist from his grasp.

"You are stronger than this."

He could see the tears building up behind her eyes. "Stop it," she sobbed. "I only wanted the knife to cut my apple in half."

Damien sat on the edge of her bed. His voice softened slightly. "Really? Why the marks on your arms, Angel?"

"I was trying to mend my wrist. I have found a new way to cure my injuries," she sniffed again, before wiping her eyes on her sleeve. "I'm sorry. Honestly, I am not self-harming, not like you think."

"Come here," he whispered. He pulled her onto his lap and placed his arms around her waist. "I'm sorry, too. You just scared me. I'm going to keep the knife, but ask me when you want it."

Rolling backwards, she squealed as she fell on top of him. The pain shot through his body as she caught his upper abdomen. Her face was only inches from his. She gave him a quick kiss before laying her head on his chest and moving her fingers to his collarbone to feel the small heart shape. The scar had kept him going for the last six months.

"Please don't hurt yourself again. It's all classed as self-harming no matter what the reason is behind it," he whispered, flicking her hair back off her face. "When I saw your arms and...well, you know what I thought. It's no excuse what I have just done, but you have been away from me for so long, and this new you... Well, it scares me. You are so fragile." Gently lifting her head, he looked deep into her eyes; tiny beads of salty teardrops lay on top of her long dark eyelashes. "I've rarely ever seen you cry, and now you cry at anything and everything." His hand touched her cheek as he wiped away a tear trickling down her face. "I love you, but I am finding this so hard to deal with." Rolling over he sat back up on the bed. "I'll leave you to sleep. You look tired. We will talk in the morning." He gave her a hug and gently kissed her forehead before standing up to leave the room.

"Damien," Angel called him back. He slowly turned around. "I lied, I don't have an apple to cut."

"I know," he replied.

For the last ten minutes, the pain in Damien's stomach had been really bad. It had been a mistake when he pulled Angel on top of him. He had nearly screamed with the pain but bit his lip and stifled it. He would have stayed in her room longer, just talking, but he didn't want her to see his pain. She could not help him, not yet, and knowing he was in pain and she couldn't help would only stress her. He needed his painkillers, and he needed them fast.

"What's wrong, son?" Damien was leant against the Macintosh chair in the communal room, or as Angel had pointed out, the chair was a Charles Rennie Mackintosh replica, originally designed as part of the Arts and Craft Movement. His fingers tightly grasped the back of the chair, nails digging into the wood. He was taking slow, deep breaths.

"I caught my stomach when I hugged Angel," he gasped. "I forgot how bad the pain can be. Could you grab the painkillers from my bag?" His father retrieved the small brown pill bottle from the top of Damien's holdall.

"Are you going to be ok?"

"Sure. These little beauties will start to kick in soon. They are better than the last lot I had." Throwing four to the back of his throat, he swallowed. He no longer required water to wash them down – four years of practice had perfected the technique. Their taste was bitter, but he knew they would help. His father was close to interrupting him, with the intention of drawing his attention to the label on the bottle that read, *two tablets every four hours,* but he held back. He guessed his son knew what he was doing. He had been in charge of his own medication for years.

"Can I ask you something personal?"

Damien lifted his head. "Sure."

"Will you show me your stomach? I want to see how the illness has developed over the last few months, and I wondered..." he stopped. "Sorry, Damien. You don't have to. You are a grown man, not a child anymore."

Damien looked over to his dad. "It's not a pretty sight."

"I am not expecting it to be."

"The sores and the state of my skin change daily." Damien explained. His father nodded as Damien started to lift his shirt. "Angel says I should think of my body as a work of art, a changing picture. You see here," he said, pointing just below his collarbone, "a heart and this here looks like a giraffe."

His dad smiled. "Your Angel is very wise. Oh look, SpongeBob SquarePants."

"Where?"

His dad pointed to his son's left side, and they laughed.

"Are you going to be ok sleeping in the communal room?"

"Don't worry about me, Dad. I'll be fine."

"I think we got the short straw tonight," said Damien's father, placing a blanket over his legs and flipping the leather recliner into a sleep position. "It reminds me of when I was on the stakeouts many years ago, although I expect this to be more comfortable." Their hotel room was named the Stevenson suite after Robert Louis Stevenson, the famous novelist. It was large with two bedrooms, one en-suite, a separate bathroom and an adjoining living room. Angel had taken the largest bedroom with its MacGregor tartan curtains and bed sheets, and Warren had taken the Campbell tartan room, which was blue and green in colour. This was his father's favourite hotel in the city. The Scottish theme ran through all the bedrooms he had stayed in, but this was the first time he had booked a two-bedroom suite, and he was impressed. Even the breakfast buffet had a Scottish influence, with Lorne sausage, oat cakes and kippers. Damien opted for the sofa underneath the window where he could stretch out quite comfortably. His father had refused the offer of the sofa bed, preferring to sit upright. Tomorrow his father would sort a second room for them to occupy. Tonight, his father wanted them all together so he could keep an eye on Angel and Warren. Similarly, his son also preferred them to be together but for a different reason.

Damien was still panicking when left alone. The only place Damien felt reasonably safe now was his parent's home, in Surrey, which was why he had not strayed far in the past six months. Spending a weekend with Tim and Laurel had been one huge step. Ever since his attack, he had felt alone and vulnerable. After the stabbing, his sleep had become restless and broken with tormented nightmares. The nightmare was always the same. A dark-cloaked figure hung suspended over his body. Saliva was dripping from its mouth onto his face; each drop burned into his skin through to the bone. Blisters formed on his skin, discharging a murky liquid. The face of his assailant was masked, with small yellow piercing eyes, which burned through his skull if he tried to look into them. The teeth were sharp and scissor-like, perfect to gnaw on the flesh of beasts. His body always froze, and he could not fight back. It was as though he was watching the nightmare unfold from outside his body. The creature would eventually consume him before he freed himself from the nightmare. The stale smell of smoke lingered in his nostrils, causing him to vomit as soon as he woke. His body was always drenched in sweat, and the bed sheets were wet from fear.

Surrounded by friends and family Damien, felt safer than he had done for a long time. It had been a long, tiring day. Tonight he would fall into a deep sleep with no dreams or nightmares. Ironically his sleep would still be disrupted by nightmares, but not his own.

"I thought you would join Angelica tonight. You look like you have kissed and made up," said his father smirking. The medical physician had obviously told everybody about his encounter in the interview room.

Damien smiled. "Yeah, I guess we got caught." Talking to his father about his relationship was weird, but he had never felt so close to him as he had in the last twenty-four hours. He had gained a certain respect for his father, seeing him at work, how he interacted with people, the planning that went on through the investigations. His father had a human side, a gentle caring nature that he had never seen before, or had never taken notice of before.

"I just didn't want to presume that everything was back to normal, and the pain..." he stopped. "Well, you know," said Damien.

His father smiled. Like father, like son. He would have done exactly the same if he had been Damien.

"Dad."

"Yes."

"What do you think of Angel?"

Looking up from his paperback, his father knew his son wanted his approval. "It's not what I think. It's what you think."

"I know but..."

His father sighed and placed his book on the arm of the chair.

"Ok, I have had two encounters with your Angelica, and both times in adverse circumstances, so I have probably not seen her in the best light. There is something about her I like. She appears genuine. She loves you. I saw that in the hospital, and again now, and I know you love her. The eyes give everything away. Angelica has some weird ideas, but I would like to get to know her more before I form an opinion. Is that ok for starters?"

Damien nodded thoughtfully. His father was about to pick up his book when Damien spoke up again.

"You know, I was hoping to bring Angel home to meet you and mam – do it properly. I guess that will now never happen. I wish you could have met her before all of this started, when she was happy."

"It never works out how we plan, but that's why life is so exciting."

"Dad, I want to tell you something, but please don't judge me. I want you to see how important Angel is too me. Before I met Angel, I was so close to calling it a day, 'throwing in the towel' as such. I was so down, and no matter how hard I tried, I was slipping further and further down. I fought. I tried so hard, but it's really difficult with the pain sometimes, and then..." he paused. "Angel came along. She was like a breath of fresh air. She was funny and...anyway, she gave me back my confidence, gave me the strength to fight. I felt different when I was with her. She had an amazing energy that I fed off. I became happy again. Does that sound stupid?"

"No, not at all. I just didn't realise how bad it had got."

"Nobody did. Laurel may have had his suspicions, but I told nobody. The person you see is not my Angel. She has lost all that energy, all that fight. I want to help her find that energy again."

His father nodded. "You survived for six months without her, and if need be you will do it again."

"What are you saying?" Damien asked.

"Your Angel may be lost, pushed too far."

"No, you are wrong. I know she will come through this," Damien protested. "She's a lot stronger than you think."

"I was just saying," his father said, not wanting his son to get his hopes up and be hurt again.

"Don't say it. What kept me going for those six months was hope, knowing one day we would meet again. I was annoyed with myself. If I had listened to her in the first place, I would have known where she was meeting Edward. I could have phoned you and had him arrested, and then none of this would have happened. I could have saved six months of our lives."

"Hindsight is a great power to have. Just don't punish yourself. We will get him soon. You'll see."

"Will we?" Damien asked. "I think he'll be back for her."

"And I'll be waiting for him."

"I wish she had never gone to meet him. I mulled it over for months. I felt betrayed. It was only when I saw her in the interview room with her brother that I realised what all this was about. It was never about me. It was about family, belonging. It's more important to Angel than I had realised, and I should have respected that."

"We learn through our mistakes, son."

Damien laid his head on the pillow. "One big mistake," he said quietly.

Placing his book down on the floor, the Chief Inspector lowered his voice, "I was thinking about the knife wrapped in Angel's clothing. I need to check, but it might be the same knife used on Warren's mother. This may be difficult to prove since the bodies were burnt, but it would explain her fingerprints on the handle. It still doesn't explain the blood from the Central Park killing, unless she is being set up."

"By who? Edward?"

"Well, there's Samuel for starters. There is obviously no love lost between them. I just can't see why she would hide a murder weapon in her own clothing, and then bring it to the police station, knowing she would be searched. It doesn't make sense."

"If it's any help, Dad, I don't believe Angel is capable of killing." His pain was now starting to subside, so they carried on talking in lowered voices, mulling over the case for another couple of hours, before retiring to bed.

A scream broke their otherwise restful sleep. Jumping up from their makeshift beds, Damien and his father knew it was Angel. Damien ran to her room, tripping over the coffee table on his way. A dark shape twisted violently in the bed, loudly screeching. Damien grabbed Angel's shoulders and shouted her name, trying to wake her from the nightmare she was trapped in. Kicking, punching and scratching hard, the demon inside had taken control. Angel was possessed by an unnatural strength for a female. Her fist landed on Damien's jaw. The linen blanket was tight around her neck. Her hands clawed the air. Damien pulled at the sheet, trying to loosen the knot that had formed. Angel's hands waved uncontrollably, fighting off the demons that surrounded her and disturbed her sleep. Her injured hand felt no pain. Her brain was controlled only by the thought, *I must escape.*

The Celtic designer lamp flew across the room, smashing into tiny pieces. Trapping Angel's arms, Damien carried on shaking her, shouting her name. She was staring straight through him towards the ceiling. There was no recognition, no realisation of what was happening. Her legs continued to kick wildly under the blankets, causing the sheets to wrap tightly around her body. It was restraining her movement, causing more panic. She drew blood across Damien's cheek. Pinning her down on the bed, his tactics changed to whispering her name. Slowly, recognition crossed her face. Beads of perspiration ran down her face and neck. The pale blue nightie she wore was now a deep blue from her sweat.

"It was just a nightmare," he whispered. Angel hugged him. The heat from her body was warm, but the perspiration was starting to turn cold and clammy.

He tucked her hair behind her ears so he could see her facial features before carefully carrying her to the shower. "Have a quick shower, and I'll sort out the bed." A faint smile crossed her face as he set the shower running. He wondered what nightmare could make somebody react so violently. Moving his hand across his cheek, the cut was slightly raised, but not deep. He placed a call to housekeeping for fresh linen.

A groan came from the bathroom. Rushing back to the room, Damien knocked on the door. He was met by silence. It was not locked, so he entered. Angel was curled up in the basin of the shower cubicle; her legs drawn to her chest. Her nightwear was soaked. The shower was still running. The droplets drummed hard on her body. He was unsure if she was crying or whether it was the water stinging her eyes. A blue substance covered her chin and ran down the front of her night-wear. He could see the liquid disappearing down the plug hole. Her eyes rose to meet his.

"Blood is on my hands," she said quietly. Damien looked down at her hands. There was no blood, only steam rising from the hot water. "Blood is on my hands," she said again a little louder. The bandage protecting her hand was wet and dripping with water but again he could see no blood.

"There is no blood, Angel."

"I can see blood, Damien. Please make it go away."

Damien stared again in disbelief. "There is no blood, Angel."

"I can see blood."

"It's your imagination, Angel. Repeat after me: there is no blood on my hands; there is no blood..." Angel mouthed the words, but he could tell she didn't believe them. "You have to say it with commitment, Angel, or I can't make it go away."

"There is no blood," she screamed quickly followed by, "I'm sorry, Damien. I didn't mean to shout."

"Ssh, it doesn't matter."

If Angel thought there was blood, then Damien knew he should be concerned. He could remember something being written in Angel's psychiatric report about having blood on her hands. There was something about how she held out her hands and whispered, "'There is blood on my hands,' staring at the wall as though somebody else was in the room with her." At least she had said the words to him, somebody real, but there was no blood. He prayed Angel wasn't slipping back, where they would have no choice but to admit her back into hospital.

"What is happening to me, Damien? Who am I?" Damien turned the shower off and sat next to Angel in the shower basin. Placing his arm around her shoulder, he held her tightly.

"I don't know what is happening, Angel, but I know who you are. You are Angel Wellingstone from Barton on Stowheath. You were born Angelica Wellingstone, but you wanted to be called Angel because you thought angels were fairies. You would pivot on your tiny toes and shout, 'My name is Angel like the fairies,' which angered your mum. 'Angels are not fairies, and it is rude to shorten your name,'" he said in a high squeaky voice.

"That didn't sound like my mum," she said, and there was almost a smile.

"I know," he kissed the top of her forehead. "Your mother was called Winifred Wellingstone. She was beautiful, like her daughter, with long dark hair."

"Longer than mine," whispered Angel.

"That's right, longer than yours. People thought she was a white witch. Her daughter, Angelica, used to find this funny because she never kept toads, newts or snakes in the house, nor did she have a cauldron or spell book." Angel snuggled a little deeper into his chest, enjoying the story. "But Winifred had a special power, the power to heal people when they were ill, and that gift was a very special gift to have. Every day between two and four, Angel's mum healed the sick. It made her very tired, but she always had time for her special Angel. Shall I continue?"

Angel nodded eagerly.

"Her daughter was never allowed to meet her guests. Instead, she was always sent to her bedroom to do her homework after school. That was why Winifred's daughter was so intelligent. She never missed a day from school, and she always did her homework, taking time and care, never rushing. When all her mum's guests had left for the day little Angel was very happy. The aroma of apple and cinnamon cookies would now fill the air. And even though sometimes Angel is unsure who she is, Winifred and I both know: she is Angel Wellingstone from Barton on Stowheath, whom I love and cherish and will protect with every ounce of strength left in my body."

She lifted her head so her eyes could meet his.

"I know who you are, Angel. You are the one I love," he said and kissed her damp forehead gently.

Angel kissed Damien on the cheek. "Thank you. That was lovely. Silly, but lovely, and you remembered everything I told you and more."

"Elephants never forget."

"You're not an elephant. You're too skinny to be an elephant," she giggled.

"Do you want to try and stand? See if we can wash away the rest of the blue liquid?"

"I'll try, but I don't feel well."

"We can't sit all night in the shower basin. For a start, we'll catch pneumonia, or at least I will. You probably won't. It must be strange never to be ill. When we all had the childhood illnesses, you could just carry on enjoying yourself."

"Sometimes it was hard to enjoy myself," Angel admitted. Edward was always at my house. He was very strict. Edward didn't like surprises or mess. He didn't like me leaving my toys in the living room; everything had its place. In my toys' case, the chest in my bedroom was where toys were kept, away from his glaring eyes. We had a strange, controlled relationship." Angel paused. "I am sorry. I shouldn't have mentioned his name."

"Don't be silly; I honestly don't mind as long as you can see what he is really like."

There was no strength in Angel's legs as Damien tried to make her stand. He was unsure what was happening or what he should do. Angel's body suddenly jerked. The flood gates opened and the blue vomit started again. This time it was not the smooth liquid he was used to, but a frothy blue substance. This time she caught him.

"Don't worry," he said in a soft tone. "It will wash out." He tried to hold her under the shower, but her legs still had no strength. Taking her full weight, he tried to wash the blue vomit out of her hair and from her face, but it was difficult to hold her at the same time.

The painkillers had worn off; his stomach and chest cried out in pain. His arms felt weak from the illness that had been creeping down his limbs recently. Still, Damien held her as he tried to wash away the blue liquid. He heard his father call his name through the bathroom door.

"Is everything ok, Damien?"

"Will you grab two of my t-shirts from my bag, mine and Angel's are wet." He couldn't let his father see Angel like this. He wouldn't understand. Damien didn't understand fully what was happening. He guessed, although he wasn't one hundred percent certain, that her body was trying to cure her own pain caused from the crushed bones in her hand. Angel was fragile, so vulnerable. Damien knew his father was watching, waiting to send her to a rest home. They had argued about what Damien could be taking on. Damien insisted he would look after her. She would be ok. She just needed to feel loved and to learn to enjoy life again.

"Stay with me tonight. I don't want to be alone," she whispered. Once they had changed into clean, dry clothes, they made their way to the bedroom. Climbing into the bed, Angel immediately laid her head on his chest and wrapped her arm across his stomach. Damien placed his arm around her shoulder and played with her wet tussled hair. His other hand moved to her arm, stroking gently from the shoulder to wrist. The bruises leapt out from her skin. He had managed to remove the wet bandage without hurting her hand too much. He could now see the damage that had been done to her hand. It was a multitude of colours with cuts dug deep into the skin. The hospital had said one of the bones was crushed beyond repair. A minor operation and a couple of screws would sort it. Not that Angel would contemplate an operation.

"Honestly, Damien, it's not a problem," she kept whispering. He looked at her hand again. This was the hand that could heal and also the hand that could kill. A cold shudder ran through his body. He pulled the blanket up so he could no longer see her hand. Instead he looked down at her face. Her complexion was like fine porcelain, not a blemish in sight. He stared a little longer as she slept. He had never realised how high her cheekbones were, and how her long dark lashes framed her eyes enhancing her beauty. How could anybody be so cruel to hurt her? He may be biased, but her heart was golden.

Angel's body started to twitch. He held her tight, knowing she was slipping back into a night of horror.

"I'm here," he whispered. "It's only a dream; nothing can harm you." The blue substance gently trickled from her mouth onto his shirt. With a shaking hand and intense pain of his own, he managed to carefully wipe the dribble from the corner of her mouth.

"Everything is going to be ok," he whispered again, kissing the top of her head. The twitching slowly eased until she was resting peacefully. Damien smiled as he remembered laughing with his brother Neil, at Puppy, their dog, when he had dreams. His body would twitch, the paws running and twitching in mid-air, while a low growling came from deep in his throat. They would lie next to their dog and do impersonations, howling with laughter. Throughout its twelve years of life their dog had always been known as Puppy, all because the brothers could not agree on a name. His dad had said their Golden Retriever would be known as Puppy until they agreed. Neil wanted Mozart, and Damien wanted Sandy or Wilson. Neither brother would back down. Both were stubborn, so Puppy became its name by default. Not that their dog seemed to mind. He still acted like a typical dog, carrying sticks whenever he went for a walk, or splashing in the water so he could shake his smelly wet fur over Damien's annoyed mother. If no water was available, then Pups, as he later became known, spent his time chasing after a half-eaten football. Damien suddenly missed him.

Damien fell to sleep with thoughts of Neil and his Golden Retriever. Keeping the same position for the rest of the night, Damien and Angel slept soundly, occasionally stirring, but neither waking the other.

Next day, leaving Angel to sleep, Damien crept silently out of the bedroom to where his father had already ordered room service. "Are you alright, son?"

Damien nodded, "Dad, I have never seen a person so bruised. Every inch of Angel's body is covered in bruising. I don't remember her mentioning a beating when you interviewed her. I remember her talking about the marks on her neck but nothing else."

"It was Samuel. He liked to practice his baton swing on Angel," said Warren, joining them for breakfast. "Samuel found it amusing that Edward said she was special, yet she could not heal herself as quick as he could. I think he was making a point."

"The son of a bitch!" Damien hissed. "I swear if I meet him, I will kill him. He may be Angel's brother, but you can't treat somebody like that."

"He could have broken every bone in her body if he wanted. Edward always stopped him. Samuel was always jealous of Angel and Edward's relationship." Warren stuffed another chocolate croissant into his mouth as he spoke.

Damien's father was confused but didn't pursue the confusion. "Are you injured as well?" asked David.

"No," laughed Warren. "Samuel wouldn't dare touch me."

Ignoring Warren's previous comment, it was Damien's turn to ask a question. "Why?"

Warren thought for a moment, "I would hit him back, of course." They all laughed. *Fighting talk from a child,* thought David.

Damien heard his name being called. He looked over to his father and stood up straight away. "It's Angel. She'll be wondering where I am."

"Don't forget what I told you. Don't take too much on"

Damien nodded. He opened the door to the bedroom and found Angel standing next to the bed. She was still wearing his black t-shirt with *rock n roll* plastered across the front. She looked cute but sexy at the same time. He wanted her there and then. Her partially exposed body was giving him all the right signals. Male urges would have to wait. Tears once again streamed down her cheeks. Running over to him, she threw her arms around his neck. He held her tight.

"I thought you had left me," she blurted out.

"I was just having breakfast with my father and Warren. I didn't want to disturb you. I thought you needed the rest, that's all."

Wrapping his arms tightly around her body, her t-shirt rode slightly higher revealing more thigh. He tried not to glance down, but his heart was beating faster.

"Cold shower time," Damien muttered. Angel looked up. "Sorry. I was just thinking aloud. Why don't you grab a shower and then join us for breakfast?" Angel glanced up and stared deep into his eyes to see if he was lying. Damien gave her a quick kiss on the forehead. "I told you I'm not going anywhere. Remember, you were the one who left me. I never left you. I came back to America for you, so I am not likely to bail out on you, am I?"

"I know. I'm sorry. I don't know what's wrong with me."

He wiped away her tears with the back of his finger. It was going to be a long, slow recovery process.

The Confrontation

There were no more incidents similar to the shower and no more self-harming. Damien still stayed close to Angel as he tried to bring happiness and love back into her life. As the days passed she grew stronger; however, at night when her back was to him, the tears fell. Curling his body around hers, he could feel her sobbing, but he never said anything. When her head lay on his chest, she didn't sob, although his t-shirt was always damp from where her eyes rested. His father kept pushing him to take Angel to see a counsellor.

"You're taking too much on," he kept saying. Damien ignored his father. He meant well, but this solution was not for Angel. It was difficult; Damien had never dealt with anything like this before, but he was coping. Every time he thought Angel was through the worst, the tears would always start again. One minute, she would be giggling and laughing; the next tears fell. He told his father he thought it was due to the substance that they had injected into her body. Angel had told him the small pin pricks on her left arm were from needles when they took samples of her blood. Later they replaced her blood with a thin, clear liquid. When he asked who they were, she didn't know.

The solution made her drowsy. It also made her mouth dry, and a sweet pear taste formed on the roof of her mouth. Paralysis resulted in her right hand and arm. Her description was chilling. She spoke of the weird feeling as the liquid entered her body, winding and curdling through the veins – an icy cold feeling. It had made his body shudder with the thought.

"Did you ask them what it was?" Damien wanted to know. It was a silly question. Of course she would have asked.

"They said it would make me mentally stronger, bring on my ability to heal quicker," was her answer. The injected substance hadn't made her mentally stronger; if anything it had made her weaker. Guilt followed by an in-ground hurt had been the next emotion. Angel said she felt excited when she thought she would be able to heal, until she realised they were not interested in her as a person, they just wanted her power. In their eyes, she was a lab rat. Going to the hospital for tests was probably the sensible thing to do, but they both had had enough of hospitals, and it was doubtful a doctor could help.

"How is she doing?" David asked each morning.

Today Damien had looked up at his father. "She is not going in a home."

"I know," his father said mildly. "You have told me enough times. I was only asking."

Angel lay asleep in Damien's arms, head on his chest, cuddled into his body. He kissed the top of her head, causing her to snuggle deeper into his chest.

"You haven't been outside for a couple of days!"

"I know, Dad. Angel isn't ready yet."

"Any improvement?"

"Yes, apart from she still isn't sleeping at night, which is why she sleeps during the day. If I hold her tightly then she seems to sleep. I'll wake her soon. There are some signs of improvement. This morning she laughed at one of my jokes."

"Nobody laughs at your jokes, son."

"Thanks, Dad," Damien said, pulling a face. "I know this is going to sound stupid, but she asked me if a mole couldn't see and couldn't hear or feel any form of vibration, could it still survive?"

His dad looked bemused at the question. "And what did you say?"

"I said yes, because the mole could still smell, so it would smell where its food was. I know it sounds stupid, but Angel used to always ask me questions like that, so I know she is getting better. The problem is, tomorrow the mole will lose the ability to smell, and I don't want to say it won't survive. I want to be positive. What would you say?" Damien once again kissed the top of Angel's head, causing her to stir.

"Interesting, Damien. I would probably say if the mole lost all of its senses, then it would adapt by giving off an odour, a smell that attracts its prey. The mole would not need to search for food because its food would come to it."

Damien nodded. "That's brilliant, Dad, the perfect answer."

"Of course," David said. As he spoke he looked to the sleeping child. She was unusual, yet Damien seemed determined to help her, and he had to admit his son wasn't doing a bad job.

Damien tucked Angel's hair behind her ear and then looked up at his father. "Angel is getting better, Dad. The tears still fall, but there are times when it is like old times. Give me more time, that's all I ask." Angel was so tense, on edge all the time. Fear and tears filled her eyes. There was depression in her movement. Her stature was often hunched. She wasn't irritable – almost the opposite, submissive in her actions. Damien hadn't lied to his father. There was some improvement, but he was worried too.

Every day at eight in the morning, Angel stood and stared out of the bedroom window. Damien didn't normally disturb this daily ritual; however, today would be different. Tears would normally roll down her cheeks, although if he asked, she would deny she was crying. He appreciated she needed time and space to heal, but the constant crying tugged at his heartstrings. Damien had observed her for the last ten minutes. Today, she had stood longer than normal, a marble statue placed strategically to the side of the window. From where he stood, not even a breath could be detected. Damien's father and Warren had gone out to purchase Warren some new clothes, so they were alone.

Should he go over and say something, or should he leave Angel to her thoughts like he always did? Angel stood slightly left of the window as though she was watching someone. If somebody was there, then surely he needed to know. He had promised he would protect her. If she was holding back from telling him they were being watched, then he needed to know.

Strolling into the room, he boldly walked over to where she stood, flicked her hair from her neck and gently kissed the now exposed flesh. Wrapping his arms around her waist, he asked, "What are you looking at?" Angel jumped slightly. She hadn't heard him approach. Without any apparent reason, she flinched. Damien quickly removed his arms from around her waist, worried in case it was the thought of him touching her that had made her flinch. It was a ridiculous thought. They shared the same bed, so why would she suddenly feel repulsed by him? Angel, as though reading his mind, grabbed his hand and then lifted her t-shirt with her damaged hand. Damien looked down to see the bruising on her body. Now he understood. He had caught her wrong.

"I'm sorry. I just wondered what you were looking at." Today he couldn't see any trace of tears in Angel's eyes, only warmth caused by his presence.

"I was just thinking about Libby," she said. Looking up into his eyes, she squeezed his hand gently. "You're shaking."

"I am losing some of the control in my hands," Damien said with a shrug. "I don't seem to be able to stop them from shaking. It's not a problem. I'm ok."

Angel gently stroked his hand. "I wish I could heal you, but my power has gone. I don't know if it will return."

"Don't upset yourself. I've told you I am ok. Anyway, right now I want to know who Libby is."

Angel squeezed his hand again. "When I was younger, Libby was my best friend." Damien nodded; the word *younger* normally referred to the psychiatric hospital. He didn't know much about her past so was always happy to glean any additional information he could without appearing to be too nosey.

"Libby was beautiful, Damien. She had long, golden hair that I would sit and plait. We would pretend she was Rapunzel, like in the story, when Rapunzel was locked in the tower. I would plait Libby's hair and then we would pretend to escape by climbing down her hair. Now when I think about it, Libby would not have been able to climb down her own hair. Don't you think it is silly what you think as kids?" Damien nodded. "I was looking out of the window wondering if I could climb down from here and could somebody really grow their hair that long. It was a silly thought."

Damien smiled. Silly, childlike and beautiful – that was how Angel's mind worked.

"What would you do when you had climbed down Libby's hair?" asked Damien.

"We would run so fast. We would only stop running when we dropped from exhaustion."

"Do you want to run now?"

"Sometimes I want to run, and other times I want to stop and fight."

"If you ran, would you take me with you?"

Angel squeezed his hand again, "Of course."

"And if you stay and fight, will you let me fight alongside you?"

Angel nodded before looking down at his hands. The shaking had almost stopped.

"It comes and goes," whispered Damien. Angel was coming back to him; he could feel it more and more. "Come sit on my knee. I can hold you better."

"Only if you don't fall backwards. I know it hurts you."

"I can't hide anything from you, can I?" he murmured. "It always makes you giggle when we fall backwards, and I love to hear you giggle. It's worth the pain." He held her tightly. "We will be home soon, and then we can do whatever you want. We'll stay with my mam and dad for a while, and if you want to train as a doctor, lawyer or brain surgeon, just say. You have the intelligence, or if you want to doss around for a couple of years and travel, we can do that as well. Whatever you want to do! My dad is trying to find Warren's wider family, and if not, he will return with us to England. Everything is working out."

Angel kissed his cheek and placed her arms around his neck. "I am so lucky to have you."

"I know," he responded; she gave his arm a playful thump.

"You are not supposed to say that," she giggled.

"I know," he laughed. "I am glad you are smiling again."

"I am sorry I can't take your pain at the moment; my power has abandoned me."

"Don't you mean the Shamanic spirits?"

She smiled. "You were listening."

"Unfortunately, so was everybody else. My father thinks you are a complete nutter."

"I didn't think you were listening. Why didn't you mention it before?"

"I don't know. The time never seemed right."

"You don't have to hug me if it hurts."

"Remember, I once said I can't hug you when I know you need to be hugged because it hurts? Well, I can hug you, and now I don't care if it hurts. When you start to smile, I will stop hugging you. Otherwise, you are going to put me through a lot of pain."

"I am smiling, look," she said, giving him a flash of white teeth. He immediately let go. A small amount of relief ran through his body. The pain had been exceptionally bad. In the last few days, the red sore patches had almost covered his entire body. The only place it rarely developed was on his face; however, lately the illness had moved up the back of his neck into his hairline and behind his ears. His face would be its next target. Damien could do with Angel's help, although he would not put any extra pressure on her. She was stressed enough. Under the circumstances, he had always felt he hid his pain fairly well. A little longer was called for, if only he could control the slight shaking in his hands that was beginning to develop.

"If I get my bandages, do you think you can help me tie them tightly around my stomach? I can't tie them as tight as I would like."

A look of concern crossed her face.

"Don't worry. It's just the knife wounds keep weeping."

"After six months!"

"Yeah, I know," Damien sighed. "It's taking longer than the doctors originally estimated. I had to go in for another operation back in the UK. The internal bleeding started again."

"But you were fine on holiday," Angel protested. "There was no weeping. The wounds were healing so well."

"I know."

"I should have been with you. Are you sure you're ok now?"

"Of course. I just don't want to ruin anymore shirts. Stop looking so serious. Smile, remember," Damien urged. She flashed her teeth as he moved to hug her.

"That's better," he laughed.

Her hands moved over his body, caressing but not healing. "You have a lot of strength, Damien," she said, kissing his shoulder blade as she spoke. Her fingertips moved across his shoulders. Angel saw beauty where there was no beauty. His body was a mess, yet not in Angel's eyes. Her fingertips moved across the slightly raised scar left from the attack. Damien closed his eyes for a few seconds, savouring her touch. Angel was showing a tenderness that she hadn't shown him in a long time. There were no tears, only an interest in him, and his body.

"Why do you think Edward did this to you?" Angel said sadly.

"I don't know," Damien shrugged. "I guess he didn't like me."

Angel's fingers once again moved across the scar, "I asked him once."

"And?"

"He laughed at me. I don't think I'll ever be able to understand why," she sighed.

"Try not think of him."

"Maybe I can heal you."

"Don't be silly. You don't have the strength. You said so yourself."

"Please let me try."

"I don't know, Angel. You will only get upset if you can't, and I know your left hand is not as strong as your right."

She looked into his eyes. "If I promise not to get upset, will you let me try?"

"You have to promise."

"I promise."

"Try my chest," Damien conceded. "I don't want to remove the bandage from my stomach." Laying her left hand on his chest, Angel started making circular movements.

"Close your eyes," she ordered. Damien closed them for a few seconds and then opened them again. Angel's eyes were tightly closed. "I can take your pain," she whispered as her fingers moved across his chest. He watched her luscious lips move as she whispered the words. He studied her face as she tried to take some of his pain.

"There is nothing there," she said, opening her eyes. He quickly closed his eyes and pretended to open them as she spoke.

"I think I felt something. Not enough to heal, but there was definitely something," he said.

"Really? I didn't feel anything."

"There was something. I'm sure."

She smiled. "That means I am getting better and then I can help you again."

"That's right," he smiled. Although, he felt awful lying, if he gave her hope then she had something to cling to, to work towards.

Angel sat back on his lap. This time she faced him and wrapped her legs around his back. "Now you can't fall backwards," she laughed. Angel tightened her grip with her thighs, placed her arms around his naked neck and shoulders and gave him a long lingering kiss. One minute tearful, the next playful and loving. Her moods were so hard to predict. He shuffled to the end of the bed.

"Hold on," he whispered; her grip tightened. Standing up, he kept her low down on his pelvis so as not to catch his stomach. "Loosen your grip, and keep that bad hand of yours tucked in," he whispered. As she released her grip, he threw her onto the bed. She squealed with delight as she bounced on the soft mattress. Jumping on the bed next to her, he flicked her raven hair from her face and continued to kiss her.

"I love you Angel," he whispered.

A knock at the door interrupted their playful loving.

"Shall I answer?" Damien asked.

"You had better in case it's important," Angel said with a sigh.

Damien grabbed his t-shirt and made his way to the door. Lieutenant Whitehouse, a young police officer, stood at the door.

"Sorry, we have to go back to the station. Some riot has started on Main Street, and it's all hands on deck. I'm sure your dad will be back soon. We sent him a message." He almost sounded apologetic until the young officer caught sight of Angel. He smiled. "Sorry again. I'll leave you to it," he said, backing away from the door. Damien doubted the young officer would be much use in a riot. A gust of wind would knock him off balance, and he certainly wouldn't be much help if he came face to face with Edward. So Damien wasn't too bothered when he and Angel were left alone.

He was about to go back to Angel when his text gave off its normal incoming bleeping. Damien picked it up immediately. "Dad wants us to meet him in the underground car park in ten minutes."

His father had left the hotel an hour earlier with Warren, making some excuse they were going shopping. Damien knew his father was giving him and Angel some private time, which he appreciated. His dad obviously thought one hour was enough time, unless he had picked up Lieutenant Whitehouse's message. Grabbing the lift, they made their way down to the car park, stopping once to let a mother with a small child in a pushchair out at the ground floor.

"Where do you think he's parked?" asked Angel as they stepped out from the lift. A figure waved, so they headed over in its direction. Damien was pleased Angel was talking more. They were deep in conversation before Angel realised it was not Damien's father they were heading towards – it was Edward. They were too far from the lift to make it back to the safety of the hotel. Angel slipped the sling off her arm and started to back up towards a concrete pillar. Damien, keeping Angel behind him, also backed up towards the pillar. He was protecting Angel the best he could from the lunatic that now stood only twenty feet away. He had feared his next encounter with Edward, but he hadn't picture it happening like this. The nightmares had always been based on the past, or of surreal images that could not be related to real life.

"Well, boy, you are becoming a right pain in the neck. No matter which way I turn, you are there, like a bad smell," hissed Edward, moving towards them. Damien did not respond. He should have realised his father would not have texted him. How could he have been so stupid? And how did Edward get his number? His mobile was new. Angel had taken his last mobile. He made a mental note to ask Angel what happened to it, if they survived this encounter. Only a handful of people had his new number. He prayed his family and friends were ok. Edward was unpredictable – a cold-blooded killer who would stop at nothing, not even killing somebody for a mobile phone number.

"Come, Angel," Edward cajoled. "Enough of this nonsense. It's time to go home." Angel's back was now pressed against the pillar. She glanced quickly around to make sure Samuel was not lurking.

Angel moved slightly to Damien's right.

"Stay where you are Angel," Damien told her, and she stopped abruptly.

"Come here, Angel," Edward held out a gloved hand.

"I said stay where you are."

"I had better go," Angel said regretfully.

"No, stay where you are."

"I would listen to her, boy," Edward spat.

"He'll hurt you, Damien," Angel said sadly.

"No he won't. He may try, but he won't. Stay behind me." Moving his arm behind his body, she moved back to the pillar. He wasn't 100% sure, but it felt like she was holding onto his jacket. "Do you want to try and make it back to the lift?" There was no answer, which he took to mean no. "I thought it was a bad idea, as well. We would be trapped with nobody around. Back to plan A," he whispered. Damien may have been acting brave, and his voice exuded confidence, but his legs felt like jelly. They always did when he was confronted by Edward. He stood his ground. There was no way Angel was going back to Edward. He said he would protect her, and he intended on keeping his word.

"You don't scare me," Damien informed the madman.

"Brave words, lad. Are you sure about that?"

Damien could feel the knife twisting in his stomach, the taste of blood mixing with the saliva in his mouth. He was reliving the horrifying experience he had gone through six months ago. Edward removed his glasses and placed them in their case.

"This is not good," whispered Angel.

"I know," Damien's voice still sounded confident, but inside he was shaking like an autumn leaf. Of course Edward scared him; he would be insane if he didn't. "Don't underestimate me, Edward. Remember, I have a score to settle."

"I am beginning to like you, boy. Brave and stupid – a lethal combination. I should have finished you off when

I had the chance, but I haven't got time to play games. Come, Angel." Once again he held out his hand and took a step closer.

Damien lowered his voice so only Angel could hear. "I am going to turn around and give you some very clear instructions, Angel. Don't take your eyes off Edward; I need to know what he is doing. You must keep giving me his distance in feet. Do you understand?"

Turning slowly towards Angel, he saw that her eyes had not moved from Edward. There was terror in her eyes, and if she looked into his eyes, she would probably see the same look. "How far, Angel?"

"Eighteen feet," was the quick response.

"Remember when we were at the lake Angel? I used to teach you some rugby moves. We are going to do the Dummy Double-Double Inside move, without a ball. You are going to take the route of the first runner and the fourth runner. Is this too confusing?"

"Fifteen foot," she said.

"When I shout now, I want you to run as fast as you can to the white Chevrolet on your left. Don't look now. Go around it clockwise and run straight up the aisle to the red estate. Cut right into the centre and run towards the white transit van with waste recycling written on the side. Before you reach it, move left again."

"Ten feet."

"Run straight as fast as you can, until you pass the barrier into the open air. Don't look behind, whatever you hear. Just keep running until you reach that barrier. Head for the hotel steps. Get help. Ask the concierge to contact the police. I will be right behind you."

"Eight feet."

"Have you got that, Angel?" Damien asked. There was no response. He prayed she understood. He could smell stale tobacco. He knew Edward was close, without Angel reinforcing the distance through her measurements. The overpowering sickly smell that clung to Edward's clothes was getting stronger.

Reaching into his pocket, he grasped the glass paperweight that Warren had given him. Maybe Angel was wrong. Maybe Warren did have a gift. Warren's last words were clearly, "Carry this, Damien. You may need it." He placed it in his pocket and thought, *It's the same weight as a baseball although crescent shape rather than circular*. He had forgotten it was still in his pocket until a few moments ago.

"Six feet," whispered Angel.

"Now," screamed Damien. He had already moved right and turned – a simple dummy move. Edward had automatically followed his movement, giving Angel a head start. She sprinted towards the white car as though her life depended on it.

Edward was now off balance. He glared at Damien and shouted, "Death to you, boy," before taking a swing. Damien's left arm came up in self-defence, and the blow glanced off his forearm. The blow should have hurt, but Damien was numb to the pain.

"Nice block, but too slow, boy." Edward's hand wrapped around Damien's fist and squeezed tightly. "Are you sure you're not scared of me?"

Damien twisted his body to try and relieve the pain in his arm, which was now being twisted with the force of Edward's grip. He reached up and grabbed Edward's collar.

"Get your diseased hands off my clothes, boy." As he spoke, his other hand slapped Damien hard across the face, making him feel stupid once again. He was so easy beaten, toyed with like a child.

"I'll be back for you later," Edward promised, releasing the grip on his hand. Damien cradled it to his body. It was not broken; his pride was hurt more than anything.

Edward started to move quickly towards Angel. After all, it was the girl he wanted. "Run," screamed Damien. This time his voice had lost its composure. Pulling the paperweight out of his pocket, his hand shook uncontrollably from the aftereffects of Edward's grip, making it difficult to line up the throw.

If he was correct, Edward would not follow Angel precisely. He would prefer to take the shorter inside line, which was what the opposition would normally do when playing rugby. This would leave Damien with a clear shot and keep Angel out of the firing line. She would only come into his firing line for a couple of seconds. This was the only way to keep Edward on the same line. Drawing his right arm high above his head, he leant back. Now was the time to see how skilled his baseball was. He used to be good, though maybe not as good as he was in rugby.

"Believe," that's what Angel would say. "Believe in yourself, Damien; you are stronger than you think." He placed his left arm in front of his body to keep his balance. His arm and hand continued to shake. He needed to gain full control or the throw would be impossible. The slight shaking suddenly stopped. He felt a subdued calmness taking over his body. He had made this throw many times. The last time was admittedly several years ago, but he had successfully managed to throw the ball to his teammate from an obscene distance on the field. He didn't dare think what could happen if he messed up the throw. He wasn't strong enough to take on Edward in one-to-one combat. He could possible tackle him and then what? Edward was also sure to have his knife with him, and a fist against a knife – his odds were looking pretty poor. He must not think like that. He could do it.

"Believe," he whispered. "Believe in yourself."

He reminded himself he had done this move hundreds of times. He heard the crowd buzzing in his ears. He loved that sound, when the entire school was there to support them, shouting and screaming their names. His heart would be pounding against his chest, knowing tonight he would either be a hero or a villain. The clock was ticking. The final whistle was about to be blown. Damien was ready. This time, it wouldn't be his team catching the object. He didn't want anybody to catch it. His timing would be spot on. It always was. The size and shape of the paperweight would make the velocity slightly different to what he was accustomed to. A forty-foot shot was not always the easiest target to aim at, especially when it was moving. His fingertips loosely grip the paperweight. His strength had to be in his wrist.

Taking a deep breath, Damien saw that Edward was now perfectly placed in his eye line. Aiming slightly in front of his target, he released the paperweight with all the force he could muster. He watched it fly through the air towards the running figure. The green blur from the four-leaf clover embedded inside the glass prison turned magically through the air. He could hear the crowd going wild. He could not afford to stand and watch.

"Follow it through," he could hear his coach bawling in his ear. He started to run towards Edward, following the line of the paperweight. Everything felt like it was in slow motion. The paperweight glided towards its target slowly, turning through the air. The paperweight hit Edward on the side of his head.

"Damn," Damien muttered. He had been aiming for the back of Edward's head. The blow knocked Edward off balance. Edward stumbled and fell forward, blood and shattered bone spraying from his head. He went down onto his left knee with such force that Damien was surprised his knee cap was not shattered.

Edward managed to stand, but he stumbled again and wildly grabbed the car to his left to stop himself falling. The force of his hand on the car bonnet started the horn blasting. Its loud, vulgar noise echoed around the car park. Damien can see a fountain of blood squirting from Edwards's head. The paperweight smashed on the floor, soaked in blood, brain, skin and bone. Damien was now gaining on Edward, and thankfully Angel had now passed the red estate and was closing on the white van. She hadn't stopped to look around. She obviously knew something was happening. The noise alone would tell her that. Edward staggered a few more steps, but the strength was now leaving his body.

The force of the paperweight had hit the parietal lobe of the left hemisphere of the brain. Turning towards Damien, Edward's speech was now incoherent, but he still managed to shout a string of words, even though they no longer made sense. Damien was tempted to knock Edward down again, but he knew Edward could still have an unnatural strength left in his body. He took a wide birth; too many movies had shown him what can happen if you approach a dying body. Edward fell once more, arms and legs splaying uncontrollably.

He was either having a seizure or swimming the 100m front crawl. His nails clawed at the ground, legs flapped rapidly at first, before slowing, and finally stopping. The blood seeped into his clothing. A large, dark pool of blood was beginning to form underneath the body. Damien had never seen a human die before. This was one experience he didn't want to see again.

Could Edward see the white light? The same white light he had seen many months ago after the stabbing? Was Edward floating towards the light, where the hazy figures stood with their hands outstretched, beckoning and drawing him closer? A cold shudder ran down Damien's spine as he remembered touching one of the icy cold fingers as it reached out to grab his hand and pull him into the light. It was an unsettling experience, one he had never told anybody about. He had been close to death that day. If it hadn't been for Angel's voice and that warm, tingling sensation her fingers created, he would be dead. Do we all see the same when we die? For a moment he considered this question. Now was not the time to ponder such a thought.

The underground car park, with its flickering fluorescent light, was closing in on him. The smell of car fumes and death filled the air. Breathing was difficult. His legs must take him to the barrier, to the daylight, where he could once again breathe the fresh air. Edward's dying breath seemed excessively loud. Damien still did not approach him. Instead, he walked slowly to the barrier. His body shook uncontrollably as he realised he had just killed a man.

Angel saw Damien from the top of the steps. At first she thought he was injured. He appeared to be staggering, but his stance changed when he saw her. He gave a small wave and then doubled over and relieved himself of his scrambled egg breakfast on the lower step. Climbing the steps, his pace quickened. Angel ran down the steps to meet him. They reached the platform together. Picking her up, he swung her around as a parent would do with their child.

"It's all over," he whispered as he held her tight. The pain stabbed through his arms, across his shoulders and down his chest and stomach. Angel's lashes brushed against his cheek as he held her close. She started to cry. It's strange how everything can change so quickly. Angel had always been the stronger one in their relationship – now she was like a child; her tears fell so effortlessly. Their roles had been reversed. Not that he minded, although he didn't feel very strong, not after killing a man. His hands began to tremble. Was it the illness or was his nerves taking over?

The following half hour was mayhem, with police and medical staff rushing around. The area was cordoned off. Damien and Angel sat still on the hotel steps, waiting to be questioned. Damien's arm was around Angel's shoulder, giving her the support she desperately needed. Not only did his body ache, but his right arm felt as though it was trapped in a clamp, which was being slowly turned, squeezing the bone and muscle until it was about to explode. The pain was pulsating through his body. Weak and nauseated, he refused to move his arm from her shoulder. Damien was locked in his own thoughts, mulling over what had just happened. Thank you, Worthington High School, for employing an American coach. The throw was almost perfect, apart from the death. Stopping Edward was his aim, but killing him had never been Damien's intention – even though he deserved it. Colour started to drain from his face.

"Are you alright?" asked Angel.

"I've been better," he responded.

Squeezing his shaking hand, Angel knew what he was thinking, and it wasn't positive thoughts. The pain showed in his eyes, along with a deep sadness and fear that he was trying hard to hide from the onlookers and her.

A figure watched them from the other side of the road. A doorway hid his whereabouts, as his body was shrouded in shadow. Today was not the time to react. He would watch and wait until the time was right, and then he would reveal his identity to Angel, and unveil his vengeful plan.

Damien's father eventually arrived at the scene after the commotion had died down. Warren ran up the steps, and Angel embraced her brother. Without any commitment in her voice, she whispered, "It's all over."

"Thanks, mate," said Damien. Warren smiled a knowing smile.

"Thanks for what?" asked Angel.

"Nothing. Just man's stuff," said Warren. This was Damien's and Warren's secret.

Insecurity

Angel had just showered. She was beginning to look much better. The dark shadows from beneath her eyes had almost gone, and her hair was starting to look healthy again. Damien's father could tell something was amiss ever since the death of Edward. He hoped Angel would open up to him again. She was an unusual child, open in some ways, closed in others. He had somehow managed to gain her trust back at the station. Could this continue? Knocking gently on her bedroom door, a confident voice told him to enter. Stepping into the room, he found Angel wrapped in the hotel dressing gown, sitting in front of the dressing table, brushing her hair.

"Oops, sorry, young lady. I'll speak to you later."

Angel laughed. "Don't be silly. The robe is firmly fastened."

"It better be, young lady, or this old man's ticker may not be able to take it." They both laughed. This was a good way to start off this difficult conversation.

He sat on the edge of the bed, and Angel swivelled her chair to face him. She continued to brush her hair. "One hundred strokes, my mam would always say to me," she said. Recollecting the memory, she managed a faint grin.

It's no good 'beating around the bush,' he thought. *Just say it.*

Taking a deep breath, he asked, "What's wrong, Angelica?"

"Nothing, why?" she responded, but her eyes didn't meet his, and he knew she was lying.

"Look at me, Angel. Are you afraid Samuel will come after you?"

"No," was the quick response. "I think," she paused for a moment trying to choose her words carefully before continuing, "Samuel would not be interested in Warren or I, unless he wanted revenge. He is too busy beating up vicars. I saw the news this morning. The vicar down Cable Street was attacked. He's not dead but close."

David frowned. *Why do the youngsters today always use the wrong grammar? Warren or me, not I.* This had always bugged him. He felt like correcting her, but this was not the time. Her grammar may be wrong, but she was right about another vicar being attacked, and this one had survived to tell an insane story of the beating he had endured.

"So what's wrong?" he asked again. She had hardly said two words in the last thirty-six hours.

There was a long pause. "William had an army of costumed dolls."

"Who's William?"

There was no direct response to his question, but she continued her story. "William would have been so angry if he heard me call them dolls. They were action figures with super-powers: the power to make themselves invisible, the power to fly, the power to run faster than any known animal on earth. The teachers were always confiscating the small six-inch figures. Next day, William would return with half-a-dozen new action figures. William must have had hundreds of dolls in his house, more than all the girls in my class added together.

"Don't you think so, sir?"

David nodded, not sure how to respond. Angel would come to the point soon. He just had to wait.

"Sir, something was not right, on that day..."

"Which day, Angelica?" But again he was met with no direct response.

"Did you know Edward had obsessive behaviour that stretched further than just the cleaning of his glasses? Did I tell you he had obsessive habits?" She continued without waiting for a response. "The way he moved, the actions he took, the clothes he wore were all bordering on being obsessive. Every day he wore a dark brown tailored wool-blend single-breasted suit. That was a mouthful, wasn't it, sir?"

David nodded. Now he was intrigued where the story was going.

"The cut complemented his frame, but every day there was a subtle difference. On Mondays, two small buttons decorated the cuffs instead of the traditional one. On Wednesdays, the chest pocket that normally displayed a neatly folded white handkerchief had a small flap over the pocket. Thursday there was no flap; this time replaced with double stitching. Friday the buttons were slightly darker. Saturday the suit slightly lighter, and Sunday a slightly longer fibre was used on the suit. Tuesday had been the hardest day for me to spot any difference, and it took several weeks studying the suits before I identified the subtle difference – the buttons on the front of the jacket were five millimetres lower than on the other days. I used to imagine Edward's wardrobe consisted of seven suits lined up in date order, like floppy rag soldiers waiting to be summoned for their weekly outing."

"And your point is?"

"Edward was wearing the wrong suit. He had Sunday's suit on. I can't figure out why."

"Maybe he had spilt something on his Wednesday suit or he had mislaid it."

"Edward would never mislay a suit."

"He could have bought a new suit to replace his Wednesday suit."

"Possibly. That would make a lot of sense, although I'm sure it was Sunday's suit."

"Damien said you were never closer to Edward than six foot."

"That's correct."

"And you still had time to see his suit?"

"Yes. To me it was important. I don't think Edward was in full control that day, which worked in Damien's favour."

The words "in Damien's favour" was a strange phrase to use. Why not say 'our' favour? thought David. There was a pause.

"Damien is in serious trouble, isn't he?" Angel asked.

David sighed, "Yes, he is."

"Will Damien go to prison?" she asked quietly.

"I don't know. I hope not but it is a possibility. We need to prove you were in danger." David was trying to be realistic. The same thought had run through his head a thousand times. The same thoughts were no doubt running through Damien's head. His son had been quiet and more thoughtful since his recent encounter with Edward. He needed to sit down with his son and run through the possibilities. It was a long shot that the district attorney would press charges, but they had to plan what they should do just in case. If only it had been him instead of Damien that killed Edward. His son was an innocent party who had been dragged into Edward's life, mainly through his girlfriend and himself. They were both to blame.

"Do you believe I was in danger?" she asked.

"Only you and Damien know that," David responded. He believed that Damien had been in danger, but going to trial with Angel as a witness was dangerous. Her responses would be unpredictable. He had heard Angel in the hospital and even now she was having doubts on the danger Edward presented. The prosecution would make mincemeat of her. His mind drifted back to Damien. His son had not spoken to him about Edward's death. An ordinary day had turned into a ghastly day that would change all their lives. As a child, Damien had always bottled up his emotions, which was dangerous. He needed to talk to Damien sooner rather than later, and he needed Angel strong to help him with this difficult task.

"Sir, if...if Damien has to serve time, I will stay with him here in America."

The Chief Inspector looked at her. "I thought you were desperate to get back to England?"

"I am, but I won't leave without Damien. He will need my support. Anyway, what sort of person would I be to abandon him? Damien came to America to take me home, so we will go home together. I won't leave him, sir, I promise."

The Chief Inspector smiled weakly. Reason told him that there was no case against his son, but his gut instinct said that if someone was powerful enough to push this incident into a trial, then the outcome was questionable. He knew his son would have to go through a lot of questioning and it would be hard for him to relive the moment again. In his son's favour the police in the US knew about Edward; Edward had already hurt his son; Damien hurled a paperweight, which any jury would call luck and not murderous intent. It was doubtful the Attorney General would press charges but going to trial there was never any guarantee of the outcome.

Staying in America to support his son was not feasible – a job awaited back home. There were so many people who were desperate for his job, who would be happy to see him fail. Inspector Halloway, the weasel who liked to report any slight hiccup to his superiors, would make the first move for his position, quickly followed by Inspector Stafford. They would have a field day when they heard about his son, and if that was not bad enough, he still had to face Claudette, his wife. He could only imagine her reaction if he didn't bring her son home safely.

He patted Angel's hand tenderly. "You are a good kid, and you're right: Damien will need you. If Damien has to serve a prison sentence, I will set you up the best I can before I fly back to England." In many ways, it was a relief to the Chief Inspector, knowing his son would have somebody close who would visit him and keep his spirits high. His son was so different when he was with Angelica, happy and confident. If the unthinkable happened, the Chief Inspector would visit when work allowed but weekly would have been impossible.

There was another long pause. "Do I need to arrange Edward's funeral?" asked Angel quietly. The Chief

Inspector squirmed at the mention of Edward's name – the man had nearly killed his son, and destroyed Damien's innocence. Here was a young girl asking if she needed to arrange a funeral for a killer. A funeral was too dignified for this animal that had destroyed so many lives.

David shuddered. "Is that what has been bothering you?"

Shrugging, Angel's face flushed with embarrassment.

"I am sorry. I didn't mean to embarrass you."

"Mr Harrington," Angel said slowly.

"David," he corrected her.

"David, you are not going to like what I am about to say, and I don't want to upset you as you have been really nice to me and Warren. I know Edward was wrong what he did but...." Her voice trailed off. "He was the only family I had," she said quickly. "I grew up with him, and I know I didn't always like what he did, but Edward was a father to me. He home tutored me, taught me to speak fluent French and Romanian, and I am sorry, but I can't help feeling a twinge of sadness."

David sighed and placed his hand over hers. "I may not like it, but I do understand you are in mourning. Edward was an evil man, you know."

"I know."

"Why Romanian, Angelica?"

She shrugged her shoulders. "He said I may need it one day."

An unusual language to learn, thought David. He had had his suspicions that Edward or Eftemie was Eastern European, and the name *Eftemie* was a Romanian name. Then again, he used several aliases. Maybe he had stumbled onto something, but this wasn't the time to press for more information.

"Come here," David stood up to hug Angel, a hug which was surprising comforting. Angel could not remember a time when Edward had hugged her. Now that she was not looking David in the eye, Angel whispered, "Edward was my biological father."

"I know," David whispered back.

"How?" Angel looked up.

"I'm a policeman."

"And yet you have been so nice to me, knowing what Edward did to Damien." At least she could not be accused of hiding information.

"We don't choose our families..." David paused. "It did take me a while to come to terms with that fact; it's not your fault."

"Sir, will I go to prison?" Angel worried.

"What for?"

"Warren's parents', possibly as an accomplice."

"Angelica, nobody knows what happened but you, Samuel, Damien and myself. I still have the tape, but I should have had a second officer in the room during the whole of the interview, so at the moment don't worry. The tape is for information only and at the moment is the least of our problems."

"Thank you," she whispered.

"And to answer your previous question, the authorities will sort out the funeral although..." he paused, not knowing how she would react to his next comment, "Edward's body has been mislaid."

"Mislaid!" she cried.

"Yes."

"How?"

"We don't know. We're trying to find it."

Angel said nothing

He could see she was thinking. "Are you ok?"

She smiled, "Yes, of course, and thank you, sir, for everything. I do appreciate everything you have done for me and Warren."

This was one busy bedroom. As his father was leaving, Damien entered the room. A friendly pat on the shoulder told Damien everything was going to be alright. Angel was back at the dressing table, brushing her damp hair. Every strand brushed one-hundred times just like her mother had said. Damien loved brushing her hair. It was relaxing; the slow movement of the brush pulling through the hair usually helped him to forget his troubles, but today forgetting the looming trial was proving difficult. He didn't want to go to prison.

Dancing Light

It started as a minor shaking in her hands and quickly spread to her arms and legs. It was starting again. If she didn't get back to the room soon, she would soon have an audience, and she didn't want that. What was happening was personal. She would share the experience with Damien, but nobody else.

"Damien, can you take me back to the room now?" she whispered. He had been deep in conversation with the receptionist and hadn't noticed Angel's change in colouring. She was now a deathly white and shaking uncontrollable. One glance and he realised something was not right. A seizure was his immediate thought.

"I'll get help," he said, standing up.

"No, the room please, Damien," Angel pleaded.

"Shall I call an ambulance?" Damien looked at the receptionist and then back to Angel.

"No, thank you. I just want to go to the room, Damien."

"We'll be fine; I'll call you if I need help," he quickly told the receptionist, who was also alarmed. Placing his arm around Angel's waist to support her weight, he half carried her back to the room.

The whole of her body was now shaking. The lack of power and co-ordination in her legs caused her feet to drag along the ground.

"Don't worry," she whispered as they approached the Stevenson suite. "When inside, remove my t-shirt and trousers, and I will show you something amazing. No matter what you see, don't lay a finger on my skin. I don't know how it will affect you." The final words were garbled and incoherent, so she hoped he understood. Damien didn't protest. Instead he steered Angel to the bed and then sat next to her and waited. He was unsure what he was waiting for, or if bringing her here was the right thing to do. The shaking was beginning to subside, and at last her body looked at peace. Her eyes had been closed for the last few minutes. Damien continued to wait. The amazing sight she had spoken about slowly started to appear before his eyes.

Angel's body started to glow. A gold streak of light danced upon her body. It was like a sparkling sequined body suit shimmering in the sunlight. The silver and gold flickered as it bounced on the surface of her skin. The light first appeared on her neck before moving slowly down her body. Splitting into two, one streak moved down her right arm, and the second moved further down her body. Mesmerised by the golden glow that her body was generating, Damien did not notice the marks on her neck had disappeared, until a couple of minutes had passed. Angel's back arched and she let out a gentle groan. Her damaged hand pressed firmly down into the mattress. There was no sign of pain, only pleasure. She groaned again, and slowly exhaled. It was surreal. He had never seen anything like it before. The first golden streak glistened and bounced around her damaged right hand for several minutes. The second streak moved quicker, heading down her legs, removing all trace of the bruising that had been left from Samuel's metal bar.

Angel reached out her left hand and grabbed Damien's hand. Remembering Angel's last words, he tried to pull away, but her grip was too strong. He watched as the golden glow entered his body. A tingling sensation moved up his arm. His head fell backwards as he let out a groan.

"Oh my god," he moaned. The glowing sparkly light had now reached his neck and shoulders. The sensation roaming through his body was out of this world. The experience was totally new.

Angel sat up when she heard him groan and started to panic. Damien's breathing was too rapid. His breaths had turned to short pants. Why had she taken the risk? She berated herself. He was struggling to take in the necessary oxygen to survive. His heart was beating too fast. Angel's panic caused her breathing to accelerate. It was now in line with Damien's. A slight pain stabbed at her chest. Through concentration and relaxation, she should be able to control his breathing, but she was losing control. The only way to break the connection was to release Damien's hand. As soon as Angel released her grasp, Damien felt himself falling. His head began to spin. Slowly, he started to gain control until he began to soar like an eagle. Now in full control, he soared across lush green fields, thick, dense forests, over snow-capped mountains and winding rivers, gradually losing height until he landed safely. It was a wonderful feeling that he longed to experience again.

Glancing down at Angel, he saw that her eyes were still closed. Her chest was moving up and down as rapidly as his. A couple of minutes passed, and she still had not said anything. He wanted to hold her, but he remembered her last words before she lost the ability to speak coherently. He didn't want to touch her again until she said it was alright. The minor pain in his chest began to subside. His breathing was returning back to normal. The tingling sensation was leaving his body. Angel's heartbeat slowed. Damien knew his heartbeat was still slightly fast, but his breathing was now normal. Feeling sexually aroused, his body ached from the sensation he had just experienced. Angel's half naked body lay on the bed. He had not had sex for over six months, and he wanted her so badly.

Angel opened her eyes and wriggled the fingers on her right hand. "Good?" she asked.

"Real good," said Damien. He couldn't take his eyes off her. "I want you so bad, Angel. Can we…" but he never finished the sentence. She had already pulled him gently down on top of her.

"What just happened?" he asked a while later.

"We had sex, silly," she laughed.

"You know what I mean," he replied, stroking the side of her face.

"I don't know what to call it, but I always think of the sparkles as healing crystals. It started a couple of months ago. I found my body could heal itself. It first happened when I had injured my arm." (What she didn't say was that Samuel had broken her arm when they were mutilating Warren's parents. The thought made her shudder in disgust and fear.) "A week later I started shaking, and then I experienced exactly what you saw today. At first I was scared. I wasn't sure why I was shaking, and then the golden glow started, and I relaxed. It was as though I knew it was a good thing. Edward told me it was natural; I was getting stronger. The same thing happened again a few weeks later when I bruised my legs." (Samuel again with his damned bar. She wished she could have taken the bar to his legs so he could feel the pain it caused.) "The only drawback, I don't know when it's going to happen, so I have no control. From the three experiences I have had, it appears between one and three weeks after the damage is done to my body.

"How do you feel?" asked Angel after she finished her explanation.

"A little light-headed, although that could be the sex," laughed Damien.

Angel smiled. "When I grabbed your hand, I was hoping the crystals would pass from me to you and cure whatever illness you have. If I am right, and this is only a hunch, where the crystals reached in your body, the illness will not appear again."

Damien smiled. He hoped she was right. No more pain in his right hand, arm, shoulder and neck would be a miracle. In the last six months, he had stepped up his intake of painkillers to the level he had been taking when he first met Angel, but he had never experienced the same severity of pain that he used to experience at school. To have no pain in certain parts of his body would be amazing.

"I'm just sorry I couldn't give you more. I didn't know how you would react with a foreign entity entering your body. I could tell you were struggling to breathe."

He nodded his head. "Maybe a little, but I didn't feel alarmed. In fact, I felt amazing, like I was floating," said Damien.

"I always wanted to heal you, Damien. My mum could heal all illnesses, and it seems so unfair that I can only take away your pain on a temporary basis."

Damien threw his arms around her. “Thank you. What you have tried to do for me is something I will never forget.” He kissed her tenderly. The warmth of his breath tingled on her skin as he whispered in her ear, “Remember, grab my left hand next time.”

She laughed. “What next time?”

*****

The weeks passed with no incidences. Angel was becoming stronger. Damien gave her all the love and support she needed. His father watched with pride as he saw his son bring his girlfriend back from the pain she had suffered. Angel was becoming independent; her laughter was beginning to fill the rooms, and she had begun to take Damien’s pain on a regular basis. It had taken time, but her ability to take pain had finally reached the level it once was. There had been no more healing, not yet. Healing was a different skill she would eventually learn; a skill that would not require self-injury.

The Court Room

Bail had been easy. Damien had handed over his passport and agreed to stay in the country. His father had paid a hefty amount, and life continued for the next six weeks, but the hearing was getting closer. Captain Henley had informed David the judge would probably be J.T. Senfield. He was not known to be lenient, but he was normally fair in his decision. Marcel Stenton was representing Edward; nobody was sure who appointed Marcel, normally it would have been a prosecutor appointed by the state. Edward obviously had friends in high places that were serious about getting revenge. Damien's lawyer was Oliver Trellis, an elderly gentleman, who in Henley's opinion was the only lawyer who could take on Stenton. He was aware of every trick in the trade, but he wouldn't come cheap.

The Chief Inspector had one more meeting with Trellis, and then he would introduce his son. So far everything had run smoothly. Henley conducted the police interview for the Chief Inspector, even though he no longer got involved with that side of police work. Much to David's relief, he had been allowed to observe the interview through the same one-way glass window Damien had observed him interview Angel.

Another five minutes, and he would leave the hotel room for his 10:30 a.m. meeting. Stepping onto the small balcony, he looked out onto the street. A dusting of snow covered the metal railing. A few flakes were still falling intermittently. He could see his son, Angel and Warren playing in the fresh covering of snow. His son's head was bent back, and his mouth was open, trying to catch the snow crystals on his tongue. Angel had watched and copied his son's action. It was a game the Chief Inspector's two sons would play before they became men; the snow tingling on their tongues as it melted. On one of the few times he had been with them as a family he could remember playing the same game; it was a strange, fascinating sensation. A slight breeze blew the small snow flurries back into the air, making it difficult to catch the flakes.

It was so nice to see his son happy again; playing like a child, making up for the childhood he had lost. It was a strange threesome. None of them had had a traditional upbringing. All had been tortured in some way, yet at this moment in time, they all seemed happy, without a care in the world. He watched his son kiss his girlfriend and drop a snowball down her top. He watched Angel shriek with laughter and then batter Damien with a barrage of snowballs before they both ganged up on Warren and bombarded him with snowball after snowball. A little further behind the small gang, David could see Detective Haines. He was hanging back, watching their every move, ready for any sign of trouble.

A Smith and Wesson 5906 semi-automatic pistol was tucked into Detective Haines' shoulder holster. Henley had said Haines was a cracking shot and fast. The Chief Inspector could see no obvious bulge to indicate the

Detective was carrying a weapon. On the opposite side of the street, an old man walked slowly, his body hunched over. A long mac covered most of his body, and a Stetson was pulled down low on his head to keep out the chill in the air. He was keeping pace with the small gang, never passing, always keeping the same distance. The Chief Inspector craned his neck to try and get a better look at the figure following his kids. Was he one of Henley's men or was it one of the Doctor's men?

The Chief Inspector picked up his mobile and made a quick call – his suspicions were not justified. The old man was one of Henley's men and apparently only thirty-nine years old, on secondment from the Canadian force. *Nice disguise,* thought David. He left the room knowing his son was well-looked after, unaware of another figure standing only feet away from the small gang hidden in the shadow of the trees. Large dark sunglasses covered the stranger's eyes. He didn't like the bright sunlight, and as the light bounced off the glare of the snow, it hurt his eyes even more. Ever since his eye was damaged when he was a child, it had hurt. Now was not the time to make his move. He was a patient man.

*****

As the trial grew closer, Damien slept less, lying awake most nights, staring at the ceiling. He was convinced he was going to prison. Focusing Angel on the trial was proving hard. He didn't want to put her on the stand, but she was his only witness, so he had no choice. He tried to explain it would take a miracle to keep him out of jail. Angel couldn't comprehend the idea. Whenever he tried to discuss the possibility, tears always began to form in her eyes. He didn't want her to tell them about her power she possessed. Threatening Angel with a stay in a mental institution or being dissected like a lab rat didn't seem to phase her.

"But, Damien."

"No buts, Angel. It will make no difference to the outcome of my trial, but it could affect the rest of your life and mine when I get out. Do you understand?"

Angel always reluctantly nodded, "You won't go to prison. I know you won't. They will understand."

She was forever the optimist, but Damien knew Angel was wrong.

The night before the trial, he held her close to his body, knowing this was the last night he would hold her this close for a long time. He prayed when she was on the stand she would not mention the power she possessed. He loved her too much for her to endure the torment of the questions and the tests they would put her through. All it would take was one fraudulent slip. Slipping his arm around her waist, he managed to find her naked flesh. Gently caressing her soft skin, he turned her towards him.

"Look at me, Angel," he whispered. Her eyes rose to meet his. They were tearful but no tears were falling. "We will get through this."

"I know," she said. Her voice was husky and strained.

Tim had been called to give evidence to strengthen Damien's case and to confirm Damien's fear of Edward. Damien perked up for a while in Tim's presence, although the thought of prison continued to haunt him. Trellis briefed them all what to say and what not to say. He warned them how Stenton would twist what they said under oath and make them out to be the bad guys.

He would suggest they had planned to attack and kill Edward in the car park, even if the weapon was unconventional. Trellis had taken them to see a trial so they could see what would happen and what the inside of a courtroom looked like. Preparation was the only way they could win this case. The courthouse was a dominating building situated in the city; the court rooms just as overwhelming. Trellis tried to reassure them. Like David, he felt that the case couldn't hold water on paper, but with the mysterious power backing Edward's side, he feared this was going to be a difficult case to win.

*****

Damien stood outside the courtroom, waiting for his name to be called. He held Angel tightly as he tried to muster up the strength to face the inevitable. He was shaking. He had not felt this nervous for a long time. He wanted Angel with him in the courtroom to give him strength, but this was impossible. Once she had given evidence, she would be there. Until then he would have to face Stenton alone. Her arms were tightly wrapped around his waist. He wondered when he would next hold her; when he would feel the warmth of her breath, the beating of her heart and the curves of her body.

They had not spoken for a couple of minutes, both deep in their own thoughts, rehearsing the answers Trellis had given them. A voice called his name, but Damien did not move. His dad came over and gave them both a hug. "Come on, son. It's time."

"I know," whispered Damien. "No matter what happens, please wait for me, Angel."

"Everything will be…" but she didn't finish her sentence. "I'll wait, I promise," she said. That was what he wanted to hear.

A commanding voice shouted his name again. His dad intervened.

"Come on, Damien. Let's not get on their bad side. Focus. Remember it was self-defence. He tried to kill you before. This time he would have succeeded if you had not stopped him."

"I'm ready, Dad," Damien managed a faint smile as he pulled away from Angel's grasp.

"Slay the dragon, Damien."

"I'll slay it for you," he whispered.

"They are waiting for you, son," his dad reminded him.

Damien nodded and followed his dad down the corridor to the courtroom.

"Why a dragon?" his dad asked as soon as they were out of ear-shot.

"I think the dragon refers to Angel's psychiatric nurse. It means go in fighting; the prosecution can be slayed."

Angel suddenly shouted, and Damien spun around. "I love you," she yelled. Damien burst out laughing. Angel rarely said those three little words but when she did it always felt so special.

"I love you too," he shouted back before disappearing from sight.

Sitting outside of the courtroom with her shoulder-blades pressed against the panelled wall, Angel waited for her name to be called. A tear rolled down her cheek and dripped onto the back of her hand. The next few days were going to be difficult. She needed to stay strong and focussed. Tim would join her soon. She hoped he would not mention the note again.

Since Tim had arrived in the United States, he had been funny with her. She only asked if Laurel intended to give evidence at Damien's trial. He had snapped at her, mumbling something about a rugby match and asking why she was so desperate to see Laurel. Then there was the note Tim had forced into her hand. A note from Laurel with the words, *I await your answer.* She had tried to explain to Tim that Laurel meant nothing to her, but her words fell on deaf ears. Only the trial was stopping Tim from telling Damien.

It was not her fault Laurel was obsessed with her. She had begged Tim not to tell Damien. It would destroy him, especially now when he seemed so insecure with the pending trial. After the trial, Tim could tell Damien if he wanted. She had nothing to hide. She would deny any attraction to Laurel, any involvement. Laurel did not want her. He wanted her gift so he could play rugby without fear of injury. She knew this, and Laurel knew this, so why did he keep making out he was in love with her? This was not the time to dwell on such matters. She needed to stay focussed. The trial was her immediate concern.

The trial was finally under way. Stenton and Trellis had a powerful presence in court. Trellis stood monumental in a beige tweed three-piece suit and a sky-blue tie. Stenton wore a dark two-piece suit, portraying sadness and mourning over the death of a client to the jury, one of the oldest tricks in the book. Enforced by his father, Damien radiated respect and professionalism with his new short haircut. A dark grey fitted blazer hung neatly on his frame. Stenton and Trellis knew the outcome of the trial would hinge on one of them making a mistake, a slight slip up on words or something one of them had overlooked. They needed to be alert at all times. Unfortunately, it was the accused that slipped up.

Nobody thought to tell Damien or Trellis that Edward was Angel's biological father. When Stenton raised this fact in court, it threw Damien off guard. The taste of bile filled his mouth. His hands turned clammy as he gripped the sides of the stand. His legs shook, and the healthy glow drained from his face. A startled rabbit caught in the headlights of an on-coming truck, nowhere to hide, nowhere to run. Until that moment, he had answered the questions confidently; now he was unsure what to say, stammering and stuttering over his words as he tried to compose himself.

"I didn't know," he finally managed to stammer.

"Speak up. We can't hear you," Stenton's voice echoed around the courtroom. Damien glanced over to the jury and then up to where Angel sat.

"I am sorry," he silently mouthed. He wasn't sure if he was sorry. Angel's father had nearly killed him, which was why her father was now dead. In a perfect world, he would be a man Damien could respect, someone he would approach to ask for the hand of his daughter. Killing your girlfriend's father was inexcusable, but Edward had tried to kill him first. He felt confused. It had been hard for him to come to terms with the fact that Edward was her guardian and meant something to her – but he had not dreamed that Edward could be her father.

Stenton was obviously leading him somewhere. At first it was not apparent, and then it hit him like a force ten hurricane. Stenton had seen his chance and started to twist the scenario; a father's love for his child, tormented by a vindictive young man who was trying to take his only daughter away from him. None of the rumours of this father's killings had ever been proven. They were just rumours created by the young man who stood in front of him and his naïve girlfriend who was blinkered by love. Trellis kept trying to step in trying to stop the onslaught. His client was losing control. Why hadn't anybody thought to tell him Edward was Angel's father? It would have changed their plan, the emphasis they placed on certain events. He may have been able to stop this onslaught! How had Stenton been privileged to this information?

David and Angel just looked at each other. "I had not given it a second thought," stammered David. "I was just so annoyed when all the case notes went missing in transit from England to here. I wasn't thinking straight." The Chief Inspector had been frantic. Detective Strangeway had parcelled and loaded the documents personally onto the Boeing 747, but the documents never reached JFK airport. The cabin crew and ground staff had all been interviewed; there were no leads, no explanation to their whereabouts.

Angel grabbed David's arm. "Don't worry. The jury will see through these lies," she whispered. David gave a faint smile and patted her hand.

"We've had it, Angel. I've been at enough trials to see the writing on the wall. Damien is going to prison. We have nothing. The stab wounds are not a strong enough defence for what Damien did. Even the initials Edward carved in Damien's arm have gone. The law is wrong. It should be changed to reflect cases like this." He glanced at Angel. "It's time like these when I just want to get out of the police."

"Silence in court," the judge ordered, and David said no more.

Witnesses followed the onslaught, confirming the love Edward had for his daughter. They painted a story of how Angel had gone off the rails since she had met this vindictive young man. How Edward had wanted her back to talk, to get her back on the right track, and to try and keep her out of trouble that she was obviously heading for. Angel had broken his heart. Angel recognised none of the witnesses, even though they apparently knew her well. Character witnesses were flown from England to counteract the venom Stenton was spouting, but because of the distance involved, they couldn't get enough to counteract the opinion the jury was forming. Trellis recognised they were one step behind, running at a pace to keep up with Stenton, never knowing what evidence would be placed in front of the jury next.

Trellis argued he hadn't seen the evidence before it was produced in court, but he was constantly overridden. He argued the evidence was not substantial, that the case was built on speculation, not fact. The facts were obvious: Damien still had scars from the knife wounds Edward had inflicted and the hospital records. They had a witness who had testified to the attack, and even though she was the defendant's girlfriend, no child would testify against their own father without good reason. Love alone was not a strong enough reason. Kurt Williams, a leading psychologist in human behaviour, confirmed this comment. Trellis purposely left out the words *murdered* and *killed*. He needed the jury to think of this case not as a father who had been killed, but a young lad who had been stalked by a man who wanted to kill him. A scared young man who was pushed too far, who eventually lashed out and thrown an object at the man who tormented him. Trellis was good, Stenton was better.

Stenton constantly pushed, and as Damien relived the event in the car park over and over again he finally snapped. "He got what he deserved," he finally yelled. "I am glad the bastard is dead." The yell turned into a sob. Stenton smiled, Damien was beaten.

When the verdict was announced, Angel's scream echoed around the courtroom. Her hands gripped the banister with such force that David grabbed her to stop her toppling over the balcony. He held her tight. She fought him to get loose, but to no avail. Angel collapsed into David's arms and sobbed. Damien was convicted of voluntary manslaughter without criminal malice. His sentence was two to three years with the possibility of parole in the second year.

Warren sat at the back of the courtroom with his new guardian, Frank. A knowing smile crossed his lips. At the back of the balcony, another figure sat watching the proceedings with interest. He smiled, a cruel smile filled with menace at the verdict. Now was not the time to reveal his identity. He was a patient man. Time was no longer precious as it once was. He could wait. He had already waited nine years. A couple more days, weeks or even months would make no difference.

Once the verdict was delivered, the figure slipped out of the courtroom as silently and swiftly as he came.

Prison

When the call first came through, Chief Inspector Harrington panicked. He hated leaving his son in America but he had no choice. He had already taken too much time off work. Angel quickly reassured him his son was coping well under the circumstances, but she had a dilemma. For the last week, she felt she was being watched. By whom she didn't know, until a man who appeared genuine introduced himself, a private eye called Todd Bradshaw. He said he had some news about her family. Her granddad and sister were expecting her back in England in a week. Her granddad had news he wanted to share, news to keep Damien safe. Todd Bradshaw had handed Angel his business card with a bold image of an eye in the top right-hand corner and a return ticket to the UK. He had told her to check him out with Chief Inspector Harrington, and then to meet him at JFK airport on Thursday at 5:00 p.m. so they could fly back to England together.

Angel's dilemma was simple. She had promised Damien she would visit him every week, and she did not intend to break her promise. Letting Damien down was not an option. She had let him down too many times in the past.

"If this man is genuine, he could help your case, sir, and protect Damien at the same time," said Angel. Angelica still struggled to call him David. He guessed he would always be sir or Chief Inspector to her.

"Read the details on the business card and describe what this man looked like. I know Todd Bradshaw. He is one of the best private eyes in the business." Todd had helped the Chief Inspector on many occasions, but he had not spoken to him in nearly a year. Once she had finished, the Chief Inspector sighed. It did sound like Todd. He tried to reach Todd on his other line; the phone went straight to an answer phone.

"You know I can't leave Damien."

"I know," said the Chief Inspector, thinking through the situation. There was a slight pause before the Chief Inspector spoke again. "Angelica, I am coming back to America. I will speak to Damien. If his life is in danger, then we need to know. We will then speak to Todd together, and if he seems genuine, we will travel back to England together. Who knows? Maybe we can find out more information, like what Edward was involved in. At the very least, we may find out who is in charge of this operation, and no buts..." he could tell Angelica was about to argue.

Damien was not as easy to persuade.

"Listen, son, I really need Angelica with me. They will only talk to her, not me. I will have her back within two weeks; I promise."

"No," said Damien adamantly. "I need Angel here with me. Her weekly visits are the only thing keeping me going. And it sounds too dangerous. I can't lose her again. It will destroy me, Dad."

The Chief Inspector put his hand on top of his son's hand. "Please, son. This is crucial. You know I wouldn't ask otherwise. I will look after Angelica. I will not let her out of my sight. I promise I will keep her safe." Angel stood in the small room with her back pressed against the wall. The pain Damien was going through was etched into his face.

"Damien, I won't go if you don't want me to – it's your call," said Angel, moving to the table. Damien stood up and placed his arms around her waist. They were not supposed to touch, but nobody else was in the room.

"You be real careful, and do not stray from my father's side. I do not want to lose you again, Angel." His embrace was firm, yet she still managed to slip her fingers inside his shirt and stroke his warm flesh.

"Oh my god," he whispered as a tingling sensation ran through his body.

"I will take your pain," she whispered back. Angel knew Damien's pain was getting worse; every visit he mentioned the pain. Normally, there were too many people around for her to help him. The three pain killers he was allowed per day hardly touched the gut-wrenching pain. Today was different. With only his dad in the room, Angel could relieve the torture. Damien brought his lips down to Angel's.

"Thank you," he murmured.

The Chief Inspector stood silently and watched his son and Angel. Finally, he could not hold back anymore. "Angelica, what are you doing?" Angel looked over to where the voice had come from and then back to Damien. Of course, Damien's father had never seen her use her gift.

It was Damien who answered. "Angel is taking away my pain. It's a gift she has."

"How?" his father asked. They both shrugged their shoulders. "Is that why you were so important to Edward?"

"Possibly," said Angel. "Edward thought I could bring life back to the dead."

"Can you?" David asked.

"No. Well, maybe."

"Can you heal?" David wanted to know.

"Possibly; I don't know. I think so."

"Still no pain in my right arm," said Damien, proudly rolling up his sleeve, revealing skin untouched by the illness. The Chief Inspector went quiet again. He knew Angel's hand had healed too quickly; however, this was way above his comprehension.

"I know you don't believe me, sir, but the next time the arthritis in your fingers is hurting you, I will take away your pain. I will show you what I can do, but please don't tell anybody."

"How did you know about my arthritis? Not even my wife knows about my arthritis."

"I can sense pain," she said quietly. Damien looked at her. Was this a new development in her gift or had she always sensed pain? It would explain why she had never hurt him when she moved her fingers across his body.

"You will come back, won't you?" Damien asked her.

Angel wriggled her arms free and placed them around his neck. Gazing deep into his eyes, she whispered, "I have never lied to you, Damien. Maybe sometimes I haven't told you everything, but I have never lied. I promise you I am coming back. You are the best thing that has ever happened to me, and I don't want to lose you."

"Even though I am in here?"

"I love you, Damien, and nothing will change that. You won't be in here forever, and who knows? Maybe through my visit back home we will find a way to get you released early."

The Chief Inspector smiled. Angel was saying all the right things to his son. Nothing would keep her away from his son for long.

Damien realised Angel would have to go. His father would not have come back to America to ask otherwise. The constant pain in his stomach had been his major problem to coping in prison. The small amount of relief Angel had just given him would help. Nobody was taking any notice of him, although this was about to change. Since the prison bus had dropped the new inmates inside the prison gates, only one of the new inmates was having a rough time.

Nobody likes a rapist, especially a rapist who brutally murders the women after the sick deed. Age was irrelevant, eighteen or eighty, a rapist would always be persecuted.

And Mickey Love had been convicted of raping and killing more than one woman. Damien heard rumours of his arrival and assumed he had changed his surname to fit his profession. He didn't speak to him. In fact, Damien spoke to very few of the inmates. It was the only way to keep his father and brother's professions a secret. A father who caught the criminals and then a brother who locked them away – what a field day the inmates would have. He might be more hated than Mickey. Slip-ups could easily be made, so it was easier to talk to nobody.

The Meeting

The Chief Inspector's large Victorian home stood majestically before them. A large brass knocker in the shape of a lion's head sat proudly in the centre of the door. Damien's mother, Claudette, answered the door. There was an air of confidence about her. She was tall and demure with natural-looking blonde highlights. Her hair was set in a neatly cut bob as though she had just stepped out of a beauty salon. Kissing her husband on the cheek, she looked Angel up and down. Unsure what to do, Angel held out her hand, but Claudette had already turned her back and gone back inside the house. Angel stared up at David, who shook his head.

"We're both in the dog house," he whispered. "Come in. I thought it best if you take Damien's room tonight. The guest rooms are so impersonal."

"Are you sure? I can always stay in a hotel," offered Angel, almost wishing David would say, *Yes, ok, That's probably for the best.*

Instead, David was insistent, "I will not have my son's girlfriend staying in a hotel when I have loads of spare room in my home."

Angel was shown to a room on the first floor with two large windows overlooking the well-kept gardens. Although it was a good size, the room still felt cluttered.

Many objects were displayed on the numerous bookcases and shelves. Picking up a small snow dome, she gave it a gentle shake. Minnie and Mickey popped up in the snow storm, causing her to clumsily fumble and juggle the dome. She smiled, wishing she could show Damien the innocent beauty of Walt Disney. Would it make him smile as well? He was struggling in prison, always so serious, never letting his guard down, always on edge even when she visited.

"I trust nobody," he had told her on more than one occasion. She placed the snow dome on the shelf, angled it slightly so it would be shown off in its best position and smiled. Her mam always told her off for picking things up in the shops and placing them back on the shelf in a different position. A sign that said 'Do Not Touch' was an open invitation to pick the item up.

Two standalone chests of drawers and three built-in wardrobes made up the majority of the room. The walking stick was now redundant, hung on the knob of one of the wardrobes. It was very different to Damien's room at school. A large sound system sat beneath one of the bay windows and a desk under the second window. A few handwritten sheets of music lay on the desk. They had been reworked several times. Scribbles and black lines crossed out the notes on different lines. A quaver, crotchet, semi-breve, minim, caesura, an f-sharp, an e-minor, all contributed to a tune. Some people could hum a tune from a sheet of music; however, the symbols meant nothing to Angel. Music was something she had never felt a passion to study. Music portrayed feeling. Now she wished she could understand what Damien was feeling through the music he wrote.

A small black file lay underneath the desk next to a small wire waste bin. Angel couldn't imagine Damien filing anything. He was normally so untidy, completely opposite to her. In the corner of the room, an electric guitar, a traditional guitar and a pair of skis rested against the wall. Did Angel really know Damien? She had no idea he could write music, play the guitar or ski, and she wondered what else she didn't know. The room in front of her was so different to anything she may have imagined, full of gadgets and interesting items.

A large mirror was tightly secured to the wall with a couple of photographs tucked into its wooden frame. The first photograph was of a young Damien and Laurel, possibly aged ten or eleven years old. They both had one knee on the ground, posing as though it was a league team photograph – the pitch was behind them. They were dressed in red and black striped rugby strips. It was the first time Angel had seen a photograph of Damien when he was young. He looked so innocent, without a care in the world. The second photograph was taken when they were on holiday in America, posing in front of Laurel's and Tim's two-man tent. Angel smiled to herself. It had taken four tries to shoot that photograph. Twice Laurel had fallen over as he had tried to beat the timer to reach his position. Laurel was funny, always larking around. Their hands were in the air, celebrating Laurel's success as the photograph was taken. The final photograph was of her. It was a head and shoulder shot, she assumed taken at the lake from the backdrop of trees. Dark hair had fallen over her right shoulder, and she was wearing her favourite pale blue capped shirt with a small collar and wide neckline. Her head was slightly turned to the left, and she appeared to be looking down. Angel could not remember Damien taking any photographs of her at school or the lake – it was a nice photograph.

A voice from downstairs called Angel's name. Leaving Damien's room Angel felt a little apprehensive. Claudette and David were already seated at the large dining room table. Angel knew they had been arguing. Their conversation fell silent as she entered the room, similar to when her mother and Edward pretended they hadn't been arguing. Angel placed a fake smile on her face and entered the room. "I am sorry to hold up dinner."

"No hold-up," came the warm reply from David. Angel felt a little guilty. Descending the stairs, admiring the hand-carved bannister and the dark wooden panels on the walls, Angel had unintentionally caught a little of Claudette's and David's conversation. Claudette had been questioning David on why she was staying in their home.

David had responded by saying, "Because she is our son's girlfriend. Just give her a chance. She is a nice kid." It would be rude to say anything about leaving, as they would realise she had been listening to their conversation. Angel slowly exhaled. At least David seemed to like her, and she liked him. Why couldn't Edward have been more like Damien's father?

Claudette had continued in an aggressive, tearful tone. "You promised me, David; you told me next time you went to America you would return with our son. You lied. It is because of that hussy our son is now locked up." David had come back at Claudette harshly in Angel's opinion. After all Damien's mother was upset; her son was in a foreign prison.

David would not let Claudette visit Damien. A mum visiting her son in prison would make Damien an easy target. It was every man for himself. Strength was key to survival. The other inmates would target any weakness. Even David did not visit through the normal visiting process. The Chief Inspector had once said the other inmates would know he was a copper as soon as they saw him. He didn't know how; they just would. The last words Angel heard before entering the dining room were from David.

"I told you. From the evidence given, our son should not have been locked up. Our case was airtight. I know I was concerned about Angelica, but she was excellent on the stand. We were set up. The jury was either bought or intimidated. I will bring our son home, I promise. It is just going to take a little time. Angelica wants Damien home as much as you do, and who knows? Through her visit, our son may be home earlier than expected. Please be civil for your son's sake."

The Chief Inspector was only partially telling the truth to his wife. The jury had not been intimidated. Angel and the Chief Inspector had made a mistake. They had underestimated Stenton and had not realised the importance of telling Trellis and Damien that Edward was not purely Angel's guardian but also her father. This was a mistake Damien was now forced to repay. Angel guessed David didn't want the aggro from his wife and a diatribe about how would she explain her son's imprisonment to her friends. Angel imagined Claudette was obsessed with respectability. The jury being bought or intimidated was probably easier to accept than your son being accused and convicted of cold-blooded murder.

The dining room was large and echoed as Angel walked across the solid wooden floor. The smell of linseed oil and polish clung to the air. An exquisite large tapestry picturing wild deer drinking from a water hole in the countryside hung on the wall, helping to absorb some of the sound. On the far side of the room hung a collection of oil paintings depicting more images of the British countryside. The dining room table was large and made of solid oak – it dominated the room, yet still felt lost. The room was partially covered in dark mahogany wooden panels. The room's windows and doors spread across two of the walls that led onto a paved patio. A hazy image of the garden furniture and leafy trees could just be seen through the windows as darkness engulfed the grand home. Angel took her place and waited for dinner to be served. She prayed the meal would be small. Her stomach was unsettled and knotted with an apprehension she could not entirely explain. Claudette made her feel nervous. Throughout the meal, her head stayed bowed like a punished child. Angel didn't make eye contact with Claudette or David. Conversation was minimal. The meal passed without incidence. The plates cleared, and Angel and the Chief Inspector were left alone. Angel wandered over to the tapestry, admiring the craftsmanship that had gone into creating such a beautiful item.

"I hope you don't mind me asking, sir, but are you rich?"

"I would describe it as comfortable. A Chief Inspector's salary is not as high as many people imagine." He could see Angel mulling over his comment.

"My mam said we were comfortable, but our house was a lot smaller than yours," she said scanning the room. "Damien once visited my house. Did he tell you, sir?"

The Chief Inspector did not answer. Instead, he invited, "Come. I will take you for a tour and show you the real beauty of the house. We started restoring it four year ago. Let's start in my study. It's my favourite room. And afterwards, we will talk about tomorrow."

The study was partially covered in dark mahogany panelling like many rooms in his home. The upper walls were adorned with framed ancient maps of the world. History was a passion Damien had shared with his father from an early age. A large over-sized Hemingway mahogany desk sat in the middle of the room with a Tiffany lamp angled at the many files on the desk. The Chief Inspector still liked to use a fountain pen and so always kept a small bottle of blue ink on the far side of the desk. The study had always been out of bounds to his two sons when they were younger. The door was always kept locked, and the key placed out of reach on a small brass hook above the door frame.

To the left of the door, there was a large mahogany bookcase extending to the ceiling. It was adorned with books beautifully bound on every aspect of law.

"Neil spends a lot of time in here when he visits, so I like to keep it stocked for him."

Angel nodded. "Does Neil look like Damien?"

"Oh no, Neil has his mum's looks. I'll see if I can find you a photograph. Damien looks more like me, but I guess you realised that." The Chief Inspector started rummaging in the top drawer of the desk; he smiled and pulled out a photograph a little creased on the corners but still clear. "Here's one taken a couple of years ago."

"He has fair hair!"

"Yes, totally opposite to Damien."

In the far corner of the room, high on the wall above an ancient map of Greece hung a small glass case. Without a small step-ladder, it was just out of reach. Angel crammed her neck to see what was inside. "Is there a stuffed fish in the case?" asked Angel.

The Chief Inspector burst out laughing. "Do I look like a fisherman?"

"I guess not."

"The case would be much larger for the fish I would catch," David bragged, and Angel giggled. "There is a gun inside, which is why it is out of reach; Claudette insisted."

"Is it loaded?"

"Always. You can't see it from here but inside, at the back of the case, there is a photograph of my father. The gun was his."

"Is he dead?"

"Yes, died on duty. My family have always served their country, usually as a member of the law enforcement for the country."

The Chief Inspector moved back to the desk and flicked on the Tiffany lamp. "It makes a lousy desk lamp, but it creates a warm atmosphere, and the colours are beautiful when they bounce off the walls and ceiling. It helps me relax; I can sit here and stare at the colours and if I angle the lamp slightly different all the colours change." Angel looked around the room. The reds, greens and yellows were mingling together, creating a wider range of rainbow colours. She walked to the nearest wall and traced a coloured diamond shape with her finger. Its edges were slightly blurred mingling in with the next colour.

"It is beautiful. I can draw but not with colour."

He switched off the lamp, "It's too distracting. Let us try with a standard desk lamp."

Angel moved to the desk. On top of the desk pad, her name was clearly written. Underneath her name were the names: Aurel Niculesco, Winifred Wellinstone (d), Edward Wellingstone? (d), and in brackets Édouard Vasser and Eftemie Vladmirescu. There were also the names: Dominique Lefevre (d), Bobby Arcos (d), Crystal Ceasar, Samuel Bennett, and Warren Malton followed by two question marks. To the right was another column of names: Petru Dalakis, Dorin Critescu, Marius Kazaku, Paul Jonker, Seamus Busby, Louis Hancock, Dr Ted Crickton and Dr Troy Eastwick. In the third column was a single name William Stenton. The Chief Inspector appeared oblivious to what she was staring at. Angel slowly moved away from the desk and stared blankly at a large ancient Greek map for a couple of minutes. The list of names played on her mind.

"Sir, I don't mean to be rude, but why is my name on your desk pad?" She had now moved back to the desk and was staring at the list. Underneath the names were the words Chameleon Enterprises Inc. and Chameleon Medical Research Unit with several arrows pointing to the names of more organisations. The Chief Inspector moved slowly to where she stood. He had forgotten about his matrix of names on his desk pad.

"Sir?" she asked again.

"Ok, Angelica, do you recognize any of the names on the list?" David asked. She nodded and pointed to all the names she had heard of. None of them surprised him.

"Is that my sister?" She asked pointing to the name Crystal Ceasar.

"I think so. Tomorrow we should be meeting Aurel and possibly Crystal."

"And the letter d in brackets after some of the names."

"Those that are dead."

"But there is a d after my mother's name. Is she really dead?"

"I'm sorry, Angelica." He gave her hand a gentle squeeze before opening an A4 card file on the desk. In front of Angel lay a collection of papers and photographs secured by multi-coloured paperclips. On every sheet, a head and shoulders passport-size photograph was stapled to the top right corner.

"Do you recognize anybody in these two photographs?" He had taken two photographs from the back of the file and placed them in front of her.

"That's Edward, and to his right with his back to the camera is Samuel. I recognise the shape of the head and his stance. He always looks like a gorilla, with his shoulders hunched over, and his legs slightly bowed. The grey haired man sitting down on the far side of the photograph I met a couple of times, but I don't know his name."

"Which one, Angelica?" David asked. She pointed again.

"That's Dr Ted Crickton, a specialist in cloning," David told her. "What about the man in the cream mac?"

Angel shook her head, "I haven't seen him before."

"This is Dr Troy Eastwick, an American who specialises in gene manipulation. I think he is one of the top scientists in his field. Often he can be found with Petru Dalakis and Seamus Busby, who are not on the photographs. They are also scientists. Seamus works in a similar field to Troy. He is good, but not exceptional like Troy.

"Petru specialises in telepathy – mind control. I think he was involved when Arnold Crabstick jumped from the Empire State building back in 2009. Petru was Arnold's psychiatrist at the time. We think Petru dabbled in mind control with his patients. We could not prove anything at the time. Arnold's wife said when he came back from seeing the psychiatrist, he was always unpredictable, with strange ideas that were totally disconnected from reality. One time he tried to walk on water. Another time he constantly spoke about a child they never had, called Henry – his wife said they had always been childless. Arnold had a vasectomy a few years previous due to a cancerous growth. I don't know if you remember the story, but the same date and time that Arnold jumped, we also had two other suicides. I don't remember their names, but one jumped from the Eiffel Tower and the other from the Naberezhnaya Tower in Moscow. It hit the news headlines for about a week. How could three disconnected people coordinate a suicide to the very second when we could not find any link between them? Don't you remember the fuss it caused back then?"

Angel shook her head. "We weren't allowed to watch the news, sir."

"Ah yes, the hospital. Sorry, I forgot they keep the news away from the inpatients. Trust me, it was a big news article back then. I am not sure how he fits in with the others as his speciality is so different from Troy and Seamus. This gentleman here," David continued, tapping the photograph, "is Paul Jonker. We think he provides finances to run their operation, but we are unsure why.

"Do you recognise these two gentlemen?" he asked, handing her another picture.

Angel picked up the second photograph and stared at the two well-dressed men in the image. "No, I would say they are Eastern European, but I can't tell you anything else," Angel passed him back the photograph.

"Tomorrow, if you meet any of the men in these two photographs, you need to be careful. Get out as soon as you can."

"I thought you were going with me. I don't think I can face them by myself."

"I am going with you," he assured her, "but we both need to be on our guard. Get out without me, if you have to."

Angel nodded. "Who are they, sir?"

"The only connection we can make is they are all on the board of Chameleon Medical Research Unit, apart from Samuel, Edward and Stenton. Currently, we have nothing on this research unit – everything appears above board. We are still checking to see if the Chameleon Research Unit and Chameleon Enterprises are connected. I think whatever they are doing is real big and extremely dangerous. Louis Hancock, who is not on any of the photographs, sits high up in the American Government. When I mentioned his name to the Captain, I could see the fear in his eyes. He said if Hancock was involved, our investigation would be shut down. Henley may seem like a pussycat, but he's the opposite, hard and focussed – that's why I like him. Now we are investigating in secret; I run the investigation to keep Henley out of it. Hancock will have more trouble trying to stop a UK investigation than an American investigation."

"That's clever, sir. I didn't think policemen were so devious," Angel stated. David didn't say anything.

"There is a name missing from your list sir, a Hannah or Anna."

"Really?" David asked, jotting it down on his pad. "When did you meet this mystery woman?"

"I didn't. I heard a woman's voice talking to Edward. She said the Doctor was getting impatient. He was running low on raw materials and when would she be ready?"

"She meaning you, I assume?"

"I think so. Edward said she is developing slower than we thought, and the drugs didn't appear to be working, but when she's ready the Doctor would not be disappointed. He told her to tell the Doctor it would be soon, very soon. She said the Doctor would be angry, and he would feel the Doctor's wrath. The woman wanted to meet me. Edward told her I was out practicing. I wasn't, and Edward knew that. When she had gone, Edward unlocked my door. I could tell he was shaken, and Edward does not, I mean did not, scare easily. He told me to get out of his sight for a while, or he wouldn't be held responsible for his actions. Raw materials is a strange phrase to use, don't you think?"

"I know Damien thinks you have something they want, possibly your blood. Is your blood type unusual?"

Angel shrugged her shoulders.

"Maybe they want you to produce babies, like your mother. Babies could be the raw materials they spoke of. It all seems so far-fetched, don't you think!"

Angel nodded slowly as she thought it through. "I don't know what they want, but if that's their intention, they won't get anything from me, sir. I'll see to that."

"I find it difficult to believe, but if you are right, we'll stop them together. Angel, do not forget: you are with people who care for you. You don't have to do this by yourself anymore."

Angel gave his hand a quick squeeze. "Do you believe Stenton is part of the group?"

"I don't know; everybody is a suspect until proven otherwise. My gut instinct is that he is just a lawyer, probably used by them on a regular basis."

"Which one is the Doctor?" Angel asked, eagerly scanning the figures in the photographs.

"We don't know; none of them would be my guess."

Angel looked disappointed. "I really want to meet him, sir. Is that wrong?"

"You don't want to meet him, Angel. He is extremely dangerous."

After an hour of discussing the photographs and what the Chief Inspector had un-covered, they moved rooms. To Angel's relief there was no sign of Claudette, who had retired early. A grand piano took pride of place in the room where they eventually chose to sit and talk. David was obviously proud of his sons. He talked about Damien playing Beethoven's Piano Concerto No. 4 from a very early age and all the sports and hobbies he once took part in.

"I don't know why I'm telling you this, but Damien was a right little action man when he was young. Unfortunately, the illness stopped everything; he was always in such pain. He shut out his family. He didn't want to come home for his holidays. I think we reminded him of what he once had. The neighbours would always ask him how he was feeling, and I think the constant reminder was too much for him." A thoughtful sadness had crossed his face. "He is different when he is with you; I see the old Damien. I want my son to be healthy, Angel. I desperately want him cured of this disease. I want him out of that place, and I want him healthy.

Is that too much to ask?" Angel shook her head. "Do you think you will be able to heal my son?" As soon as he said it, he could have kicked himself. He didn't want to encourage such silly talk or to believe in false hope, but for some reason the words had already escaped from his lips.

Angel nodded, "I hope so, sir. I will do everything in my power to heal Damien, but I am scared. I am not in full control yet and I could end up hurting him instead of healing him. I know I must wait, but it is difficult when I see him in pain. It tears at my heart. I am close, but not close enough to attempt it. Do you know what caused the illness?" David shrugged his shoulders, annoyed with himself for encouraging such hopeless talk, but he answered Angel's question.

"We have had the top specialists working on this, yet they come up blank every time."

Their conversation continued into the early hours, and eventually the discussion turned to David quizzing Angel on her past life. He was not intrusive, but he digested everything she said in his slow, quiet manner. His brain cogs were turning, joining pieces of information, positioning the jigsaw pieces together. Angel was getting used to how the Chief Inspector processed information. His decision-making was a slow process, weighing up all the alternatives before deciding how to proceed. His brain processing was quite methodical. Angel had once read this was what made the best detectives. Sherlock Homes was a key example, never leaving a stone unturned, always thinking one step ahead, processing the information slowly. As Angel pondered this thought, reality struck. Sherlock Holmes was a fictional character, although the character was inspired by a real person, Dr Joseph Bell. Angel could not think of a non-fictional example.

David noticed her silence and apologized. "I am sorry if you think I am prying. I don't mean to. It's the policeman in me. I am just interested in who my son has chosen as his girlfriend."

Angel smiled, "I don't mind, sir."

David continued, "Your relationship is strong. What you both have is special. Most relationships would not have survived what you have been through. I believe you are good for my son."

"And Damien is good for me," grinned Angel. David could not argue with that statement. He had seen how his son had cared for Angel the night she awoke screaming. How he had taken control of the event and even now, in prison, he was proud how his son was handling the situation. He was stronger than he could have imagined. He wasn't just his sick son. He was a son he was proud of.

"Do you have any other files on me, sir?"

"Yes, I am a policeman, and you do have a police record."

She nodded her head slowly. "Did you know Damien and Laurel had a file on me?"

The Chief Inspector wasn't sure where the conversation was going, but he answered honestly.

"Yes, but that was a long time ago. What on earth made you think of that?"

"I don't know. Do you think Damien burnt it?"

"Was he supposed to?"

"Yes."

"Then I am sure he would have done. Did you see it?" asked David.

"No."

"Were you curious?"

"Of course. I thought about it for a long time, but if I read the hospital notes, and they were negative then all those happy memories I have would be destroyed. I didn't want that to happen."

"It makes sense and possibly very wise," said the Chief Inspector, who had seen her notes but he was not going to tell her that.

"Can I ask you a question, sir?"

"Of course."

"Why do they call you the Rottweiler?"

David burst out laughing. "Did Damien tell you that?"

She nodded.

"Well, I really don't know. I talk loud. Some say when I have an idea I won't let go, a bit like a dog with its bone. Some may say I am overpowering and have an aggressive manner especially with criminals." He looked at Angel. "Do you think Rottweiler's are handsome animals?"

Angel burst out laughing, "No."

"Oh well, I guess that's one similarity we don't have." They both laughed. If he had a daughter, he would have liked one similar to the young lady sitting in front of him. Somebody to talk and laugh with, who had an innocence and strength. David wished his wife would accept Angel. She never accepted their sons' friends immediately. It was always the same; it had taken her five years to accept Laurel. He gave an exasperated sigh. Claudette was so protective of her sons. She mothered them too much, in his opinion, but she cared for them deeply.

Tiredness and a long flight began to take its toll. The seven-hour difference was hard to adjust to quickly.

As Angel turned to say goodnight, David reminded her Todd was picking them up at 9:00 a.m., not that she was likely to forget. Although tired, Angel hardly slept. Damien's bed was comfortable, but apprehension kept her awake.

*****

Angel woke in a house she did not recognise, sitting in a leather chair she had no memory of. A large open fire burned in front of her. A brass coal scuttle stood on the hearth, brimming with lumps of coal and pieces of wood. Her hands and legs were not bound, but an old man sat in front of her, a walking stick by his side. Standing slightly behind his chair was a female with fiery red hair. Her hand was placed on the old man's shoulder. Behind the female, Angel could see two more figures. Her eyes were still slightly blurred from whatever they had given her. She recognised Todd immediately, and she was sure Dr Ben Wilson was with him. They were laughing and helping themselves to a decanter of some sort of alcohol. Angel glanced around but could not see the Chief Inspector. Angel remembered the Chief Inspector sitting next to her in the car, and she remembered Todd stopping for fuel. After that, nothing, no recollection, no memory. Her neck felt stiff. There was no sensation in her legs and right arm.

The female was the first to speak, "Don't worry. In ten minutes you will feel as good as new."

"Where am I?" asked Angel with a slightly slurred speech that sounded like "wer m y." The old man laughed and then stopped suddenly, waiting for Angel's reaction. There was no reaction; instead she chose to sit and wait.

It was the redhead who broke the silence, "My grandfather wants to talk to you. I'm Crystal."

"Where is..."

Crystal responded before Angel had time to ask her question. "The invitation was for you only. He is probably annoyed, but he is safe, so don't worry."

"Am I a prisoner?"

The old man laughed again – and again, it was Crystal who answered.

"The door is open. You can get up and walk out at any time. We are not kidnappers. My grandfather has to be careful who knows his whereabouts, which is why the secrecy is necessary."

The old man was now staring at her. His hair was white and thin on top; red veins were starting to appear on his cheeks and nose, which made his elderly face look jolly. His eyes were dark and tired, although he seemed happy. Assisted by Crystal, he adjusted the rug over his legs to lay flat and pulled it up to cover more of his body. The old man patted Crystal's hand affectionately for this assistance, which gave Angel a feeling of warmth to her current situation.

The first time the old man spoke, he spoke in Romanian, "*Buna Ziua domnişoara, numele le meu este Aurel Niculesco.*"

Angel recognised the language, and without thinking replied in the same language. "*Buna numele le meu este Angelica Wellingstone.*" Her hand grasped the small gold locket that hung around her neck, praying her mother was right, praying it would protect her.

The old man pointed at the locket. "My daughter's," he said more to Crystal than to Angel. They continued their conversation in Romanian. To Angel's surprise, she could communicate at an advanced level. Edward had insisted she practice her Romanian regularly – the lessons had obviously paid off. Crystal appeared to be following most of their conversation. The two men moved toward the old man and listened for a while before retreating to the drinks cabinet. Angel assumed from their actions they could not follow the conversation, or were not interested in their discussion.

"We would like you to stay tonight and continue your conversation tomorrow; my grandfather is tired and must rest now," said Crystal, moving to the door and calling the name Sarah. Another lady came to the door.

"Nurse Green," gasped Angel. "What are you doing here?"

"Hello, Angelica, ain't you all grown up? Please call me Sarah. I am your grandfather's private nurse."

"But..."

Sarah looked to Aurel, who nodded, before she spoke. "I was sent to look after you, keep an eye on you, protect you if needed. Aurel has always known about you, Angelica. There is so much we need to tell you."

"Please, Sarah, no more. It's too much for the lass to digest in one go." Aurel sounded tired. Taking an arm each, Sarah and Crystal escorted the old man from the room. "Tomorrow, Angelica, you will meet my son," he called out as he disappeared from sight.

Angel watched and then shifted uncomfortably in her chair. "Can I phone the Chief Inspector and let him know I am ok?" she asked.

Crystal popped her head back around the door. "Todd, lend the kid your phone and don't stay on long. I don't want the line traced." Both Todd and Angel obeyed her instructions. Crystal dominated the men and ran the household efficiently. It wasn't just Crystal's fiery red hair that gave her a presence. Her attitude and actions held a controlling power. Could Crystal really be her sister? None of their features looked remotely similar, and her manner and personality was so different. Crystal was confident and forceful. Did Crystal have the same gift? If she did, was it a gift or a curse in her eyes? Angel didn't want to ask, not in front of her two male colleagues. Crystal may not answer truthfully, in any case. Angel could just be setting herself up, opening up her secret to others – she chose to keep quiet.

It was slightly uncomfortable waiting for Crystal to return with Ben watching her every movement.

"This young lady has amazing DNA," Ben told Todd, loud enough for Angel to hear. "Blood cells a little heavy on white cells but nothing too abnormal but her defence mechanism is something I have never seen before." Ben moved towards Angel, who immediately coiled her legs up onto the chair. "See how she goes into a defensive position. Inside that small body, she has a system that can create a unique defensive shield around the essential organs. I have never seen anything like it. I would love to study you, young lady." The smell of cognac was evident on Ben's breath. Angel wished Crystal would hurry back.

It was Todd who finally stepped in. "Come on Doc. Have another drink. Her boyfriend's father would make mincemeat of you if you laid a finger on her." Todd nodded over to Angel.

"I wasn't going to do anything. I was just saying. You must admit, it's a brilliant defence mechanism that could do with further study." Ben moved back to the drink's cabinet, where he and Todd continued talking in hushed voices. Throughout the evening, Ben kept glancing over to Angel, but he didn't approach her again.

Angel did stay the night, although she slept little. Her mind was too active, trying to digest all that she had heard. Next day with fewer people present, Aurel switched to English so there would be no misinterpretation.

"I am trying to find a child who has more than one gift. We were not sure if it was you or Bobby," said Aurel.

"What do you mean, two gifts?"

"I'll let my son tell you."

"You do know I am not like my mum."

"You mean you can't heal like your mother. Don't worry, we know all about you."

"I can hardly do anything," said Angel.

"No, not at the moment, but we assume your time spent in the hospital has hindered your advancement, although Sarah used to give you vitamins during the day instead of Pericyazine. We probably overdosed you on vitamin C. You nearly blew Sarah's cover when you attacked that lad. The Pericyazine should have curbed any aggression you may have had. Sarah had to tell them she had forgotten to give you your medication that day." Aurel sighed. "Edward was a fool, pushed you too early, which was why you ended up in there, although we were thankful in some ways as it kept him away from influencing you."

"What am I supposed to be able to do?"

Crystal and Aurel looked at each other. "Let's wait and see if you have two powers."

"My son was keeping an eye on Bobby, monitoring his progress to see how he was developing, and boy, was he skilful. Once again, they pushed him too hard. This time it was Flaviu, not Edward. There was always too much competition between them; always trying to impress the Doctor. Here's Sandu, my son." Aurel watched Angel's face change as she realised who had just entered the room.

"Stan, do you work here as well?"

"How's my little Angelica?"

"Not so little now."

"I guess not. Do you still remember who Jazz is?"

"Why the off-spring of Gala of course. She's the pretty one," was the quick reply. "Do I call you Sandu or Stan?"

"I answer to both. It was my father's joke when he named me Sandu. It means 'the defender of mankind.' I have never forgiven him for that, have I, Aurel? Forty years I have lived with that name!"

Aurel waved his hand dismissively. It was interesting meeting her new family. On the surface, they appeared like any other family, yet there was more, a difference that she could not pinpoint.

"Does the dragon work here as well?" Angel asked.

Stan glanced at Sarah before asking Angel, "Is she still giving you nightmares?"

Angel nodded.

"You will be glad to know the old witch, or should I say Nurse Drayton, retired last year," Sarah told her.

Angel gave a sigh of relief before realising that the room had fallen silent. All eyes were focussed on her.

"Can you hear me, Angel?" a voice asked. Looking around the room, nobody looked like they had spoken. They were all waiting for something or someone. The voice was Stan's. Angel looked over to Stan, who had his back to her. He slowly turned around.

"That's right, Angel. I am telepathic. Nobody else can hear me. This is my gift, my power. Your mother, who was my sister, had the power to heal. I have the power to communicate through my mind. I can control people, make them do things. Watch Crystal. She will start to scratch her right arm." Angel let out a giggle as Crystal scratched her arm.

"Stop it, Stan," snapped Crystal. "You know it's not funny."

Stan smirked. "Ah, come on, Crystal. It is funny." This time he spoke aloud so everybody could hear.

Giving Angel a wink, he switched back to communicating telepathically. "Now, Angel, listen to me. Can you answer me? Focus your mind and try to talk to me telepathically."

"How?" she asked aloud. All eyes once again focussed on her.

"Concentrate, Angel. That's all it takes, concentration and practice." A couple of minutes passed. Stan let out a frustrated sigh. Approaching Aurel he whispered something in his ear, too quiet to be overheard by anybody else. Aurel also sighed and leant back in his chair.

"Ok, Angel, maybe Bobby had two powers. An educated guess based on genetics tells us a person with dark hair and eyes may have both powers, although even then we are not one hundred percent sure on that information; it's more a feeling than fact."

"And who is to say any of them have two powers?"

"You're right, Sandu, as always."

*****

Angel had no memory of the return journey. They had no doubt drugged her last coffee. Little of the day stuck in Angel's mind. She remembered wondering why Stan approached Aurel to discuss her lack of telepathic skills instead of relaying the information telepathically. She could also remember Crystal's voice as she drifted to sleep. Crystal's voice had been very clear.

"Don't waste your gift, Angel. Let it develop naturally. In time you will give your young man what you both want. Push too hard too soon, and you will destroy everything." These words were the last words she would hear from her sister for a long time.

Arriving back at Scotland Yard, Todd accompanied Angel into the building to find the Chief Inspector, to apologise for his actions and to explain he had no choice. All the staff at the headquarters seemed to recognise him. It was an impressive building with a large security desk dominating the foyer. Todd waved to the security guard and headed right towards the lift to the third floor to the Chief Inspector's office.

"He used to be on my team before starting to work here. I give all my rejects to the Chief Inspector." Angel glanced behind them. She could see the gentleman Todd was talking about, limping slightly, left leg slightly longer than the right, compensated by a thicker sole on the boot. Todd had seen her turn.

"Gunshot," he said as though reading her mind. "He was a first-class private eye until..." he stopped; the lift doors had opened and a pile of people were spilling out into the reception area. "Shift change," he said, as if he felt the need to explain the large number of people.

Within seconds, they were delivered to their destination. Another security desk, and once again Todd just waved. A large sign hung over the reception desk that read, 'Don't waste my time.' Somebody with a sense of humour, or was it a warning? Angel deliberated this for a moment before speeding up to catch Todd. There were many people around, and she didn't want to lose Todd because of dawdling.

"Do you want me to let him know you are here?" shouted the security guard.

"Best not," was the reply. "Tip the old bugger off and he'll go for my throat." Todd headed down the corridor, poking his head into different offices to say hello. Everybody on this floor appeared to know him.

"You're not in the Chief Inspector's good books," and "I wouldn't like to be in your shoes right now," greeted him. The offices he didn't enter, he tapped on the windows and raised his hand, making the shape of a gun. Angel guessed it was a policeman's friendly signal, not that it looked friendly.

The Chief Inspector's office was at the far end of the corridor. The door was closed, yet she could hear raised voices coming from the other side. A red-faced man burst through the door. Glancing at Angel, he muttered something to Todd, who nodded.

"He's in a foul mood this morning. Probably an argument with the misses before leaving home."

"Come on. Let's get it over with." Todd gave Angel a gentle push into the room and followed her in. A half-eaten tuna fish baguette and a can of Coke sat on the end of the desk. The can's ring was pulled, but the can looked full. She always thought of Damien's father as a sandwich box man, freshly prepared in the morning, possibly with the crusts removed.

The Chief Inspector's office was a mess, piled high with papers and files, not like his study at home where everything was kept in its place. The Chief Inspector was fairly subdued.

"Pull another trick like that, Todd, and I will have you thrown into prison for impeding police investigations."

"No harm done," answered Todd.

The Chief Inspector gave him a sneer. "Get out of my sight."

Angel assumed the Chief Inspector's pride had been hurt more than anything.

When Todd left the office, the Chief Inspector's mood changed, a smirk followed by laughter. "Did you see his face?"

Angel managed a tentative smile. His mood had changed so abruptly, it was confusing. The can of Coke was thrust under her nose, which she graciously declined by shaking her head. Angel was determined to relay all the information before she forgot, but the Chief Inspector appeared in no rush.

"Did you have a nice night?" he asked.

She nodded. "It was a strange night, not as I expected. I have so much I need to tell you that I am unsure where to start."

The Chief Inspector held up his palm. "Stop, I have had a translator working through the tape recording all night. And might I add, costing the department a fortune, so we know what was said," laughed the Chief Inspector.

Confusion crossed Angel's face before realising, "You planted a bug on me." Flicking up Angel's collar, he revealed a small metal circular disk.

"I placed it just before we got in Todd's car. Remember when I adjusted your collar?"

Angel nodded.

"I knew Todd was up to something, and I couldn't take a chance. After all, I promised my son I would look after you. I know exactly where you have been and what was said. I know you were not in danger. Todd's a first-rate guy. He just underestimated Chief Inspector Harrington and his new Sirus bug with built in GPS tracking. The only thing it's not equipped with is a visual image, so try and explain visually what you saw."

The Chief Inspector made a mental note to thank Brian. He had designed the bug. It consisted of a tiny metal disk that transmitted conversations clearly to a larger recording unit situated two miles from its destination. The Chief Inspector knew Brian would be advantageous for the department – bring them into the twenty-first century. Several years ago, the Chief Inspector had recognised Brian was more than just a hacker. Brian had a skill, an intellectual brain far advanced than other personnel in the department. He accepted a few of his colleagues felt threatened by Brian's presence, and some of them felt he was only offered a job because he found and probably saved his son's life. This wasn't the case; Brian was technically more advanced than any of his department would ever realise.

Aurel's phone line was tapped, and a team watched the comings and goings from the house. The Chief Inspector hoped Aurel would give him another lead to follow. "Now what do you think of Flaviu?"

Angel considered the question for a moment before grasping the connection. "Oh no! Do you think it is Frank?" she asked.

The Chief Inspector nodded. "Too much of a coincidence. His hair is yellow; he closely matches the description with a few minor differences. A moustache can be shaved off. A hair style can be altered. He turned up out of the blue and claimed he was a relative of Warren."

"But Warren knew him," argued Angel.

"Yes, but only because Warren had met him before. Think what Aurel said: they move in with your family, gain your trust. What did Edward do? He moved in with you and your mam."

"But Edward didn't live with us."

"Not physically, but Edward was close enough to have control. What is Frank doing right now?"

Angel nodded, "I think you might be right, sir."

"I have arranged for Frank and Warren to be watched. I do not want to scare Frank off. He may lead us to the Doctor."

"Or the game-maker," said Angel. Aurel had called the Doctor the Game-Maker, without any explanation other than he played with games with serious consequences.

The Chief Inspector laughed, "Or the game-maker. Do you realise how close we are, Angel?"

Angel nodded.

"Ok, I want you to do something for me," he requested, pressing a button on a computer. Aurel's voice filled the room. "Tell me what I don't hear. As I said before, I have had a translator on this, but now I need your story."

Cocking her head to one side as though listening intently, Angel turned to the Chief Inspector. "The phonemes and morphemes of Aurel's speech are unusual. They suggest he lived in the same district as Edward and Frank, in Romania. They say their p's and r's the same, which is unusual if they lived in different districts."

"I probably phrased that wrong. I meant what is Aurel doing? What is he showing you? But I am more interested in what you thought I was asking. You were analysing his speech, which takes years of practice. Tell me what you can gather from his speech."

At the end of the analysis, the Chief Inspector nodded, unsure if what Angel had said was true or just a wild guess. He would park the information for a while and regurgitate it, if and when required. Now to Angel, who had continued to grow on him steadily over the last few weeks. Angel was obviously more gullible than many kids her age, and it was up to him to sort out the facts from the fiction.

He started by praising Angel for the information she had brought back and then he expressed his concern. "I am worried Angel. You must not believe what these people are telling you; everybody is special in their own way. I know you believe you can take away pain and possibly heal, but you can't, Angel. It's all to do with pressure points. If you believe you can heal, then they will start to manipulate you, ask you to do things which are illegal, like Edward was doing. In my opinion, they are no better than Edward. They are feeding on your vulnerability. Your hair and eyes are dark, but so are many people's. I know we all want to think we are special, and you *are* special, but not like they are suggesting. Be careful, Angel. I think you are too clever to believe such rubbish." He stared at her for a while, hoping she was listening, understanding what was being said.

Angel's mouth slowly fell open. "But you have seen what I can do!"

"No, Angel, I haven't."

"Damien's arm and Edwards initials!"

"Coincidence," David dismissed it. "The initials may not have been cut as deep as we originally thought."

"And Damien's pain!"

"I have told you, pressure points. Be clever, Angel. There is always an explanation." Angel knew it was useless to argue. Maybe Damien's father was right, and it was all just coincidence.

The negativity Damien's father was conveying was not going to dampen Angel's mood. Aurel had given Angel the one item she had always wanted – a photograph of her mother. Standing in front of their old home in Barton, Angel, who would have been no more than three or four years, stood holding her mother's hand, smiling at the camera. Angel still had doubts whether or not Aurel was her grandfather. The photograph had caused some confusion when Aurel said they never met before, and her mother had not spoken to Aurel since her son Dominique was adopted. Working backwards, it was obvious Aurel would have been in prison around the time the photograph had been taken, so how did Aurel have the photograph? Angel knew she should have asked, but at the time she had been so delighted with the photograph, the flaws in the story seemed unimportant.

The Release

Angel glanced up at the large dreary-looking building. It was cold. The people inside were cold, too, apart from Damien. He shouldn't be locked-up in such a miserable building, an evil place, where rapists and murderers resided. This was Angel's first visit since her trip to England. Damien would not be pleased. She hadn't phoned him as promised. It wasn't through lack of trying. The phone wouldn't connect, and now she had to tell him he could not appeal against his sentence. It was going to be a difficult visit. Detective Haines sat with her, occupying the driver's seat. He gave her a reassuring nod as she swung the passenger door open.

"I still feel like I am being watched," Angel said as she peered through the steamed-up window.

"It's just the regulars," said Haines. "Don't worry I'll be here when you come out."

This time Angel nodded. She liked Haines' unassuming character. He rarely spoke unless spoken to. And he never asked questions, but was conscientious with a capital C. Haines tended to speak to Damien more than her – she didn't mind.

Feeling uncomfortable, Angel joined the other visitors trooping to the prison. Although anxious to see Damien, her stride was hesitant. Somebody was watching her, she was sure of it.

The smile that crossed Damien's face indicated he was pleased to see her. Her previous visits he had shown little emotion in front of the other inmates, but today was different. A red mark covered the lower part of Damien's face. She ignored it, although she knew something must have happened. Damien's mood constantly changed throughout Angel's visit, which was unusual. She knew he was happy to see her, scared of his situation, but she wasn't expecting sarcasm mixed with anger. Maybe she should have. He took the information about the appeal badly.

"Damien, it is the only way. If we appeal, we 're afraid they'll uphold your guilt, and you won't be eligible for an early parole," declared Angel.

"How, Angel? Everybody said I shouldn't be in here. Trellis said we could use my illness as a way to get released. And when my father has collated the case notes again, and I am prepared for the questions and accusations about your father, I could be released."

"I know, but they have the power, Damien. You need to slip under their radar. If we appeal they might decide to accuse you of another murder."

"Who has the power?" he asked.

She shrugged her shoulders. "Look, Damien, my grandfather served twenty-five years for molesting children, a crime he strongly denies. If he had not appealed, he would have served fewer years. It is a game to them; they pull at people's emotions to see how far they can push them before they snap. It destroyed my grandfather emotionally and killed my grandmother. My mother never spoke to my grandfather again; it destroyed my family. Please, Damien, your dad and I have had long discussions about this. Serving your time and hoping for an early release is the only way," said Angel.

"Maybe I should be involved in these discussions. After all, it is my life," Damien replied sulkily. Angel wanted to hold him so badly; he seemed so helpless.

Their hands were in front of them on the imitation wooden table. The table had been screwed firmly to the floor. Even their chairs were screwed down. Their fingertips slightly touched. If the guards spotted them, Damien would have to leave immediately and miss the rest of the visitation time. He withdrew his hands and placed them on his lap. His head hung down like a rejected dog.

"They found out who my father is," he said looking up at Angel. "I won't last five more minutes in here. My dad is not just a common policeman; no, he has to be a Chief Inspector, which makes it twice as bad."

Her heart sank. Now she understood why he had been so moody and snappy during this visit; his life was in danger.

"I cannot stay in here. The bruising on my face is just the start. I wasn't bitch-slapped by some thug just trying to establish dominance. I was sought out and punished, which means there is worse to follow," he whispered.

The creep, Mickey Love, who preyed on women, had landed the lucky punch. Damien wasn't expecting it. They would not catch him off guard again. This was a promise he had made to himself. Next time he would leave his mark on the culprit. 'Eyes, throat and testicles are the three most vulnerable parts on a man, aim for one of those and you will win any fight' he remembered his father's advice clearly. Damien had never yet failed with those words of wisdom. He doubted the creep would land the killing blow. Mickey punched him to take the attention from himself – an act of self-preservation. A cop's kid or a rapist – who was hated the most? Damien guessed a 50:50 split.

"What about solitary confinement?" piped up Angel.

"What, for two years?" he snapped. They sat in silence for a few minutes.

"Let me speak to Captain Henley. I have an idea," she finally responded.

"Hopefully better than solitary confinement," he muttered under his breath, thinking, *Or how about a prison break or smuggling in a file in a cake.* This was not one of her stories; this was his life. Maybe he should not be so cruel. Angel meant well, but he was the one who was suffering. Without thinking, his fist slammed down on the table in frustration causing a loud thud. The prison guards stirred, but no action was taken.

"Keep it together, Damien," Angel whispered. "I promise I will get you out of here. I may not be here next week, but I will get a message to you." She stood up to leave; visiting time was over.

"Don't," he whispered. It was too late. The look in Angel's eyes said it all. Angel's idea was simple – she would offer to cure Captain Henley's wife on the condition Damien was released. The Captain had contacts in high places who could surely have Damien released if he wanted to. On the recommendation of Damien's father, Angel had taken the role as a live-in carer for the Captain's wife, Agnes. Angel cooked, cleaned and generally took care of Agnes Henley. The Captain's wife's brain tumour was malignant and far too advanced to cure, according to the doctors. Angel regularly cured Agnes' headaches and sometimes the involuntary muscle jerking she was prone to. Agnes was privilege to Angel's secret from the beginning, but they had not divulged this secret to the Captain, although with Agnes' memory, she probably could not remember how Angel helped her. Angel realised she needed Agnes on board to help persuade the Captain.

*****

"I think I can do it, sir, but there is no guarantee. I have not practiced this, and if I take it too far, it could kill Agnes rather than heal." The Captain looked over at his wife, who nodded.

"This is no life. I'm totally bed ridden. My memory is failing, and I would be in constant pain if it weren't for Angel. I feel nauseous most of the time. If there's any chance at all, I think we should at least try. I am dying anyway." Angel was thankful Agnes was having one of her better days and actually making sense.

"This is blackmail, young lady; I should have you thrown in prison."

"I know, but I have nothing else to trade. I'm desperate and this could be a win-win situation for all of us."

"This sort of thing only happens in films, not real-life. It isn't possible to have somebody released from prison. There are procedures and protocols to follow," the Captain explained. Angel stared at him, waiting for a positive response. He was considering the possibility. She could almost see him working through the options just like Damien's father would do.

Two years left and then the Captain could retire on full pay. He could not afford to mess up. He wanted to spend his retirement with his dear wife, but this was starting to look unlikely. Angel was giving his wife and him a lifeline – the chance of a new life. Could the young girl standing in front of him really cure his wife? He wanted desperately to believe in miracles. Could this be the miracle he had been waiting for? If there was any chance at all, he could not let it pass him by.

"Do what you have to do, and I will do what I have to do," he said as he got up and walked out of the room to the phone. His first call would be to his old friend, the District Attorney.

*****

Damien realised he needed to hold it together, especially alone at night when his imagination ran wild. He had now come to the conclusion that Warren was in partnership with Edward, which was a ridiculous idea. But everything fit together. If Edward had not used Warren's name on Angel's note, she would never have left him to meet Edward. If Warren had not given him the paperweight, then he would not have thrown it and killed Edward, and he would not be in prison. After all, why did Warren give him the paperweight? What did he know? Was it all planned? And why was Warren not taking any credit for the killing? Then again credit was probably the wrong word to use. It was a damn mistake – that's what it was. At first Damien had felt privileged to share a secret with Warren. He felt as though he had been accepted into Angel's brother's confidence – now he was having second thoughts. He didn't trust Warren.

There were other examples which again pointed to Warren being in partnership with Edward. Warren would have had access to Angel's belongings. Could he have hidden the knife in her clothing? And when the riots kicked off, his dad had not received the message from Lieutenant Whitehouse. At the time, his father had expressed surprise that his mobile was on silence. His phone was never kept on silence due to his work. Warren would have had access to his father's phone. There was also a coldness to Warren. How could a child show no emotion over the death of his parents and not even want to know what happened? It was strange. If it had been his parents, Damien would have wanted to know every detail. There was no way he could have hidden his emotions. He may have even strived for revenge, but Warren was cold towards their deaths. Damien needed to put these thoughts out of his mind. His dad and Angel trusted Warren, and that should be enough. Sometimes the thoughts became more depressing. On really bad days, he was sure Angel was against him. She hadn't removed his scars out of love; no, it was out of spite. Removing the scars on his arm left from Edward's attack had made him defenceless in court. There was no proof of the evil he had been subjected to.

*****

The cell doors were locked; the lights were out. He had survived another day. More of the inmates were ignoring him, taking a wide berth when he was present. Rumours spread fast. Nobody wanted to be caught in the finale when he would eventually come to blows. They would come for him soon, though. The atmosphere was tense, the pressure building. Who would strike the killing blow? His money was on the biggest chap in prison, over six foot tall and built like a tank, not the brightest but probably the deadliest. The other inmates called him

Python, but not because of the colourful red and green tattooed snakes winding up his arms to a thick broad neck, their fork tongues pointing to a square jawbone. No, the other inmates reckoned he could squeeze the life out of any living creature without breaking a sweat. It was for this exact reason he was serving a twenty-five-year sentence. With facial features chiselled out of rock by a mason who had no comprehension of beauty, he was an ugly, hard-faced killer. Then there was the Mexican, smaller in stature, but he had the eyes of a killer. He was always within a fifteen-foot radius, watching his every movement. Was he waiting for his chance? With no close allies, very little was known of the Mexican. He had been admitted two weeks after Damien. A solitary figure serving his time, but his constant watching was making Damien feel uneasy.

Damien knew he must think positive thoughts. His father was right. At night prison could screw with your mind, make you paranoid. It was the clank of the heavy metal door, the sound of the key turning, the cold concrete floor underfoot and the smell of disinfectant. All these factors and many more contributed to the paranoia. *I must block out the negative thoughts,* Damien repeated silently over and over again. The only positive memory he could recollect was the same memory he thought about every evening. The day he took Angel to see a Super League rugby game between Wigan Warriors and St Helens, Wigan won. Not that Angel had taken the game seriously. She had giggled at how tight the players' shirts were, claiming she could see all their muscles and when he had suggested flexing his pecks later, she had collapsed into another fit of giggles. That was what Damien loved about Angel. She always giggled at silly things. Damien wasn't sure if Angel understood or enjoyed the game; she had said she had, but comments like, "It's a rough game. They look like they just want to injure each other the way they pick each other up and slam each other down onto the ground," made Damien wonder. Angel had found the game difficult to watch. She had continuously talked about the players swiping the legs from underneath their component.

"They must get hurt," she had quietly remarked, followed by, "I can't imagine you doing that."

He had laughed, "I am harder than you think." Watching rugby with Angel was very different to watching it with Laurel. With a man, you could shout and yell obscenities, punching the air when your team scored. With Angel, he had found himself quite subdued. Seated throughout the match, he found himself explaining the game and pointing out the position he used to play, shirt number four, and explaining how his role was to support the winger through tackling, passing the ball and speed. He pointed out the ten-metre law and the dummy runner, pass and tackle moves. He even explained in a calm, controlled manner that was almost a whisper how he drove the ball forward, to support the winger where possible – Laurel's position. Everybody around them appeared to be acting like chimps who had just experienced their first signs of freedom, but Damien had been calm during the match. He was happy that Angel was with him experiencing one of his greatest joys – rugby. If he could have held onto that memory he would have, but then his mind would drift to the uninvited memory – the killing of Edward. The man was still mocking him even when dead. He always forced his thoughts back to Angel. He had promised Angel he would take her to a Four Nations game so she could see Australia play. Would this still be possible one day? Australia, the top team in the world, was so far advanced compared to other teams. Would he ever play again? His assumption was probably no. His mind would then drift back to school when he played alongside Laurel. They were an excellent team. At this point, he would let out a gentle sigh and bury the back of his head into the tiny flat pillow. Plumping it up would make no difference. There were no feathers or goose-down, not like his pillows back home. These were synthetic, hard as rocks, impossible to rest the head on, impossible to sleep on.

Forgetting the pillow for a moment, a smile crossed his face. Another letter from Laurel had arrived that afternoon. University sounded like it was all women, partying and drinking, which would suit Laurel. Laurel had been fourteen when he lost his virginity to a then sixth former. Admittedly she thought he was older. He boasted long and hard over that conquest, kept going on about it until Damien had finally lied and said he had also had sex, not that Laurel believed him. He wondered how many more women had fallen under Laurel's charm. Eighteen years old, and he must be close to thirty. The letter didn't say much about his training with Wigan, which was a disappointment. Going reasonably well, hard work, ached after every training session, was about as much as he could glean from the letter. Damien made a mental note to write to Laurel in the morning, not that he would have much to say.

Damien lifted his right arm into the air and slowly turned it from left to right. Still no sign of the illness, not even a blemish. Edward's initials had disappeared from the surface of his arm. That constant visual reminder was now gone, but the memory was deeper than the skin's surface. His arm was beautiful, so disease free. It felt strong and powerful. If Angel could do this to his arm, then there was always hope she could eventually cure him. Could this be what Tim meant when he said every object was symbolic, whether we realise it or not? Laying his arm across his body, his eyes closed.

*****

Another break to her arm and within two weeks Angel had kept her promise – Agnes was cured. The brain tumour had disappeared. Unfortunately, some brain cells were destroyed during the process. A small part of her memory lost, but nothing too serious. Agnes and the Captain could once again enjoy their life together.

*****

No knock, no privacy. Damien's cell door opened without warning. Two guards stood blocking its entrance.

"Grab your stuff now," one of them bellowed. Damien could hear the other inmates moving behind their cell doors – listening to what was going on. A few shouted abusive comments. Were they aimed at him or the guards? He was unsure. At one stage, he thought he heard Edward's voice.

"You're mine, boy," the voice hissed.

The mind can play strange games when stressed. "Edward is dead. He can't hurt me anymore," he muttered under his breath.

What did the guards want? Oh no, he had seen the films. Two guards drag an inmate from his cell and they rape or beat that inmate close to death. Sometimes the guards took part, and other times they turned their backs and let the inmates do the beating, paid off handsomely for their trouble. Damien tried to convince himself it does not happen in real-life, but he was still concerned.

Damien thrust his hands together, waiting to be handcuffed. It was useless to struggle. He was well aware of the procedure. To Damien's surprise, he was marched down to the large, impersonal visiting room, un-cuffed and left. The room looked different at night, larger and colder. The shadows created by the bright moonlight stretched across the floor, bouncing off the furniture and making eerie shapes. There was nobody lurking in the corners of the room, and the tables and chairs were in lines, preventing anybody from hiding. There were no nooks or crannies to hide in. The entire room was visible from where he stood. This was where the guards stood on visiting day, observing all that went on in the room, making sure no illegal substances, drugs or weapons were being sneaked into the aging prison under their nose. The door on the far side of the room creaked open. A good oiling was required. In walked Captain Henley. Damien slowly walked towards him, unsure if he should be scared or happy. The Captain did not look pleased.

"Don't say anything. Just sign the document they put in front of you, and we will walk out of here," were the instructions. Small beads of perspiration were forming on the Captain's furrowed brow, a look of concern etched deep into his ageing facial features. Damien walked out of prison, released into the Captain's custody after serving only six weeks. He was never to return.

Part 3

Freedom

Damien took a deep breath. Fresh air had never smelled so good. Glancing towards the Captain's red clapped-out motor, Damien stifled a laugh. Surely this wasn't the car his father had spoken about – 'the Captain's pride and joy.' The Captain was already seated in the driver's seat; his head rested on the car's aging headrest. He too was taking deep breaths, not from the relief of freedom but from fear of messing-up his retirement plans. Damien opened the passenger side door and sat down gently on the faded leather seat. He was afraid the stitching would not hold with the sudden impact of his weight.

"Well, Damien, don't let me down. I am doing this for my wife and because I have the deepest respect for your father. My career can go up in smoke if you let me down."

"I won't, sir. I will do anything you ask."

"Ok, first we are going home to my house where you will stay the night. I hope my wife is cooking dinner. That girlfriend of yours is not the best cook."

Damien laughed, "No, I guess she's not."

"Tomorrow the work begins. Do you want me to call into the pharmacy to pick up some more painkillers? Your dad said you were struggling with the pain."

Damien shook his head, "I have Angel. I'll be ok. How is your wife, sir?"

Henley closed his eyes and pressed his head deeper into the headrest, leaving an indent. The stitching held. He didn't start the car immediately, choosing instead to sit for a while in silence. When he did decide to speak, he spoke in a slow tone in case they were overheard. "Agnes went for her next course of Chemotherapy today. The doctor said there was no sign of the brain tumour; it has just disappeared."

"That's good, isn't it?"

"Yeah, but Damien, it's not natural, is it? It's freaking me out. A couple of days ago I went to work as normal, and when I returned home everything had changed. My wife was cooking dinner, just like the old days. It's like the last twelve months of hell never existed. Not only that, your girl and my wife are so close, I feel like an outsider. My wife is obsessed with your Angel, worships the ground she walks on. The other day she taught Angel to bake a cake, and I know there is nothing wrong with that, but on top of the cake Agnes had used sugar-paper to create Angel's face. I had to sit at the table with the cake staring up at me. If I glanced left, there was your girlfriend looking at me. If I glanced right, there was a picture of Angel hung on my wall. Agnes has removed the photograph of our daughter and replaced it with a photograph of Angel. That graduation photo has hung on our dining room wall for over ten years. I feel like Angel is haunting me. Everywhere I look, she is there, and yesterday evening Agnes spent all night teaching her to knit. She hardly spoke two words to me all night. It's as if I don't exist. They are so close; Agnes is treating Angel like she's our daughter. It's weird, Damien. I am not sure what to make of it all.

"Did you know that girl of yours broke her arm? She calmly placed her arm on the small wall in my back garden, picked up a brick, and smashed it against her forearm. There was no shouting or screaming. That's not normal; it was done so coldly. It was broken for about a week. I could see the bone pushing against the swollen, bruised skin. She didn't go to the hospital, even though I tried to make her. Instead, she constructed a sling out of a tea-towel and carried on as normal. For god's sake, Damien! A sling out of a tea-towel! It's not normal. Then when Agnes recovered, Angel's arm was no longer broken. I admit she looked dreadful, pale and weak for a few days but suddenly overnight, she had fully recovered. I know it's all connected; it's not the devil's work, is it?"

"No, sir. It's not the devil's work," Damien assured him.

"I will never forget her eyes. They are normally so dark, but they had turned the colour of cats' eyes. You know the colour, almost an emerald green. They looked straight through me. There was a coldness I hadn't seen before."

Damien made a mental note to mention to Angel the change in her eyes' colouring. He had noticed it a couple of times before. Originally, he had assumed it was due to a change in lighting, but now Henley had confirmed what he had only suspected. Angel's eyes drained of the dark colouring when she was stressed or when healing above her means. The act of healing puts her body under strain and brings out the green in her eyes. They weren't cold like Henley described. They were a beautiful, deep, rich green. This discovery had to be connected to her gift. Damien knew Angel would be fascinated by this finding – if she didn't know already.

Henley lowered his voice once more, "I think your girlfriend destroyed part of my wife's brain on purpose so that Agnes would no longer remember our daughter, Sylvia. I think Angel is trying to take my daughter's place." He looked up at Damien, who was staring back, totally shocked at what Henley had just told him.

"No, no you are mistaken," stuttered Damien. "Angel is not like that."

"There are other weird instances. She moves everything on my shelves and dresser. My personal belongings are moved and placed in a particular order. I moved them back to where they were, and she has gone and moved them again. They are all placed at a 90° angle. I am sure she is challenging me."

"It's just Angel's way. She's not challenging you, sir. She has always moved things. She does it to me all the time, kept my room tidy at school. Who needs a housekeeper?" Damien managed a fake grin, but the Captain could not see the funny side.

"I am scared of her, scared of what she is, and what she could do, if she is not controlled," continued Henley.

"Don't be scared of Angel. She can't hurt you. She wouldn't hurt anyone intentionally. We don't know why or how Angel can do this, but she can. Without an injury to her body, she can't heal. Please don't let her broken arm bother you. When Angel moves out, I am sure your life with Agnes will return to normal."

"I know I should be grateful, Damien. It's just so hard to accept when you don't understand."

"I know Angel will be heartbroken if she thinks she is scaring you. Angel hates being able to do this. I know she longs to be normal, yet I think it's a beautiful gift."

"Will you get her out of my house, son, and real soon?"

"Tomorrow. We will leave tomorrow, I promise. Please don't make Angel feel uncomfortable tonight." Damien could see Henley had a lot on his mind. He was building himself up into a frenzy. Damien needed to keep him calm or he would ruin everything for Angel.

It was Damien's turn to place his head on the headrest. How could Henley be so ungrateful? Angel had given Henley's wife her life back at a great pain to herself. Surely he should be grateful rather than wittering on about the devil's work and being scared of her. At that very moment, Damien would have loved to speak his mind; to holler at Henley, tell him how selfish he was. No matter how angry Damien felt, he knew he couldn't afford to upset Henley. The Captain was his only life-line to freedom and he wouldn't destroy that for anything.

"How come she has never healed you?" asked Henley, interrupting Damien's thoughts.

Damien smiled a fake smile. So far he had told Henley the truth. His intention was to continue to be open and truthful. Maybe then Henley would realise Angel was no threat.

"A couple of reasons. She feels my illness is too close to my heart, and my heart always starts to beat so fast that she starts to lose control. If she loses control, well, I guess the worst will happen. Angel has tried, and we will try again, but I won't have her injure herself for me, and she knows that. I am sorry to say I was totally against her injuring herself for your wife."

*****

The night with Angel had been worth waiting for. She was as tentative and loving as always. That night, his pain had been taken slowly, allowing him to savour the tingling sensation as her fingers moved across his body. Afterwards, they made love, slowly and quietly so as not to disturb Henley and his wife. It felt so good to be back together.

Next day they arose early. Henley was already waiting impatiently at the breakfast table, which was laid out with a wide range of food, although nobody was particularly hungry, even though the food smelt appetising.

"I have decided we are going to use you as bait. I want you to pay Frank a visit with the intention of loosening his tongue," said the Captain. An uneasy feeling sat in the pit of Damien's stomach, and although Damien didn't say anything, the Captain could sense his uncertainty. "Remember what you promised me," the Captain reminded him. Damien nodded. He had hoped for a couple of hours freedom before starting work.

"Of course I will visit Frank. I gave you my word, didn't I?"

The Captain smiled and patted him on the shoulders. "Don't worry. You will have back-up within a close vicinity."

Damien looked relieved.

"Is Frank dangerous?" asked Angel.

"No, we are just testing a theory, that's all."

"In which case, can I go as well?" chipped in Angel. "Frank will wonder why Damien is visiting Warren alone."

The Captain looked at Damien. "She has a point," said the Captain.

Damien glanced towards Angel. "Don't give me those pleading eyes. It is not a social call," he muttered. He could see she desperately wanted to go with him. Angel would want to see her brother, whereas he intended to push Frank into submission until he eventually contacted the Doctor. If he could not break Frank, then he would have no choice but to tackle Warren and test his own theory – a theory he had not shared with anybody else. This would upset Angel, and he didn't want to upset her. In many ways, he hoped he was wrong for Angel's sake. Damien sighed, knowing Angel and the Captain had a point.

"Will you do what I ask and don't argue? Just go along with whatever I say," Damien requested.

Angel nodded. "I love it when you are masterful," she whispered, giving him a quick nudge.

"I mean it, Angel. It could be dangerous." She nodded again with the intention of arguing. Henley had stated it wasn't dangerous, but she didn't. Instead she was serious. Damien had no intention of telling Angel of his suspicions about her younger brother being part of the Doctor's clan. If he was right, she would find out in her own time.

*****

Frank's home was in a rural setting on the outskirts of Newburgh. There was no suggestion from the outside of the house that this home was run by a dangerous man. The garden was immaculate. The hedgerow was trimmed flat on top by a hand with precision. A large rhododendron bush stood in the corner of the garden next to a tree with small green and red stripped leaves. Angel did not recognise the tree, which was unusual. After all, she had read many books on flora in the Northern and Southern hemisphere. In the small front garden next to a pond that once held water a garden gnome stood, a fishing rod tucked under its arm, with turquoise trousers and a jacket painted in a fire-engine red. A small three-foot-high white fence secured the garden's boundary and protected the gnome from gnome snatchers. The whole place seemed quaint, with a woman's touch. They found Warren in the garden. A look of shock followed by delight crossed his face.

"So how did you manage to get out of prison?" asked a bewildered Warren. Angel was about to respond when Damien jumped in.

"They decided I was not guilty. It was all a big mistake, so I'm a free man," he said jovially.

"But you admitted it."

"I know. It's funny how it works out," laughed Damien. "Anyway, shouldn't you have said, it's great to see you, Damien?"

Warren smirked, "Yeah, of course. I am glad to see you both."

"Do you like it here?" asked Angel.

"It's cool."

"And Frank?"

"I like him," said Warren. Angel smiled, obviously happy with the response.

Frank approached the group, and although they had met him before, he seemed older than they remembered. He was a tall, thin man, with sharp facial features. His eyes were not as piercing as Edward's. They lacked the intensity in colour. His iris was a pale slate grey and a little watery, giving his sharp features a slight softness. He wore an old tweed jacket with corduroy patches on the elbows.

"Please excuse my appearance. I was planting some more fruit trees and vegetables at the back of the house."

He looked over to Angel and grinned. She returned the smile. "Home grown fruit and vegetables give you far more nutrition than shop bought groceries," he uttered.

"Did you know there are around eight American varieties of apple that are home grown yet there are over 65 varieties of American eating apple and…." Angel began.

"And 7,500 varieties in the world," joined in Damien. He looked over at Angel and winked. Put Frank at ease so he lets his guard down, and then hit him hard to see if they could unsettle him; a simple idea and hopefully an effective one.

"Are you going to invite your friends in?" Frank asked, directing his question at Warren. It all sounded very innocent and natural.

"Yeah, of course," responded Warren, looking confused. Did Damien sense a little irritation in his reply or was he desperately searching for something that was not there? They followed Warren into his home.

"Sorry we didn't phone," said Damien. "We didn't have your number."

"Not a problem," responded Warren, mustering a smile.

Inside of the house was as well-kept as the outside. There were very few possessions, but the house was clean and lived in. The furniture was a little worn but served its purpose. A large overflowing bowl of fruit stood out in an otherwise dark living room. It was a multitude of colour with a variety of fruits.

"Would you like an apple?" Frank had lifted the glass fruit bowl and placed it under Angel's nose.

"No, thank you. Not at the moment." Frank nodded and returned it to the table. Damien smiled. He had never seen Angel turn down an apple before. She was obviously taking her role seriously – no distractions.

"Did you know a Gala apple must only be eaten from the Northern hemisphere in Autumn?" Angel asked. "In Spring, you must eat Gala apples from the Southern hemisphere. It's their taste, you see. They change through the seasons."

"I have heard that as well, but I have never tested the theory, have you?" Frank asked. Angel shook her head. Damien looked at them both in turn. Did Frank also have an obsession with apples? Surely that was impossible, a strange coincidence. Probability surely had to be at least a million to one.

Now the pleasantries were over, as planned Angel opened the conversation.

"I hope you don't mind me asking, Frank, but is that an accent I detect?" Frank sat quietly not answering. "You roll your r's very slightly, and your tone rises on the last syllable when you ask a question ending in a verb. Now let me guess, there is definitely an accent. I am fascinated by accents." She paused for a couple of seconds as though she was thinking and then continued. "I think it's Polish. No wait, it could be Italian, as it has a romantic tone. No, it can't be, you always pronounce your i the same, no matter what the word is, which is particularly unusual in the English and French spoken word. It's Romanian, definitely Romanian. The accent and sound are almost identical to Italian; I know it is Romanian. If I am right then they would have called you Flaviu after your yellow hair. I always wished my hair was a golden yellow." Angel twisted her fingers through her hair, looking totally relaxed and innocent whereas Frank's face was beginning to redden with anger. Warren had never seen Frank angry. He wasn't sure how he would react with Angel's comment. He had no choice but to intervene.

"Stop it, Angel. Please leave Frank alone," Warren spoke with authority. Damien looked over at Warren. Was he trying to protect Frank? Warren spoke as though he was the master of Frank, not the other way around, yet he was still calm, not rattled. He spoke respectfully.

"I am sorry, Frank. I didn't mean to offend you," laughed Angel. "It was just an observation. Nobody should be embarrassed by where they come from. Edward, my father, was from Romania. Did you know him? He was known as Edward Wellingstone, or Eftemie Vladimirescu when he lived in Romania. He is dead now. Oh but of course, you know that. You were at Damien's trial with Warren. I think he was from Northern Romania; his accent was Northern." Frank glanced towards Warren. Sweat was forming under his checked shirt. What did these people know? Warren was playing it cool, giving him no sign on how he should respond.

"What are you trying to say, Angel?" Warren asked inquisitively.

"Oh nothing, I was just making an observation." Damien looked across again, unsure if Warren was playing on the innocent child image – pretending not to understand what was going on.

Angel hoped she had not upset Warren. She couldn't understand why Damien wouldn't let Warren into their secret. If Frank was part of the Doctor's group then surely Warren was not safe with his new guardian.

As they got up to leave, Angel turned to Frank and whispered, "I know who you are."

"*Nu împingeți-vă norocul* [do not push your luck]," hissed Frank. Angel smiled. The Chief Inspector was right. Frank was not who he said he was.

*****

"You were great, Angel. Where did you learn to act like that?" asked Damien proudly. Angel nearly responded by saying the psychiatric hospital, but then thought better of it. Instead she smiled. "Do you think I provoked him enough?" she asked.

"Oh yes, he didn't know what to do. I had a quick snoop around when I asked to use their bathroom. I didn't find anything unusual, although I did pick up this."

"A blank page!" Angel exclaimed.

Damien laughed. "You wouldn't make a very good detective. It's the top page of the notepad next to the telephone. I thought somebody may have made notes from a telephone call. I am sure they can rub over the sheet with a pencil to reveal what was written down."

"I think you have been watching too many films," Angel shook her head.

Damien laughed, "You'll see I'm right."

"We make a great team," said Angel, giving Damien a quick hug.

"The best," responded Damien.

"What next?"

"We wait. It's their move."

*****

Warren studied Frank. "You are pathetic. All you care about is that stupid garden of yours. What is my father going to say?" His father – the Doctor – had been so proud of him. At least, he thought the Doctor was his father. Then again, over the last few years, he had heard so many conflicting stories that he wasn't sure who he was. He had infiltrated into the Harrington family, gained their trust. Now the Doctor could play his game, tease and play with their emotions until he finally broke them. Was that what he really wanted? Warren was unsure. He liked Angel, liked her a lot, although today he had seen a different side to her. She was play-acting, and Frank had fallen for it. Then there was Edward's death, which hadn't been planned. He had received a lot of praise from his father for his part. It was a stroke of genius giving Damien the paperweight. Warren knew as soon as Damien took the object that his fate was written. He knew Edward would go back for Angel. He always had a soft spot for her, and that would always be his downfall. His father had wanted Edward disciplined. He was showing weakness, and the authorities were beginning to close in on them. The inner circle had no place for any weakness. The Doctor had liked Edward's games. The clues left at the crime scene had been amusing. Now his father had tired of them, but this was a new twist. What did Damien and Angel know? His father had not planned for this unexpected turn in events.

After a few minutes, Warren stomped into the hallway. He preferred everything to be planned, laid out in front of him, just like Edward. And what about his father! What would his father say? How could Damien have gotten released from prison? The plan had been to put the Harrington family through hell, to keep their attention on their own problems, allowing the Doctor to move his plans forward – now that had changed. Sometimes Warren wished his adoptive parents were still alive. From an early age, he had understood their destiny, but that didn't stop the grief. They had been decent parents. He hoped they had not suffered, although he doubted this would have been the case with Samuel taking care of them. He was a thug, but his father seemed to like Samuel's aggressive nature. Warren smiled. He was the brains; Samuel was the brawn. He needed to think.

His father had the telepathic gift of control and manipulation. Being able to draw on his gift whenever needed was important in his line of work. Warren couldn't control his telepathic power, not yet. Time was required to nurture and develop this ability, although he realised it was becoming stronger.

"What should we do, Warren? They know who I am. The Doctor will have me removed like he did Edward."

"How many more times do I have to tell you that he didn't have Edward removed? It was an accident."

"Please, Warren, tell him I am blameless. He will listen to you."

Warren walked over to Frank and slapped his face hard. A red mark started to form on his right cheek.

"You are weak, Frank. Why did you respond? Why didn't you just play along with her? Laugh as though she was saying something funny. Tell her you were Italian – anything but confirm your Romanian ancestry. They can now link you directly with Edward." Warren took a deep breath. Damn! He didn't want to contact his father. Frank was going to make him appear incompetent just when he was starting to impress his father and gain his trust.

Warren marched outside, picked up the gnome and threw it at the front door of the house. The door splintered, and a large gash appeared above the letterbox. The gnome suffered worse. Its tiny legs and black boots separated from the rest of its body, and the arm shattered into tiny pieces. Inside the house, Frank flinched. He didn't like violence. The gnome had been with him since the loss of Bobby, and for some strange reason, the gnome had felt important. The only stable part of his life that he still controlled was in his garden, represented by the gnome, and now that had gone. Warren marched back into the house.

"Do you know where the twins are?" he hollered.

"I don't know. I have never visited them. I was supposed to be their guardian, but your father always wanted me to keep my distance. He had other ideas for them. I am not even sure if they were ever placed with their adoptive parents." Frank was sitting in the chair, head in his hands. He glanced up every now and again to respond to Warren's questions. Frank needed time to think through his options. Sometimes he wished he had never got involved with the Doctor. At first it had been easy money, keeping an eye on Bobby, bringing him up as his own, developing his power, reporting Bobby's progress regularly. In return, every monthly report yielded a handsome sum of money, compliments of the Doctor. The time he had spent with Bobby's mother and later with just Bobby had been the happiest times in his life. If only that time could have continued, but as the old saying goes 'all good things must come to an end.' The Doctor had been so annoyed when Frank had lost Bobby. At the time Bobby had been their strongest prodigy. His gift had been close to perfection.

The call would have to be made, and Warren knew this conversation was going to be difficult. The voice on the end of the phone was demanding yet controlled.

"You failed me, son. Redeem yourself. Bring me Angelica. It's time to test her power before she causes me anymore problems."

"I know she won't come," Warren was desperately trying to sound confident and in-control like his father.

"Well, don't give her a choice. The stupid b**ch has caused me enough trouble. Take Samuel with you."

Warren glanced to the far side of the room. Samuel had come in, and was swinging his bat, trying to perfect the swing to get as much power behind the force of the bat as he could muster. He was a nasty, dangerous piece of work, with a brain in his fist instead of his head. Nonetheless he could be useful sometimes. At least he had had the sense to stay hidden during Damien's and Angel's unwelcome visit.

"What happens now?" asked Angel.

"We wait," responded Damien. There was no wait. Within twenty-four hours the powers had shifted.

The Trap

Damien could feel the blood pulsating through his veins. He was trapped once again, like a caged animal.

"Come on then, Samuel. Why don't you hit a man instead of a woman?"

Now back on his feet, Samuel moved towards him. The bat swung by his side.

"Take me on like a man," shouted Damien. His hands beckoned Samuel to take another step forward. Dislodging the metal bar from Samuel's grasp was his only option if he was to stand any chance. Angel's body lay in the dirty alleyway ahead. Why did she head down the alleyway? As soon as he heard Warren's voice shouting for help, he had realised it was a trap. Damien's reactions had been slow. Angel had a ten metre start on him before he realised what was happening. Maybe he should have warned her of his suspicions.

A figure had stepped from the doorway. Damien tried to shout out a warning. Angel's head had turned, and then he saw the bar come crashing down. Angel's legs crumbled beneath her body as she fell. He ran towards her still body, straight into a trap. The alleyway led to a dead end. Angel's attacker stood in front of him, blocking his passage. The bat was swinging. Damien knew he was facing Angel's older brother, Samuel. The description given in the interview room had nearly been perfect, apart from the scar across his cheek – she had failed to mention the scar.

"How could you do that to your sister?" Samuel did not respond verbally, nor did he glance to where Angel lay. Instead, the bat swung in Damien's direction. Intuitively, Damien ducked. The baton caught him again across the right shoulder. Once again the blood pounded through his veins. This time he didn't go down. His left hand moved to his right shoulder, and he pushed hard with his palm. A sharp stabbing pain followed by a loud click forced the shoulder back into place. It felt sore, although he had suffered worse pain.

Another figure stepped out from the building, but no weapon was in this person's hand. The figure moved towards Angel and scooped her up off the ground. The physique of the stranger suggested male. He was stronger than he looked, although Angel was not heavy. Her limp body fit comfortably in his arms. An educated guess was Frank. The face was in shadow. He was wearing a long dark coat with a hood pulled over his head, disguising his appearance. Damien bellowed one single word, "No!" The echo of his voice bounced off the enclosed buildings. The figure glanced up. Even though Damien could not see the face, he was now sure it was Frank.

Damien rushed towards Samuel to stop Frank from taking Angel. Stopping short, he scrutinised the surroundings to see if Warren was hanging around. He was not scared of Warren as he was physically stronger, but he did not want to be trapped. Ducking again, the baton swung fiercely towards his face. This time it missed. Damien brought his foot up between Samuel's legs and he kicked hard. Samuel let out a scream. His hand immediately covered his testicles. Unfortunately, the baton stayed firmly in his grip. The figure was now disappearing back into the building. Angel's head had fallen back over her abductor's arm. Her long dark hair swept the ground. Without any co-ordination, the figure slammed Angel's head against the wooden door frame. There was no blood, which indicated the baton had not struck her head. If they were going to the trouble of taking her, then they must want her alive.

"Please, no brain damage," Damien uttered under his breath. He had promised Angel he would protect her; that her so-called family would not hurt her again. Faltering at the first hurdle was not his style. Damien yelled again. Angel was out cold. He glimpsed a swinging arm before Frank and Angel disappeared from sight.

With Damien's concentration lost for a second, Samuel came at him again. This time the bat was aimed lower. Damien leapt into the air and threw himself at Samuel. Aiming high, he 'spear-tackled' him to the ground. It was an illegal-move in rugby league, although this was no game. Using Samuel's body to protect his fall, he managed to deflect the bat and grab Samuel's arm. Pounding the arm on the floor, Samuel's hand smashed hard onto the cobbled alleyway. Samuel was strong and stubborn. He held tightly onto the metal bar as though his life depended on it. The smell of urine rose from the cobbles. The foul odour clung to Damien's nostrils. Samuel kicked Damien in the shin and grabbed a handful of hair, which he pulled like a man obsessed. The movement gave Damien enough room to swing his fist at Samuel's face before Samuel could go for his throat. He landed a perfect punch, busting Samuel's nose and splitting his upper lip.

"That's for the beating you gave Angel," he hissed, smashing Samuel's hand down again onto the ground. This time Samuel released his grip on the baton. Damien leant over to grab it, but the baton rolled beyond his reach. Samuel now landed a perfect punch in the ribs. Damien's hand sprung back and landed another punch in Samuel's face, but with less force than his first punch. Samuel's face hurt. The bridge of his nose was caved in, and his nasal passage was leaning slightly to the right.

Two more figures entered the alleyway. Damien was about to shout over to them and then he realised they were also carrying batons. Staggering back to his feet, he fell into the garbage cans as he tried to gain his balance. A grey furry creature scurried from its current location, distressed by the sudden movement of its home. Its scrawny tail was twice as long as its whiskers. Stopping, its nose twitched, attracted by the smell from the rotting meat and vegetables. Sensing danger, it quickly disappeared into a small gap in the wall, its hunched back flattened, allowing the creature to squeeze through the hole to safety. Damien wished he could have followed, shrink like Alice in Wonderland, Angel would have said.

Scrambling to his feet, Samuel waved the newcomers over.

"Let's see how you do now, Damien," he taunted. The words sounded nasal, his breathing raspy. *Where are the police? They should be here by now,* Damien worried, and then it hit him. He was not wearing the tracking device. As far as the police were aware, they were still back in the hotel. Damien prayed Angel was wearing hers. He remembered them stripping off their t-shirts and leaving them in the bathroom. It had been Damien's idea. He wanted some quality time with Angel where they could talk and laugh about stupid things without everybody listening to them. Without thinking, he had grabbed the first t-shirt he could find when they decided to pop to the café.

Damien made a move for the baton. Samuel saw him and counteracted the move. They both quickly withdrew, knowing if they bent down it would put them at a disadvantage. He was trapped; the only option was to run. The two guys were still moving down the alley towards them, kicking empty cans and bottles out of their path. The guy to his left kept close to the buildings as he moved down the alley. The guy on the right – the larger guy – dragged his baton along the wall. The baton made a loud thudding noise as it bounced across the walls of the buildings. The sound changed to a clanking as it caught the garbage cans or a drainpipe. If the noise was meant to scare him, then he was succeeding. As they drew closer, he realised the guy on the left was carrying a cricket bat rather than a baton. Damien knew if he rushed him, he would not be able to swing the bat in time to hurt him. He waited until the figures were within ten metres before making a move. He sprinted towards them, making a couple of dummy moves, confusing the two figures before taking the left line up the alleyway. Slipping past them had been easy. The figures took chase, but he was already in full stride. It was amazing. Less than eighteen months ago he could hardly walk – now he was running. Turning left as soon as he reached the end of the alley and then left again, he headed towards the shopping mall, unsure what he would do when he got there. All he knew was he needed people around him.

*****

Angel was now awake. Frank was stood over her. She sat up quickly, making her head thump.

"Are you ok, Warren?" she asked immediately. Warren was sitting on the table, swinging his legs. He laughed and then Frank smirked. Laughter emanated from behind them, where two more men stood guard near the door.

"Samuel says hello, but he's a little tied up outside. He'll be back soon," said Warren. "Please say hi to Samuel's friends," he invited, signalling behind her. Angel didn't say anything. She glanced over again, but the pair hadn't moved. Warren was in charge. How could that be? Angel's right arm and ribs had a sharp pain running through them, and her head was pounding from where it had hit the door frame. She could still move her arm, so it was not broken, but her ribs ached.

"A couple of Samuel's friends are visiting your grandfather, Aurel, in England. We should have killed him a long time ago. The pervert deserves to die. Maybe your sister will want to join us. Does she have the power, Angel?" There was no answer. "Do you think she can heal?" asked Warren calmly.

Angel shrugged her shoulders. "I don't know," she finally muttered. "What has happened to you, Warren? Why are you doing this?"

Warren stared coldly at Angel, "You killed my mother."

"No, Samuel killed your parents."

"You knocked on the door, and you entered my house. You killed my parents and then you burnt my house down. Did you think I didn't know?"

Angel looked shocked, "It was Samuel, not me."

"You will suffer for what you have done, but first my father's brother needs healing, and you are the only one who can do it."

"But your father is dead."

"No, my adopted father is dead. I mean my true father, Angel," his eyes lit up and a wicked smile crossed his lips. "My true father, the Doctor."

"The Doctor is not your father."

"How dare you call me a liar? He is my father, and I am his son. I am not a nobody like you. I am somebody."

Angel sighed; it was pointless to argue. "What has your father's brother got?"

"Marasmus."

"No," gasped Angel. "I won't. I can't heal Marasmus; it will kill me."

"I know. That is why it has to be you," laughed Warren.

"And if I refuse?" Warren stopped and considered the question for a moment. "Then we will kill that boy-friend of yours, if Samuel hasn't already." A cold shudder ran down Angel's spine. She could not heal Marasmus. Anything but Marasmus. Her thoughts turned to Damien. Not knowing what was happening was the hardest thing to deal with. Was he alright? Were the police on their way?

*****

The police van doors flew open. A large burly detective grabbed Damien as he ran past. Damien was about to throw a punch when he heard his name.

"Damien, what are you doing here? I thought you were with Angelica."

"They've got her; I couldn't stop them," he managed to blurt out in between breaths.

"We know they have her, but I thought you were with her."

Damien shook his head.

The detective who grabbed him was Walter, a sad rundown man who had more than his fair share of pain. Damien glanced down the road. His two assailants had stopped their pursuit. From their location, they would be able to see he was talking to someone. Would they guess it was the police?

"Get in," barked Walter. "We are in the open; too many prying eyes." Once in the van, the doors were hastily closed. The van was kitted out in surveillance gear. *Brian's dream van,* thought Damien. "Clinton, turn the van around and head up Fifty-Fourth Street."

"No," shouted Damien. "What the hell are you doing? We need to get Angel out of there!"

"Listen," one of the smaller guys passed Damien the headphones. He could hear Angel and Warren clearly.

"What's happening? Why don't you get her out of there?" Damien demanded.

"They're going to lead us to the Doctor. We just need to be patient. Don't worry. We will move in if we think Angelica is in danger," said Walter.

"It's Angel, not Angelica," Damien snapped quickly followed by, "Sorry, I didn't mean to sound rude. I'm just worried. I should be with Angel. I was so sure they would come after me, not Angel, after the incident with Edward. I was wrong. Why now? They could have made a move for Angel a long time ago."

"Don't beat yourself up, kid. We were all wrong. She's doing fine. Your father is heading over to Angelica's, I mean Angel's grandfather's. We understand they have gone after him."

The Attack

Bollards and police tape blocked the road ahead. Crystal pulled off the road in her small Fiat and watched. One-hundred metres up the road, she could see flashing blue lights – something had happened. An ambulance pulled out of her grandfather's driveway. Crystal knew her grandfather was dead. Engulfed by sadness, Crystal sat and continued to watch. Death had a habit of following her. She owed everything to Aurel. He had taken her in, looked after her, re-educated her, and in return, he asked for nothing.

A knock on the Fiat window made her jump. She lowered the window slightly to hear what was being said. A young uniformed police officer was standing next to her car. Leaning forward, his hand slipped into his pocket. Crystal assumed it was to reach for his badge, but the shape in his pocket was bulky, too large for a badge. Her dark green eyes rose to meet his. He was smiling. His eyebrows were thick and bushy, but underneath his police cap his head was almost bald. Behind him, another police officer approached.

"Why?" she whispered.

"You have a choice: join us or die." His hand was now fully inside his pocket. He was slowly drawing the object from his tunic.

If you feel like you are in danger, make sure your attacker sees you as a person not an object; he will find it harder to harm you. At that moment, Wenlock's advice rushed to her defence. Wenlock's words of wisdom could be vital to her survival.

"Is your name Tyrone?" she asked, giving him a friendly forced smile. "I noticed the badge on your uniform." Without losing momentum, Crystal continued, "I have a brother called Tyrone. He lives three miles from here. His two young lads, Ben and William, want to be policemen one day."

Her assailant stared in disbelief. "What the hell are you wittering on about? You don't have a brother called Tyrone and my name is..." He stopped suddenly. "You are a clever b**ch. Think you can catch me out, do you?" He stared at her for a couple more seconds. "You have ten seconds to make your decision," he hissed as he swung around to face the police officer approaching. A metal bar was now fully exposed. The baton caught the police officer off guard and smashed down across his face. Crystal saw the stranger's face twist to the right. Blood dripped from the mouth. His left cheekbone was smashed into tiny pieces. Major plastic surgery would be required if he survived the attack.

The uniformed stranger fell to the ground, clutching his face. His assailant placed his metal capped boot deep into the guy's ribs. Crystal heard a crack and a groan. The stranger's bones were being broken. She wanted to help, but to get out of her car was sure to mean her death. The assailant smiled. He had initially argued with Samuel. He had wanted to carry a gun or at the very least a knife, but now he could see the benefit of a baton. It was a silent, deadly weapon. No mess like a knife, and yet more enjoyable.

His attention turned back to the car. Crystal put her foot back onto the accelerator. The small blue hatchback jumped forward and stalled. The handbrake was still in an upward position. Knocking the gears into neutral, Crystal tried to turn the ignition key. The baton slammed down hard on her side window, shattering the glass. A menacing hand forced its way through the broken window. The hand tried to grab her arm. Across the left knuckles, she could read the word F**K; across the right, the word KILL was tattooed deep into the skin. Was it old school to have LOVE and HATE? She didn't have time to contemplate this thought.

His hand was close to grabbing her. Throwing her upper body on the passenger seat to get out of his reach, the handbrake dug uncomfortably into her stomach. She tried to lay flat to open the glove compartment, but it was locked. He brought the baton down again, smashing out more of the window so he could reach her. Crystal's lap was covered in tiny pieces of glass, but she was not cut, only shaken. This time there was no mistake. The ignition key turned as her foot pressed hard on the accelerator. The car surged forward at a speed. The police line was her target. As she surged forward, a feeling of relief rushed through her body. The sudden movement knocked her assailant to one side. She heard the word *bitch*, but no more. Through the rear window, she could see the man she had called Tyrone holding his arm. Her car door had obviously caught him. She hoped it had cut him badly. Easing her foot slightly off the pedal, she slowed. Control was of the essence. There were two police officers near the police line staring up the road. She hoped this time they were genuine.

Crystal heard a single gunshot. It made her jump, but her front windscreen was still intact. Glancing behind, the rear windscreen was also in one piece. Through the rear mirror, she could no longer see the man she had called Tyrone.

Crystal gathered herself together. Her hands started to shake. They felt wet and clammy on the steering wheel, leaving greasy marks. If the steering wheel was a clock face, it would show quarter to three. Not the perfect driving position. Maybe the salesman was right. A leather steering wheel cover would have been beneficial. The yellow and black police tape was getting closer. The bollards didn't look right. Surely police bollards are normally larger and brighter. Panic started to take over. Aurel always said she had to keep her wits about her.

Was it safe to head towards the police-line? There were too many doubts, but she couldn't turn around. Tyrone waited behind her, and there was no other road to turn into. She was trapped like a canary in a cage with nowhere to go. Ben stepped in front of the police-line and waved. If Ben was there, then surely it was safe. A faint smile crossed her lips. No more teasing, this time she would give Ben a chance. She had no feelings for Ben. Then again she had no feelings for anybody. Ben wanted her. She could tell by the way he watched and flirted with her, and maybe over time she would grow to love him. He was a decent man, even if he was a little obsessed with his work.

For six years she had not let herself get close to anyone. Maybe now, with the death of Aurel, it was time to change. Aurel had sensed her reluctance. He had not pushed her, and maybe deep down he understood what she had been through. Aurel was a wise old man, frail but wise. He had warned her they would eventually come for them – to kill him, and to take her. He said she would have to make a choice to join them, or run. If she ran, she would be running for the rest of her life. Unless Aurel was right, and Angel would be the one to stop the feuding. Her decision had been made. She would run.

Crystal exhaled slowly and deeply. Why Angel? It wasn't as if Angel could heal. In fact, her power was non-descriptive. Stan said Angel was showing no signs, so why had Aurel been so adamant? Taking another deep breath she waved at Ben. Only time would tell.

The Operation

With blood boiling, Damien sat in the back of the van. He couldn't understand why everybody was sitting so calmly, just listening. The surveillance team took it in turns to glance over in his direction. They were no doubt waiting for another outburst. Would he disappoint? He wasn't sure. All he was sure of was that it was getting harder and harder to just sit quietly and wait. Wait for what? That was the burning question. Samuel's baton was lethal. It would only take one swing and then death was all that was left.

"Your girlfriend is clever. Listen, she has remembered she is bugged. She has already told us there are two of Samuel's men plus Frank and Warren, and now she has indicated Samuel has just joined the select group. Verbally Samuel is coming down hard on her. Physically there has been no contact," one of the men explained. Damien took the earpiece to listen to the conversation, but anger continued to build inside.

"He's hurting her. We must go in now," he almost shouted, ripping the headphones from his ears.

"No," said Walter sternly. "They need her so they won't hurt her."

"I'm not going to sit here and let you use her."

*****

"Put the bar down, Samuel, and leave our guest alone." Angel looked towards Warren. Thankfully he had stepped in.

"Who the f**k put you in charge?"

"My father, or have you forgotten? Do you want me to ask him to remind you?" Warren placed his body between Samuel and Angel, much to Samuel's annoyance.

"Ok, nothing meant by it," he muttered. Why was he scared of a man he had never met? Edward had been scared of the Doctor – everybody was, but nobody seemed to have met him.

One day I swear I will challenge Warren, and the Doctor will do nothing, thought Samuel. Warren would not belittle him again in front of his men, and especially not in front of the bitch that got Edward killed.

*****

"We must move in now," pleaded Damien. "It will only take one swing of Samuel's bat and she will be dead."

Walter grabbed Damien by the arms and shook him viciously. "Angelica, I mean Angel, is ok. I told you they won't hurt her. This is our chance to close this case. You heard what the kid said. He won't let Samuel touch her." Damien lashed out and punched Walter hard.

"Don't you ever place a finger on me again, or I swear I'll..." he stopped suddenly as he remembered who he was threatening. The other members of the team were on their feet, ready to restrain him. Walter signalled them to carry on monitoring the event unfolding before them. He was in control of the situation.

"I'll give it a few more minutes. If I think Angel is in danger, I will go in myself, with or without you," Damien said. Walter did not respond. As far as he was concerned, the kid was upset, and he didn't want to upset him further. He knew his Captain had taken a liking to the kid. After a few uncomfortable seconds, Damien apologised.

"We won't let anything happen to Angel," Walter repeated, "but Damien, you must understand there have been many innocent killings." He nearly followed this up with, "including my partner," but he didn't. He could not show this was personal. "We don't know what the Doctor is planning. His name is always cropping up. If we can get close to him and his men, maybe we can stop these pointless killings and whatever else he has planned." Walter spoke calmly and precisely as he rubbed his cheek, which was now red and starting to sting.

Damien nodded. "What would you like me to do?" he asked.

"Just keep calm, don't get in the way and let the experts do their job," was the reply.

"They are on the move, heading up Straight Street," said a woman's voice from the front of the van.

"Strap yourself in, son. Now it gets interesting." Walter made a quick call to make sure everybody was ready, and they knew their individual jobs. Walter was not taking any chances; this was one large operation. A promotion depended on the outcome. He had already been overlooked twice, and he wasn't getting any younger. Sometimes he yearned for an office job where he could drink coffee and eat donuts whenever he wanted. He liked donuts, especially powdered sugar from Dunkin Donuts. An office job would take him away from all the madness. How many times had he put his life on the line? Too many times in his opinion.

He had lost one partner, and he remembered it as though it was yesterday. He had replayed the scene over and over again. Could he have done anything differently? Luke had been a faultless partner – his death had shaken Walter up. Two years, five months and two days ago, that's when his partner had died in his arms. Walter enjoyed his job until then. Now he often wondered if it was all worth it. The criminals were becoming devious, more violent.

His job had also cost him two divorces. He could not devote the time to a family as well as to work. Always on call, never able to plan anything with his family. It was a lonely job being a police officer. Somewhere out there he had a son who must be close to fifteen. He had not seen him since his ex-wife remarried. She had a new life in Seattle, with a banker, and his son had a new father. Walter snorted. A banker was a safe bet. He sighed and turned his thoughts back to the current operation. He would not lose another life.

"They are turning into King Street, sir. I think they are heading to the interstate," called out the woman.

"Ok, officer, keep your distance," Walter replied. The audio was a little crackly, yet the words were clear enough to understand. Small beads of perspiration were forming on Walter's brow. Taking a hankie out of his trouser pocket he dabbed his brow before blowing his nose. The conversation they were listening to was uncomfortable. He remembered the game. Last time they played it, they lost, which was why his partner lost his life. A shiver ran down Walter's spine.

"Are you ok, sir?" asked Babs, the only female surveillance officer in the van. Walter looked up abruptly aware. They were all watching him.

"I'm fine. Turn the audio up so we can all hear it."

*****

"My father likes to play games, particularly chess. Now that Edward has been sacrificed, I am his key chess piece, and you are his new opponent. I have the power, Angel, a power I have never had before. People listen to me," explained Warren.

"I don't understand," said Angel. "How do I play against somebody that I have never met? I don't even know the rules of the game."

Warren laughed. "That's simple; there are no rules. My father chooses his people, and then he chooses his opponent. His opponent will change when he tires of the game, or if the game is too easy, and then he moves onto the next opponent. You amuse him, Angel. You throw unexpected obstacles in the way and then he has to change his plans. He has never used one of his own as an opponent so this is a new challenge. Tell me, Angel, how did Damien get out of prison?"

"I don't know," said Angel.

"I nearly forgot. I think this belongs to you." He passed her Damien's old mobile phone.

"Thank you. I thought it was broken," she muttered, slipping it into her pocket.

"I have lost all audio, sir," called out the surveillance officer, "but the satellite is still picking up their location."

"Probably in a tunnel. It sometimes happens," said Walter calmly.

"Where are we going, Warren?" Warren didn't respond.

"You know I can't cure Marasmus," repeated Angel.

"Don't worry," laughed Warren. "It was just one of my father's little jokes. He thought it might freak you out, especially after your time in hospital."

"So what is my next move?" asked Angel.

"That's up to you. Chess is about protecting the king. So who is your king, and how are you going to stop him reaching your king? And don't forget, your king may change."

"I don't have a king. Surely you need to tell me who my king is?"

Warren laughed. "That's not how we play the game, Angel. Anyway, enough talking. It's time for you to leave us."

The car turned off the interstate and took a couple of turns before pulling up next to the kerb. Angel stepped from the car and scanned the surroundings. The road was dark and deserted. A couple of large houses stood behind a tree-lined avenue. No lights could be seen from their windows. Curtains drawn, shutters down, kids tucked up in their bed. Their parents either watching television at the back of the house or out at some social event. It was not late, but it was one of those days when time passed quickly.

"Oy, Walter, I have left Angel on Lombard Street," shouted Warren.

"I guess you thought you were real clever. I know you are hiding a tracking device. You're too damn calm. Remember, I know you and your weaknesses. Your first move and you have failed," he said smugly. "My father does want to meet you, but now is not the time. Not unless you tell me where you are hiding the device."

Angel shook her head. "I don't know what you mean."

"Oy, Walter," Warren shouted again. "My father tells me Luke squealed like a pig when he died. Did you know, Angel, the American police force is so predictable? They always use Walter for this type of operation. The big fat oaf can't do much, not since his partner died. He just sits on his arse eating and listening, don't you, Walter!" and with those final words Angel was left standing by the roadside. As the car pulled away, Warren threw a clear plastic bag out of the window. "A souvenir," he shouted. "Tell Harrington he should be more careful where he leaves things."

Angel picked up the bag from the kerb. Inside was a knife, its carved ivory handle clearly visible. On the plastic bag, the label had a date, the reference number SW507942 and the name Stacey Wilson. Angel quickly dropped the package. This was the knife that had killed her friend; the crucial piece of evidence that had her committed. She hoped Walter was listening. It was a long walk back to the hotel. She couldn't leave the knife on the pavement in the middle of a residential area where a child could pick it up, but she didn't want to touch it again. The thought of carrying it through the streets back to the hotel was a task she did not relish. A cold shudder ran down her spine. The thought alone brought her out in goose-bumps.

Dropping the knife back onto the pavement, Angel contemplated her options. A black Cadillac pulled into the street. She didn't see it at first. It was driving slowly past and pulled over to the kerb one hundred metres further up the road. Nobody stepped from the car. The engine ticked quietly over. The young driver sat and watched. This was more fun than he could have imagined. He wasn't sure what was happening. Angel had obviously upset somebody else, and this time her female charm was not working. He watched as she stared at a small package on the pavement. He was a patient man. He would wait a little longer. Now was not the time. As he pulled away from the kerb, Angel heard the engine. She looked up and watched the car for a second before turning her attention back to the object on the pavement.

Ten minutes later, the surveillance van pulled up beside Angel. She was still staring at the clear plastic bag on the pavement. Damien leapt from the back of the van and ran towards her.

"Angel, are you alright?" he asked softly, but she didn't answer. "Angel," he repeated. This time she responded by turning towards him. A smile crossed her face, and her arms reached out to him. He could see the bump on her head clearly; it was not bleeding.

She pointed to the knife on the pavement. "The knife that killed Stacey," she whispered. He glanced at the object in the small plastic bag and then turned away. Angel followed him back to the van.

*****

"So what did he want?" asked Damien. They were both now back at the hotel, trying to make sense of what had just happened.

"I don't really know; something about a game and my king." An apple sailed over in Angel's direction.

"I am afraid it's American, not an English variety," he laughed.

"I have eaten American apples for nearly a year, so one more won't make any difference." Taking a bite

Angel suddenly spat it into her hand. "It's horrid! It's burnt my mouth. Look," she said, sticking her tongue out. Tiny white blisters were forming on her tongue and roof of her mouth. Damien dragged her to the bathroom.

"Rinse and spit; don't swallow," he said, sounding like his mother. Concern crossed his face as he realised somebody had been in their room. The apples had been tampered with.

"I need to get you to a hospital."

Angel shook her head before spitting out another mouthful of water.

"Head back, tongue out," Angel did as she was told. The back of her throat was not swollen, and the blisters seemed to be disappearing.

Picking up the apple, he turned it over in his hand, smelt it and then passed it back to Angel. "What do you think of the smell?"

"I can't smell anything, apart from a slight tangerine scent, which is what you would expect from a Newtown Pippin. It has a sweetness which balances the tartness, but it should not burn."

"It's strange. You would expect it to smell of something if it burned you." He turned the apple over again. "No wait, Angel. It looks like it has been injected with something." A small pin prick was evident on the rosiest part of the apple. "It's a good job you didn't bite this side or you would have had its full contents."

"But I never bite the reddest part of the apple first. I like to save it until the end" was Angel's immediate answer. Thank god for Angel's peculiarities, was Damien's first thought. The person who had tampered with the apple obviously didn't know Angel that well, was his second.

"I'll take it to Henley for analysis, find out what it has been injected with."

"Do you think it's the Doctor playing his game?" she asked.

Damien nodded. "I think you ought to be extra careful what you eat and drink from now on."

A quick call to Henley, and Angel and Damien found there had been a new turn in events. Frank had handed himself in at the police station and asked for witness protection.

"Why?" asked Angel.

Damien shrugged his shoulders. "All I know they are talking to him now, and he has asked to see you."

*****

"I'm sorry, Angel. This has gone too far. I didn't sign up for any of this." It had only taken forty-five minutes from the initial call to get to the station, and now Angel sat alone in front of Frank; the same room she had sat in many months ago with Damien's father. Frank's eyes were bloodshot and more watery than last time she had seen him. He was tired. His eyes looked strained. Watching and waiting for the Doctor had sapped his energy. He was not a young man anymore. Though not exactly old, the last few years had taken its toll. The anxiety he carried around was a burden that had aged his fifty-one years.

"I wanted to see you because..." he paused for a few seconds trying to decide how best to explain, "Bobby told me about you."

"I don't know a Bobby," said Angel impatiently.

"I know, but he spoke to you in his dreams. Bobby was your brother; he died many years ago." Angel could vaguely recollect a Bobby in her mum's letter and on the Chief Inspector's desk pad, but she was sceptical. Frank was probably one of the Doctor's pawns, playing the game. "He dreamt of you, and I know you were a great comfort to him. I wanted to tell you because he had a child, a young girl who we called Stephanie. She has the same power as you and Bobby. I know she is confused and can't understand why she is different from the other children. I can't help her. The Doctor is not aware of Stephanie, and I don't want to draw his attention to her. I want her to have a normal life without the Doctor's influence. I owe Bobby that much."

"If she has the power, her life will never be normal. She is cursed like the rest of us."

Frank looked shocked. "Bobby was not cursed! He used his power for the good of mankind. I am surprised you think like that."

Angel blew out her cheeks and exhaled slowly, "So am I; I don't know why I said that."

It took Frank a couple of minutes before deciding to continue. "I knew Carla was Bobby's girlfriend, but I did not know she was pregnant. Carla told me after he passed away. One day I hope you will go and see Stephanie, help her understand who she is. Carla is confused about her daughter. She doesn't know what to do. I don't think Bobby told her what he was capable of."

"Do you have an address?"

Frank scribbled the details on a scrap of paper, "Please don't let the Doctor find her."

"I won't," said Angel with a hint of scepticism.

"The Doctor will come after me; I have let him down. I gave away who I was, and I know he is mad. I can feel it. Very soon, he will remove me, which is why I have asked for protection. I do feel you can beat him, Angel, but you need to think smart. Did you know the Doctor can control you telepathically?"

"No, how can he control me?"

"He can control everybody, but his power is starting to weaken as he gets older. Warren is close to taking over. His mind is becoming powerful, yet he still lacks the control that is required."

"How can Warren...?"

"You don't know what you are up against, do you?" butted in Frank.

"I didn't choose any of this," snapped Angel.

"I know," he paused for a second. "The Doctor is only strong because of the people he has around him. The skills they possess are the skills he created them with. Do you know much about the Doctor?"

"Not much."

"Do you know why he is called the Doctor?"

"No."

"He genetically changes DNA to create children with specific gifts."

"Was I genetically created?"

Frank stared at her, "Truthfully, I don't know. I know your mother gave birth to you, and I know she had the gift, but if you are asking me whether your DNA was manipulated in some way," he shrugged. "Angel, I can tell the police where the Doctor is; however, they won't be able to reach him. The children are too strong. Many people will die trying."

"If you don't, they won't give you witness protection."

"I know, but people will die."

"That is their choice to make, not yours."

"If I tell you what you are up against, will you try and prevent the deaths?"

"I don't see how but I'll do what I can," Angel said, thinking of her brothers and sisters, whom until recently she hadn't known existed.

Frank placed his elbows on the table. His head slumped into his hands. Ingrained dirt tainted his fingernails from the hours spent in his garden. The thumbnails had been bitten down; their ragged edges with red patches of skin underneath. The skin looked sore and swollen. Angel almost felt sorry for him. "Listen carefully, Angel. There are two groups of children who are extremely dangerous. I don't believe the others will pose much of a threat. One of the groups I only met once, and I don't want to meet them again. They are creepy. So controlling, you can feel them probing into your mind. Have you ever cleared your mind?"

"What do you mean, like when you think of a brick wall?"

"No, deeper than that. The Doctor's children can control your thoughts, but first they have to get into your mind. They can make you do and see things. This is why you must be able to block them out. To do that, you must clear your mind completely. A brick wall is useless. They will make you think it is falling down on you. The dust will sting your eyes so you can't see. The dust will get trapped at the back of your throat, and you will begin to choke. It is your imagination, but it will kill you because you will believe it is truly happening."

"What if I just think about the colour white?"

Frank shook his head again. "They will make you think you are trapped in an ice block. You will feel icy cold, your heart will slow down, you will feel hypothermia setting in, and you will lose the feeling in your toes and fingers. They will turn blue then black, and you will suffer intense pain; your body will slowly begin to die and then you will drop dead.

"These children are very dangerous. You have to clear your mind so there is nothing they can grab hold of. It takes practice, but it is the only way to fight them."

"How do I clear my mind, Frank?"

"Stare at an object and let your thoughts disappear into it. Your mind will eventually go blank and then you need to hold it for as long as you can. It's like sometimes when you're driving – you can drive from A to B and you don't remember how you got there. It's all done subconsciously."

Angel stared at him.

Frank laughed. "Bad example. You don't drive, do you? Just blank your mind. As you become more competent, you will be able to move around and do things. They cannot get in to control you if your mind is blank."

Angel tried one second, two seconds then released, "This is stupid. It's impossible. Thoughts keep entering my head."

"I would recommend you keep practicing, and get Damien to do the same thing. The Doctor knows Damien is your weakness. He may target him to get to you."

"Is he my king?"

"I don't know. I would guess not because he is the obvious choice. The Doctor does not normally go for the obvious. That is another important piece of information – don't assume the Doctor will go for the obvious. "

Frank paused for a few minutes, "Edward cared about you in his own way, just like I cared for Bobby. I know Edward never showed his emotions. We were programmed that way. Edward would never have stopped killing. It was in his blood, and he enjoyed it too much. I think it was the buzz factor."

"Have you ever killed, Frank?" Angel asked.

"Who me? Oh no, that is something I could never do, which is why I don't fit in with them. They are too focussed on death and killing. It was not like that at the beginning. We just wanted to create children who could do amazing things."

Angel felt a vibration from inside her pocket. She had forgotten she still had Damien's mobile phone. Removing the phone from her pocket, she glanced over to Frank and then turned her attention to the small white screen. There was a strange text message. The words meant nothing to begin with and then realisation set in.

"I think its code using Romanian letters; there's also an image at the end of the message. I think it's a picture of a chess piece," she said aloud.

Stranger Revealed

The meeting with Frank played on Angel's mind. Different names were now entering the equation. Now there was a Stephanie, who nobody had mentioned before, and telepaths, and to top it all, somebody calling themselves the Doctor had texted her. If Aurel and the Chief Inspector were correct, the Doctor ran the show. Why would the head person target her to play his stupid game? There were stronger, clever and more interesting components for the Doctor to pursue. Angel still felt she was being followed even though Damien and Detective Haines insisted it was her imagination playing tricks. Was it the Doctor that was following her?

"I really fancy a coffee, Damien. A real strong black coffee, that will make the spoon stand to attention."

Damien laughed, "Your taste buds are weird, but if you want a strong black coffee then that is what you will have. On the way, you can tell me what Frank said, and what the police are doing with that text message you received."

"It's in code, so they are trying to decipher it. I will try as well. I am quite good with codes."

Damien brushed Angel's hair back from her face. "Promise me you won't stress if you can't work it out. You put yourself under a lot of pressure sometimes."

Angel smiled. "I won't. I promise," she said, crossing her heart with her fingers and blowing him a kiss.

The coffee shop was a quaint place, decoration closer to a typical English tea shop than an American coffee shop. Inside was laid out in an L shape, wider at the front of the shop and narrowing to the back to where the toilets could be found. A large selection of pastries and finger-licking cupcakes that tempted all customers were for sale as well as a large range of exotic coffees. Candy-Ann, the proprietor, was a fifty-something rounded lady who enjoyed sampling her own products, if her waistline was anything to go by. During the week, the coffee shop attracted the office staff from the high-rise buildings that surrounded the small premises, and at the weekend the local residents. It was a strange place, full of life. Damien and Angel had been in a couple of times, but still they could not get used to the soul music playing quietly in the background.

"I think we always enter at the same track," giggled Angel as James Brown sang out, "Papa's got a brand new bag." The café was full. A throng of murmured voices blended with the music.

Angel watched the assistant measuring out the coffee before placing it in the machine for its final mix. It was a simple task, but fascinating to watch. The aroma drifted over to where they stood.

"I think my next challenge is to try all the coffees in the world," she declared. Damien smiled. There was no doubt Angel would try to get through as many variations and blends of coffee possible. The coffee she chose tasted exquisite; a smooth dark Columbian with a warm, mellow flavour made entirely from the Arabica bean. It was still a superb coffee, even though the spoon did not stand up straight.

Damien stood. "Can you give me a minute? I am just going to pop next door for some chewing gum." He had only just left when Angel was joined by a stranger.

Dark glasses shielded the stranger's eyes. His face and hair were hidden by an over-sized hood. "Good afternoon, Angel."

"Do I know you?" she asked innocently.

The figure slowly removed his sunglasses. "Don't you recognise me?" She stared for a moment. There was a familiarity but she could not place from where. The left eye, a pale grey in colour, was glazed over and slightly out of sync with the right eye. A small scar was evident under the left eye. "Think back ten years."

"But I was in..." she suddenly stopped. "Peter Holden, is that you? You look so different. How are you?" asked Angel.

"How the hell do you think I am? You took my eyesight! You destroyed my life, remember?"

Angel was shocked at such a fierce response. "It was an accident! We were young then."

"You will pay for this, you b**ch," he hissed at her. "I will make you scream like a baby, just like they said I did. I didn't scream, did I? Tell me I didn't scream."

"You didn't scream, Peter. I didn't hear you scream," answered a shocked Angel.

His tone calmed slightly. A cold smile of satisfaction crossed his badly scarred face. The left eye began to itch, but he ignored this small annoyance. The constant itching had given him aggro for over ten years, so why should it bother him now? He didn't need reminding what the bitch had done to him. His lips were now pursed. He drummed his fingers slowly on the table to the Led Zeppelin classic 'Moby Dick.'

"Do you remember this tune?" he asked.

Angel shook her head. "What do you want, Peter?"

The smile moved to a grimace, and then in a menacing manner, he asked, "Did you get the gift I sent you?"

"What gift?" asked Angel.

"The apple, of course. Are you stupid?" his voice rose again.

The coffee shop door opened with the tinkling of bells. Damien entered and walked towards Angel, unaware of the potential danger that was to greet him. Back facing him, Angel sat rigidly.

"Ah, the young man who kills people and then gets away with it. You must have some very influential friends," her companion greeted him. Damien looked down at Angel, who was shaking her head.

"This is Peter Holden. We met ten years ago," she spoke quietly. For the first time she hoped Damien had read her psychiatric file notes and would make the connection.

"I was just asking Angel if she enjoyed the apple I sent her."

"You sent the apple? Why?" Damien placed his hand on Angel's shoulder for comfort. Looking up at him, she shook her head slightly. She didn't want him to say anything else.

"Females control us. Did you know that? She," he spit out, pointing at Angel, "just flutters her eyelashes and men fall at her feet. We will do anything for them. They flick their hair, making sexual gestures towards us and what do we do? We are totally controlled by them. We must rid them from this earth. She was given an apple every day from that orderly guy. What was he called? Sam? I know it began with an S."

"It was Stan, Stan Cauldron," Angel said quietly.

Peter continued. The name was unimportant. "It wasn't just any apple. It was always the largest, rosiest apple available. He was a pervert; did you know that? Liked young girls, so I was told. I saw him mopping the floor, watching you when he thought nobody else was watching, sitting and talking to you at every opportune moment, but I was watching Angel. Did he touch you, Angel? Is that why he gave you one of his apples?"

"Slay the dragon, Stan. Make him go away," Angel whispered to herself. Angel glanced up. She could see the dragon looming over her, hands on hips, a stern look on its face, a wart the size of a saucer covered the side of the nose. "Please go away," Angel whispered again to herself.

"All the females were given apples, but us lads, we didn't get anything. What did it taste like, Angel?"

"Slay the dragon, Stan."

"I said, what did it taste like?"

"It was a Gala apple picked fresh from a tree that day."

"I said what did it taste like, not where was it from," shouted Peter.

"It had a sweet punchy flavour," answered Angel quickly.

"Ah, I was right. I thought the apple I sent you was a nice touch. Don't you? Was it sweet and punchy?"

"No, it burnt my mouth."

Peter's eyes widened with excitement. The scar under his left eye appeared to grow. The eye moved further out of sync with its partner. Saliva appeared at the corner of his mouth. Angel swallowed, repulsed at the sight.

"This isn't about me getting an apple, is it?" she managed to stutter.

"You're learning quick, Angel. You were never punished for what you did to me. Females get away with everything, but not this time. Sit down. Damien, right? Well, Damien, I am going to see how vain Angel is. Let us see what she will do to keep her sexual power." Damien didn't move. "I said sit down now, or this goes in her face." Damien glanced towards Angel, who nodded, before returning his gaze back to Peter. A small corked test tube was in Peter's hand. Leaning over the table, he poured a small amount of the liquid into Angel's coffee cup.

"Why don't you take a drink, like a good girl?"

"Is it sulphuric acid, like what was in the apple?"

"It's not water, that's for certain," snapped Peter. "If you take a mouthful, I will leave you alone." Angel glanced towards Damien, who shook his head.

"And if I don't?" she asked.

"Then I will throw the rest in your face. It's simple. If you swallow some, it will burn your insides and destroy your organs. It is doubtful that you will survive, but you will die keeping your looks. You could even have an open casket. Now, if I throw acid in your face, it will burn that pretty little face of yours off. You will look grotesque; no man will ever look at you again. Can you live like that, Angel? Can you? It may even splash into your eyes so you will no longer have your sight. This may be a blessing in disguise. At least you won't be able to see the monster you have become, but you will be alive. Have you ever smelt burning flesh, Angel? It smells like charcoal, but the smell of hair when that burns is magnificent. The sulphurous odour clings to your nostrils. Being feminine flesh, it has a disgusting smell. It is burning away your power and control.

"I was thirteen when I threw acid at my classmates. They never locked the school's science lab. It was always open for me to take what I wanted. I left them scarred for life. I remember the smell. It felt so good, knowing they could no longer control us men, their power destroyed. I hate girls. They are vain, tarting themselves up so they can control us men; using their sexual influence like prostitutes." He stared at Damien. The scar under his eye was reddening. "Are you listening to me?" Damien nodded. "My mother was always with different men, flaunting her ample cleavage, skirts only just covering her arse. She disgusted me, and she disgusted my father. He tried to control the bitch with a belt and fist. I personally prefer acid. It's quicker, scars the body for life, but you already know that. Do you recognise this?"

Angel nodded. "It was Christie's," she said quietly. In Peter's partially crippled hand lay a small, limp, dirty white rabbit that had seen better days. Its ear was clumsily sewn on with large black stitching. One of its eyes hung from a single thread.

"Shall I pull its eye off, Angel?"

"No," said Angel quietly. "Christie would be upset. I don't want Christie to scream. I didn't like it when Christie screamed hysterically." Peter looked at the rabbit then flicked the loose eye with his fingernail; the thread still held.

"Nah, you're right, another time maybe."

"Why have you got Christie's rabbit, Peter?"

"Why do you think?"

"Have you hurt Christie?"

Peter gave an evil grimace. "What do you think, Angel?" There was no answer.

"I said sit down," screamed Peter.

A gentleman rose from his chair as though he was going to intervene; instead he reached for his mobile and started to press its numbers with rapid speed. He looked over again at the man shouting at the two teenagers. With mobile to his ear he rushed out of the shop.

Damien sat down, pulled his chair away from Angel and the table, then sat on the edge of the chair. Trying not to make it obvious, he leant towards Angel, so he could grab her hand that was laid on her lap if they needed to move fast. He hoped Peter hadn't noticed, but if he sat where the chair was originally placed, Angel would be trapped against the wall in the space she currently occupied. There would be no escape route. At least this way she had a fighting chance of dodging the acid – if Peter threw it. A fighting chance was surely an overestimation. More like a split second before it hit and burnt her skin.

Damien could now see Peter's hand clearly – it was badly scarred and disfigured. Never would you have known it was a hand of a young man in his twenties. The skin had dissolved away on the thumb and index finger revealing the white of the bone. Small flaps of skin and fat grizzly lumps had formed at the joints of the fingers. Damien was surprised Peter could still use his hand. It looked red, sore and useless. Even his wrist was badly damaged. *The perils of messing with acid,* thought Damien.

"Don't do this, Peter. This is stupid. They will lock you up again," said Angel.

"Stupid, stupid is it?" shouted Peter. "Look at me, Angel. Look at what you did to me." He pulled his hood down to reveal thin, patchy clumps of hair and several circular scars that could be mistaken for ring-worm.

"I didn't do that."

"I had to wear an eye patch for years. I had to endure the constant bullying because of what you did to me. Did you know they sent me to a youth custody centre? Do you know what it is like in one of those places?"

The remaining customers in the coffee shop were beginning to get agitated. Many of the earlier customers had left, obviously uncomfortable with the atmosphere that was being created. Nobody wanted to intervene. A pretty young assistant in a pink and white pin-striped pinafore and a crisp white apron tied tightly around her waist asked them to keep their voices down.

"Another female is trying to control me," shouted Peter. "Do you want some of this as well?" He waved the test tube in her face, and she quickly backed away and rushed into the kitchen.

"Drink it now," hissed Peter, pushing the coffee cup closer to Angel. A small drop of the contaminated liquid splashed over the rim onto the saucer. It looked harmless, yet it was deadly.

"Put the bottle down slowly, son, or I will pull the trigger. I have a gun pointed at the back of your head." Damien had never felt more relieved than when he saw Detective Haines sneak up on the man sitting in front of them. "Sorry it took me so long. I couldn't get in through the back door, and the front door – well, as you know, is a little noisy," said the Detective, turning his attention back to Peter. "Put it down on the table now slowly."

Peter lifted the test tube.

"I will pull this trigger if you don't put it down."

The bell above the door rung as the last customer tried to sneak quietly out into the safety of the street.

The noise did not break the detective's concentration. He was focussed on the small container of acid and Peter's actions.

"Angel, move away from the table slowly," Haines said calmly. Damien stood up and made more room for her exit. Peter glared, oblivious to the Detective's threat.

"You will face your crime, whore," he screamed, releasing the test tube. Damien grabbed hold of Angel's arm as the test tube flew through the air, its contents spilling across the table. He pulled her arm so hard and so fast that her body flew towards him into his arms. Spinning his body around to shield her from the acid, he was prepared to feel the burning on his back but there was nothing.

A gunshot fired. Its loud piercing sound echoed through the air. Peter's body slumped forward onto the table into the shattered glass and the clear acid splattered on the table.

"Is he dead?" whispered Angel. Detective Haines jumped in quickly with a reply. He didn't want Angel freaking out at the thought of a dead body.

"No, it was a dummy bullet. The close range has knocked him out, that's all."

"You were fast, Detective. I think you pulled the trigger as he released the acid."

"You were just as quick."

"Who is he?" asked the Detective.

"Peter Holden, somebody Angel knew a long time ago. He always held a grudge after a misunderstanding," Damien explained.

"Some grudge," said the detective, fastening the handcuffs onto the body before calling the station.

Damien held Angel a little closer. "Thank you for not telling him," she whispered.

"He doesn't need to know; the detail is unimportant," he whispered back.

Peter was right. The smell of burning flesh was disgusting.

"I only left you for five minutes. Anybody else I should know about from your past who may want to kill you, or is that it?" asked Damien.

The Games Begin

Angel pondered over the code for several hours with no luck. Whatever she tried led to a dead-end. There were no real words forming, only nonsense words, utter 'gobblety gook.' She had just put her latest workings down to take a much-needed break when Damien popped his head around the door.

"How are you doing with that code?" he asked.

"Not good. It's a hard one to crack. Maybe the thinking is different for a Romanian. Edward never showed me how to crack a code in Romanian. I know the letters are a modification of the Latin alphabet, and I have tried to apply the same principals as you would to a code in English, but it does not seem to work out. I know I am working with 31 letters, but it should not make any difference."

"Did you know it was the Spartans in 400BC who first pioneered Cryptography in Europe?" Damien asked.

"Was that the scytale?" Angel responded.

Damien nodded. "I might have guessed you would know that already."

"Have you seen Detective Haines this morning?"

"No."

"Didn't he say he was only having one day off?"

"I think so."

"It's strange. He's never late; I think I'll give the station a ring to see what has happened." Angel dropped the small silver trinket she had been studying.

"Damien, I think you have found the key to the code. Haines is my king. Warren said I was the queen. In chess, the queen always protects the king but in a battle. Take your Greek battles. It is the king who protects his people and his queen. Haines was protecting both of us." Angel grabbed pen and paper off the table and started scribbling. "I assumed *seniah* was a spelling mistake made in haste. It is easy to hit the wrong letter when texting, but it is obvious – it is Haines written backwards."

Angel was talking fast as the realisation started to sink in. She had worked out the code. It was simple. Her mind was working fast, and she spoke just as quick. "Look, this would mean the first word, the second word, fourth word, eighth and finally the last word which is the sixteenth word are all English words spelt backwards. These words read: 'It's Haines you should protect.' The numbers corresponding to the English words gives us our timescale. 12:40 p.m. 1 = first character, 2 = second character, 4 = fourth character and the date is today – 16th August."

"Where did the 0 come from?" asked Damien.

"0 is insignificant and can be used anytime anywhere."

"Did Edward teach you that?" Angel nodded.

"It is now 10:20 a.m. That means whatever is going to happen will happen in just over two hours."

"How do you know the 0 goes there, and it's not 10:24? Or 1:24?"

Angel explained, "I asked the same question. Time will always end in 0 rounded up to a whole number."

Damien nodded, "Ok, so how do you know it's the 16th August, the 8 is before the 16."

"Yes, but that is how the Americans write their dates. It's just us English that do it the other way around."

Damien nodded again, "Ok, it makes sense, so what else does it say?"

"I'll tell you in half an hour. I haven't worked it all out yet.

She started to think out loud, "If I take out all the English words, which are a distraction, the rest of the words and letters should be easy to work out. The rest of the letters are Romanian, so if I work out the code I should be able to work out the words in Romanian, and hopefully they will tell us where Haines can be found. I can then translate it to English. Unfortunately, they are using a different code to the English words. If only all the words were written backwards." The original code read:

Sti seniah timpul uoy se scurge încercaţi dluohs barge depozit trausprazacae

strada etajul treilea dacă sunteţi tcetorp târziu el moare

Angel placed the code into a table made up of six columns and six rows and started working on it fastidiously. Damien watched in fascination. Her mind and hand were working quickly; letters were scribbled out and replaced with new letters and then crossed out again. After twenty-five minutes, she put down the pen and stared up at Damien.

"It's easy. He has only changed letters that we class as English vowels. Look. If I change the e to a, the a to e, the I to u and the u to an I and keep the o the same. It says:

"Timpul se scurge încercați barge depozit fortieth strada etajul treilea dacă sunteți târziu el moare

"And when translated to English it reads:

"Time is running out, try barge warehouse, thirteenth street, third floor, if you are late he dies."

*****

Who was this annoying, demanding little man standing in front of him? His children were less demanding. Were they right to use an outsider to kidnap Detective Haines? For some reason, Samuel's men did not inspire confidence. They managed to kill Aurel, but the old man was an easy target. Crystal, the one he really wanted, had managed to get away. He had no choice. This time it had to be an outsider. He could not afford to take any chances. But now he had to smile and humour the man standing in front of him. At least the job had been done, and admittedly he had been impressed with the thoroughness, but now his removal was the only option. All the loose ends must be tied up; destroy the link to him and his empire.

He was a sick motherf***er, cutting the spinal cord. The Doctor smirked at his use of 'street language.' He was obviously spending too much time conversing with Samuel. The Doctor had wanted the Detective kidnapped and stabbed a couple of times with one of Edward's knifes, to wound rather than to kill. As a tribute to Edward, the body would be placed in a crucifix position. At 12:40 – the same time Edward had died – the body would be burnt alive. If Angel was a suitable opponent, she would work out the code, and this code was fairly easy. Edward said she had a natural gift for code breaking, so it would test her ability – was she a worthy opponent? By severing the spinal cord, the Detective would not feel the pain of the fire, which was not what the Doctor wanted. Then again, if Angel tried to heal the Detective, her ability could be tested on two separate, unrelated skills.

"I believe we agreed $150,000 for my services."

The Doctor nodded his head, trying to stifle the grin that was beginning to form across his lips. He knew what was coming next. "Have you met the twins?" he asked.

The man turned around to face the two teenage children. When he saw their snow-white hair and pale skin, a cold shiver ran through his body. There was something about these children that made him feel uncomfortable. His heart started to pound fiercely. Panic rose through his body. His skin turned clammy, and all colour drained from his face.

"Please pay the man, my children." They moved forward in unison. The man tried to take a step backwards, but his body had frozen. A pain stabbed at his heart. What was happening? As he fell to the ground, the children stood over his body. They looked to their father for approval as blood trickled from the man's eyes and mouth.

"Well done, my children," the Doctor praised them. "You are getting stronger."

*****

"You don't mind, do you? I feel like we owe it to Detective Haines to tell him everything. He always said he would protect us, but nobody told him why and what he was up against. I felt so guilty not telling him," Angel muttered.

"Don't blame yourself," Damien replied. "It was Henley who decided nobody should know, and even if Haines had known, this would still have happened."

"It must be so scary, knowing you will spend the rest of your life as a quadriplegic. Do you think he will hate us?"

"I hope not." Damien and Angel had just reached the main reception and had been directed to the second-floor.

"Oh my god. It's happening again."

"What's happening?"

"My body is starting to heal itself; it must be the cut on my head."

"No, not here, not now. I can't protect you," said Damien, glancing around.

"But, Damien, we can try again! I can try and heal you. I just need to find somewhere quiet away from prying eyes. If we can control your breathing, we could eradicate your illness. I just wish I knew why it being so close to the heart makes the process difficult."

"It's got to be my left side or my stomach," Damien whispered excitedly. "My stomach is really painful sometimes." He stopped suddenly. "Do you think you could help Haines?"

"I guess so, but what about you?" Angel asked. She had wanted to heal Damien of his pain since she met him.

He looked into her eyes. "You know what I am thinking."

She nodded. "It is the right thing to do, isn't it?"

Damien nodded. "There will be other times for me."

"Are you sure?"

He nodded again.

"You know it will bring me very close to Haines, don't you? We will have a certain bond."

Damien nodded, "You won't have sex with him, will you?"

Angel giggled, "Of course not."

Her body started to shake. She had entered the first phase. Placing his arm around her waist to support her weight, Damien pulled Angel's body into his. To an outsider she would appear like somebody mourning a recent death.

"Keep your head turned into my body," whispered Damien, who was trying hard not to draw any unnecessary attention to their predicament. Slowly and without incident, they make their way to the small room occupied by Haines. Thankfully there were no other visitors.

"Hiya, kids, what are you doing here? You haven't come to gape at a quadriplegic, have you?"

"Glad to see you have kept your sense of humour," said Damien.

"There's not much else I can do. God, you look ill, kid, worse than me," Haines said, directing his comment to Angel. Damien moved the high-back visitor's chair closer to Haines' bed. The back of the chair faced the door so nobody could see Angel. Damien steered Angel to the seat just as her body moved into the second phase of the shaking.

Damien knew Angel's speech would now be incoherent, so he explained. "We are going to help you, Detective, but whatever happens in the next ten minutes stays within these four walls; you must tell no one."

"You have my attention, Damien," Haines said. "I am intrigued."

Damien moved to the door and checked the corridor to make sure they would not be disturbed.

"Now I am very intrigued."

It was dangerous for Angel to heal in public. She would never be left alone if people knew what she could do. There was also the problem that Haines might not be able to accept what Angel could do, like Henley. If Haines made a similar comment to Henley, it would destroy Angel's confidence. It was hard enough for Angel to accept her power without casting any negative thoughts into her mind. This was a risk. Damien had made the suggestion before thinking it through, but backing down now was not an option. If he tried to change Angel's mind, she would want to know why.

"Remember, you once asked why they want Angel? Why were you protecting us? We are going to show you; Angel is going to make you walk again."

Haines burst into laughter. "Nice one, kid. It's going to be hard enough accepting this condition, and now you come up with a cock and bull story that you are going to make me walk again. It's cruel, Damien. Don't you know my spinal cord is cut?" Haines wanted to turn his body away from his mocking visitors – but he couldn't.

"Close your eyes and accept what is about to happen," Damien instructed. "Don't fight it." Angel had now entered phase three. The golden sparkles were beginning to dance across her face, moving down her body. Haines had squeezed his eyes closed, not because of what Damien had said, but because it was his only way to escape from his visitors.

"Leave me alone, Damien," Haines muttered.

Angel grabbed the detective's hand. The healing had begun. A small ounce of jealousy flowed through

Damien's body. It could have been his body being healed, feeling that sensuous tingling sensation. Damien averted his gaze and moved to the door to check the corridor was still clear. Angel's hand slipped under the bed clothes to Haines' lower back. His pyjama top made it difficult to reach his naked skin. Finally, Angel's fingers were in the correct position. She gently moved her fingers up and down the spinal cord, massaging the spine. The position Haines lay in made it difficult to get much movement. If only he was laid on his stomach. A tingling sensation that felt like tiny pinpricks ran down her arms, through her fingertips to his lower back. Haines didn't move. His eyes stayed tightly closed, unaware of the miracle that was about to happen.

Five minutes passed, and then Damien heard Angel's voice.

"I'm sorry, there were not as many healing crystals this time." Damien moved to where she was seated. "It must depend on the severity of my injury," she said, directing her comment to Damien.

"Is he cured?"

"I think so, but he may have to go through rehab. I don't think he can jump out of bed and run around."

"I can hear you, you know," Haines said. "If you're going to talk about me, at least call me Robert. What just happened?"

Angel smiled. "Try wriggling your fingers, and you will soon find out. Remember, it's our secret, Detective. I mean, Robert."

Robert suddenly sat up and gave out an excited cry. He grabbed Angel and kissed her swiftly on the lips. "Is this real?"

"It's real."

"Oh my god, am I dreaming?"

"No," Angel assured him, and he kissed her again.

"I am indebted to you."

"Please, Robert, keep calm."

"You were telling me the truth, weren't you, Damien? You are special, Angel! Now I understand why you needed protecting."

Damien watched, pleased Robert had acted so positively, but jealous at the same time. Angel had said there would be a bond between her and Robert straight after the healing, just like there had been with Agnes. He watched Angel pull away from Robert. She glanced towards him, giving him reassurance the kiss meant nothing.

"Robert, we have got to go before somebody puts two and two together," Damien said.

"You are amazing, Angel." Robert was now staring at her.

"Yes, she is," said Damien, slipping his arm around her waist. "Your eyes are green," Damien whispered, remembering the information he was meant to share.

"Do they look nice?"

"Gorgeous, not as light as I have seen them, but gorgeous all the same."

Angel gave him a quick kiss on the cheek. "Could they bewitch you?"

"I am already bewitched," he assured her.

She burst into a fit of giggles. "You are funny." Angel seemed stronger and full of life after this healing, which was unusual.

"Any side effects?" he asked.

She shook her head. "My back aches slightly, and I feel a little woozy. Apart from that I feel great."

Damien realised for the first time that although Angel bonded with those that she healed, they would always be closer. It was love that had brought them together. He didn't worship her like the others. Her healing power was just an additional benefit. Angel would always be special to him, with or without her gift. They were about to leave when Damien stopped dead in his tracks.

"Robert did they take an x-ray?"

"Yeah, of course."

"So how do we explain the original x-ray?" asked Damien.

Angel shrugged her shoulders. "I don't know. Does it matter?"

"It could," he responded. "I think we need to start being careful. Robert where's the x-ray room?"

"Down the corridor, through the double doors and then it's..." he paused as he visualised the location, "fourth door on the left. It's marked."

"Ok, we need to get hold of that x-ray."

"They will have moved it by now," Robert stopped him.

"Are you sure?" Damien asked.

"Yes, after 48 hours they normally file them for future reference."

"Where do they file them?" asked Damien impatiently.

"Behind the reception desk, they have a store room where all the patients' notes and x-rays are stored. Every year they clear them out and store them in the basement. Nurse Manouz was telling me some of the files are over twenty-five years old."

"Shall I..." Robert started to sit up again.

"Stay in bed, Robert. You still need rehab for your legs."

Robert swung his legs back into bed.

"Ok, you're the nurse, Ms Wellingstone."

Angel smiled.

"Stop the flirting, will you? We need a plan," butted in Damien.

"If it's any help, the nurse is Caroline Manouz. I reckon if you flirt nicely, she will get you the file."

"You're not suggesting I chat her up, are you?" Damien asked.

"Why not? She keeps coming on to me, and I am, I mean I was, not exactly desirable. Who would want a quadriplegic? Unless she was trying to make me feel better, which it did."

"No, I couldn't," Damien protested. "I wouldn't know what to say."

"It worked on me, didn't it?" said Angel smiling.

"Yes, I mean no. It just happened between us. No, I can't do it. I would be hopeless. We'll have to think of something else."

"Ok, I'll do it," said Robert. "She was coming onto me earlier. I'll say as a detective I need to check the information they hold on me and then we could swipe the x-rays from the file."

"Will she believe you?"

"Move aside. Watch the master in action; all women fall for my charms, especially half-soaked nurses, and anyway, you will see she is not the brightest member of staff. Angel, could you go and get Nurse Manouz? I'll try and not move a muscle, keep the quadriplegic act going a little longer. I am just so excited; I feel as though I have been reborn. Are you ready, Damien?"

Ten minutes later they had the x-rays in their hands, and the file minus the x-rays had been returned to Nurse Manouz for filing.

The Plan

Everybody thought the vicar batterings had stopped – they hadn't. Samuel was still trying to perfect his technique so he could pay the flawless tribute to Edward. He was attempting to bring together everything Edward had taught him, to have elements of Edward's trademark combined with his own unique style of killing. "You're not a copy-cat killer," Samuel could hear Edward's words clearly.

"Why couldn't you forget Angel? I could see you were obsessed. Why couldn't you see, Dad?" shouted Samuel. "I hid your suit so you wouldn't go. I know you like everything planned, laid out with no surprises. I didn't think you would go after Angel, not with the wrong suit on – I was wrong. I underestimated your stubborn streak," Samuel laughed. "Maybe that's our trademark – we are stubborn. You were not thinking straight; you died because of your obsession. Damien would not have stood a chance if you had been on top of your game. Revenge will be sweet. This is the only way I can redeem myself, Edward. I know you will like what I have planned." Samuel adjusted his position and then decided to pace the empty factory floor, mulling over his cunning plan.

"Soon, Edward, it will be soon," he shouted. "The vicar first and then him, Damien, the one who took your life. We will have our revenge." Samuel paused then sat down on the floor next to his father. The lifeless body was slumped in an old battered armchair rescued from the local dump. The hole in his head gaped wide open. "You'll like this, Edward; you'll like this a lot." Samuel pulled the ring on his can. The white frothy liquid spilled slightly over the edges. Gulping the liquid greedily, he let out a loud belch. "Sorry, Dad," he said, laughing. "Beer never agrees with me." He lifted the can in the air and saluted his hero. "Let me tell you my plan." Absurdly, he lowered his voice so nobody would overhear him in the abandoned factory.

"I have been reading, Dad, reading the bible. I have found a perfect verse in Job 1:6. I am going to pay Reverend Brainstow a visit. You know the one; he has the largest flock of followers in this state. I will crush every bone in his body to a pulp. I will make him think I am the devil by hurting him and then I will take his pain just like you taught me. I will do this six times – the devil's symbol. Now this is the bit you will like. I will place his body in the shape of a cross, just like you used to do, Edward, and then, and this is why I have been reading the bible, I will lay a copy of the bible on the Reverend's chest. It won't be closed. Oh no, it will be open, and I will highlight the passage: 'One day the angels came to present themselves before the LORD, and Satan also came with them.' Job 1:6. Isn't that funny, Edward? I will even leave a map reference like you did, but this time it will lead to the Harrington's family home. Can you imagine their faces when they realise they are my next target? If they don't realise immediately, under the body I will leave a photograph of the Harrington's house, printed from Google Streetmap.

I have seen his house, Edward, and the bast**d has one big mansion."

Samuel was starting to show an unnatural intelligence. The white, cloudy liquid Dr Kazaku had given him was working, but now Kazaku was dead, beaten to death for his refusal to give him more. "'The brain can't take too much; small doses only,' according to Kazaku. I proved you wrong, didn't I, Doctor!" Samuel laughed.

The left side of Samuel's face began to twitch as he raised his can. In the corner of the room, Dr Kazaku's body lay propped against the wall, his neck twisted at an unnatural angle. The lifeless eyes appeared to watch Samuel's every move. Samuel gave him the finger and then laughed – a loud chilling laugh that would scare the hardest person.

"Who's the man now, Doctor? Who's the man?" he asked, tapping his chest before throwing the empty can in Kazaku's direction.

Spilling the 'Beans'

It felt great to be back on duty. The doctors had been adamant he would never walk again, but here he was, in front of a key suspect. He felt fit and healthy; in fact, healthier and stronger than he had ever felt before. He felt invincible, all thanks to Angel.

"So Mr Jonker, Chameleon Medical Research Unit is under investigation. We have uncovered some disturbing evidence that suggests the medical research being carried out by Chameleon might seriously compromise National Security. I understand you are a board member. What can you tell me about the research being conducted by this company?"

The hawk-eyed gentleman shuffled uncomfortably.

Chief Inspector Harrington had asked him to visit Paul Jonker to find out about Chameleon. He hadn't meant to keep the visit a secret from Henley. He just didn't get round to telling him. Detective Haines would do anything for the Harrington family. After what Angel had done for him, he reckoned he owed them. If reprimanded by the Captain, so what! Protecting Angel was his main priority. Her healing powers were amazing, but if they fell into the wrong hands... A shiver ran down his spine. He didn't want to think about the consequences. She needed protecting, and that was all there was to it. Damien's heart was in the right place, but he wasn't strong enough or equipped to protect Haines's Angel. If he could reach the core of the operation and close the medical research down, work to the same plan the Chief Inspector was working to, then maybe they could remove the potential threat.

Detective Haines sat in Paul Jonker's expensive apartment on the sixth floor, watching Jonker shuffle across the large open-plan living area to a mirrored cabinet. Haines immediately unclipped his holster and placed his hand on the semi-automatic pistol just in case immediate action was required. Paul Jonker returned with two large tumblers of malt whiskey. Haines relaxed his grip on the pistol, disappointed Jonker hadn't tried anything. Blowing away scum like Jonker was very tempting.

"Can I offer you a drink, Detective?" He thrust one of the tumblers into Haines's hand.

"No thank you, I never drink when I am on duty," Haines quickly replied, placing the drink on a silver coaster on the tinted-glass coffee table. There was something about Jonker that Haines did not like. He was a confident bloke, so sure of himself, with more money than sense.

"Of course, silly me. Maybe a coffee, Detective?"

"Thank you, black, one sugar," Haines accepted. He was feeling disgusted. It was becoming more and more difficult to keep an air of professionalism in Jonker's presence. Would anybody notice if he blew the scum's brains out? After all, nobody knew he was there but the Chief Inspector, and he wouldn't say anything. They both were working towards the same goal; the Doctor's operation had to be destroyed.

"Priscilla, coffee for the Detective," shouted Jonker through to another room. Disappointment crossed the detective's face. Somebody else was in the apartment. *Could he claim self-defence?* he pondered.

"Now where were we? Ah yes. You were asking about the medical research." Haines could have kicked himself. Jonker had been wasting time, planning what to say; no doubt working out an alibi if asked about specific dates, not that Haines had any dates in mind. In fact, he had very little information, other than a hunch and some flimsy information from a man who was desperate for police protection. "It's like any other medical research facility. We are trying to cure some of the world's deadliest illnesses."

"How?"

"I can't pretend I am a scientist, Detective, but I believe in layman's terms we are separating the diseased chromosomes away from the healthy chromosomes. I am told it's quite simple really."

"And do you conduct these experiments on children?"

"What? No, of course not. Thank you, Priscilla."

A mug of hot steaming coffee arrived and was placed in front of the detective. The young blonde must have been twenty years Jonker's junior.

"My wife, Detective."

Haines gave a friendly nod. The young woman looked nervously at him, and then back to her husband, before disappearing into the room from which she came.

Haines stood, cupping the mug of hot coffee. A perfect weapon was placed in his hands if needed. Slowly he moved to the large window that led onto the balcony and stared out over the wooded backdrop. His feet were planted firmly on the wooden floor; a one foot gap between his feet giving him the perfect balance. A policeman's stance, his superintendent would say. "We were talking about the experiments you conduct on children, Mr Jonker."

"I have told you that I know nothing about any experiments on children."

"Really? And what if I tell you I have evidence that proves otherwise?"

Jonker stopped sipping his drink. "What evidence? You can't prove anything."

"We have photographs and a witness statement that says different, and we know it's your financing that is funding this sick research."

For the first time, Jonker didn't say anything.

"What's in it for you?"

Jonker paused for a moment. His mouth twitched, almost nearing a smile, as if unsure to answer.

"I said, what's in it for you?" Haines repeated.

"I have been promised eternal life," Jonker blurted out, unable to contain his excitement.

"That's impossible. There's no such thing."

"There wasn't, but now it's almost possible. A few more months, a few more tests, and then we are there."

Haines narrowed his eyes. "You are sick, Jonker; however, it's not you that I am after. I'll cut you a deal if you tell me what I want to know. Otherwise, you are going away for a long time, and it will feel like eternal life."

Obsession

Damien loaded, pointed and fired the gun. A loud thud sounded again. The board behind the target took another pounding. Detective Haines pointed and jerked his hand upwards. Damien knew what he was doing wrong without Haines pointing it out, yet again. He was squeezing the trigger too hard, causing his hand to jerk upwards.

"I know," said Damien with a certain amount of frustration. Detective Haines had insisted they learn how to shoot, even though neither one owned a gun or had any intention of owning one. In the last few weeks Angel, Damien and Detective Haines had grown close. The bond between them was strong after the healing. Too strong, as Damien was about to find out.

"I am sorry, Damien. I...I know I said I would show you and Angel how to defend yourselves but," Haines paused, "I can't spend any more time in Angel's presence."

"Why, Haines? You get on so well!"

"Too well, and call me Robert," uttered Robert looking away.

"I don't understand."

"Nor do I, and I know this sounds stupid, but since you both visited me in the hospital... this is really hard for me, Damien. Since Angel laid her hand on me, I have had an attraction to her."

"So!"

"It's not like any other attraction I have ever experienced. I will end up doing something I shouldn't."

"You can control yourself, can't you?" Damien asked, suddenly worried.

"That's just it. I don't think I can."

"We need you, Haines – I mean Robert. Angel needs you and I need you."

"I know. Don't you think I have thought long and hard about this?"

"Yeah, but..." Damien said slowly.

"There are no buts, Damien. I can't do this."

"So you are just going to dump us?"

"No."

"So?"

"I will train you; I will show you what you should pass onto Angel, but I can't get too close to Angel. It's dangerous for her and for me."

"You feel that strongly about Angel?" Damien had known this was a possibility, but he hadn't taken into account how strong the feelings could be. This was more than a crush or gratitude for the healing.

"Yes, it's bordering on obsession: I'm sorry, Damien."

Damien didn't say anything for a few minutes. He sat on a wooden bench next to the firing range to collect his thoughts. The target in front of him showed one hit out of six, and that was in the outer circle. A lot more practice was required. He knew Angel would be back in a minute. *Obsession*, the same word Henley used about his wife's relationship with Angel after she was healed. This was more than a meagre bond. Haines was right; an obsession was dangerous.

"Ok, Robert, train me, but will you do me a favour? Don't tell Angel. Leave it to me. And will you keep me informed if this obsession develops any further? It could be to do with her healing you. I think something similar has happened before."

Robert nodded. "I can help in other ways you know."

"I know."

"I only grabbed a coffee for myself; you didn't want one, did you?" Angel was moseying down the gun range corridor towards them. Damien saw Robert take a step backwards.

"You two look guilty. What have you been talking about?" Robert and Damien glanced at each other.

"Women," they said in chorus.

"Robert is not feeling well, so we are going to finish for the day," Damien explained.

"Oh, that's a shame. Can I help?"

"No," they responded in unison.

"Ok, I was just offering,"

Damien glanced over to Robert, who was starting to undress his girlfriend with his eyes.

"Robert," whispered Damien.

Robert looked at him. "I had better go."

"I think you had," Damien said with a sigh. "I'll see you tomorrow." Robert had no choice but to walk past Angel to get out. He walked slowly, head-down, trying not to catch Angel's eye. His cheeks reddened, and as he passed, he could smell her perfume. His heart was beating fast.

"Robert, are you ok?" Angel asked, placing her hand on his shoulder. He pulled away quickly.

"Yeah, I'm fine," he muttered, his cheeks reddened deeper. "I'll see you tomorrow." His eyes raised to meet

Angel's. He gave her a warm smile and then looked down again.

"Is Robert alright?" she asked after he left.

"Yes, fine," replied Damien, "but I need to talk to you." She linked her arm through his and blew gently across the surface of her coffee, making mini ripples before taking a sip. They walked to the exit. "Let's find somewhere quiet," he suggested as he turned to give her a tender kiss on the lips. "You taste of coffee."

"Italian or Columbian?"

"I would say Columbian, deep roasted, strength four."

"You are getting good at this," she giggled.

"That's because you always chose the same coffee," he laughed. "Who else have you healed apart from Henley's wife and Robert?"

"Nobody but you, and I still haven't finished with you yet," she gave him a gentle squeeze.

"What about when you have taken somebody's pain?"

"I don't know. Mainly you and a couple of kids when I was younger, but my mam wouldn't let me, so I never practiced. What's this all about, Damien? Why all the questions?"

"I am thinking through something. Just answer my questions as best you can and then I'll explain," Damien requested. "Did your mother have to injure herself before she healed people?"

"I don't think so, but I was very young,"

"Ok, and that brother of yours, the one Frank was talking about – Bobby, wasn't it? Frank said he healed daily. He can't have injured himself that many times. You said yourself you don't know when you have the power to heal. It can come two or three weeks after an injury whereas your mum and Bobby were healing daily."

"So?"

"So your gift is different to theirs."

"Maybe."

"I think you should stop healing altogether."

"Why?" Angel asked, curious and confused.

He took a deep breath. "Robert has become obsessed with you."

"So maybe he finds me attractive, or is that so unbelievable?" she said fluttering her eyelashes.

"No, of course not," Damien said, not wanting to hurt her feelings. "Let me finish, Robert is obsessed with you. That's what we were talking about at the firing range. He's afraid he will do something he shouldn't, which is why he is going to stay away from you."

Flabbergasted, Angel managed one word, "Really."

Damien placed his arm around her shoulders. "Don't worry. Now let me ask about Henley's wife, Agnes. When Henley picked me up from prison, he told me his wife was obsessed by you. She worshiped you. His words were 'it's an unnatural obsession. My wife treats Angel as though she is our daughter.' That is why I wanted us to move out quickly. I am sorry, Angel. I know it's a lot to take in."

Angel sat for a while thinking through what he had said. "Are you obsessed with me?"

"It's different for us because we are in a relationship. Truthfully, since you healed my arm, my feelings have not changed. Maybe it's only a full healing or the type of healing. I don't know, but Robert is really worried about how he feels."

"Do you think I tricked you into loving me, when I took your pain for the first time?"

"I never thought about it. The night you stayed in my room when I was in agony. Was that the first time?" Angel shook her head.

"Ok," he thought long and hard, trying to remember when he had been in severe pain and for some unexplainable reason the pain had subsided. "The day we sheltered from the rain, and I thought it was an Indian head massage, was that the first time?"

Chewing on her bottom lip, Angel nodded reluctantly.

Damien smiled, "Then no, I was falling for you long before then; what I feel is genuine."

She threw her arms around his neck, "I am so pleased you said that. I knew it was real."

"I don't think taking a person's pain is the problem. It's just the healing. Let's just monitor the situation and maybe you should try not to heal."

"What about you?"

"I'll survive. I have so far, haven't I? And who knows what will happen in the future?"

She smiled and gave him a long loving kiss. "I love you," she whispered.

The Children

The police were ready to raid the Arboreal Research Partnership complex. Damien and Angel had been given strict instructions to stay well away, a task that was going to prove difficult for Angel.

"Damien, please don't let your father go. I have a real bad feeling about this."

"I can't stop him. He has been after the Doctor for as long as I can remember. Maybe even longer than Edward, I mean your father..." his voice trailed off. "I am sorry. I still can't get used to Edward being your father."

"Don't worry. Neither can I."

"I know my father is not going to listen to me."

"I think he will die if he goes. Have you told him what Frank said about the telepaths and how dangerous they are?"

"Yes, but you know what he is like. He is sceptical. He thinks its rubbish. If you can't touch it then it isn't real."

"Does he believe what I can do?"

"Truthfully, I don't know. If he doesn't think about it, the situation doesn't exist. You know the truth, and I know the truth, and that's all that matters."

Angel nodded. "I just have a real bad feeling."

"It will be worse when my father finds out we are here; annoyed will be an understatement."

Angel laughed. "He cannot ground you. I'm sorry if I cause a rift between you. I'll explain it to him later. I'm sure he'll understand that I need to know what's happening. I also want to see the Doctor's face. I want to slap him so hard after what he did to Detective Haines."

*****

Security was slack. They had sneaked unnoticed into the complex with ease behind Henley's men. Frank Arcos and Paul Jonker had led the officers to the complex that was known to the locals as Coldits – people went in and never came out. The wall around the building was not scalable from the outside, or the inside. Nobody knew what happened inside the complex except those that worked there. Jonker had asked that the Chameleon Medical Research Unit was not touched until he had stepped down from the board. Haines had agreed although he doubted Jonker would step down. Eternal life was one big pull. Haines had listened as Jonker expressed concern if his name was dragged through the mud. Based on the information Jonker had given, it would have been a waste of time targeting Chameleon. Coldits was the place to hit.

Chameleon was a front, according to Frank. It was the smaller specialist units where all the experiments took place. Coldits, registered name Arboreal Research Partnership, was currently the most active of all the units. Situated on the outskirts of New York, Coldits was taking the lead on mind control and was the likely place where the Doctor would be found. The police had half a dozen units across several different continents to visit. If they had the resources, the raids on all the units would have taken place simultaneously. Cutbacks prevented the ideal solution.

Armed officers surrounded the complex. Their bulletproof vests made them stiff in their stance, hindering their movement. Their robotic movements made them look ridiculous and sluggish. With guns holstered and covers unclipped, they were ready for action – an army of transformers that could evolve into combat machines. The double cast iron gates that separated the outside world from the inside were open. A large coat of arms was mounted in the centre of the gate. A shield shone bright in blue, yellow and red. In the centre of the shield, a golden eagle spread its wings. A small cross lay in its beak. The letters W M T B C were clearly identifiable – a symbol of the historical Romanian provinces.

The open gates were an invitation for them to enter. Was the Doctor expecting them? The complex was beautifully landscaped, surrounded by an eight-foot stone wall. A coiled razor wire clung to the top of the wall. A nasty surprise for any intruder. Was this to keep people out or to keep the research participants in? Visually the building was not noteworthy. Its architecture was typical 1970's. It was a clinical, square, bland box which served its purpose.

The Doctor was annoyed. The attack on his complex was unexpected. Frank had betrayed him – he was a weak man who should have been eliminated from his position many years ago. The warning had come through two hours before the police arrived, thanks to Jonker. His preparation was rushed, but with ruthless efficiency he was ready. The Bunsen burners burned fiercely, heating the Diethyl Azodicarboxlate liquid compound. Two more hours and the magical 100° Celsius would be reached, and then boom! The toxic substance, DEAD, would explode, obliterating the complex and half the police force with it. The Doctor stored enough of this liquid to take out a small community. Before vacating the premises, the Doctor had left a small team of children in place. It was their first serious test. A sacrifice he was willing to make to protect his research. Sometimes it was best to sacrifice a couple of pawns to protect the key pieces. How many chess pieces would his component be willing to sacrifice?

It had been a brilliant idea – burn the complex to the ground. Let the police or their forensic science team find the kidnapper's body in the ashes. The police were so stupid. They would probably think it was him, the Doctor, who had died in the fire. A chemical reaction gone wrong – a simple mistake. They could re-start the game whenever he wanted, when they least expected. That was the beauty of chess. The shift of power would be with him. Now he needed time to consider his next move and change tactics. The last few months had tested his patience. Nothing seemed to be going to plan.

*****

Half a dozen children marched from the main entrance, controlled by something that could not be seen or heard. They moved without fear into a defensive line to protect their home, a ten-foot gap between each child. Their positions seemed well rehearsed. They all knew their role. Two were female, and the rest were male, but this was the only visual difference. They were dressed in white clothing, with white shoulder-length hair and thin twig bodies. From the back, they would have been mistaken for old people. From the front there was no doubt they were still children – but children without emotion. Their expressionless faces stared through the officers. The police officers moved slowly towards them, their apprehension clearly evident. An uncomfortable anxiety began to form – the odd glance from one police officer to another. Nobody could have guessed what would happen next.

Benton Hailey was the first to die. Louis Cransley took his revolver out of his holster and blew a hole into Benton's forehead at point blank range. Benton felt nothing. Louis then placed the tip of his gun to his own temple and blew his brains out. This was the start of the bloodbath that Frank had spoken about. One of the women officers, known affectionately as Babs, the surveillance officer, had frozen. Her eyes never left the children. Mesmerised by what she was seeing, hearing and feeling, Babs was under their control. Suddenly, her body started to cavort spastically. Crying out in excruciating pain, Babs fell to the ground, rolling and snorting, like a pig in its sty who was heading to the slaughter house.

Sidney Denver screamed. His right leg buckled. The shin bone splintered, cutting through the flesh on his leg. A large flap of skin hung loosely on his leg. It all happened so fast.

"It's them. Get them out of there," screamed Angel. Damien saw his father collapse to his knees. Hands over his ears, a loud painful cry escaped from his lips.

"Dad," shouted Damien. He started to move towards his father. Angel grabbed his arm.

"Wait," Angel scanned the line of children. "The second one from the right has hold of your father. How long can you clear your mind for?"

"Ten minutes maximum."

"Me too."

"Angel, what should we do? I have to get my dad out of there. He will die if I don't, and your premonition will come true."

Angel thought for a moment, "Damien, do you think you can blank out your thoughts long enough to stop the kid controlling your father? I'll clear your father's imaginary pain. Then you can drag your father to a safer place. You are much stronger than I am. For god's sake, why are they sending more police officers in? Can't they see they are like lambs to the slaughter?"

Damien gently pecked Angel on the lips. "If your mind opens, then you must get out of here."

Angel nodded. "You too."

He kissed her again before disappearing to the right. The plan was to stay close to the boundary wall, out of sight. His heart pounded fast. He had to get his father out of the complex. The bushes would give him ample cover. His speed was rapid and controlled, as he made his way around the garden. He stopped only once to stare at a pile of rotting apples. Fresh apples that hadn't reached maturity lay scattered on the ground, old and new lay side by side. The umbrella effect from the numerous trees made it appear darker than it was, giving him some cover from the mind-controlling freaks. Apples hung from the branches. The mature trees appeared so well established in their surroundings. Red in some trees, green in others, all slowly ripening. It looked quite beautiful. Why apples, what was so important about apples? Angel was obsessed by them, Frank grew them, and now at the Doctor's centre all the trees were various varieties of apples. Apples had to be the key to the research that was taking place.

No time to contemplate. He had to keep moving. At that very moment, a bullet whizzed past his ear. He had been spotted. It didn't matter anymore. Now on a ten minute timer, he headed across the open land to the mind-controlling freaks. An armed policeman was now facing him – a marionette masquerading, controlled by an invisible puppeteer, arms and legs moving with no self-control. Another bullet fired in Damien's direction. He ducked just in time. The marionette was squeezing the trigger, aiming in Damien's direction. A warm unwelcome sensation of air touched his skin as another bullet whizzed past the side of his face. Angel would have said the dragon's breath had caught his skin. Glancing to his left, he saw Angel was picking her way through the bodies. His attention returned to the immediate problem. Soon the officer would have to re-load. Could a child control a man to that level by thought alone? Was the officer fighting this intrusive child who was trying to take him over? Was that why the bullets were missing him, or was he just a bad shot? He had to keep moving. It was the only way to dodge the bullets. Eventually, the child would have full control. Speed was the essence, a blank mind essential.

Another policeman fell to his knees, crying uncontrollably. His hand moved to his throat, squeezing the very breath that was keeping him alive. Coughing, his forehead touched the ground as his body doubled over. His grasp tightened around his own throat, squeezing harder. Tears kept falling, and his lips started to turn grey. Two more lifeless bodies to step over, then Angel would be with his father. Don't, Angel, my father is your priority. He could see Angel slowing down, looking around at the bodies, but her legs kept moving towards his father.

Angel tried to communicate with Damien's father. His hair was dark, although grey hairs were starting to take hold. Lifting his head, his face was strong and his jawbone was slightly squarer than Damien's. A faint smell of his aftershave lingered. It was different from Damien's, an older gentleman's. It was nice, not overpowering.

Damien had now reached the child who was probing deep into his father's mind, trying to find a way through. Fighting hard to stop the intrusion, Damien continued to block him out. As he moved closer to the children, he realised they were much stronger than he had imagined. Raising his fist to shoulder height, he was ready to strike the child. He suddenly stopped and instead shoved the child hard. A flash of white, and the child fell backwards onto the hard ground. It felt wrong hitting a child, even if it was a freak of nature. The kid appeared shocked and winded, the first sign of any emotion. The child lay on the ground, not moving, waiting for his next order. His once white trousers were now grass-stained from the fall. Another child turned to face Damien, trying to reach and probe into his mind. Damien tried to move towards him, push him over as he had the first child. He couldn't move. An invisible force field blocked his passage. Taking a step backwards, Damien turned and sprinted in the direction of Angel and his father. The freaks were too strong for him.

"David, listen to me," Angel's hands cupped his face, forcing him to look into her eyes. She never normally called him David, always Chief Inspector or sir, but from this moment he became David. His hands still covered his ears. "David, I will take your pain. Listen to my voice. You must let me in." Her hands now covered his firmly placed hands. To have more power, her fingers needed to be underneath his hands not on top. "David, look at me; I will take your pain," David's eyes met hers. "Please, David, relax; I will take your pain," she repeated again. His eyes were glazed over, but she knew he was listening. Suddenly, she felt the imaginary pain lift from his body and enter her hands. The pain slowly moved up her arms. It was a strange feeling. His eyes began to lose their icy-glazed stare. "Let me take your pain," she whispered again. Damien was now back beside Angel, who instinctively moved to one side, allowing Damien to grab his father and pull him to his feet.

"My mind is open," he shouted to Angel. "I can't close it."

"Get out," she screamed over the mayhem.

Angel glanced around, taking in the scene as she wiped the blue substance from her lips. The officer behind her started scratching at his face, drawing blood as his fingernails dug deep into his skin.

"Don't," she whispered. "Please don't." The sight was disturbing, making Angel feel sick to the stomach. A child tried and failed to penetrate her mind. Officer Denver was dragging his body across the grass. His broken leg was hindering his every movement, yet he felt no pain. Grabbing Angel's leg and then her arm, he tried to pull himself into a sitting position. The uncontrollable wails and screams broke her concentration. Angel tried to shake off his grasp.

"I'm sorry," she whispered. From the corner of her eye, she could see another officer running towards her, yelling abuse. His hands and arms flapped widely. He was using the rifle in his hand as a battering ram on the officers blocking his path. Could this be the one who broke Denver's shin – the man who was desperately trying to hold on to her leg? The barrel could easily break bones used as a manual weapon. A couple more seconds, and then this controlled nutter would connect with her. What was he programmed to do?

Denver released his grip on Angel's leg. She turned and walked slowly towards the children, ignoring the battering ram that was heading in her direction.

"I command you to stop," she yelled. "I am in charge now, and I am telling you to stop." One child stopped and stared at Angel. There was no probing of minds. "Stop now. That is an order." The child glanced left to another child, who also abruptly stopped. The policeman nearest to the child stopped punching his colleague in the gut. A fine mess had been made of his face. The officer running towards her suddenly slumped to the ground. He lay on his stomach, not moving, not even a muscle spasm. He was not dead, although the body appeared lifeless. Both children stared at the last three children, who were still standing and controlling the officers.

"Stop, I command you," shouted Angel again. Adrenaline pulsated through her body. She was unsure what she was doing, but it appeared to be working. A couple of head nods and all the children had stopped. Crossing their legs, they sat on the ground, waiting for their next instruction. Angel took another step towards them and then halted. Their faces were a deathly white, matching their hair and clothes. White slacks and tunics hung loosely on their twig-like bodies. White plimsolls were tied in a double bow on their feet; however, it was their eyes that stopped her from getting any closer. Their eyes were dark and piercing, almost predatory with a threatening glare. Their lips were thin. They were pure evil.

The officers started to take control of their bodies and actions, brushing themselves down removing the dust, twigs and leaves from their clothes. Back on their feet, the chaos calmed, the officers moved reluctantly towards the children. Their hesitant stride indicated the uncertainty of what may or may not happen next. Some of the officers who had taken the brunt of the mind probing appeared startled. They stared down at their injuries and then to their colleagues' injuries, unsure what had just happened. The police vans were waiting outside the complex as the children were led away. No officer laid a hand on a child nor looked them in the eye. They would need the body bags for the carnage that was left.

Damien had now joined Angel, "What made you do that?"

"I don't know, instinct I guess." Her eyes met his. He wiped the small trace of blue liquid from her lips and pulled her close to him. "Damien, I thought I heard Aurel's voice telling me to take control of the children. It was a strange sensation. I kept thinking they have to have a leader. Every group, every team, has a leader who gives them direction, yet none of them appeared to be leading. I thought if I made them think I was their leader then I could take control of them. It was a wild guess – a hunch that worked."

Damien didn't say anything. His only response was to pull her closer. Her body was icy cold, yet his was so warm from the recent physical exertion and the sun's heat that was now in the high twenties. Moving his hands up and down her arms, he rubbed gently, trying to bring warmth back into her body. The movement caused goose-pimples, and then a shiver, but no warmth.

"I'm so cold."

"I know. I can tell. Can't you think yourself warm?"

She giggled. "That's just silly. Anyway, how is your father?"

"He'll survive. Maybe next time he'll listen to me." Damien rubbed a little quicker and harder, but still no warmth generated from her body.

"Fathers never listen," she replied harshly, and then shivered again. "So what do you think now – curse or a gift?" asked Angel.

Damien paused for a while and thought it through before answering. "Gift, definitely a gift." They would agree to disagree, although she was coming around to it being a gift.

"You never cease to amaze me," he murmured bringing his lips down to hers.

Damien glanced over to the children to make sure the officers still had control before closing his eyes and letting his mind absorb itself into the kiss. It was all over. A group of armed officers were now making their way into the main building. There was no gun shots, no obvious resistance.

"Do you think the Doctor is in there?" asked Angel.

"We'll know soon enough," he replied.

They turned their backs to the building, and hand in hand headed towards the open gate. A shout from behind, and they both swiftly turned around. A large ball of fire glowing red and orange was clearly visible inside the building, moving swiftly through the rooms. A peculiar green flame flickered on the lower floor of the building. The flames soon escaped, licking the outside walls, blackening their once white coating. A colossal explosion, and glass from the windows shattered. The officers piled out of the building, falling over each other as they tried to reach safety. Another larger explosion shook the land. Everybody including Damien and Angel was flung to the ground. Instinctively, Damien went into protective mode, shielding Angel's body with his. The heat started to build. An unfamiliar chemical smell poisoned the air.

Debris was hurled high in the sky before landing on the lawn, setting off small fires. Black, dense smoke clung to the air, destroying all living matter, burning the oxygen that once occupied the space. The fire had taken hold quickly. Cinders and embers danced rhythmically in vertical patterns up into the sky. Damien's hands and upper body covered Angel's head and body.

"Stay down," he whispered before flinching as a piece of burnt timber landed inches from his body. Another piece of timber landed near their heads. He started to cough. Realising it was unsafe to stay where they were, Damien leapt onto his feet. Dragging Angel onto her feet, he held Angel's hand tightly as they ran to the open gate. He had no intention of letting go. She stopped to cough. Damien pulled her hand hard, forcing her to continue moving. The main gate was slowly closing. The automated lock clicked into place seconds after they had managed to squeeze through. The gate proudly displayed its coat of arms to all those on the outside of the complex – the coat of arms that indicated the Doctor's triumph over the authorities. The sirens from the fire trucks wailed in the distance, their blue lights rotating high in the air. At least a dozen officers were trapped behind the gate. Nobody else made it out of the building alive.

Damien grabbed a blanket and dragged Angel away from the fifty-plus shocked officers who stood peering through the gate. Somehow he had to warm up her icy-cold body. "Did you do that? I said think of something warm, and then boom! All that shit happened."

Angel burst into a hysterical fit of giggles. "Oh god, you are serious, aren't you?"

"I'm asking a simple question, Angel. Did you do that?"

"No, of course not. I wouldn't know how to do that."

Relief crossed Damien's face. "Thank god for that. You had me worried for one awful moment. When you controlled those kids and with your ability to heal, I just wondered if there were other things you could do."

"Like big booms," laughed Angel.

"Yeah, like big booms. It sounds so stupid when you say it like that," he cradled her body in his arms. "I'm sorry," he whispered.

"If I could do something like that, would it scare you?"

"Yep, I would be petrified. I would never want to argue with you because you would always win by controlling me."

"If we argued, I would use my power to make you love me more," Angel threatened.

"I couldn't love you more, no matter how hard I tried," was the quick reply. Their lips met once more. Warmth was finally beginning to return to her body.

"Oy, you two love birds. Your father is looking for you, and he is pissed. Apparently he told you to stay at the hotel," Detective Haines informed them.

"I told you he wouldn't be happy," whispered Damien into Angel's ear before answering Haines. "Can you tell him you couldn't find us? Anyway if it wasn't for us, he would probably be dead."

Haines nodded, "Yeah, of course I saw what happened. Your dad is just like my Captain when he is annoyed. It's quite funny to watch as long, as you are not the person taking the brunt of the anger." Damien smirked then squeezed Angel once more. Haines gave Angel one last fleeting glance, before disappearing from sight to find the Chief Inspector.

"Where are the children?" asked Damien scanning the area. One of the officers within hearing distance pointed to a transit van, parked over the road.

Damien grabbed Angel's hand and wandered over to the van.

"I don't want to see them," Angel said pulling him backwards.

"They aren't here," Damien exclaimed. "Look! The back doors of the van and the driver's door were wide open." Peering in the back of the van, she saw it was empty of children. There was a man sitting in the middle of the floor. His peaked cap was turned backwards. He hummed the tune 'The Enemies Within.' As a new verse of the song was reached, his body rocked backwards and forwards aggressively. His eyes were open but glazed. He stared at a piece of chewing gum stuck to the floor of the van. The gum took precedence. He was oblivious to whatever was going on around. His eyes were transfixed as he hummed the tune over and over again.

"It's a message from the Doctor; he's telling us we can't stop him," said Angel.

"How do you know?" asked Damien. "The Doctor might have been in the building when it blew."

"You could be right. I have a feeling that this isn't all, though. Anyway, we can't leave him like this," said Angel.

Damien quickly skirted around the van; the children had vanished.

"I'll send a cop over to talk to him. Let's see if we can find my dad first, get it over with."

*****

"Was the Doctor in the building?" Angel asked the Chief Inspector.

"We don't know. There are half a dozen dead bodies, burnt beyond recognition. A pathologist is trying to perform an autopsy on what is left of the bodies. We also have several forensic criminologists combing the scene, trying to piece the information and evidence together. Maybe then we will know more, but I doubt it. We don't know who the Doctor is, or was. We don't know his age, what he looked like, if he's black, white, Asian or green! Frank received messages from the Doctor but never actually met him. We do know he was male and over the age of forty. His body could be any of the ones found in the remains of the building."

"Did you find a child's body?" asked Angel.

"No, I don't think so, but until we get the final report back nothing is conclusive."

"Are you thinking about Warren?"

Angel nodded. "I can't believe Warren turned so quickly against me, after all we went through. When he spoke to me in the car, there was still something there. The old Warren I once knew. I felt like he wanted to tell me something, but he couldn't."

Damien gave her shoulder a quick squeeze. "Forget him, Angel. Let's move on."

They turned to leave when Angel swung around. "Sir, I have one last question. The chemicals in the building, what were they?"

"We don't know yet. Why do you ask?"

"Oh no reason, I was just curious."

Epilogue

As Damien lay in bed that night, staring at the ceiling, thoughts of the last eighteen months ran through his mind. Before meeting Angel, he had been so depressed with the constant pain. He had hated his life, but now his whole life had turned around. Bouts of pain still manifested themselves regularly, but with Angel's help it was controllable. In the last eighteen months, he had been shot at, stabbed, placed in a coma and served time in prison. The list was endless, and yet he would go through it all again, as long as he could have another eighteen months with Angel. She laid curled up in his arms. Before falling asleep, she asked if the red mark on his chest hurt.

"A little," had been his reply.

"It will be gone in the morning," she whispered. Her fingertips moved across the reddened patch. He had felt the routine tingling in his body. He knew he would always love her. It did not matter if she could never heal him. He was happy, and that was all that mattered. She had given him a lifeline to ease his illness. One chapter in the book was closing; another was about to begin. He did not know where life would lead them. All he knew was that life would never be straightforward with Angel, but with her by his side, he was ready for anything.

He had longed for the day when they could have some normality to their life. Tomorrow was the start of that normality. They had an 11:00 a.m. flight back to England, where they would spend time with his family before visiting Angel's sister. He hoped Angel had found a real friend in her sister. A sister who would not let her down as her brothers had done. It was so obvious Angel was still confused about who she really was, and he could see it sometimes played on her mind. By finding her sister, he hoped it would take away some of the confusion.

Crystal had reluctantly agreed to try to heal him, even though she had not tried to heal in over ten years. She was breaking the promise she had made to herself many years ago. He declined her offer, which had shocked Angel. He had seen how Robert and Agnes reacted to Angel when she had healed them – they worshipped her. He didn't want to worship Angel's sister. He didn't want to miss his chance of having his illness cured, as he had dreamt of the day when this would happen; however, it had to be Angel if it was anybody. It had been a difficult decision to make.

Not only did he want Angel to cure him, he was also concerned if his heart would be able to take the strain. Angel would be careful. She knew his body and his heart maybe even better than himself. Angel would be able to judge when he could take no more – could Crystal? Did he want his heartbeat to regulate with Angel's sister's heartbeat? He still had time to change his mind. Deep down, he knew he would wait for Angel's gift to develop, and if it didn't, she would continue to take his pain. Anyway, he would miss the tingling sensation Angel's fingers generated when taking his pain. A faint smile crossed his lips. He loved the feelings she gave him.

All charges against him had officially been dropped. He was a free man, yet deep down he knew it wasn't over. The Doctor and Edward were no longer a threat, and Frank had been given a new life, a new identity, shipped off to some remote part of the world. Angel had said she hoped it would be a lush, green place, where he could grow his own vegetables and fruit trees. Nobody would tell them where he had gone, and deep down Damien did not want to know.

A small sigh escaped from Damien's lips. Angel stirred slightly but did not awake. He sometimes felt she could sleep through an earthquake. Glancing down to her head of thick, dark hair, he twisted several strands around his fingers. He loved playing with her hair. It was so relaxing. A faint smile crossed his lips. He was feeling exceptionally happy, so happy he wanted to shout it from the rooftops.

Damien knew there were others who would try and carry on the Doctor's work. For some reason, it no longer bothered him. Would he see Warren or Samuel again? Would they try and continue with the Doctor's work? He doubted Samuel would have the brains to run such an operation. At least the vicar battering had stopped. The last time he read about a vicar being tortured was over three weeks ago, and as for Warren, the whole episode was confusing and disappointing. He had deceived them all.

He guessed there would come a time when Angel would want to find Stephanie or possibly the twins. He could hear her argument already: 'but they are my brother and sister and the only family I have is your family and Crystal. Please, Damien, I really want to meet them. I promised my mother I would take care of them.'

Damien knew he would once again stare into her dark bewitching eyes, nod his head, and reluctantly agree to find them. Maybe Peter was right; females do control the male species.

Giving Angel a gentle squeeze, he remembered the one thing Angel wanted when she got back to England – an English Cox's Orange Pippin apple.

"Best in October," she had commented. He had laughed and then reeled off the description of a Cox's Orange Pippin apple – "one of the finest dessert apples with a unique flavour and an orangey-red colouring." Angel had been impressed, but there wasn't much else to do in prison but read. He wondered why the Cox apple and not the Russet apple. He made a mental note to ask Angel in the morning. Then there was the other question he needed to ask, not that Angel would know the answer, but he had to ask. Why apples? Why did everything revolve around apples? Angel was obsessed with apples. Even now Damien could see a half-eaten Benoni apple on the bedside cabinet, the once yellow flesh turning brown as the oxygen penetrated deep into its soft flesh. Rarely did Angel consume a full apple. She almost appeared to crave one or two bites of a crisp, fresh apple. Even after the acid attack, Angel still craved the humble apple. It wasn't just Angel that was obsessed with the apple – the Doctor and Frank had apple trees. The apple tree was not ornamental or beautiful in any way. They were just apple trees that served no other purpose than producing edible fruit.

Maybe his mind was overactive, reacting to the excitement of going home. Maybe it was all just coincidence. Apples were healthy. Everybody appeared to like apples. Nevertheless Damien knew there was more to it. The apple was important. He didn't know how or why, he just knew. One day it would all become clear. Until then he had to be patient, and wait for the answer to be revealed. Damien gave a long, deep sigh and closed his eyes; tomorrow would be a long day.

*****

"Guess what?" shouted Ben. Crystal made her way to the living room.

"What now?"

"The telephone call, I have just been offered an interview at that new medical research centre. It is in my area of expertise – DNA and gene manipulation. I will be working with my old colleague, Troy. You will like Troy. He is a genius, so focused. The director wants to meet us both tomorrow."

"Why me?"

"I guess he wants to see that I am secure. You know, a family man, my background that sort of thing."

Crystal smiled. "You are a very intelligent man. I know when he meets us, he will offer you a job."

"So you will come?"

"Of course," Crystal winked and wandered back into the kitchen to finish dinner.

*****

"Who's that you are drawing, honey?"

The young girl looked up at her mother. Her thick eyelashes framed her dark eyes, her raven hair long and thick.

"It's the lady who visits me at night."

"Can I have a look, honey?"

The young girl passed her mother the drawing that she had been working on for the last twenty minutes. It was drawn in crayon, a rough child's drawing of a female in the centre of the paper. Carla could clearly see the long hair that had been scribbled in black, the dress in green. The facial features were unrecognisable. Two eyes, a nose and a mouth, but they could have been anybody's. Carla glanced again at the drawing and then at her young daughter who was now munching on a small crisp apple.

"Why does she visit you, honey?"

Stephanie shrugged her shoulders and continued to crunch on her apple.

"So what does the lady say to you when she visits?"

"I don't know; I can't hear the lady." Carla blinked back a tear. Could this be the same young woman that her Bobby had spoken about?

"Finish it later, honey," Carla scooped her daughter off the floor, revealing a small scar on the child's hip, the number nine clearly visible.

Every story, every saying is inspired by a real event.
Maybe there was something in the old saying:

'An apple a day keeps the doctor away'

#

Child One - Dominique x suicide
Child Two - Bobby x death thru healing
Child Three - Crystal - ~~Jessica~~?
Child Four - Samual

The Groomers:

'Edward Frank'

Their Boss:
The Doctor

~~Samuel~~?

Lightning Source UK Ltd.
Milton Keynes UK
UKOW01f0034030816

279839UK00001B/1/P